T0146607

tropical Lure

tropical Lure

DUANE A. EIDE

iUniverse®

TROPICAL LURE

iUniverse books may be ordered through booksellers or by contacting:

iUniverse
1663 Liberty Drive
Bloomington, IN 47403
www.iuniverse.com
1-800-Authors (1-800-288-4677)

ISBN: 978-1-5320-3543-2 (sc)
ISBN: 978-1-5320-3542-5 (e)

Library of Congress Control Number: 2017916273

Print information available on the last page.

iUniverse rev. date: 11/08/2017

Table of Contents

Chapter 1

"What the hell did I do?" Dane Barton asked himself as his elbows rested on top the check-out counter. The question occupied the very edge of his consciousness, accessible during moments of reflection. Lately, Dane found himself far too often in a reflective mood.

For three months he endured a series of dreadful eight hour, grave yard shifts, 11:00 P.M. to 7:00 A.M.,which dragged endlessly through the night. But, hey, it offered a pay check. Without one, his parents threatened to sentence him to the street. At least their recent conversation suggested as much.

Since checking in at 11:00, he waited on very few customers. "Who does any shopping at a convenience store in the middle of the night?" Without customers, Dane tried to pass the time in some constructive way, such as sweeping the floor again or arranging the morning paper piled on the rack next to the front counter. Only after several days on the job had he learned the location of the hundreds of items shelved in three aisles stretching from the check-out counter back to the soda, water, and beer coolers. Tending to those shelves stacked with candy and other snacks served as one of Dane's many duties.

Though he tried to keep himself busy with these duties, he found impossible ignoring the clock positioned over the soda, water, and beer coolers in the far end of the store, a perfect place for him to count the minutes since the last time he looked.

A particularly slow night at the store, in the past two hours three customers entered to buy petty items like soda, cigarettes, potato chips, even tampax. People's shopping habits intrigued Dane. He considered if stopping at a convenience store in the middle of the night defined shoppers as victims of poor planning, victims of repeated emergencies, or simply compulsive about what they needed? Before this job he never imagined people spending time in the middle of the night doing anything like shopping. Oh, he realized other people worked the nasty hours he did. He couldn't understand so many needing a drink or a cigarette at three in the morning. Despite his thoughts on the matter, Dane understood all-night customers delighted his boss.

He glanced again at the clock over the coolers at the far end of the store, pondering where he would have been now if he had resisted the temptation to drop out of the community college. He knew for sure he would be in bed sleeping. However, his decision to give up on the two year Associate in Marketing program gave him a chance to relax from the pressure of his classes and the pressure of his parents.

His eyes seemed attracted to that clock on the back wall. "The minute hand must be stuck," he thought. On the counter in front of him small items, such as gum, breath fresheners, small bags of chocolate hearts, and a rack of salted peanuts offered the customers a last minute purchase. Dane reached for the tray of gum, repositioning it next to the breath fresheners. Only a short time ago he repositioned the chocolate, something to do with restless hands.

Though it annoyed him, the bell connected to the front door did keep him attentive to arriving customers. The bell sounded announcing the arrival of a customer, this time a young man in his late teens or early twenties. Dressed in a sport suit, white shirt and tie now hanging loose at his neck, he likely came to the end of a night on the town. Tall and well built, probably a frequent visitor at some fitness center, he displayed a two to three day growth of whiskers, dark to match his hair slicked back with some kind of hair product.

Dane greeted him. In return the young man merely nodded his head. Dane watched as he headed straight for the soda cooler, "What the hell is a young guy doing out in the middle of the night?" Dane rolled his eyes in recognition of a stupid question he ought to quit asking. Nonetheless, at twenty-three, he could recall doing nothing at three in the morning except sleeping; that is until he took this job.

The young man lingered around the snack shelves, reaching for crackers then for chips. While he did, the door opened again, this time to two older man dressed in grubby T-shirts and shorts and wearing hiking boots. One towered over the other. The bigger one, with bushy, gray hair, an out of control look, and a mustache giving him a distinct identity, paused only steps inside the entrance. He made a visual survey of the store, his eyes traveling from the check-out counter where Dane stood waiting for questions around to the coolers lining the wall and across the back.

His shorter companion, with dark beady eyes peering out from under a floppy hat pulled tight over strands of greasy hair, stood obediently behind his apparent leader. Dane speculated whether they were ending their night or starting their day. They greeted Dane with a smile and a mumbled, "Good morning." Like the young man before them, they moved to the soda cooler where they lingered in obvious indecision. They turned to locate the young man standing several feet away near one of the snack shelves.

The two men moved by the line of coolers to stand before one filled with energy drinks. They studied the contents of the cooler, their attention divided between noting the location of the young man and now also checking on Dane's position behind the counter. They both stood with hands on hips; their eyes made another complete search of the store. The bigger of the two dragged his hand over his mustache, dropping his hand to wipe it on his shorts. The smaller man looked up at his companion as if to receive directions. They both drifted through the aisle toward the counter. Dane watched them approach.

"May I help you find something?" he asked.

The taller of the two men reached behind his back and from under his shirt he pulled out a hand gun. He rushed to the counter shouting, "Yes, you can. Give me all the money in that cash register!"

Dane stood paralyzed in shock. His eyes wide, his mouth open, he could only stare at the intruders.

The partner of the man holding the gun on Dane immediately accosted the other customer, commanding him to back up against the cooler with hands on his head.

"You deaf?" screamed the man whose gun pointed in Dane's face.

Dane shook his head, "No, no." His hand trembled as he punched the key to open the cash register.

"Now scoop up the money and throw it in this bag!" Mustache tossed a canvas bag onto the counter. "Move! I haven't got all night!" He waved the gun in Dane's face.

Backed up against the cooler, the young man locked his eyes on the gun pointed at his head. The moment the beady eyes looked to the front of the store at his companion who held Dane hostage, the young man acted. He rushed the unsuspecting assailant who fell back against a snack shelf which collapsed into the next aisle but failed to dislodge the gun. A shot echoed through the store, the bullet slicing through the neck of the young man who collapsed in a pool of blood. The shooter ran to the front counter.

At the front counter, his companion panicked, grabbed the plastic bag filled with money from the cash register, pointed his gun at Dane, then at close range pulled the trigger. Nothing happened. For an instant mustache gazed at the gun in his hand. Raising the gun he reached across the counter, clutching Dane by the neck. With a broad swing of his right arm he bashed Dane across the head two, three, four times, each time the weight of the gun cutting into Dane's face and head. Bruised and bloody, Dane sank behind the counter.

With money in hand the two men rushed out the door to a waiting car. The squeal of tires marked their escape.

Chapter 2

Eleven year old Dane Barton sat with his mom and dad around the kitchen table. Dane's mom, Beatrice, insisted they eat dinner as a family. A small family of three, for Beatrice it represented her family regardless of size.

Her family lived in a small but modern house where she took charge, particularly in the kitchen. Milo, her husband and Dane's dad, an over the road trucker, often left her in charge of the home. Like the house, the kitchen, too, was small. Lined on three walls with cupboards interrupted by the traditional kitchen appliances as well as displaying more contemporary, time saving devices, such as her favorite, a food processor, the kitchen offered the Barton family a place to share healthy, specialty dishes Beatrice took pride in preparing.

Besides the kitchen, the first floor of the Barton house included a living room, a half bath and two closets. The living room gave Milo the chance to watch Viking football on a large screen TV, his most important appliance. A typical fifties farm house, the Barton home included a second floor with three bedrooms and a master bath shared by the entire family.

On this autumn evening the three Bartons ate in silence, intent on one of Beatrice's specialties. Only that morning Milo returned from several days on the road. He took his time chewing his food. Then looked at his son seated across the table.

"So, son, tell me what happened this time." He took a swallow of milk, set the glass down on the table, and waited for his son's response.

Not a harsh man, still Milo Barton rarely displayed tender feelings. He loved his only child but worried about Dane's tendency to fall victim to the taunts and, at times, physical abuse from his peers. An over road trucker, Milo often was away from home several days in a row. That afternoon he completed a five day trip to Texas and back. These long trips afforded him abundant time to reflect upon his family, especially his son's relationship with his peers.

Twelve years ago Milo expressed reluctance to his wife's request they think about starting a family. Married only two years, they faced a list of financial obligations, one a large mortgage on the ten acres on which sat their home. New in the trucking business, Milo's salary gave them only enough money each month for essentials. However, Beatrice brought in additional money from her job as an accountant with the same trucking company Milo worked for. The introduction of a baby would likely require her to quit her job and would definitely add another mouth to feed, imposing further strain on their meager budget.

Beatrice persisted in arguing that though she loved her husband dearly, she could not envision living their lives without sharing it with a family. She reminded her husband of his two siblings, of her four, and of the benefits derived from growing up in a home crowded with family. Her persistence won. Twelve years ago that mouth, Beatrice came home jubilant from the doctor's office. She was pregnant.

Milo's concern for providing for another member of the family faded during those moments when Beatrice urged him to place his hand on her stomach to feel the movements of their first child. She requested and received a leave of absence from her job with the trucking firm. When his schedule allowed, helping his wife prepare the house for the expected baby weakened further his initial objections to starting a family.

Only a forty minute drive from downtown Minneapolis, the Bartons' small home, located on ten acres in western Hennepin County, needed only minor alterations to accommodate their baby. The most important was converting one of the bedrooms into a nursery. Beatrice attached considerable importance to the creation of a nursery, fully aware of the critical need for sensory stimulation even for a tiny infant. Milo willingly did what his wife told him to do. His road schedule demanded careful planning to ensure his availability for those jobs only he could do.

Beatrice's pregnancy advanced without complication until near the seventh month. Then nausea and severe cramps caused grave concern about the growing fetus. Her doctor prescribed bed rest for as much of the day as possible, suspending any more preparations for the baby's arrival. To spend more time with his wife, Milo sought a modified schedule. Though he needed the money his full schedule provided him, tending to his wife assumed more importance.

At the beginning of the eighth month of her pregnancy, Beatrice's condition declined, more nausea, more cramps, even some bleeding. On the night of August 10, eleven years ago, her condition became a crisis. Milo rushed her to Methodist Hospital in suburban St. Louis Park where at 11:29 p.m., August 10, a son, named Dane, arrived one month premature. Weighing only three pounds six ounces, the newest Barton would spend the first three weeks of his life on earth in infant intensive care. Beatrice recovered quickly after Dane's birth. Milo suffered fears, questioning if a baby so tiny could survive to lead a normal life. The staff at Methodist Hospital tried to allay those fears, guiding Beatrice and Milo through learning to respond to the special needs of a premature baby. One day short of three weeks after his birth, Dane Barton arrived at his new home.

Chapter 3

Dane stared at his plate, making quick glances at his dad. He chewed slowly, favoring the left side of his mouth, his left cheek discolored by a bruise.

"Son, can you tell me what happened?" Milo asked the question, stripped of any hint of criticism, yet devoid of any expression of sympathy.

Looking up from his plate, Dane winced, the natural sparkle in his deep blue eyes dulled by tears and by realizing he was again a disappointment for his dad. He tried to formulate some response to the question. Nothing came.

"Come on, son, you don't have a problem talking most of the time," a reference to Dane's proclivity for conversation. Milo reached to clasp his hand over his son's resting on the table. "What happened?"

In despair, Dane pushed himself away from the table and rushed from the kitchen, leaving his parents in confusion.

Beatrice moved her plate to one side and reached for her cup of coffee. She took a swallow. "You don't have to be so harsh with him. You know how sensitive he is to conflicts with his peers."

"Harsh? I was harsh?" Milo spread his arms, palms up, in a gesture of surrender. "All I did was ask."

"I know dear, but please remember how hard Dane tries to live up to your expectations."

Milo settled back in his chair, ran his hands through his thinning hair. "All I want is for him to stand up for himself. I don't want to hear he's smaller than others his age. I don't know what happened again today. All I know is he comes home with a bruise on his cheek. He doesn't go to school to get physically picked on."

Milo Barton came from a family that took shit from no one. Born and raised on a farm in northern Minnesota, he learned early to fend for himself, to look out for himself. His dad and two older brothers, by their actions, pushed him toward a life of independence and self-reliance. Achieving that independence came with a battle. When other boys his age enjoyed a growth spurt, Milo's size advanced in tiny intervals. He discovered early the importance of size. He envied those his age who stood above him. He also discovered early the need to compensate for size he would never achieve. His ultimate five feet eight inches, one hundred fifty pounds molded that compensation into a defiant often belligerent response to people and situations he considered a threat.

Though Milo wouldn't admit it, others saw him as handsome. His small frame was well proportioned, his shoulders square and his hips narrow. Deep brown eyes peered out from under thick eye brows. His cheeks tapered to a moderate chin. In moments of defiance his chin assumed more prominence.

Through the years of an elementary, a middle school, then a high school education, Milo took his place next to his dad and brothers on the farm, a six hundred acre spread in the fertile Red River Valley. Over the years the tedium of farm work, the desire for change, awakened thoughts of a different kind of life. Only a high school education narrowed Milo's choices.

Out of frustration and four years out of high school, he answered an ad for an over the road truck driver. His years on the farm equipped him with a familiarity with most motorized vehicles from motor scooters to tractors to trucks. However, none of his driving experience would include commanding a huge semi. Nonetheless, with completion of both written and road tests, he earned his license to drive an eighteen wheeler.

Beatrice pushed herself away from the table. She paused to look at her husband. "I don't know all the details. I can tell you what I know after checking on our son." She hurried up the stairs to Dane's bedroom where she knocked quietly on the closed door. Hearing no reply, she inched the door open to find her son face down on his bed. She moved closer to where he lay, placing her hand on his shoulder.

"You okay, sweetheart?"

"Yeah," came the muffled answer.

She sat down at the end of the bed. "Look, honey, your dad wasn't scolding you. He only wanted to find out what happened today."

Dane rolled over on his back. Rubbing his tear streaked eyes, he said, "I know he thinks I'm a sissy. Always getting picked on." He looked away. "I can't help the way I am."

Like his father, Dane would likely grow into a small man. Even after eleven years his frame hinted at his potential physical size. Clear-blue eyes like his mother's gave his face childish vitality. His mother insisted on keeping his curly blonde hair precisely trimmed, a job she often did herself. With a small nose above full lips over a slight over bite, Dane occupied a privileged place in the Barton family even though his dad didn't always acknowledge it.

"Sweetheart, I love the way you are, and so does your dad. Don't you ever forget that." She stood up from the bed. "I know your dad sometimes, ah, sometimes isn't the most gentle. But he can't help the way he is either."

A smile lightened Dane's sad face.

Mom shared her son's smile. "You okay now?"

Dane nodded his head.

"Do you want to come down to finish your supper?"

He shrugged his shoulders.

"When you decide, it will be waiting for you."

Beatrice returned to the kitchen where Milo rinsed dishes in the sink.

Turning to address his wife, he asked, "He's all right, isn't he?"

"Yes, of course he is." She sat down at her place by the table. "You know how sensitive he is to being picked on. He's also very sensitive about pleasing you. When things like today happen, he thinks he's let you down."

Milo breathed deeply, stacking another dish in the dishwasher. Perplexed, he turned to face his wife. 'I don't know what to think. I do know I don't want others pushing our son around. He's a great kid with a big heart for his age. I can't stand others taking advantage of that."

"Honey, I understand. We need to make sure our son does too."

For Beatrice, acquiring that understanding came much easier than for Milo. Beatrice Graves, too, grew up on a farm only miles from the one on which her husband did. A plain, petite girl, with sparkling, blue eyes and a pretty face surrounded by brown curls, she prided herself on her academic talent establishing a record as one of the best students in her class. Through the years her persistence and dedication culminated with her graduating valedictorian of her class. Along with her academic talent, she possessed a marvelous capacity for conversation. Give her the chance, she loved to talk, making her a favorite among her classmates.

Four years at the Bemidji branch of the University of Minnesota earned her a cum laude degree in accounting. Her impressive academic record, her friendly, engaging personality, and her tendency for loquacity opened wide employment opportunities. Her search for employment took her to the Twin Cities where she accepted an accounting position with a national trucking firm. There she met Milo Barton.

"I've tried to understand that for years." Milo leaned against the kitchen counter. "Incidentally, what did happen today?"

Beatrice rested her elbows on the table. "I don't know many

details, but, I guess, it started on the bus when this older, bigger bully named Dwight or something objected to Dane taking his seat."

Milo scoffed at her explanation. "They have assigned seats on the bus now?"

Beatrice smiled. "Of course not. At least, I don't think so. We would have heard about it." She paused. "It's this kid who has a history of picking on younger, smaller ones."

Milo shook his head. "Can't somebody do something about that shit?"

Beatrice eased herself out of her chair. "If someone could figure out a way to prevent bullying, he'd probably be rich and famous."

"Yeah, I suppose. How did he get the bruise?"

Standing next to her husband at the sink, Beatrice attempted to offer a brief explanation having to do with a scuffle on the slide during recess, maybe a continuation of the bus thing. She announced in conclusion, "Dwight was disciplined by the playground supervisor."

"Well, that's good," Milo agreed.

Chapter 4

His body refused to respond. Opening his eyes admitted flashes of light. His head throbbed in pain. His mind wrestled with where he was and what happened. Bile left a bitter taste in his mouth. With only his arms he urged his body up. Pain thundered through his head. He risked opening his eyes, bracing himself for the stabs of pain each time light penetrated them. A desperate grasp for reality produced the last thing he remembered, the gun pointed at his head.

"The store! His job! Who was watching the store?" Grabbing for the edge of the front counter where typically he controlled the store, he eased himself to his knees, pain crushing his skull. With the gradual return of consciousness, Dane Barton stood up behind the counter, knees weak, pain cascading through his head. He stared at the scene in front of him, a familiar scene which he observed for eight hours nearly every night. Imposed upon that scene he saw a gun pointed at his head. He saw a big man, a mustache draped over his lips, in shorts and a T-shirt demanding money, definitely a scene he wished to avoid even though he knew the vulnerability of convenience stores open twenty-four hours.

His eyes stopped on the legs protruding from an aisle midway to the coolers in the back. A person lay sprawled on the floor. Dane remembered the shot, the one he heard before the resounding blow to his head made his world black. He steadied himself on the counter. In the fog of his mind he knew he had to do something about the person on the floor, maybe the young man who entered alone. Inching his way around the counter, he stopped to lean on the counter's front side. A closer look through blurred eyes revealed a pool of blood collected under the man's legs. With clouds in his mind starting to clear, Dane decided rather than attempting to stumble back to investigate the body on the floor, he should call 911. He reached for the phone.

Within minutes he heard screaming sirens in the distance followed by the flicker of strobe lights through the store's front windows. Police officials instantly declared the store a crime scene while emergency medical staff attended to the person on the floor, presumably the young man who entered the store shortly before the two older assailants.

Police attempted to glean from Dane details of the incident, descriptions of the robbers, time of entry to the store, and the amount of money taken. However, besides informing them of the robbery, he could provide few details. A brief examination by the emergency medical staff determined Dane's need for medical attention before anyone could expect him to answer any more questions. An innocent victim, the young man on the floor in a pool of blood needed only the coroner to verify his death.

At Methodist Hospital in suburban St. Louis Park Dane rested comfortably in Room 319, a typical, private room with the usual amenities, such as chairs, wall-mounted TV, a closet, and a small bath. The bed and the monitoring equipment, of course, reigned as the most important. Dane dozed in the bed, his mind drifting, considering the irony that not since his birth twenty-three years ago had he spent time in Methodist Hospital or in any other hospital for any reason. Now he would spend time there for a very good reason, to begin healing from serious head injuries. An examination by the emergency room doctor revealed a mild concussion, deep lacerations above the left eye, a broken nose, and damaged left ear drum, according to the doctor, all the result of a series of blows to the head with a blunt instrument, in this case a hand gun. Though the emergency room staff had yet to inform him, none of his injuries were life threatening but demanded sufficient time to heal, even the ear drum.

Dane glanced at the monitoring devices connected to his arm by clear plastic tubes. He lay back waiting for the arrival of his parents whom the hospital staff had notified after Dane's room assignment. Also the hospital staff informed him someone from the police department would soon arrive, eager to discuss details of the robbery, a routine requirement.

Dane ran his hand gently over his nose, then his forehead. A bandage circled his head, concealing the deep bruise which caused the concussion. Tape secured his broken nose; a bandage covered the deep cut above his left eye. After all the agony of the last twelve hours, Dane managed a smile, induced by remembering the day, years ago, he received a cut over the same left eye.

He couldn't remember exactly his age, but he did remember playing Little League baseball. Remarkably fresh in his memory, too, he glimpsed his dad standing with fingers entwined in the chain link fence surrounding the baseball field. Despite Dane's small size, nobody expected more from him than his dad. "What you lack in size, you make up for in determination." was his dad's philosophy, one he adhered to with fervor.

Through the haze of Dane's memory, the scene emerged, a beautiful sunny day perfect for a baseball game. He played right field when he played which, of course, for his dad wasn't often enough and only squandered his son's talent. On this day, however, the coach put him in the game in the third inning. The score of ten to two gave Dane's coach confidence in a victory even with reserves.

Standing with his feet planted firmly in the batter's box, Dane eyed the pitcher who stared down at him with hostile eyes. In Dane's opinion anyone nearly twice his size looked at him with hostile eyes. With his dad yelling encouragement, Dane waited for the first pitch. He hardly saw it flash by. "Strike," announced the ump. Dane stepped out of the batter's box to tap his shoes with the bat the way the big league guys did. Back in the batter's box he waited for the next pitch. The pitcher stretched, leaned backed and threw, the ball exploding from his hand. The pitch never did reach the plate. Instead it struck Dane on the forehead just above his left eye, slipping mysteriously under the brim of his batting helmet.

Remembering the excitement the incident created brought another smile to Dane's face. His dad, his coach, the ump, even the pitcher rushed to Dane as he lay motionless in the batter's box. A headache and seven stitches above his left eye marked the conclusion of his baseball season.

A knock at the door to his hospital room rescued him from his reverie. A middle aged nurse dressed in a white uniform with a name tag identifying her as Dorothy pushed a small cart through the partially opened door. With practiced diligence, she moved with little hesitation to check Dane's vital signs.

"How are you doing?" she asked.

"Okay, I guess." Dane shifted his head on his pillow.

"I'll take just a minute to check your vital signs. How is your pain level?" She noted the monitor readings. "Things look good here."

"Still a little headache but better." Dane's eyes followed her around the bed.

Dorothy reached for a bottle positioned on top the cart. "Here, let me give you one of these."

"What is it?" Dane asked.

"Just a Tylenol to help reduce that headache." She handed Dane a plastic glass of water. With one swallow he downed the tablet.

"That should take care of you for now. Is there any thing else I can get you?" The nurse moved toward the door.

"I don't think so." Dane settled back against his pillow.

"Good, I will check back a little later. Bye for now." She smiled as she slipped through the slightly opened door, closing it behind her.

Dane settled back against his pillow and closed his eyes. Still he could see that gun pointed at him, its size growing bigger every time he thought about it. He saw in his mind the legs sticking out from beyond the snack aisle. He shook his head, knowing the young man's decision to stop by the store, perhaps, on his way home, cost him his life. Dane found frightening believing he witnessed a murder. He could have been the victim. In his mind he heard the click of the gun the robber pointed at his head. "Why did it fail?" Dane thought little about fate or destiny; however, as he drifted off into a shallow sleep, certainly fate may have had something to do with his surviving a close encounter with death.

When he awakened, his parents sat one on each side of his bed. He opened his right eye, his left nearly swollen shut as a result of the deep laceration above the eye brow. Both parents stood up from their chairs while Dane shifted in his bed.

His mom stepped up to the bed, placing her hand on her son's arm, the one free of monitoring tubes. "You doing all right?" she asked.

Drowsy from the ordeal he experienced only hours before and from the pain medication, Dane only nodded his head. He gazed with dull eyes at his parents, unable to piece together exactly why he was there. A short ambulance ride to Methodist Hospital, an examination in the emergency room to determine the extent of his injuries and the assignment to Room 319 found Dane trying to reconstruct in his own clouded mind what had happened earlier that morning. Though cautioned by the emergency room doctor to avoid pushing for details, Dane's parents desperately wanted to know what happened. They waited for their son to regain full consciousness before inquiring. That a robbery occurred at their son's store, that a man ended up dead on the floor was the extent of their knowledge of what had happened. With shock they realized their son could have been the victim. Still they thirsted for more detail.

Noting his son was fully awake, Milo approached the bed. "How you doing?"

Dane mumbled, "Okay, I guess. Sore and a little woozy."

"Can you take a couple questions?"

"I suppose," Dane mumbled.

"What about the robbers? Did you recognize them at all?" Milo studied his son's bruised face.

Dane rolled his head side to side, cautious about any rapid movement. "No."

Persistent, his dad asked, "What about the young man they shot? Did you know him?"

Dane restricted his answer to another soft roll of his head.

"Milo, let him rest. There's plenty time for those details when he feels better," Dane's mom advised her husband.

"I know." He lowered his head and returned to one of the chairs in the room. "I know he shouldn't have taken a job in one of them all night places."

Dane looked over at his dad but said nothing.

Beatrice glared at her husband. "This is not the time or the place to bring that up."

Milo stared down at his hands folded in his lap.

Beatrice rose from her chair and stepped closer to the bed. "Son, you need to concentrate all your energy on healing. The doctor told us your mild concussion will heal on its own." She paused to study her son's face. "You have to take it easy."

A smile relaxed Dane's dry lips. In a voice little louder than a whisper, he said, "I know, Mom. I want to heal as much as you do."

"You know, don't you, the police will come by to talk to you about what happened."

"I know. The doctor already mentioned it." Dane pulled on the sheet that covered him.

"Your dad and I will go home for a while. We'll come back later today. Maybe the police will have completed their job by then." She reached to touch her son's arm, "Remember, you need your rest."

Dane's eyes closed followed by a gentle nod.

Chapter 5

"Sorry to disturb you." A harsh, gravelly voice apologized for entering Dane's room. "I'm Lieutenant Alvin Lewis of the Minneapolis Police Department." In his hand he held his badge. "With your permission I need to ask a couple questions about last night. The hospital staff should have informed you of my visit." Tall, stout, in his late fifties with strands of grayish blonde hair inadequate to cover his balding crown, Lieutenant Lewis paused near the door waiting for an invitation to enter.

Dane boosted himself into a near sitting position in his bed. "Sure, come on in."

The lieutenant stepped closer to the bed. Dressed in a business suit stretching over an ample stomach, a white shirt, and a tie loosely encircling his bulky neck, the officer reminded Dane of the stereotypical TV detective. A broad smile prefaced his first question. "How you doing? I understand you sustained a concussion." His eyes drifted toward Dane's face. "And obvious injuries to your forehead."

Dane returned the smile. "A bit sore but a whole lot better than last night."

The lieutenant stood closer to the bed, feet planted wide and firm on the carpet, an image of authority. "I don't intend to take much of your time, just a few questions about what you recall from last night's incident." He reached into his suit jacket to withdraw a small note pad. "Do you mind if I sit on that chair?" He pointed to the one just inside the door of the room.

"Yeah, sure," Dane invited.

Lieutenant Louis sat down, loosened his suit coat then looked up at Dane. "First, I need to remind you of the seriousness of last night's robbery. Besides the assault with a deadly weapon, the perpetrators also face a murder charge. The young man in the store did not survive his wounds."

Dane shook his head. "That's what I heard. What a damned waste."

"It sure was." The lieutenant cleared his throat. "I understand the trauma you faced last night, but can you recall anything about your assailant?"

Dane closed his eyes grasping for an image of the man who pointed a gun in his face. "Well, it all happened kinda fast. The store was empty about two this morning when these two men walked in." Dane studied the blank TV screen suspended from the ceiling across the room. "I don't remember much about them except one was a lot bigger than the other, ah, with this mustache that almost hid his mouth." Dane ran his fingers through his hair. "Something about them made me a little suspicious. The bigger guy stood at the front of the store kinda surveying the place." He paused to consider his next comment. "Maybe I was just thinking that anybody shopping for anything at two in the morning is suspicious."

Lieutenant Lewis chuckled. "Yeah, I can relate to that. These all night shops serve as prime targets for those looking for a quick buck. Your store was the third in the last week."

"I think I heard that earlier. I think about guys out for a quick buck a lot during my long shift." Dane pulled on his sheet. "I try to remind myself that robberies happen only at other places."

Again the lieutenant smiled and nodded his head. "Yes, that's a common reaction. Sadly, these robberies have almost reached an epidemic. As I said, yours was the third in the last several days." He paused and looked up at Dane. "So these two suspicious looking dudes enter your store, the big one looking like he is surveying the place. Then what?"

"Well, they headed for the soda coolers in the back of the store." Dane continued. "They stood around the cooler for a couple minutes just looking at the sodas and water."

"Did they wear anything that would in any way identify them with any particular job, such as with the street department or with some delivery firm?" The lieutenant jotted a few notes on his pad of paper.

"I don't think so. They both wore shorts, T-shirts, and I believe they had on some kind of hiking boots. It was a warm evening."

"Can you be more specific about what these guys looked like, any special identifying features?"

The question forced Dane again into deep reflection. "As I said before, things happened awfully damed fast." Dane fumbled with the edge of his blanket. "I said before that when they entered the store I could see this one guy, with the mustache, was much bigger than the other.

"By bigger do you mean just taller or heavier or both?" The lieutenant asked.

Dane thought for a moment. "Maybe a little of both. The big guy was the one who pointed the gun at me. At the time I wasn't in any mood to consider special features with a gun in my face. But, you know when I look back on it, that big brute also had some kind of mark on his cheek, a scar or mole of some kind. I didn't have much time to look at him. I couldn't miss the mustache." Dane scratched his head and touched his tender nose. "I really didn't see much of the other shorter guy."

"What did they do by the cooler?"

"Not much. This young guy who walked in just before them got their attention."

"What exactly did they do?"

Dane breathed deeply as if to stimulate his memory. "I don't know. I guess they just moved around to another cooler, kinda keeping an eye on the young man."

Lieutenant Lewis wrote more on his note pad. He looked up at Dane. "Tell me. When did their intentions become obvious?"

Dane ran his hand over his tender forehead, touching the bandage over his left eye. "I think the two moved toward the front together. For the first time they paid some attention to me. I asked if they needed help in finding something. That's when the big guy rushed to the counter. He pulled a gun from behind his back. He pointed it in my face, then he said something like, 'You can put the damned money in the bag.' He threw this plastic sack at me."

"What did you do?"

"Almost shit in my pants." Dane rushed the answer then dipped his head. Looking up at the lieutenant, "I'm sorry, but it was one of those scary moments in my life, really scary."

"I can understand that," he acknowledged. He tapped his pen on the pad. "I know with a gun in your face you aren't concerned about being able to describe your assailant." He cleared his throat. "Do you remember anything else about what this guy looked like?"

The strain of recollection creased his damaged brow. "All I can think of is the bushy mustache, that mark on his cheek and glaring eyes. Oh, he may have had bushy hair. I can't remember clearly. I do remember he was one scary guy if that means anything."

"It all helps," the lieutenant stated. Turning very serious, he leaned forward with his arms resting on this knees. "Did you see what happened to the young man? As I noted earlier, he didn't survive the gun shot to his throat."

"I know and what a damned shame. I didn't really notice what happened in the back of the store. The big guy had my attention." Dane took a deep breath, calming emotions aroused by recalling the sequence of events. "I did hear the shot but had no idea what had happened until the police and emergency medical guys showed up."

Lieutenant Lewis rose from the chair he occupied for the entire interview and stuffed his pad of paper back into his suit coat pocket.

"Mr. Barton, I thank you for taking the time to talk to me about this robbery. I know how difficult it is remembering details of an experience you would rather forget." He stepped closer to the bed. "Just a couple things I want to leave you with. First, if over the next few days more details occur to you, please contact me at this number." He handed Dane a business card.

"Second, I must remind you that the two perpetrators of this serious crime face charges of assault with a deadly weapon, robbery and murder." His eyes opened wide and his arms stretched in front of him, palms up, reflecting the seriousness of his comments. "These charges could land them in jail for life. In that regard, please remember since you are the only eyewitness, the Hennepin County Attorney's office will eventually contact you about the event, seeking your testimony about exactly what happened that night." He paused to adjust his suit coat. "I tell you this only because you could conceivably identify them as the people who robbed your store. This could cause them to seek you out in an attempt to keep you quiet." He stepped back toward the door. "I don't wish to alarm you. I only wish to alert you to reality. If and when you return to work, please use extra caution. Consult with your boss about store security."

He moved a few steps closer to the door. "Again, thank you for your time. If I can help in some way, please don't hesitate to ask. You have my card. Incidentally, if it brings any comfort, the department will contact your boss or manager advising him what I've explained to you about security." He finally reached the door where he stopped. "Thank you and have a speedy recovery. You think of anything else, let me know." He closed the door behind him.

With the lieutenant's departure, an air of mystery lingered in the room. He impressed Dane with his gentle but thorough interview. Obviously he had considerable experience in doing his job. Dane settled back into his pillow. His journey back to the horrible events of the early morning left him physically and emotionally tired. Reflecting on the precautions referred to during the interview, Dane doubted the job at the convenience store was worth the risk. He breathed deeply and closed his eyes, thinking about what would happen next.

Dane dozed, nearly reaching the threshold of sleep. Another tap on his door interrupted his slide from reality. The door opened. A nurse stuck her head through the narrow door opening.

"Excuse me, Mr. Barton. I'm sorry but you have a visitor."

Dane emerged from the fog of near sleep. "Could his parents have returned?" A vague thought skipped through his mind. Someone told him, he recalled, of restrictions on visitors other than family members. He nudged himself up against his pillow. "Who is it?"

"A Mr. Reynolds," the nurse announced.

Dane's attention focused on the door as his boss and owner of more than one convenience store (Dane didn't know how many.) stepped around the nurse and approached the bed. Unprepared for a visit from his boss, whom he hardly knew, Dane fumbled for something to say. All he could manage was "Thanks for coming."

"You're welcome." Chester Reynolds stepped forward, short of the bed. "How ya doin?"

"Okay," Dane nodded, curious how Chester somehow circumvented the hospital's visiting schedule. Maybe those business people who own stores have special privileges. He dismissed the thought.

Dane met with Mr. Reynolds only once before, shortly after a subordinate hired Dane. That meeting lasted only minutes in the store where Dane worked. Though brief, that meeting carved in Dane's mind a distinct image of Chester Reynolds.

An anemic, pale man, smaller than Dane, he was bald except for a rim of hair around his head giving the impression of balancing above his ears, the resting place for heavy, round, aviation type glasses giving emphasis to penetrating eyes. Besides giving him better vision, they also created an image of authority for a frail, intimidated, little man. His narrowed eyes did not simply focus on people or objects, they burrowed into what he looked at. A reluctant smile guarded yellow, crooked teeth.

Standing before him now, Chester wore the same wrinkled vest over a white T-shirt turned gray he had worn when they first met. His heavy woolen trousers, secured by a belt much too long for his skinny waist, hung over shoes scuffed and dull from months of neglect. Dane found difficult understanding why a man presumably with enough money to dress presentably allowed himself to look like a vagrant.

Chester risked a momentary smile. "I don't want to take much of your time today. We can talk more later." He stepped hesitantly closer to the bed. "I wanted to check on you as soon as I heard about the robbery." He guided his beady eyes over the part of Dane's body not covered by his blanket. "You seem okay. A concussion, right? Obvious cuts on the face."

'Yes, thank you for coming."

Chester stepped back from the bed. "As I said, I don't want to bother you here. We can talk about details later." He paused to adjust his heavy glasses. "Any idea who the big guy was who hit you?"

"No, none." Dane answered.

"How about the money they got away with. Any idea how much?" Chester asked.

"No," Dane admitted again.

"The police were here?"

"Yes, just before you arrived."

"I thought so." Chester looked down at the floor as if searching for what to say next. "What did they ask?"

Dane closed his eyes more out of impatience than out of thought. "The officer asked for as many details as I could remember."

Chester shrugged his narrow shoulders. "Well, I gotta go. Just wanted to check on you. We can talk later." He turned without further comment and slipped through the partially opened door.

Dane stared at the door left open by Chester's departure. In his mind Dane asked, "What did he really want?" Strange questions from someone who should have some idea about the amount of money stolen. "What about his big guy comment? How did he know the guy was big? Maybe he got it from reports in the paper."

Dane rested his head on his pillow. Conversations with the police officer and Chester took their toll on his energy. He closed his eyes, thinking again about what would happen next.

Chapter 6

"What the hell were you assholes thinking?" Chester Reynolds, owner of three convenience stores, shouted. His voice penetrated the thin walls of the humble dwelling sending into flight birds resting in a tree outside the front door. He stared at the two men seated across the table. "Our agreement did not include bullets. You know that." He scraped his hand across the table as if sweeping away crumbs. "Now look at the fucking mess you face." He banged his fist on the table, his eyes magnified behind his glasses. "Murder is a damned serious crime around here! I want no part of it!"

Silence dropped over the cramped kitchen; a stiff breeze fluttered the curtain over a closed window. The three men huddled around a wiggly table in the middle of the kitchen floor. A free standing cupboard, a portable sink, a stove, and a small fridge occupied space around the perimeter of the room.

Tony Harris and Sylvester Ramirez, together, owned this aged building they called home. Located near Lake Independence in northwestern Hennepin County, the building at one time served as a garage. Years ago, Tony assumed ownership through a barter deal with a man for whom he did carpentry and maintenance work. Over the years Ramirez bought into the place, joining Tony in converting it into a livable four room house.

The exterior of the building did little more than keep out rain and snow. Suffering from years of neglect with siding cracked or missing and shingles curled and discolored, the small building obviously received little attention from the two maintenance men who lived there. A short distance from the lake, the sagging house sat in the shadow of towering maple trees. Indeed a humble home, it suited two Vietnam veterans in their sixties who still waited for whatever society could give them.

Tony Harris, a big man with a distinguishing mustache under flaring nostrils, and Sylvester Ramirez, slight in build with a look of perpetual submission, sat resisting Chester's vehemence. A plan to defraud an insurance company, viewed as ingenious by all three men, now faced exposure and disillusionment for the men involved. The route to this critical moment began years ago in a small rural community thirty miles north and west of the Twin Cities.

Though they shared the same public education, at times even the same classroom, not until high school did the lives of Tony Harris and Sylvester Ramirez intersect. That happened when they discovered a mutual academic apathy and overall indifference to high school. During lunch breaks as well as before and after school, they shared their disinterest in their education. By their senior year in high school they found, in each other, an identity, celebrating their rejection of any responsibility as students as well as any self-discipline to control their sluggish advance toward graduation. Nonetheless, they stayed out of trouble and did enough to get by to graduate. Upon graduation, they floundered in a world for which they lacked little preparation.

They learned during their years stumbling through high school of parallels in their lives. Both occupied the position of oldest of three siblings. They also lived a life in a lower, middle class family where both parents worked, providing adequately for their children. Where in their maturation Tony and Sylvester lost touch with the values representing dedicated parents, nobody bothered to explore. They stayed out of trouble while negotiating the jungle that at times confronts adolescents. Tony found some satisfaction playing high school football. Sylvester was content to watch others play.

Graduation left them searching for some way to support themselves. They pursued different paths. Tony sought work to the East in the big city, Minneapolis, first at a car wash then at a parking ramp. Sylvester hung around his home town, washing dishes at a local restaurant.

Months of unrelenting boredom, of almost daily conflicts with transportation into his Minneapolis job, Tony began to question where the hell he was going in his life, a question he realized he should have asked years ago. Those private moments before sleep at night or riding the bus to work in the morning invoked mature thoughts about the future and the past. Though no great patriot, Tony heard almost daily reports on the war in Vietnam, a war even he, who took no part of political conversation, watched as the war in this far off, remote country divided America. Months of introspection and reflection found Tony at nineteen years old a member of the United States Army.

Sylvester's decision to enlist arrived much more abruptly than did Tony's. The months following graduation saw only infrequent contact between the two high school friends. One of those contacts came in a local beer parlor when Tony mentioned his thoughts about the future and about Vietnam. Two weeks after Tony's enlistment, Sylvester followed his friend into the United States Army.

At the conclusion of a three-year enlistment, they returned to their home town with the expectation the country owed them a living. After all, in the seething jungles of Vietnam they had put their lives on the line for their country. Despite what they assumed about the country's debt to them, their lives reverted to a previous idleness.

Their military service brought them together with Chester Reynolds, a lean, serpentine man with bulging, penetrating eyes behind large aviation style glasses. Chester served in the same company as Tony and Sylvester. Along with the dark shadows of Vietnam memories, Chester often talked about making money. His ideas impressed the two refugees from a small rural town.

Chester grew up in St. Paul where he and one sister lived with their parents, his father employed by the city, his mother a cook in the St. Paul School District. Unlike his two military friends, Chester carried on a tradition of ambition and independence resulting in, after several years of sacrifice, determination, and three years in the Army, the ownership of three twenty-four hour convenience stores

At a time when business declined and mortgage payments eroded his diminishing bank account, Chester happened to meet up with his Vietnam buddies in a suburban, Maple Grove bar where Tony and Sylvester had stopped for a beer. Since their discharge from the Army, both had resumed a frustrating search for profitable employment. A nation, plunged into a bitter dispute over the war in which they had put up their lives, offered little in retribution. They tried various options, none working out. Desperate, they decided to combine their meager talents in establishing a maintenance service which unmistakably excluded their home by the lake.

Their day entailed repairs to rain gutters on a home near the bar. Seated in a booth on one side of the dim bar, the three engaged in talk renewing their friendship. Eventually, the conversation drifted to economics, bad economics. Chester entertained his friends with his narrative describing the convenience store enterprise. However, business was weak he admitted; without business no money came in. Out of this discussion emerged what to these three men was an ingenious plan. For Chester it promised to rescue him from the burden of mounting debt. For Tony and Sylvester it promised a better living than the scattered days of employment they faced.

The plan was simple. Chester carried thousands of dollars in risk insurance, including robbery, on his convenience stores. A burglary would conceivably entitle him to a potential, lucrative claim. The conversation with Chester awakened Tony and Sylvester's thinking about the life the country owed them. They carried no criminal record, not yet any way. A couple petty thefts lost in the haze of memory represented their only step into the world of crime.

Chester glared at his partners in crime as the wind whistled through the aging house. "Everything we discussed made the job so goddamn simple. All you had to do was use your stupid heads." He pushed his chair away from the table, scraping the rough, hardwood floor of the small four room house. At the front door he turned to face his coconspirators, hands on hips, eyes narrowed in anger. He said no more.

Tony, in silence, had listened to Chester's raving. Finally, he pounded the table, pushing his chair back against the wall. With arms outstretched, face red, eyes wide, he spoke, "All right, we fucked up. I don't know what the hell you expected Sylvester to do. The goddamned kid was on him. He had to do something. He pulled the trigger."

"And where in hell were you?" Chester shouted.

"Taking care of your guy who ran the damn place."

"Yeah, you took care of him all right, a perfect witness."

"What're you gonna do about him, the perfect witness?" Tony stepped around the table to confront Chester.

"Probably not a fucking thing. He's your problem, not mine." Chester turned to open the door.

"Not so fast. When do we get our money?" Tony urged.

"I will submit a claim after the final police report. If you're still around, you'll get your cut. Until then you'd better hide some place." He pushed on the sagging wooden door. "I'll contact you. Don't try to contact me."

Tony turned back to his friend still seated at the table. They stared at each other then at the door left half open, both considering what they would do now. They never intended to use the guns. The situation demanded they do something. Ramirez believed he had little choice than to shoot the young man who threatened to attack him. Finally, what about the guy tending the store? Chester declared him as their problem. He could make a hell of a difference in their future. Maybe the situation compelled them to do something about him. Tony reached over to close the front door.

Chapter 7

Dane waited with his parents for the arrival of the doctor, Dr. Amos Hunter, who for the last three days vigilantly tended to Dane's condition. Today would mean his release, he hoped. At least confirmation had come from the nurse who that morning stopped by to disconnect the monitoring devices attached to his arm.

Dressed in shorts, tennis shoes, and a golf shirt for the first time in three days, he had shed hospital gowns open in the back and designed to expose rear ends of any size. He sat with his mom in the straight-backed chairs provided in his room. Dressed in jeans and a sweatshirt, she took time off from work to assist in her son's return home. His dad leaned against the bed, every few minutes seeking another spot to lean on.

"What time is he supposed to stop by?" Milo glanced at his watch. Time for him always carried with it a near crisis. His over the road schedule allowed little latitude. By mid-afternoon that schedule required his presence behind the wheel of a rig destined for Chicago. Dressed in his overalls, thin, truck-driver-blue, cotton shirt and working engineer boots, he was ready to head for Chicago when they checked out of the hospital and delivered Dane home without any more drama.

Dane shifted his position in the chair. "They told me he'd stop by about 9:00 this morning. What is it now?" He looked to his parents for an answer.

"8:45," His mom glanced down at her watch.

Silence dominated the room. Milo paced from one side of the bed to another. He then made his way to the restroom, only steps from the bed.

A firm knock on the door broke the room's silence. Fingers appeared on the edge of the door as it opened only a few inches. A young man, perhaps in his late thirties, squeezed through the door. Dressed in his white doctor coat, with a clip board in hand and a stethoscope hanging from his neck, he identified himself.

"Good morning. I'm Doctor Hunter. I've been keeping an eye on Dane the last couple days." A handsome young man, he stood about six feet tall with a full head of curly hair that appeared a perpetual mess or very likely simply resisted management. Dark framed glasses contributed to his professional look, softened by a smile that weakened barriers.

Miles emerged from the bathroom.

Dane assumed responsibility for introductions. "Dr. Hunter this is my mother, Beatrice Barton. Obviously, this guy over here," he pointed to his dad coming out of the bathroom, "is my dad."

Dr. Hunter reached out his hands to shake those of both Beatrice and Milo. "Pleased to meet you, Mom and Dad."

Milo, studying the young doctor, declared, "Nice to meet you." He assumed the position next to the bed. "By the way, has this guy given you any trouble?" A rare attempt at humor.

The doctor smiled, " No, not at all."

"Thank you," was his brief reply.

The doctor stepped back to address all three members of the family. He glanced at his clipboard. "I want to take a few minutes to talk about Dane's recovery and about any restrictions to his activity. Please make yourselves comfortable. This won't take long."

Milo sought his station next to the bed. Dane and his mom sat in the chairs. Dr. Hunter stood near the door in a place where he could command the attention of all three Bartons.

Seeking eye contact with each of the family members, Doctor

Hunter began, "First, I assure you that Dane has made impressive progress in responding to his injuries. Also I want to assure you we don't anticipate any unexpected consequences from the concussion." He paused. With arms spread wide, palms up, he emphasized. "Don't get me wrong. Concussions can be dangerous injuries." He looked at Milo and Beatrice. "That's not the case with Dane. Please understand that brains can tolerate little abuse. That's the reason for the thick skull we some times make fun of. Dane's brain received only a mild bump, but still something to treat seriously. We have done that here."

Evincing a bit of impatience, Milo interrupted. "When will he get back to normal?"

The doctor smiled. "Oh, he's normal right now. He only needs to rest for a few days before resuming his usual routine."

"Does that include work?" Milo asked.

"Yes, at least for a few days. I'm going to schedule an appointment for Dane in ten days. By then we should know for certain about his return to work."

Milo shuffled his feet and nodded his head.

"What about his nose and that gash above his eye?" Beatrice spoke for the first time.

"I don't have a concern for them. Time will heal both." He looked down at Dane. "Just don't run into any doors." He smiled. After a pause he looked to each member of the family. "Do you have any more questions?"

They responded with silence.

"As I mentioned earlier, I want to see Dane in ten days. Until then make sure he gets plenty rest. Take the mild pain killers if needed for any headache," the doctor smiled, "ah, ah, which is normal under the circumstances."

The doctor stepped toward the door, turning one last time to thank the Bartons for their patience and attention. He then disappeared into the hall.

"Well, son, let's get out of here. What do we have to do next?" Milo, eager to leave, rested his hands on the edge of the door.

"Check out at the nurses' station down the hall, I guess." Dane stood up as did his mom.

Beatrice moved closer to her son, placing her arm around his back. "How do you feel? Ready to go home?"

Dane looked down upon his mom only a few inches shorter. "You know it, Mom. I've been here long enough."

"Was it that bad?" Milo asked.

Dane slid his chair out of the way. "No, it wasn't bad at all. It's just a little confining."

"You'll have to face a bit more confinement at home," his mom reminded him.

Dane smiled. "I know, Mom."

After three days Dane received his release, walking out of the hospital with a bandage over his left eye, a tender nose left to heal on its own, and a mild headache that would gradually disappear with rest and healing. He would take his doctor's advice to spend several days considering a return to his job at the convenience store, a position, more each day, fading in its appeal.

On their walk toward the parking ramp, the family passed the emergency room where only days before Dane lay barely conscious, striving to recapture what had happened.

Chapter 8

Released from the hospital the day before, Dane rested in front of the TV, relishing the familiar comfort of home, this the only place he ever called home. The attention he received during his brief stay in the hospital impressed him. Still a hospital failed to compete with the attraction of home. Home for a few hours following Dane's release, his dad left for a haul to Chicago. His schedule had him returning in four days. From experience Dane knew he and his mom couldn't depend on that schedule. Far too many unexpected circumstances could alter it.

Staring at the TV screen, Dane reviewed the events of the past five days, events he would likely remember for some time. Already he lost count of the number of times he replayed the dramatic scene at the front counter in the convenience store. When he pushed himself away from that reflection, he thought about his injuries. They amounted to nothing in comparison to what the young man suffered from the shot to his neck. Dane found senseless wasting a young life for a few dollars. Though what the robbers did run off with remained a mystery to him, no amount could justify the killing of an innocent, young man.

Nonetheless, the concussion worried him. In the past he read about people with long-range disabilities as a result of a concussion. He took some solace from the words of Dr. Hunter, who assured him that with time his brain or whatever part of his head suffered the damage would heal. In a few days he would revisit Dr. Hunter, who supposedly would remove the stitches from above his left eye, another scar to join the one from the baseball injury so many years ago.

When not reinventing the events of that fateful night at the store, Dane contemplated the future, immediate and long range. The weeks devoted to his grave yard shift at the store reinforced his aversion to those hours as well as to the duties involved which demanded little if any thinking. No genius, Dane considered himself a relatively competent, intelligent person capable of handling responsibility. However, at various times during his short life responsibility eluded him. He needed to work on correcting that flaw. Giving up on his venture into higher education did little to address that flaw. Without the degree another few months would have earned him, his options narrowed to the kind of job he had in the convenience store. Where would that lead him? Recently, it led him to the hospital.

His mom and dad both retained rewarding jobs. At least his mom did with her position in the accounting department of the same firm for which his dad drove. As far as driving a truck, Dane had serious reservations. He considered, perhaps, his dad shared those reservations. However, his dad's tenure as an over the road driver guaranteed him a good income. The days ahead, days dedicated to healing, offered him the opportunity to think about his future. At twenty-three he stood at the threshold of that future. Of that his dad reminded him with regularity.

Dane stood up from his place on the sofa, stretched, walked to the nearby kitchen for a glass of water, and returned. Before he could sit down to resume his desultory, TV entertainment, the phone rang, not his cell phone within easy reach but the land line phone resting on a small table across the room. A few quick steps brought him to the phone.

"Hello," though the explanation eluded him, his voice often attracted some comment, such as "You should take that voice on the air." or "Where did you pick up that distinctive, mellow voice?" The quality of his voice failed to assume any importance for Dane.

After all, what great benefit does a special voice offer? He could find no answer to that question. Apparently others could. He never really dwelled on the significance of his voice even though during his school years he heard comments he didn't even understand about the mellow tone of his voice, a mellifluous quality, a word he had never heard of. Perhaps he benefitted from what a teacher long ago called his mother's loquacity. Dane shuttered to think such a word applied to him.

"May I speak with Mr. Barton please?" the speaker's voice deep yet without a hint of threat. He remembered the precautions given by Lieutenant Lewis regarding Dane's potential vulnerability to two desperate crooks.

"Speaking," Dane replied.

"Mr. Barton, my name is Andre Harrington. I'm a reporter for Channel 11 news. You familiar with our station?"

Dane's mouth dropped open with the mention of a TV reporter. "Yeah, yes, of course."

"I'm calling about your resent experience with robbers at a local convenience store. I'm preparing a report on the string of robberies. Would you have time for a few questions?"

Dane shifted the phone in his hand, his immediate reaction to a call from a reporter weakened by his misgivings about more publicity and its potential effect on his safety. But what could it hurt? "Ah, Ah, yeah, sure. I think I have time."

"Great. Would you be willing to discuss the incident on camera?"

Dane stared into the empty space above the TV. What should he do? Silence filled the phone line.

"Perhaps, I could let you think about it. I could call back later." Mr. Harrington's voice retained its calm, reassuring quality.

"No, I, I don't think you have to do that." Dane closed his eyes to aid his thinking. "What did you have in mind?"

Over the phone Dane heard the reporter exhale, a sign of relief. "As I mentioned earlier, I'm doing a story on the recent rash of robberies of all-night convenience stores like the one where you worked. With your permission, I would like to interview you here at our studio or if you prefer, at your home." He paused waiting for a reply.

Dane shuffled his feet. "Yeah, I think that's okay. Could we do it here? It's a bit easier for me. I'm kinda confined. No driving for a while and both parents work"

"Absolutely, that would be perfect," another hint of relief in the reporter's voice. "I don't mean to push you, but could you be available tomorrow morning? I'm under a rigid time restraint."

Considering Dane's commitment to recovery at home, he could see no complications for a morning interview. "That sounds good to me. About what time?

"How about 10:30 tomorrow morning?" Mr. Harrington suggested.

"Sounds good," Dane confirmed. "By the way, do you know where I live?"

"Yes, the wonder of GPS will guide me out to western Hennepin County, right?" Harrington emitted a chuckle.

"That's right."

"Well, Mr. Barton, I'll see you tomorrow morning at 10:30 and thank you for your time."

"You're welcome and thank you. See you in the morning."

Dane replaced the phone then leaned against the wall, considering if he made the right decision, if the publicity would do him more harm than good, or if the two crooks would watch the interview on TV, whenever it played?

Dane walked back to the living room sofa, preoccupied with the decision he made, feeling a hint of confidence that maybe he shouldn't worry about the robbers. Maybe the police would find them before his story aired. Maybe, too, his moment on TV will reap benefits; what kind, he had no idea.

He smiled, thinking about his morning appointment with a TV reporter. He never for the world entertained any idea he would ever sit for an interview with a reporter. He reached for the remote and switched on the TV, wondering what he would look like on the screen.

Chapter 9

Dane rested with his mom on the living room sofa. For Beatrice it marked the end to another long day of recording numbers and checking them twice. For Dane it concluded another day of idleness. Tomorrow's appointment with Dr. Hunter, he hoped, would free him to consider a return to work. That return he still contemplated with ambiguity. Dane envisioned no future working the grave yard shift or any shift at a convenience store. What his future did hold eluded him. He already squandered one route to the future when he dropped out of the community college. Nonetheless, the first step of the return to some kind of work depended on Dr. Hunter's assessment of Dane's physical as well as emotional condition.

Dressed in her robe in preparation for an early escape to bed, Beatrice sat restlessly waiting for Channel 11, ten o'clock news. Never had she personally known anyone she saw on TV. Now she anticipated the rare opportunity to watch her own son. Though she tried, she failed to control her fidgeting with the buttons on her robe or fluffing the sofa pillows or adjusting the TV volume.

Dane handled his anxiety with more discretion, simply doing a better job of concealing it. On the floor near the TV he sat on his hands undecided about what to do with them. Five days had elapsed since the interview session with Mr. Harrington. The excitement he felt waiting for the news matched the excitement he experienced waiting for the arrival of Andre Harrington, even the name carried with it some intimidation.

That morning five days ago, Dane got up when his mom left for work, much earlier than the news reporter's scheduled appointment at 10:30. Though he refused to admit any excitement over his interview, he found sleeping impossible beyond 6:30 a.m. Mr. Harrington arrived precisely at 10:30, accompanied by a crew of two, a camera man and another technician whose job Dane didn't understand. The equipment and people needed for a simple interview amazed him. "My god," he thought, "what do they need for a really important interview?"

Handsome with hair cut short, and vivid blue eyes that joined his lips in a smile, Andre Harrington expressed his gratitude for the chance to talk with Dane about the recent rash of burglaries. Harrington, dressed informally in a plain Polo golf shirt and khaki trousers, helped make Dane more comfortable in the reporter's presence. The only hint of any special status, a huge watch covering his wrist, grabbed Dane's attention, giving him pause to consider if the watch served some important function since time imposed rigid restrictions on TV broadcasting. Maybe it added simply a mark of distinction. Dane confessed to himself the watch made absolutely no difference. It attracted his attention probably because of his expectations about the type of person he would meet in Mr. Harrington. After all, a big time TV reporter must attend to image. Dane concluded Mr. Harrington projected little concern for image. Quite the opposite, he was unassuming and engaging.

Mr. Harrington introduced his staff, seeking Dane's approval to set up special lighting in the living room. Large cables snaked out to a van parked in the driveway, declaring on its sides, "Channel 11 News." Dane watched the process with disbelief in the extent of the preparation, positioning of lights, testing of microphones, adjusting cameras, for an interview with him.

Waiting now for that interview to play before him on the

TV, Dane recalled the well orchestrated approach employed by Mr. Harrington. Of course, he asked many of the same questions asked by the police lieutenant in the hospital. However, he tastefully avoided pressuring Dane into commenting about details he did not fully remember. He reached for spontaneity, avoiding always the appearance of rehearsed responses. Dane discovered, in the days since the incident, details he hadn't remembered gradually gained more clarity. Perhaps the enhanced memory had something to do with psychological calming; the reduction in tension released from his memory details at first suppressed. Also Harrington's professional technique helped stimulate Dane's memory.

During the interview the gentle verbal maneuvering by Harrington helped Dane recall or bring into sharper focus a couple details previously buried in his memory. A mustache required no verbal priming. He would not soon forget that detail. Linking carefully the sequence of events awakened details previously inaccessible. This applied definitely to the crucial moment when Dane stared into the barrel of a pistol. Likewise with Harrington's careful urging, Dane admitted that the smaller of the two robbers may have walked with a limp, and the one who accosted him had some kind of mole or scar on his cheek.

To his credit, Harrington, aware of the sensitivity of the subject, devoted very little time to the tragic death of the innocent, young man. Only in establishing the sequence of events did he mention the young man and, relative to Dane, his location in the store.

"Milo, are you going to get in here? The news is on." Beatrice sat up straight on the sofa, her hands folded on her lap.

"Yeah, in a minute. Is our celebrity on already?" Milo hovered over the kitchen table concluding records for his recent haul to Chicago. His return earlier in the day demanded he complete the necessary expense records. Since his wife managed the trucking firm's accounting department, he applied careful attention to his mileage and expense reports.

"No, but it could come at any time," Beatrice cautioned.

Suddenly, the TV screen filled with a picture of their living room, the very one where they now all sat, Dane on the floor off to one side of the TV, his parents on the sofa. The camera focused on Dane, a smile suggesting a degree of relaxation he didn't feel. Watching now, he relived the tension he felt at the time, the perspiration around his neck and forehead. He recalled, also, the calming words of Mr. Harrington, who introduced Dane to the TV audience and described the extent of his injuries before explaining the purpose for the interview, to explore the recent increase in burglaries hitting all night businesses.

"You look so handsome," his mom declared.

"A real celebrity. Did they powder your nose and spray your hair?" A playful grin stretched his dad's lips.

The interview progressed with Dane doing most of the talking, a result of Harrington's professional interviewing talent. The family listened intently to the five minute segment, well aware already of the details Dane discussed. All the time and energy that went into a five minute report again amazed Dane. Nonetheless, he took pride in his part of the interview. His only misgiving centered on the potential for the miscreants who faced serious criminal charges seeing the report and learning his name and maybe even something about where he lived.

The newscast moved on to other news items then weather and sports, only Milo paying much attention.

"Son, you did great. What a delight to see you on the screen. I didn't know you could speak so, ah, ah, mellow, yet distinct." Beatrice settled back in the sofa.

"Was it rehearsed?" Milo, for a moment, looked away from the TV. Laughing, he looked at his wife. "He sounded just like you."

"Oh, stop it," she reprimanded. "He sounded like himself, clear and confident. He didn't stumble once."

Milo stood up still dressed in his driving overalls and pale blue, denim shirt. He looked down at his wife still seated on the sofa.

In another of his rare moments of humor, he laughed. "You know, sweetheart, maybe he has some of that stuff you had." He scratched his head in thought. "You remember someone wrote this word in your yearbook. Something about your talking. Ah, Ah, shit I can't think of it."

"Loquacity," Beatrice smiled, then rose from the sofa to make a playful jab at her husband, picturing in her mind the teacher who started the rumor that survived all these years.

On the floor Dane grinned, pleased with his part in the interview but unable to dismiss the potential harm from the publicity. Staring but really not seeing what now appeared on TV, he pondered if those two thugs had watched his interview.

Chapter 10

Dane's moment in the sun set quickly. By the next day the excitement generated by the interview faded, leaving him with a feeling of self-satisfaction. He did well. What effect the interview would have on the resolution of the robbery he questioned. At least Mr. Harrington's report should awaken the concern of residents in those areas where the robberies had taken place. Right now the search for a resolution rested with his boss, Mr. Reynolds, and the police. Dane's concern centered on his impending appointment with Dr. Hunter, the one to determine the timing of his return to a normal routine. In the morning, since his concussion suspended his driving privileges, his dad, in between truck hauls, would drive him to Methodist Hospital and the meeting with Dr. Hunter.

The usual congestion of cars and people greeted Dane and his dad as they moved, foot by foot, through the parking ramp, seeking the first available stall.

"God, is everybody sick?" Milo turned to address his son slouched in the seat next to him.

Dane glanced over at his dad. "A big place."

Nearly running out of floors in the ramp, they spotted a place. An elevator ride down to the first floor, a long walk to a receptionist desk, another elevator ride to the third floor finally brought them to Dr. Hunter's office. Another receptionist greeted them, checked Dane in, and requested they have a seat.

In minutes a nurse, with Maggie printed on her name badge, introduced herself to Dane and his dad. She directed Dane to Dr. Hunter's examination room, suggesting his dad would be more comfortable in the reception area. In the examination room she faced Dane, smiled, and asked, "How you doing today?"

"A lot better than the last time I was here." Dane waited instructions.

"Please take a seat in the chair next to the desk. The one under the desk is for me." Maggie laughed.

Dane relaxed in the straight back chair designed for convenience, not comfort. Without hesitation, Maggie checked his blood pressure, then asked, "Any more headaches?"

"No," Dane watched as Maggie recorded his responses.

"How about your nose? On a scale of one to ten, where would you rank any pain, nose or other places?" Maggie waited for Dane's response.

"Oh, maybe a two, nothing is perfect," he smiled.

"That's great. Today we get rid of those stitches above your eye." Maggie reached for a small package of instruments presumably for that purpose.

"Will it hurt?" Dane asked, not all together serious. Still the area around the eye was a tender area.

Maggie jotted a few words on her chart. "Only if you move." She laughed. With that comment she unwrapped the small package of instruments, a small tweezer and scissors designed to remove stitches without producing pain.

She positioned herself directly in front of Dane then leaned closer.

Dane licked his lips, tense in anticipation of pain.

Placing her hand on Dane's forehead, she urged, "Hold still, now." With lips clinched, she snipped. "That's one; that's two; that's three, four, five, six, and seven." She sat back in her chair. "There, now that wasn't so bad was it?"

Dane ran his hand gently over the healed wound. Maggie

handed him a small mirror to inspect the scar. He positioned the mirror to include the area above his left eye. "Kinda matches the other one," he joked.

"Yeah, it kinda does." Maggie studied the area of the new scar. "Where did the other one come from?"

Dane smiled, "It's a long story. A baseball game and a wild pitch that hit me on the head."

"Ouch!" Maggie shivered. Her function concluded, she left the examination room with the promise Dr. Hunter would be in shortly. He was.

Dressed in his usual doctor attire including the ever present stethoscope, Dr. Hunter greeted Dane with an out stretched hand. "How you doing?" he spoke with a smile. "Saw you on the news the other night. Nice job."

"Thank you," Dane sat back down on the chair next to the desk squeezed in the corner of the room.

Dr. Hunter took the chair in front of the desk. He switched on the computer attached to the wall above the desk. He studied the image for a few seconds. Looking over at Dane, he asked, " Have you experienced any more headaches?"

"No, not really, at least not in the last few days." Dane sat forward in his chair.

"Any discomfort in the nose?" The doctor selected a cone shaped device he used to inspect inside of Dane's nose. "Looks good."

The doctor studied the recently exposed scar on Dane's forehead. 'The scar looks good. It should fade a bit in time." He rolled his chair back away from Dane. 'Ready to go back to work?"

"Yeah, I sure am."

"Well, as far as I'm concerned just go for it."

Dane released a deep breath. "Thank you. I've waited to hear you say that."

The doctor rose from his chair. "Just take it a bit easy at first. Your body still needs time to heal that head completely. Otherwise, you're as good as new." A couple steps toward the door and the doctor paused. "By the way, any word on the guys who invaded your store?"

"No, I've heard nothing from the police since the lieutenant talked to me in the hospital."

"Sometimes these are tough crimes to solve."

Dane stood up and nodded his head. "I guess so. The toughest part is with the young guy shot."

"What a shame." At the door, the doctor stopped. "Remember, you have any questions, please call. Also in about six weeks, I'd like to see you again for a final check." He stepped through the door then turned, "Have a good day. In fact have several good days." He closed the door behind him.

While Dane spent time in the examination room, his dad waited almost patiently in the room designed for that purpose, the waiting room. Dane entered all smiles.

His dad stood up and stretched. "Well, how did it go? You gonna live?"

"I'm afraid so," Dane echoed the humorous intent of his dad's comment.

When they arrived home, a message awaited them on the land line phone. Since the televised interview, Dane tensed whenever the phone rang. Nothing threatening happened thus far. Still, he could not dismiss the thought of the two burglars finding his phone number or even worse finding where he lived. The red light blinked reminding Dane of a phone message from someone. He stepped to the phone resting on an end table across the living room from the sofa. He stared at the blinking light, his hand reaching for the phone. Picking up the hand set, he checked the caller ID, a Mr. Monty Carmona.

He searched his mind for a Monty Carmona. He ran his hand through his hair, touching the new scar above his eye. With a name like Carmona who knew what kinds of mischief captured his time. Dane positioned his finger over the delete button. He paused in doubt.

"Screw it." He deleted the message, with a little guilt for falling victim to name stereotyping.

Milo's rigid trucking schedule reduced the time he could share dinner with his wife and son. The evening following Dane's appointment with Dr. Hunter gave him that chance. Her position as assistant manager of accounting at the same trucking firm for which Milo drove limited her time to prepare meals for her family. With Dane's help, this evening she prepared a family favorite, a special baked chicken breast. Intent on enjoying the meal, the Bartons sat around their kitchen table eating in silence, their individual schedules limiting them to enjoy only occasionally the rare chance of sharing a meal as well as thoughts about their lives.

"You had a good report from the doctor." Beatrice set aside her fork to reach for her glass of milk. She looked across the table at her son. "What specifically did he say about the concussion?"

Dane sat back in his chair, chewing slowly. "Not much. Just report back to him any severe headaches or dizziness."

Beatrice fixed her eyes on her son's new scar. "They did a nice job of sewing up that nasty cut on your forehead."

"I guess so." Dane took another bite of chicken.

"They had to save his pretty face to go along with his pretty voice." Milo's lips spread in a typical caustic grin.

"Oh, stop it, now. That's enough of your smart tongue. Your son is lucky. Now stop making fun." Beatrice scolded her husband, who hung his head in mock shame.

Silence returned to the Barton family table. Dane looked at his parents. A crease formed above his new scar and across his forehead. 'Do either of you know anybody with the name like, ah, ah, Monty Carman or no, ah, ah, I think it was Monty Carmona?"

"What's the name?" Milo asked.

"I think Monty Car … something." Dane shrugged his shoulders.

Beatrice rolled her eyes. "Where did that name come from?"

"When Dad and I got back from the doctor's appointment, there was a message on the answering machine. I checked the caller ID." Dane shrugged his shoulders. "Never heard of that name so I didn't listen to it."

"Probably a good thing. Just another sales job." Milo laid his fork off to the side of his plate. He studied his son. "What's going to come of this damn burglar stuff? Have you talked to the police again?"

"No, I haven't heard a thing."

Milo leaned his elbows on the table. "What about the little creep who owns the place? Has he talked to you again?"

Dane shook his head. "No, he said we would talk later after I healed a bit."

"Well, you've healed now."

Dane's shoulder slumped. "I know, Dad. What I don't know is if I want to go back to that dead end job."

Milo pushed his chair back from the table. "Yeah, it may be a dead end job, but it is a job."

Beatrice got up from her chair to address her husband. "Please, Milo, be a little understanding. Dane's trying to decide what to do." She picked up her plate and set it near the kitchen sink only a few steps from the table. She turned to look at her son and husband. "All this talk about jobs. What about those guys who robbed the place, injuring our son and killing an innocent man?" She inhaled then crossed her arms over her chest. "What do you think, Dane? Will they try to find you? I'm no lawyer, but it doesn't take one to realize these guys are in deep shit. Forgive my language."

"There you go again with that, ah, loquacity," Milo chuckled.

Beatrice dropped her arms then gripped her hips. "Milo, this is not funny. Dane could be in trouble if these thugs decide getting rid of a witness to their crime will keep them out of jail."

"Mom, Mom, settle down." Dane clasped his hands behind his head. "You make a good point. Don't think I haven't considered it. So have the police. Lt. Lewis told me in the hospital to keep in touch about any suspicious cars around here or phone calls. That's why I didn't answer the message this afternoon."

"I guess we all have to watch out for a while." Milo pushed farther away from the table. "I've got an early trip tomorrow. Got to get to bed. Son, you gonna take me to the garage?"

"Yes, I am." Though Beatrice worked for the same trucking firm, her schedule as well as the location of her office failed to match her husband's.

The doctor's visit also included a clearance for Dane to resume driving a car.

Chapter 11

Dane yawned, arching his back as much as his seat belt allowed. Despite his job or maybe because of it early mornings carried little appeal for him. His drive home, however, gave him a glimpse of the recently risen sun casting a pinkish glow across the eastern horizon. The early morning hours at the convenience store usually found Dane occupied inside, shielded from the simple splendor of nature. This morning he committed to driving his dad to the trucking garage where he would step into a huge cab to begin another extended trip over the road.

Dane relaxed in the driver's seat, reflecting on his return to a normal life free from the restrictions imposed by doctors and nurses. He anticipated the meeting with Chester Reynolds to discuss his future at the convenience store. Ambivalent about that future, he was sure about one part of it. He would not return to the same store where he most recently worked. The fierce, threatening eyes behind the gun pointed at his face raced through his mind. What possible dangers Dane still faced lingered, much too accessible, in his memory.

With a slight shake of his head, Dane jerked himself back to the reality of driving home in the freshness of the early morning air. Returning home, he greeted his mother, who readied herself for another day in the accounting office.

"Morning, son. Mission accomplished, right?" Beatrice rinsed her coffee cup at the kitchen sink.

"Yeah, delivered with plenty time to spare."

Beatrice faced her son. "Can I get you anything for breakfast?"

Dane opened the fridge door, grabbing a carton of apple juice. "No thanks. I'm fine with a little juice and maybe some toast."

"I need to take off for work. What are your plans for the day?" She searched in her purse for her car keys.

Seated at the table, Dane chuckled, "Not much. Maybe read a little. Maybe try to figure out if I want to go back to the damned store."

Beatrice paused before opening the door to the garage and her car. "It'll work out. You don't have to rush into anything."

"Yes, I know." He took a swallow of juice. "I've got to get in touch with good old Chester, I suppose."

"Okay. See you later." Beatrice stepped into the garage.

Dane slid his chair away from the table, stretched out his legs and dropped his hands into his lap. Just what would he do today, tomorrow, or the next? Chester, he assumed, would contact him. At least, he thought that was the arrangement. Either back to the convenience store or someplace else. He couldn't continue living in some kind of vacuum. He drank the last of his juice. Easing himself out of his chair, he moved toward the sink. From the living room the phone rang. He glanced at the clock on the wall next to the fridge, 8:45. The early morning call produced before his eyes visions of that beast who pointed a gun in his face.

Placing his glass in the sink, he hurried to the unrelenting phone. He checked caller ID, "Monty Carmona." Dane stiffened. The phone rang repeatedly. He reached for the receiver; at the same time the call went to voice mail.

"Hello. I'm calling for Mr. Dane Barton. My name is Monty Carmona. I would like to talk with Mr. Barton about a position with my company."

Dane listened to the distinct, mellow tone of Carmona's voice.

"I would like the chance to explain this opportunity. Thank you." He closed leaving his phone number and extension.

Dane stared at the blinking red light on the answering machine. His finger hesitated over the delete button as he contemplated the identity of Monty Carmona, who could have something to do with the robbery. Dane closed his eyes and shook his head, pondering the possibility of the job offer only a ploy to confirm his phone number.

He dropped onto the nearby sofa. With hands clasped behind his head, he pushed his legs straight in front of him. In his mind, the question replayed, "What would he do today, tomorrow, or the next day?" He pulled his legs back, slapping his hands against his knees. "Screw it," he uttered aloud.

He quickly stood up, walked to the phone a few steps away, and dialed Mr. Carmona's number. After the sixth ring, a sweet, female voice answered. "Fore Sure Telemarketing. My name is Carmen Hinton. How may I help you?"

Dane explained the reason for his call, prompting Carmen to transfer him quickly to Mr, Carmona's extension. His distinct already familiar voice greeted Dane. "How are you today?"

"Fine," came Dan's terse response.

"Thank you for returning my call. Let me be brief. I caught your interview on TV the other night. Very nice job. Your composure and articulation impressed me." He paused.

Dane gripped the phone. "Thank you."

"Please accept my concern for your injuries. I trust you are recovering."

Again Dane said, "Thank you. Yes, I am."

"Excuse me, but I don't wish to take up much of your time. Do you have a couple minutes?"

Already Mr. Carmona had consumed a couple minutes. Dane nodded his head. "I guess so."

"Good, then let me be brief. I own a telemarketing firm in suburban Plymouth. We can always use composed, articulate voices like yours. If you have some time, I would like to invite you to my office where I can explain in detail what we do at Fore Sure Telemarketing." A pause. "I realize this is sudden. Of course, you can take a little time to think it over."

Dane stood up perplexed by this man with the strange, Hollywood kind of name. "Ah, yeah, this is a bit sudden." He ran his fingers over the new scar above his left eye, pondering what he had to lose? "Okay, let me think about it, and I'll get back to you." His voice sounding more confident.

"Great. Can I expect to hear from you in a day or two?" Carmona asked.

"I think so," Dane confirmed.

"Thank you. I'll await your call." The conversation ended leaving only the dial tone.

The rest of the day Dane debated the request. He almost laughed out loud when he thought about acquiring a job based on the tone of his voice. Though it wasn't the first time reference was made to, what did his dad call it, "loquacity." This Carmona avoided a pressure sales pitch. Dane scolded himself for such indecision. His attitude toward Chester Reynolds and his empire of convenience stores served as no justification for his delay. Almost anything would surpass the grim hours he worked at a job that could have gotten him killed. Lounging around the house, he carried with him this internal debate, more annoying as the day progressed.

Upon her return from work, Dane explained his dilemma to his mom. She concurred with his skepticism. She also reminded him of the need to move on, to find a path toward employment satisfaction and security. At twenty-three he needed direction and stability. Through the evening they did not return to the subject. The next morning they did.

"Well, what do you think?" Dane's mom asked as they shared a light breakfast.

Dane closed his eyes and furrowed his brow, lips pressed together, then relaxed in a smile. "You know, will it make a ton of difference if I call back? Who knows, maybe I can find out something interesting."

"I don't know much about telemarketing except it's kinda a bother sometimes, those pesky calls at dinner time," Beatrice admitted. She placed her hand on her son's shoulder. "You're probably right, though. What damage can it do?"

That afternoon Dane called Mr. Carmona to set up an appointment for the next day at 11:00 a.m.

Up early the next morning, greeted by a clear, early autumn sky, Dane viewed, with a bit of excitement, the prospect of the meeting with Carmona. A plunge into the unknown did that sometimes.

"Good luck today," his mom said as she left for work.

At most, Dane figured a drive of no more than thirty minutes would deliver him to the address Carmona gave him. At 10:45 he pulled into the parking lot of a small strip mall adjacent to I-494 in suburban Plymouth. Made up of a variety of businesses including an insurance company, a real estate office, and a chain grocery store, the area reflected merchants who valued image. No debris littered the parking lot and sidewalks. Professionally produced and installed signage identified each business. Dane's destination occupied the second floor of the real estate office, the only two story building in the development.

An elevator stood ready to transport him up one floor. He elected to take the stairs. On the second floor he faced a door imprinted with "Fore Sure Telemarketing" in bold letters. He opened the door to look into the bright eyes and engaging smile of an attractive young woman who introduced herself as Carmen Hinton.

Dane approached the reception desk. "I'm Dane Barton. I have an appointment with Mr. Carmona at 11:00."

"Yes, we've been expecting you." Carmen rose from her chair behind the desk. Slightly taller than Dane, she appeared more elegantly dressed than necessary for someone sitting behind a desk all day. Still, to Dane, she looked damned good sitting there.

"Please follow me," she invited.

A few steps down a short hall brought them to an unpretentious metal door proclaiming the office of "Monty Carmona, President." Carmen's light tap on the door produced a muffled, "Yes?"

Carmen opened the door enough to announce the arrival of Mr. Barton.

"Come right in," the voice deep and accommodating.

She pushed the door open, moving aside to allow Dane to enter the office. He stood in the center of a small room, no bigger than a master bedroom suite, meticulous in furnishings. To his right, Dane glimpsed a window decorated with a flamboyant curtain, reminiscent of a stage curtain. A modest wooden desk occupied the better part of one wall, lined with book shelves made from the same wood as the desk. On top of the desk sat the replica of an old wall mounted, cranked phone, the kind common in the 1940s and 1950s.

Mr. Carmona, with hand extended, stepped around his desk. "Mr. Barton, I'm Monty Carmona. I'm so pleased to meet you." He turned to Carmen standing off to the side. "I assume you've met Carmen, one of my very versatile assistants."

Dane smiled. "Yes, we've met and pleased to meet you too."

Carmen smiled then slipped through the open door, closing it behind her.

Dressed in a blue sport coat, gray trousers, a button-down collar shirt open at the neck, Mr. Carmona made an instant impression of calm, self-assurance. Taller than Dane, true of most men except, perhaps, for Chester Reynolds, Carmona's dark hair, combed straight back, lay just over his collar. Dark eyes danced with his smile exposing sparkling white teeth.

From Italian ancestry, Monty Carmona grew up in rural Iowa in a small town only miles from Minnesota's southern border. In search of a better life, his grandfather left Italy to settle ultimately on land vastly different from that in his homeland. Determination and diligence rewarded the Carmona family with a farm specializing in corn fields stretching for miles. From an early age Monty evinced an affinity with the dramatic. He delighted in long lectures to the family dog or standing in front of a mirror watching the movement of his mouth as he read aloud passages from his collection of children's books.

Throughout his education he found great satisfaction in losing his own identity to assume that of a character in some dramatic production. Upon graduation from high school, Monty moved onto the University of Iowa where he majored in theater. His college experience refined his acting talent and strengthened his voice. With a move to the Twin Cities in search of an acting career, Monty discovered fierce competition for work even in a cultural environment rich in community theater. Spending long nights waiting tables did little to fulfill his dream of theatrical success. After a few stints in several neighborhood theaters around the Twin Cities, even minor roles at the internationally acclaimed Guthrie Theater, he surrendered to the realization that theater would not provide him a living.

A few stumbling starts in advertising and for one season the voice of the St. Paul Saints baseball team, Monty signed on with a telemarketing firm where his dramatic talent made him a quick success. In time he set off on his own, establishing a company he named Fore Sure Telemarketing.

"Please take a seat, Mr. Barton." Monty pointed to the chair in front of his desk. He returned to his place behind the desk. Folding his hands on top the desk in front of him, he fixed his eyes on Dane. "Have you recovered from your injuries?"

"Pretty much so." Dane settled into the narrow chair.

Monty smiled. "As I told you on the phone, your interview on TV impressed me. Quite a traumatic experience."

Dane nodded his head.

Monty pulled his hands back to rest in his lap. "Mr. Barton, I've asked you here to acquaint you with our telemarketing business. We are young, but we are good." He emphasized the point by stabbing his finger on top his desk. "I think you could make us even better." He paused nudging his chair closer to the desk. He cleared his throat. "I know some telemarketers have acquired a bad reputation. The business can lend itself to abuse. Here, we try to satisfy the needs of our clients without intrusion into private lives."

Dane listened, repositioning himself on his chair. "I don't pretend to understand much about your business. I do know we have received calls in the middle of dinner."

Monty shook his head. "I know, and I wish there was some way to avoid that kind of call. When you have to access as many potential customers as possible, avoiding a dinner intrusion isn't always possible."

Dane nodded his head then ran his finger next to his tender nose. "What exactly would the job involve?"

Monty smiled, uncovering his pure white teeth. "Great question." He tipped back in his chair. "Of course, you know the basic purpose of telemarketing is sales. We offer a service to our clients which includes personal contact with customers who might need our clients' services or products."

Dane listened, fully aware of the purpose of telemarketing.

"With us," Monty continued, "you would exploit that theatrical voice of yours to communicate by phone with potential customers."

Dane chuckled. "Theatrical?"

"Absolutely, I know about precise articulation. How you acquired yours I've not sure, but you have it. I'm sure of that."

Dane grinned, looked down at his hands squeezed together in his lap.

"The routine is simple." Monty pursued his explanation. "Our clients, some selling windows, some selling remodeling, some selling vocations, hire us to promote their products. We have a data base of possible customers whom we call with an offer to try a product or to seek more information." Again the smile. "We don't always call at dinner time either."

Monty discussed in detail the role of a caller, hours on the job, and compensation. Rising out of his chair behind the desk, he moved around to stand beside Dane's chair. "Look, enough talk. Come with me. We'll take a look at the operation."

Monty guided Dane out of the office, back toward the reception desk, and into a larger room, maybe the size of a large family room, without windows. Located around the periphery of the room, Monty pointed our four phone stations each equipped with phones, a panel of blinking lights and other electronic items Dane found curious. Seated at three of the stations, two young women and an older gentleman managed the phones. Far outside prime time to call prospective customers, late morning and early afternoon gave callers the chance to prepare any presentations or to practice those already prepared.

Along side Dane, Monty stood in the middle of the floor. "Excuse me for a minute." Three heads turned to face their boss. "Pardon the interruption. This is Mr. Dane Barton. He's here to consider filling our empty chair." He touched Dane's shoulder. "Permit me to introduce my hard working staff. Over there that stunning blonde is Ashley Ryland. Next to her is Misty Snow, whose voice everyone finds irresistible. And around on this side is Emile Molina, the one who takes control when these ladies get out of hand. Laughter rippled through the room. All three voiced a greeting of "Welcome" or simply "Hello."

Monty clasped his hands behind his back in a mild commanding gesture. "Dane and I have been talking about his joining us. Perhaps we will know in a few days." He turned to Dane, smiled and applied a playful tap on his shoulder.

Monty followed Dane out to his car in the parking lot. He leaned his hands against the roof. "Thanks for taking the time to talk with us. Consider my offer. Let me know soon. We could use you, especially for the approaching fall season."

Dane started the car. "Thank you for the information and the offer. I will get back to you."

Driving west toward home, Dane reflected on the nearly two hour meeting with Mr. Carmona, who offered him an alternative to Chester's stores, an alternative he most assuredly would consider.

Chapter 12

Dane stared at the plain faded door with the name "Chester Reynolds" affixed near the top. Years of hands had worn any color off the doorknob. He made a quick survey of the area around the door, scattered candy wrappers, a lone pop can resting in a corner, linoleum worn through exposing bare wood. In the short time Dane worked for Chester Reynolds, he had no reason to visit what Chester termed "his corporate headquarters." All previous contact took place in the store where Dane eventually worked.

Turning to view the entire lobby, Dane smiled as he compared this office complex with that of Carmona's in Plymouth. The first sight of the building containing Chester's office, awakened Dane's suspicions about his convenience store enterprise. Located at the far south end of Hennepin Avenue in Minneapolis, the building joined a series of three to five story structures of 1930s vintage. Of brick construction, the buildings suffered the ravages of time, small pieces of brick accumulating around the foundation, joining neglected bushes with curled leaves and dried twigs where once leaves grew. Heavy mesh screens protected foggy windows. Uncontrolled vine growth wrapped around one corner of the building.

The irony of Chester Reynolds' call yesterday afternoon gave Dane a chuckle. Only minutes after his return from the interview with Mr. Carmona, the phone rang. Chester suggested they meet the next day to discuss Dane's future with the company. The invigorating meeting with the people at Fore Sure Telemarketing infused him with a fresh flow of doubt and misgiving about continuing in the convenience store business. Nonetheless, he believed he did have an obligation, at least, to discuss the question of his returning.

In addition, he carried with him concern, perhaps even fear, for his safety from retaliation by the vermin who robbed the store. More important, they killed an innocent man and, in Dane's mind, messed up his own life. The short, phone conversation with Chester did end with an appointment the next day in early afternoon.

For much that remained of the day, Dane reflected on that conversation and on the meeting scheduled for the next day. He frowned when he thought of all the meetings and appointments dominating his life since the fateful moment in the convenience store. He decided in his own mind that if he derived any benefit from the robbery experience, it related to how the event provoked deeper consideration of his future. Even before the robbery, he knew his future lay in a world far removed from the world of convenience stores.

Standing before the faded door, Dane harbored little doubt about his decision to leave Chester's world. He raised his hand to knock firmly on the door.

"Come on in." The voice that filtered through the door sounded more masculine than the familiar strained squeak of Chester Reynolds. Dane turned the knob and pushed open the door.

Seated behind what appeared an Army surplus desk, dark green in color, Chester Reynolds looked up from a stack of papers to squint at Dane but refused to rise to greet his guest.

"Come in. Take a seat," he gestured toward a folding chair off to the right of the desk.

A five story building, it housed three offices on the first floor; only one belonged to Reynolds. Apartments filled the four upper floors of the building. From what Dane could observe, Chester's office contained minimal furnishings: the desk, two steel filing cabinets, two folding chairs, a chair on wheels behind the desk, and a book case supported on one end by two bricks.

A skinny, anemic looking man, one of the few in Dane's acquaintance shorter than he, Chester wore his round, trade mark aviation glasses that accentuated probing eyes. Dressed in a gray shirt open at the collar and a wrinkled vest with two missing buttons, Chester, somewhere in his early sixties, had changed little since his days growing up in St. Paul. He rarely identified with any social group. What he lacked in size he made up for in ambition and determination. Those qualities, combined with an occasional disregard for rules and ethics, eventually found Chester Reynolds the owner of three convenience stories scattered around the Twin Cities.

Chester fixed his intimidating eyes on Dane seated on the other side of the desk. "You look healed. How you doin?"

"Fine." Dane crossed his right leg over his left knee.

"Terrible thing that happened. I only hope they catch the bastards who did this before they strike again." Chester pushed the stack of papers off to the side of the desk. "Have you talked any more to the police?" his eyes large behind his glasses.

Dane shook his head. "No, I've heard nothing." He dropped his right foot back on the floor. "I don't know how they solve crimes like this." He scratched his head. "Happening here among a couple million people can only make it worse."

"For sure," Chester grunted. "You know, Dane, you're probably as important to solving this mess as anyone, the only living eye witness."

Dane touched the still tender spot above his left eye. "I know that. It scares me."

"I understand." Chester leaned back in his chair. "Your TV interview was good but maybe not such a good idea. The big guy could get a better look at you."

Like a sudden electric shock, the comment raced through Dane's body. His body stiffened; his eyes froze open. He restrained himself from a more animated response, wondering where the hell he got this idea about the big guy. Dane vaguely recalled a similar comment by Chester on his visit to Dane's hospital room. Dane's throat tightened. "I know, but the interview just might make people pay more attention to these burglaries. It happened to two of your stores, right?"

"Yeah," Chester nodded his head with reluctance to pursue the topic of other stores.

"Have you had any more contact with the authorities?" Dane settled back in his folding chair, careful to avoid its tipping, his stomach still jittery from Chester's suspicious comment.

"No, I haven't. Just trying to get back to business as usual." Chester paused and adjusted his glasses. "Does business as usual include you?"

Dane gazed down at his hands clinched together in his lap. The decision he had already made. How to convey it to Chester concerned him. His comments about the big man damaged further Dane's tenuous trust in his former boss and reinforced Chester's potential resistance to Dane's quitting. Dane envisioned some surreptitious plan or strategy or plot to entangle him in a world he wanted no part of. He took a deep breath reaching for courage. "No, I don't think it will include me." He said it. He relaxed, ready for however Chester reacted.

Chester's mouth dropped open, his eyes even wider than normal. His voice strained. "Are you sure that's what you want?" Chester's jaws moved as he clinched his teeth. "Just damned ungrateful, the opportunity I gave you …" His voice drifted off.

Dane searched for any justification for Chester's expression of ingratitude, dismissing any notion that his employment constituted some kind of gift? "I'm sorry." Dane's voice reflected his resolve.

"Maybe you had better think about it for a couple days," Chester advised, hands gripping the arms of his chair.

"Oh, I have," Dane declared. "For days, I have thought about it long and hard." He clamped his hands over his knees. "I intend to look for a different future."

Chester grimaced and thought to himself that Dane may not have a future. He rose from his chair. "Well, I guess that's it. I'll have to find a replacement." He rested his hands on top of the desk, leaning closer to Dane. "I would suggest you watch your back. Good luck."

Dane stood up to return Chester's intimidating stare. "I will and hope you can find the crud who interrupted my life and wasted another." He stepped back, bumping to the floor the folding chair.

In his car Dane gripped the steering wheel, trying to calm his raging emotions. "He is up to something," he whispered to himself. For a moment he rested his head against the steering wheel, inhaled three times then started the car to pull out into traffic, confident to drive home without incident.

As he gazed through the windshield, studying the traffic in front of him, in his mind the scene of the big man whose gun pointed in his face replayed again.

Chapter 13

Heat waves danced on the horizon, for Tony and Sylvester the sun much too slow in making its ark across the southern sky. Sylvester, perspiration dripping off his nose, leaned against the shovel he used to remove worn shingles. "Did we have to do this job on the hottest damn day of the year?" he pleaded with Tony, who opened another square of shingles.

"You want to eat. You work." Tony fixed his eyes on his partner. "Pay attention to the job. It's about done."

"Yeah, but it's hotter than a bitch up here."

"No shit? Don't you think I can feel the heat?" Tony grabbed another shingle.

For nearly two months Tony and Sylvester scrambled to make a living doing odd maintenance jobs. This one took them to a home near theirs not far from Lake Independence to repair a small section of deteriorating shingles. The heist of the second Chester Reynolds' convenience store halted their criminal careers at least temporarily. Sylvester ardently preferred another late night plunge into Chester's pocket rather than suffer on top some damned roof under a blazing, early autumn sun. Ambiguity shadowed both of them since the early morning hold up which threatened to impose a dramatic change on their lives.

"When do we get the damned money?" Sylvester pleaded more

impetuous than normal. "I thought those late night things would solve any money problems. It sure as hell ain't happened."

Tony straightened up from a kneeling position and stretched his back. "Yeah, so you thought wrong. Now hand me that bag of nails."

Sylvester fumed, angered over his useless life and insulted by Tony's arrogant rejection. He placed his hand on his hips in a posture of defiance. "Have you talked to that asshole Chester?"

Tony stepped closer to his partner. "You know I tried lots of times. He don't answer."

"Why not?" Sylvester's voice echoed against the steamy roof.

"How the hell do I know?" Not mentioned was the warning issued by Chester never to contact him. He would contact them. Tony turned away, removed his cap to run his hands over his balding, sweaty head.

For the next half hour, the demands of the job commanded their attention. Loosen worn shingles, scrape the bared roof boards clean of nails and shingle debris, apply new tar paper, fit in new shingles secured with roofing nails. Only a small part of the roof of this single family home required repair. Still the heat of the day and the pitch of the roof added difficulty to the job.

Reaching the end of the day on the roof, Sylvester stopped and reached for their water cooler resting at an angle near by. A healthy drink brought a smile to his sunburned face. He set the cooler down on the roof.

"Say, Tony, why don't we visit Mr. Chester at his office?"

Tony's eyes lingered on Sylvester. "Why don't you tell me where it is?"

Eyes wide, Sylvester asked, "You don't know?"

Tony shook his head in disbelief. How many times had they discussed the prohibition imposed on them by Chester? They were not under any circumstances to contact him at his office or any other place.

The job finished, they gathered their meager tools and collected all the old discarded shingles and tar paper. Placed in a large tarp, the debris would eventually end up in a landfill supervised by Hennepin County. Weary, sweaty, and impatient about money, they drove to the shared, converted garage they called home. Not until they sat at the table in the middle of the small kitchen did the subject of money resurface.

Tony reached for his bottle of beer wet with condensation. He took a long drink then set the bottle on the table. He leaned back in his chair, eyes fixed on Sylvester. "So you think we should visit our friend Chester?"

Sylvester gulped his beer then burped. "Why the hell not? He owes us money for two jobs." With his finger he rolled off the condensation on his beer bottle, moving it in a tight circle through the small puddle of water on the table. He placed his elbows on the table, staring at Tony. "Shit, do we even know how much?"

Tony shook his head in disgust. He tired of repeating details to Sylvester, of Sylvester's fragile memory. He was worse than a kid. He knew or should have known the answer to his question. Chester's claim on the insurance company took time, too much time. The two robberies of Chester's stores garnered about three thousand dollars which, with Chester, they split three ways. Their take from the insurance settlement hung in mystery.

Tony jumped up from his chair, walked to a corner bench on which rested the phone. From under the phone he extracted the hefty Minneapolis phone book. With the phone book under his arm, he took the few steps back to the table, plopped the phone book in front of Sylvester. "Here, smart ass, you see if you can find Chester's office."

Mindful of the prohibition on contacting Chester, Tony decided enough was enough. They had waited for weeks to hear from Mr. Reynolds. They would wait no longer. Paying Chester a visit would maybe hasten receipt of the money they had coming, money they had earned. Besides, though they faced no immediate threat of identification and arrest, the face of the wimp interviewed on TV along with the potential consequences of the unexpected events of the last burglary festered in his mind.

In mild consternation, Sylvester looked up at Tony standing over him. "What the, ah, we already know his phone number. Just call him."

Tony rolled his eyes. "Done that." He pounded his finger on top of the phone book. "Look up his damned address!"

Sylvester averted his eyes then stared at the phone book as if it posed some kind of threat.

"Go ahead, look for the address." Tony placed his hands on the table, leaning closer to Sylvester. "You're so damned worried about the money."

With pleading innocence, Sylvester looked up at Tony, "Ain't you?"

Tony straightened up and turned his back. "Just look up the damned address."

The next morning after a night of restless sleep in stuffy bedrooms with poor ventilation, they abandoned their work clothes of overalls and blue denim shirts for shorts and T-shirts. However, they couldn't face the day without their work boots. Sylvester rode, gripping the pad of paper on which he had written Chester's address. Tony drove east to downtown Minneapolis, determined to visit their elusive colleague.

"What was the building number again?" Tony asked.

Sylvester glanced down at his pad of paper and announced the number.

"We gotta be gettin close." Tony alternated between watching the street ahead then the rows of buildings, much too similar in appearance.

"There it is, I think," Sylvester blurted out.

They approached the five story structure, which, according to the phone book, represented the office of Chester Reynolds. Tony pulled up to the curb, stopped, then peered through the windshield at the decaying building. He switched off the motor and reached for the door handle. "Well, let's find out about our friend." Sliding out of the car, Tony paused on the sidewalk. "Let me check that address to be sure."

Sylvester dug in his pants pocket then handed Tony the piece of wrinkled paper. They stood before the main entrance, slightly puzzled by Chester's office located in such a decrepit building. Clouded glass panels on each side of the door allowed them a peek at the inside lobby of the building. They tried the door. It opened to a narrow hallway bordered by three more doors. Tony moved close enough to read names printed on the doors. There it was, "Chester Reynolds" in bold letters. Tony grinned with success then glanced at Sylvester.

"Go ahead. Let's see if good old Chester is in."

Sylvester knocked on the door. They listened. Nothing. He knocked harder. With an ear pressed to the door, Tony listened. He heard movement inside. The door knob turned. The door opened a crack. Two eyes behind large glasses peered through the crack. The door started to close. Tony thrust his foot between the door and the frame.

"Hey, Chester, is that you in there?" Tony held his shoulder against the door.

"I told you guys never to come here. Now, get the hell out of here!" Chester roared behind the partially closed door.

"Where's our money?" Tony roared back.

The danger of the confrontation arousing other tenants in adjoining offices compelled Chester to open the door where he stood glaring at the two intruders. "Get your asses in here before you wake up the dead!" He slammed the door behind the two, his face glowing red, his eyes locked on his coconspirators in an intimidating stare. "I told you dumb shits never to contact me here or any other place." His eyes narrowed, first on Tony then on Sylvester.

"Where's our money?" Tony straightened up to his maximum height, towering over the much shorter Reynolds.

Undaunted, Chester stood firm. "How many times have I told

you I'd contact you?" He stepped back away from Tony and moved toward the protection of his desk. "Insurance claims take time." His eyes locked on Tony. "You gotta third of the take from your late night visits. Wait for the rest."

Sylvester had not moved since entering the office. From just inside the office door, he asked, "How damned long do we have to wait?"

Chester stood behind his desk. "How the hell do I know? All I do know is I don't want you two around here. Now get the fuck out. I'll contact you when the insurance money gets here."

Silence crowded the office. "Have you heard anymore from the cops?" Tony folded his arms across his chest, refusing any intimidation from a weasel like Chester Reynolds.

"No. Now get outta here." Chester leaned over his desk for emphasis.

Tony moved a little closer to the desk. "What about the wimp who worked at the store, the little shit who spilled his guts on TV?"

"What about him?" Chester asked. "He don't work for me any more."

"Where the hell did he go?" Sylvester stood beside Tony, his source of courage.

"I have no idea. Now either you two get outta here, or I'll call the police."

Tony laughed. "Yeah, you sure as shit are going to call the police on us. Remember, you're into this up to your ass."

Chester pounded on his desk. "Don't you threaten me. Who the hell's gonna take your word over mine?" Saliva dripped from the corners of Chester's mouth. "Worry about the little wimp, as you call him. He has you by the balls ready to squeeze. Now get!"

Tony turned his back, nudged Sylvester, then headed to the door. He stopped with his hand on the door knob. "Chester, oh boy, you're dumber than I thought. Remember, watch your skinny ass. I'll be in touch if we don't hear soon about the money." He pointed his finger at Chester frozen in rage behind his desk. "Don't even think about bull shit with us."

He left the office door wide open.

That was not the only door Tony left wide open, at least figuratively. The first floor of the old building the owners subdivided into three offices. Chester occupied one, a struggling collection agency occupied another, and Rory Weldon occupied the third, the one next to Chester. Designed more for expediency than for privacy, the partitions often permitted sounds, even conversations, to filter from one office to another

Rory Weldon, a young lawyer celebrating six months since passing the bar exams, specialized in divorce, DWI, and bankruptcy cases. So far his office in an ancient five story building attracted few clients. However, on the day of Tony and Sylvester's visit to Chester Reynolds, Rory welcomed a potential DWI client, a young man twenty-one years old and recently arrested for driving under the influence. As Rory attempted to unravel for the offender the complications involved in a DWI, the turmoil next door interrupted their conversation. Mostly, only voices rather than distinct words penetrated the thin partitions. Still, words like "money," "time," "get out," and assorted vulgarities were clearly decipherable and attested to the hostility of the voices.

Rory's innate curiosity guided him into a law degree. That curiosity compelled him to investigate what was going on in the next office. He excused himself to his potential client to step to the door to his office. He opened it only far enough to glimpse the door of Chester's office next to his. When he did, a big man, sporting a bushy mustache, stomped through the door. Rory ducked back into his office, pulling the door closed. The brief glimpse of the big man triggered something in his memory. Something he read or something he saw on TV about a guy with a big mustache.

He furrowed his brow reaching for this tiny slice of memory. With apologies to his potential client, he returned to his place behind his ancient desk. He smiled, "The price you pay for less than luxury office space."

The young man shrugged his shoulders, more concerned with his legal problems than with the lawyer's office neighbors.

With the departure of the young man, Rory tipped back in his chair, convinced he had secured a client. He closed his eyes to see again the bushy mustache, his legal mind reluctant to give up on the search for the source of that memory. He switched on his small office TV where Channel 11 reporter Andre Harrington reported on a fire in downtown Minneapolis. Seeing Andre Harrington clicked the switch which awakened Rory's memory to the interview weeks before with a victim of a convenience store robbery. It was there he heard about the bald man with the big mustache.

Rory shook his head. "I'll be god damned," he mumbled. He dropped his hands on top his desk. "It can't be. Just coincidence," he scolded himself for permitting a flight of imagination. Still, his imagination would not let go. The next day he contacted the Minneapolis police.

Chapter 14

With headphones cupping his ears and a tiny microphone adjusted immediately below his mouth, Dane listened for the dial tone then the ringing. The recipient of the call, of course, had only a name, a Mr. Adam Peterson, who resided in Bloomington, a Minneapolis suburb. Six rings ended in a "Hello?" Though the dialing depended on an automated, computerized system, the success of the call depended on the skill of the caller including voice quality and gentle persuasion.

"Good evening. Could I speak with Mr. Peterson?"

"Speaking," came the skeptical reply.

"My name is Dane Barton. I'm calling about your home there in Bloomington." A brief pause made room for exhaling on the line. "We are offering a special on replacement windows, a full forty percent off the regular price." A momentary pause armed Dane with his smoothest, most distinct delivery. "We can have a technician visit your home to offer a professional opinion on the condition of you windows."

A harsh voice replied, "I don't need new windows and don't need any technician around to tell me that. Thank you."

The dial tone indicated the abrupt end to the call. Dane smiled. His three weeks as a telemarketer softened his disappointment in the sudden conclusion to many of his calls. He studied the lighted board in front of him. He punched button number two then waited as the automatic system selected another possible customer from the Bloomington area. This time a woman's voice answered the phone.

Dane identified himself. "May I speak with Mr. Monroe?"

"I'm sorry, he's not here right now."

"Am I speaking with Mrs. Monroe?" Dane inquired in a gentle, nonthreatening voice.

"Yes," came the terse reply.

"I'm calling to offer you an attractive discount on replacement windows."

"I don't know anything about windows. Good bye." Dane could almost feel the vibration of the phone slammed on its base racing through the phone line from the Monroe home.

At first these callous responses bothered Dane until he realized the very small percentage of people called who accepted the offer. This was the reality of the business. Of course, the offer changed with each new client. Sudden rejection was still not easy to accept even though he realized it as part of the job. That job had begun three weeks ago following a short period of consideration of the role of a telemarketer. Rejecting any further association with Chester Reynolds proved easy. Not so easy was dealing with the threat of possible retaliation by the goons who assaulted him and murdered an innocent customer.

In the weeks that passed since the robbery, Dane realized he couldn't live his life looking back at who might follow him. He couldn't hide at home. He needed to get on with life, to suppress the fear of retaliation.

Dane's parents presented conflicting attitudes toward the telemarketing business. His dad labeled them as predators, determined to interrupt dinner to sell products to gullible people. His mom, more generous in her appraisal, believed Dane should make his own decisions. At nearly twenty-four he needed some job, some occupation, some career to pursue. Though afternoon and evening working hours would require getting used to, they were far better than the wretched grave yard shift of the convenience store. In addition, the staff, from Mr. Carmona to the callers at Fore Sure Telemarketing, impressed Dane. A week following his interview with Mr. Carmona, he called to accept the position offered.

Gaining an acquaintance with the technology of telemarketing, learning about the strategy that produced the best results, and identifying with his fellow callers dominated the first few days of his new job. He met his colleagues in passing on the day of his interview. Now he would acquire greater insight into those with whom he would spend his working hours.

Of his colleagues, Ashley Ryland assumed the responsibility as his mentor. At five feet six inches, she stood about the same height as Dane. Thick, dark brown hair hung nearly to her shoulders. A plain looking young lady, two years older than Dane, she compensated for average looks with a vivacious personality. As a testament to that quality, her high school classmates declared Ashley Ryland Miss Personality in the annual Hall of Fame election, an important part of each year's annual. A prominent nose called attention to her full lips and a slightly receding chin. Ashley's commitment to exercise helped maintain if not a seductive figure at least a physically fit one.

Ashley grew up in a small community near Duluth where she graduated from high school. Rejecting the chance to attend the branch of the University of Minnesota at Duluth, she sought a degree in marketing from the University of Wisconsin at Stout. Upon graduation, she found positions in marketing scarce for someone with no experience. Telemarketing offered an alternative marketing job, not a career but a job. Already, she was the most senior of the callers at Fore Sure Telemarketing. That distinction made her the best choice to train Dane for his new role as caller. Dane and Ashley worked well together, she patient, he eager to learn.

Emile Molina, the other male on the calling staff, floated aimlessly through the Minneapolis Public Schools and later the Hennepin Technical College. A second generation Latino whose parents immigrated to the United States from Mexico, Emile lacked the motivation and tenacity of his parents. In his mid-thirties, he found in the telemarketing business an outlet for his glib, fast talking talent.

The charming twenty year old Misty Snow completed the caller staff. A part time employee, she attended the University of St. Thomas in St. Paul, majoring in education with a goal to teach English to high school students. A refugee from Bismarck, North Dakota, she came to the Twin Cities fulfilling a dream to test life in the big city. Misty Snow represented a perfect name for her light blonde hair cascading around delicate shoulders. At five feet eight inches, her figure dispelled the mist from anyone's vision to view her captivating beauty. Her sharp blue eyes glistened under full, sharply defined eyebrows. The tantalizing tone of her voice served her well as a telemarketer.

Dane had very little contact with Carmen Hinton, receptionist, except to greet her each day when he came to work. He did know Carmen was an original member of Mr. Carmona's staff, and she played a significant role in assisting him in acquiring new clients. Mr. Carmona made himself available wherever he was needed, a characteristic making him a favorite with the entire staff.

Each week, almost each day, the calls promoted different products or offers and required different scripts prepared in conjunction with the client. On this day replacement windows received the most attention. All calls by both Dane and Ashley during their late afternoon early evening session involved replacement windows. Dane registered three customers agreeing to a window evaluation and to an appraisal by the client, a good day for a novice caller.

For a usual six hour shift, Dane and Ashley sat at adjacent call stations. That arrangement enabled her to lend any assistance Dane might need. It also enabled him to get to know her more than simply as a fellow employee. In three weeks Dane's courage reached a level permitting him to suggest that he and Ashley share a drink or a coffee after work. Seated at a small table in the dim light of a popular bar near the strip mall where they worked, Dane sipped a cool, refreshing beer, Ashley a glass of white wine.

Ashley smiled as she set the wine glass on the coaster in front of her. "Well, what do you think about the telemarketing business?"

Dane clinched his lips in a grin. "Not bad if you don't count the number of unsuccessful contacts."

"You've done fine so far. I remember my first few weeks. Lots worse than yours." She took another sip of wine.

Through the years Dane avoided any close relationship with women. He couldn't explain the resistance to relationships. Except at times, in response to his mother's concerns, he didn't have to supply any explanation. When he did consider the question, he speculated it had something to do with independence or maybe with his size. He never felt confident with girls even in high school. However, at nearly twenty-four, for Dane life demanded much more than a concern for the quality or depth of relationships with women. He had wasted enough time squandering a chance at a better life equipped with a college degree. In virtual desperation he had taken the job with the enigmatic Chester Reynolds. That ended in near disaster for him. Though he yearned to dismiss his apprehension, he still harbored concern for retaliation from the scum who injured him and murdered an innocent customer.

Over a second drink for each, Dane and Ashley talked briefly about their lives, avoiding any detailed explanations of schools, jobs, and parents. He ignored his traumatic moment with hoodlums, and she didn't ask about it. Their casual conversation hinted at the ease and comfort they both felt in each other's company.

Ashley drank the last of her wine, sliding her chair away from the table. "I've got to get going. Work to do cleaning my apartment. I just can't seem to keep up with that. Thank you for the drink and the conversation." She rose from her chair, clutching her purse.

Dane stood up. "Thank you for joining me and thank you for all your help on the phones." He pushed his chair up to the table. "We'll have to do this again."

"Yes, we will."

They walked together to the parking lot where they said good bye before heading to their respective cars. The drive home to his parents' place in western Hennepin County gave Dane the chance to think anew about women and relationships. Ashley impressed him more than any other woman he could remember. He touched the tender spot over his left eye. Maybe she could fill the void in his relationship with women or maybe she represented just another brief fascination.

Dane pulled into the driveway to park behind his mother's car. Since his dad spent so much time on the road, his car served Dane's needs. The front door of their home entered into the kitchen. Seated at the table his parents shared a late dinner, Milo's latest trip concluding earlier that day.

"Welcome back, Dad," Dane announced standing near the kitchen table.

"Thanks." His dad set down his fork and looked up at his son. "You got a hard ass message on the phone."

Dane closed his eyes, grimaced, and shook his head. "What'd it say?"

"Something about those rats that robbed the store." Milo shrugged his shoulders. "You'll have to listen yourself."

The fierce eyes and the mustache flashed through Dane's mind. For a moment he stood immobile staring at the space above the kitchen sink, fighting against the fear of retaliation that had shadowed him for weeks.

"Go listen," urged his mom.

Dane turned and made his way toward the living room and the land line phone where the red light signaled a waiting message. His stomach muscles tensed. He punched the replay button. The familiar strain and scratch of Chester Reynolds' voice gave Dane a jolt.

"Mr. Barton, Chester Reynolds. Just a reminder to give up any ideas about hero shit. Your life's much fucking safer if you forget the god damned robbery." The message ended.

Chester had debated making the call to Dane Barton. Keeping him at a distance from the investigation eliminated another source of trouble. In recent weeks trouble was a frequent visitor to Chester's door. First, he had to contend with an investigator from the insurance company that carried his risk insurance, in Chester's opinion an arrogant smart ass who nosed into areas that were none of his business, such as the number of employees and their average hourly wage. His stores got robbed twice. Insurance covered both of them. The insurance company needed to pay up without bothering him with smart ass investigators and all their fucking delays.

In addition, only days ago a Lieutenant Lewis from the Minneapolis Police Department called. He asked for another meeting with Chester to review new information about the incident. The memory of that meeting was etched into his mind. Besides the probing inching closer to exposing Chester's fraud and conspiracy, he resented dealing with those who towered over him, like Tony Harris and now Lieutenant Lewis. He interpreted their gestures and comments as intimidation. He tolerated Tony, whom he considered strong in body but weak in mind, subject to manipulation. Officer Lewis was not subject to manipulation or deception.

His call had caught Chester overwhelmed with paper work required by the insurance company as well as the petty intrusion of the two miscreants, Tony and Sylvester. He needed no more prying into his business or questioning of his integrity, thinking, "What businessman always played by the damned rules? Rules only deterred success."

Previous conversations with Officer Lewis following the robberies established him as thorough and efficient. He spent little time on irrelevancies, intent on Chester's knowledge of the men Dane Barton had described and reminding him of the severity of the crime committed at one of his stores. Seated in Chester's office,

Lieutenant Lewis plunged again into the subject of the big man with the mustache.

Chester tensed in his chair, eyes bulging behind his large glasses, averting the officer's steady glare. The weeks since the robbery and homicide at his one store had intensified rather than reduced his apprehension about exposure. The plan he assumed would rescue him from his economic difficulties had instead only burdened him with the threat of having to face the penalty for his miscalculations.

Officer Lewis rested his elbows on the arms of the chair. "Mr. Reynolds, do you now or have you ever met a man who fits the description given by Mr. Barton?"

Chester wiped his hand across his mouth. "No."

The officer moved forward on the chair. "Was there a man fitting part of that description recently here in this office?"

Chester caught his breath then choked and coughed. With eyes the size of quarters, he pounded his fist on his desk. "What the hell, is this some fucking game? That's so god damned stupid it don't deserve an answer." Chester moved his chair back away from his desk. "You mean the guy who robbed my store hanging around this office? How damned stupid do you think I am?" He slapped his hands on the arms of the chair. He pushed himself up. "I have nothin more to say. When you got somethin that makes sense, come talk to me. Otherwise don't waste my time." He walked to the door, opened it, then faced Officer Lewis. "We're done, Leave!"

The officer rose from his chair, smiled at the irascible Mr. Reynolds. Lewis thought a feathered tail would complete Reynolds' identity as a bantam rooster. Approaching the door, Lewis looked down upon the seething Chester. "We shall meet again, I'm certain."

Chester slammed the door causing it to rattle on its tired hinges. He kicked the chair used by Officer Lewis as he lurched back to his desk. "That little shit, Dane Barton, shootin his mouth off." He reached for the phone.

Dane clinched his fists in anger and dismay, trying to access the reason for the message. Chester's obvious attempts to cover his ass came to mind. Dane reached out for the nearby couch, easing himself onto the soft cushion. He closed his eyes and leaned back, perplexed by the vulgarity and intimidation of Chester's message which hinted at little interest in resolving the burglary. Chester's comment a long time ago about the big guy with the gun and the mustache surfaced for the first time in weeks.

Milo stood in front of his son. "What's with that bastard? What's he got to hide? Obviously something." He placed his hands on his hips. "He's worried for some reason about you, the only witness."

Dane rolled his eyes, extending his arms in a gesture of surrender. "All I know is I'm going to contact Lieutenant Lewis. I don't care what that prick Chester says."

Chapter 15

Dane tossed the TV remote onto the sofa arm. Television served only as a distraction, not a very good one. Morning programming offered little besides people sitting behind desks talking, conversations with little relevance except, perhaps, for those entranced by pretty faces and women wearing sleeveless dresses. Not even the news brought any escape from a house shrouded in silence. Early that morning Milo left on another date with his semi while Beatrice left for her day at work in the accounting office.

Chester's disturbing call the previous evening made impossible a good night's sleep for Dane. Perplexed by Chester's apparent reluctance to resolve the robbery, Dane debated his hasty decision to contact Officer Lewis. With time to think about such a contact, Dane struggled with a decision that could possibly force his further involvement in a crime he would rather forget. The sad incident had already taken a bite out of his life. His dad insisted contacting the police was the only decision, one that refused to allow Chester to get away with threats. Honest people didn't do things like that. Still, Dane wavered in deciding what he should do.

The previous night, indecision followed him to bed to hang suspended in his room throughout the night while he wrestled with tangled sheets and an elusive pillow. The morning brought him no closer to a decision. Alone, now, in a profoundly quiet house, he shifted from the living room to the kitchen to the bathroom.

Standing before the bathroom mirror, he saw a distraught face, red drooping eyes and pronounced furrows around his mouth. He stared at the image in the mirror, questioning the time cowering in the house because of some asshole like Chester, a blatant crook. Police dealt with crooks.

With resolve Dane rushed out of the bathroom, slamming the door against the wall. In the living room he grabbed the phone book to find the number for the Minneapolis Police Department. In minutes Officer Lewis answered his extension. He agreed to meet with Dane the next morning at police headquarters in downtown Minneapolis.

Though the call engendered some relief for Dane, it offered him no more protection from the threats disrupting his life. It did, however, satisfy his need to make a decision. Maybe, too, it would ultimately lead to freeing him from the images of that early morning brush with death.

The hot shower helped to sooth nerves agitated by the unrest of the last twenty-four hours. It prepared Dane for his three to nine shift at Fore Sure Telemarketing. Nearly a month on the job had given him confidence in his role as caller, one with what the staff humorously referred to as eloquence touched with gentle persuasion. Yesterday's message from Chester damaged that confidence by imposing the burden of anger and apprehension. His preoccupation with the threat and with the meeting with Lewis would surely haunt each of his calls.

He stepped out of the shower to wrap himself in a towel, some protection against the chill that filled the morning air. The sudden approach of autumn brought with it a chill that demanded getting used to. As yet his body hadn't made the adjustment. More important, the shower had softened the frown that creased the area around his mouth and erased most of the redness from his eyes. It even induced a smile.

Unlike his job at the convenience store, Dane enjoyed the one at Fore Sure Telemarketing. The challenge of dealing with potential customers, many overtly hostile, and the companionship of fellow callers made going to work something to anticipate rather than dread. Special among his calling colleagues was Ashley, who continued in her role as Dane's mentor. Though the speed with which he adapted to a caller's responsibilities reduced the need for a mentor, they both favored the relationship. Their occasional sharing a drink after work enhanced that relationship.

Dane dressed in his usual casual work attire, a golf shirt, jeans, and loafers, his voice, not his appearance, the only factor that mattered on the job. Concentration on his impending shift rescued him from thinking about Chester or about his meeting with Lt. Lewis. Nonetheless, the moment he relaxed his defenses the images of both rushed back into consciousness. A simple passing through the living room and glancing at the phone tore into that defense. Backing the car out of the driveway, he promised himself his meeting tomorrow with Officer Lewis would not cloud his day.

Two hours into his shift, Dane already had made fifteen calls, most to suburban St. Paul and most to recalcitrant, resistant customers. Few professed any interest in what he considered an attractive offer, three days at an Arizona desert retreat for merely listening to a sales promotion. To his satisfaction four accepted the offer.

The end to the two hour rush of calls found Dane moved away from his station, ear phones and microphone grasped in his hands resting in his lap. He stared vacantly into the ceramic tile floor, his resistance to Chester Reynolds weakening.

"You okay?" Ashley, sitting only a few feet away, inquired of her partner.

Her question jerked Dane back to reality. "Huh? Ah, ah, yeah, I'm fine." He turned in his chair to face his friend and mentor.

"I didn't want you to fall asleep." She laughed.

"No, I don't think that'll happen." He fitted the earphones over his head and repositioned the microphone just to the side and below his mouth.

Each shift carried a quota of calls, more of a benchmark than an absolute requirement. Nearing the end of his shift, Dane approached the quota with relief. His voice strained by the number of his calls but, as a slight boost to his confidence, countered by the few producing a productive conversation with a customer, Dane watched the clock as the hands inched their way to nine o'clock and the conclusion of his shift.

Throughout the evening Ashley took note of Dane's occasional drift into another world, his uncharacteristic moments of reflection or escape into memory. He just didn't seem his usual convivial self despite the relative success of his calls that shift. As they prepared to leave for the evening, Ashley joined Dane in storing their phoning equipment in the shelves at one end of the calling room.

"Are you sure you feel okay?" she asked placing her hand on his shoulder.

He smiled. "You're almost as bad as my mother." He placed his hand on her shoulder in return.

"How about a drink?"

Dane's eyes opened wide at the invitation. Several times they had shared a drink after their evening shift. This was the first time she made the invitation. "Are you asking me for a date?" he grinned.

"If going out for a drink after work is a date, I guess I am." Standing firmly before Dane, Ashley straightened her shoulders to emphasize her resolve.

"I'm sure not one to turn down a date with a beautiful girl."

Ashley rolled her eyes and turned her head in response to Dane's compliment, serious or not.

With conversations swirling around them, silence hung over their table as they enjoyed their drinks, beer for Dane and white wine for Ashley.

"You had a good night the way it sounded to me." Ashley positioned her wine glass on the paper coaster.

"Yes, I guess it was. More people than usual, at least, asked questions." Dane rested back on his chair, a far away look invaded his eyes.

Ashley sipped her wine. "Dane, I don't mean to pry, but does something bother you tonight?"

He reached for his glass of beer, brought it to his lips, then set it back down on the table. "Yeah, something does. I'm sorry if I'm a drag."

Ashley moved closer to the table. "No, no, I don't mean that at all. It's just you seem different."

Dane moved his beer glass aside. He rested his elbows on the table, his eyes fixed on Ashley. He took a deep breath and exhaled. "About six months ago, before I signed on to the telemarketing business, I worked at one of those twenty-four hour convenience stores. I worked that awful grave yard shift."

Ashley sat entranced by his story.

"One night, oh, about two or three in the morning, two older guys came in." Dane described the events of that horrible night including his own injuries and the death of the young man. He concluded with a brief reference to the recent mysterious message and his scheduled meeting with the police officer.

With eyes wide, Ashley listened to Dane's description. "Oh my god, that's horrible," she exclaimed when he finished. She confessed to knowing nothing about the burglary or its media coverage including Dane's interview. "I don't know how I missed the whole thing."

A smile brightened Dane's face. "Watching the news isn't my favorite either. Besides, a robbery and a murder around here happen more often than we think."

Ashley reached across the table to place her hand on Dane's. "Are you in any danger?"

He settled back in his chair, reached for his beer, and this time took a long drink. "I really don't know. Maybe tomorrow this officer will know more."

"Have you talked to this Chester guy?" Ashley shifted in her chair.

"Only once. That was about going back to work for him after I recovered. I don't think he was happy about my decision not to." Dane glanced at his watch. "I'm sorry, but I think I should get home. Big day again tomorrow."

Outside, Dane walked Ashley to her car. They stood face to face in the cool, autumn air. Ashley place her hands on Dane's shoulders. She stared into his face obscured in the darkness of the evening. "I'm so sorry. I hope you can get some answers tomorrow."

She leaned closer. Dane could smell the sweetness of her breath and the fragrance in her hair, the street light that cast a shadow over her face created a sparkle in her eyes. Her hands reached around his head, pulling him closer. Despite the many evenings they had shared a drink, they had never given in to the power of emotion.

Dane's heart raced, a tingle rushed from his throat to his stomach. He leaned into Ashley's body, tense and incredibly warm. Their lips brushed. He pulled back. Her hands behind his head urged him toward her, their bodies drawn together in intense desire. Their lips met in a prolonged, passionate kiss, one each had yearned for and one fulfilling their fondest expectations. In the shadowed darkness, they lingered in a firm embrace, her breath a strong whisper in his ear, his arms locked behind her back, chasing away thoughts of Chester and of Officer Lewis.

Not accustomed to spending time in a police station, Dane was intrigued by the rigid security. Just inside the door he faced a glassed-in reception counter attended by a young female officer. Dane explained his reason for being there. The young officer checked a computer screen then reached for the phone. She dialed. "You have a visiter," she announced. She hung up the phone. "Lt. Lewis will be here shortly." She then released a door which opened into a large room divided into cubicles, each one apparently occupied. Standing just inside the door, Dane observed the number of officers sitting, standing, or talking on the phone. For an instant he stood mesmerized by the activity, wondering who was watching the streets. From a distance he recognized the tall, stern figure of Lieutenant Lewis dressed in a dark blue suit, white shirt open at the collar, and wearing a reassuring smile.

With introduction completed, Dane followed Lt. Lewis to a plain office furnished with the minimum, a desk, dominated by a tangle of phone cords, a file cabinet and three chairs, one behind the desk. Officer Lewis directed Dane to one of the chairs while he sat in the one behind the desk.

"Well, Mr. Barton, you have healed well. No lingering effects?"

Dane sat straight in his chair, uncomfortable about the mission that brought him there. "No, I'm fine."

"Yesterday's call mentioned a message you received from your former employer. Can you tell me more about that message?"

Dane shifted his position in the chair, folding his hands in his lap. "Yeah, it was a message left on the answering machine, ah, ah, from Chester. He told me for my own good to lay off the robbery. Something about what he called 'hero shit'." He paused.

Officer Lewis listened with interest. "Anything else?"

"No, not really." Dane scratched the side of his head. "I don't know, but it's strange to me why he would threaten me? I'm the only witness. Wouldn't I be someone important to finding the guys who did this?"

With a slow nod of his head, Lewis cleared his throat. "That's a good question. I'm not sure I can answer it right now."

They stared at each other in silence. Dane slid to the front of his chair. "Mr. Lewis, something Mr. Reynolds said when I was still in the hospital has bothered me for a long time. He mentioned the big guy with the gun." Dane's eyes glanced down at the floor then up at the lieutenant. "I've wondered how he knew anything about a big guy with the gun. I had said nothing about that." He stopped.

He gripped the edges of the chair. Officer Lewis made no response. "Anything new in your investigation?"

Officer Lewis shook his head. "No, I'm afraid not." He avoided mentioning the call from the young lawyer or his recent meeting with Chester Reynolds. The crime still under investigation prohibited him from doing so. Nonetheless, Dane's comment gave support for a disturbing theory emerging in the officer's investigation, a theory of conspiracy and complicity. "Have you noticed any suspicious people around home or work?"

Dane cocked his head to one side. "No, not that I can think of. I guess if I did see something suspicious, I would remember it." He smiled in acknowledgement of the obvious.

Silence returned to the small office. Officer Lewis rose from his chair to stand tall behind his desk. "Mr. Barton, I thank you for sharing your information. Every little bit helps." He moved around to the front of the desk. "I don't wish to alarm you, but I would remind you to watch carefully for suspicious activity of any kind around your home, at work or on the road."

Dane stood up. Lewis guided him to the door. "I think these guys who committed this crime are amateurs subject to impulse. You just never know what to expect." At the door Lewis faced Dane. "You live in western Hennepin County, right?"

Dane nodded his head.

"I'm going to alert the Hennepin County Sheriff's office to increase surveillance in that area."

Dane responded with another nod of his head. "Thank you."

The lieutenant pushed open the door. "Please keep in touch with anything else you might think of."

Dane left the office with a bit more confidence than when he entered it. Until the guy with the bald head and mustache sat in jail, he supposed he would never really relax.

Chapter 16

Dane backed out of the driveway under heavy clouds and the threat of rain or maybe even snow. The passage of days had reduced but not eliminated the tension and anxiety of Chester's threatening message and the subsequent meeting with Officer Lewis. Dane found time to relax his vigilance when working or when at home. The officer's advice about caution Dane took seriously. However, he had noticed nothing suspicious since his meeting with Officer Lewis.

On this cloudy afternoon drive to work, Dane still could not overcome a hint of paranoia, his eyes darting from side to side, checking one rear view mirror then another. At three in the afternoon, he avoided the morning and late afternoon crush of traffic, making easier his casual watchfulness. He welcomed the clouds, a harbinger to the arrival of autumn, one of his favorite seasons of the year. His twenty-four years had weakened the excitement of the first snowfall. It hadn't dulled the memories of that excitement. Dane smiled thinking of those mornings years ago when his mother would announce the arrival of snow. Nothing motivated him to get out of bed faster than the chance to climb into his layers of sweatshirts, coats, and scarfs, anticipating a slide down the hill making up part of his back yard.

A frown displaced the smile when the image of Dwight Perkins pushed away the image of his backyard snow slide. Dwight Perkins ruled the playground at Dane's elementary school. Much bigger than

Dane, much bigger than most others his age, Dwight took advantage of his size, particularly with smaller kids like Dane.

Dane's attention returned to his driving, his eyes making a quick check of the rear view mirrors. Nothing suspicious. He squeezed his lips in a grimace remembering the incident years ago with Dwight and the slide. One of the first significant snow falls left the school playground rich in snow activities. One involved a long, steep slide. When dusted with a layer of snow, the slide made for a fast, thrilling dissent. Dane's classmates stood in line to await their turns, all except Dwight Perkins.

The image grew more vivid in Dane's mind. He stood waiting at the bottom of the ladder, waiting for the climb to the top and the thrilling slide down. He stepped on the first rung of the ladder. A hand grabbed him around the neck. Dwight Perkins towered over him.

"My turn, runt," he sneered into Dane's face.

From Dwight's firm push, Dane stumbled on the first rung; his face bounced against the ladder railings. Blood spurted from his nose. Dwight stood on the first rung, looking down at Dane writhing in the snow, crying, covering his nose with his mittens.

"Did the runt get hurt?" Dwight sneered. "Next time get out of the way."

Dane shook his head to erase the memory of the humiliation. Recent events in his life reminded him of those who would intimidate. He gripped the steering wheel, vowing that assholes like Chester Reynolds would not get by with Dwight Perkins shit.

Of course, now, no amount of snow would lure Dane out to the hill behind his house or certainly not to the slide on the school playground. Instead, if snow did arrive, he would likely spend a bit of time brushing it off his car parked in the parking lot serving the strip mall where he worked.

He pulled into the parking lot, alert for a place close to the entrance to Fore Sure Telemarketing. He had no objection to walking a short distance. He did resist the damp chill in the early autumn air. Squeezing between a pickup and a SUV, Dane stopped, shut off his car, and prepared to get out when he noticed two men engaged in autumn cleanup of the grounds surrounding the parking area. One man was much larger than the other. The larger one turned to look in Dane's direction. Though the man wore a heavy winter cap and the collar of his jacket was tight around his neck, what he wore failed to hide a bushy mustache.

Dane held his breath. "What the hell!" he mouthed, his memory replaying the fateful moment when a big guy with a mustache pointed a gun in his face. For seconds Dane sat in his car, frozen behind the wheel while images of the scum who disrupted his life and killed a young innocent man raced through his mind. The big guy turned and moved away from Dane's view. Sharp twinges invading his stomach, he opened the door and stepped out onto the blacktop. He looked again at the two men gathering debris into small piles. Shrugging his shoulders, he headed for his second floor duties as a Fore Sure Telemarketing caller.

He greeted his calling companions for the evening and seated himself at his usual station next to Ashley, who smiled in a greeting to her friend and colleague. Studying the script and the client for the evening, Dane prepared for his series of calls. Though he tried, he could not dismiss the thought that the robbers might be right outside in the parking lot nor the speculation about who the hell hired them. Through the evening the brief encounter haunted him, a distraction from his usual calm, articulate delivery.

During a brief break in their calls, Dane moved closer to Ashley. "Excuse me. Did you see those two guys out by the parking lot?"

Ashley looked at Dane, confused. "When?"

"This afternoon when you came to work."

"No, I didn't. Why?" She turned her chair to face Dane.

He shook his head. " I don't know. Maybe I'm just seeing things." He moved closer to her. In a near conspiratorial tone, he asked, "Remember our talk the other night about that robbery a few months ago?"

Her eyes widened. "Sure."

"When I parked this afternoon, I got a good look at one of those guys." Dane paused and cleared his throat. "He looked like the guy who tried to shoot me."

Ashley brought her hand to her mouth and inhaled. "Oh, my god," she exclaimed. "What are you gonna do?"

He place his hand on her knee. "I, ah, ah, I really don't know. Maybe it's just my mind playing tricks."

They sat together in silence. "Maybe you should talk to Mr. Carmona. He might know something about who they are."

Dane's eyes brightened. He stared at Ashley. "I don't know. I don't wanna create problems with him."

"Oh, I don't think asking him would create problems. Maybe he knows how they got here."

Dane and Ashley returned to their respective stations where their calls kept them busy for the rest of the evening. Though occupied, Dane could not escape the idea that just maybe the culprits were so very close. As they prepared to leave for the evening, Ashley joined Dane at the shelves where they stored their phoning equipment.

"Any more ideas about this guy?"

"No, not really." Dane hung his head.

Ashley grabbed his arm, turning him to face her. "Look, I know Mr. Carmona. Mentioning your concern will not disturb him or make him mad. Ask him if he knows anything about these guys." She looked into Dane's troubled face. "If it makes any difference, I'll go in with you."

Mr. Carmona, laughing, expressed delight that two of his top callers wished to talk with him on their own time. Dressed in his typical blazer and golf shirt, he directed them to chairs in front of his desk, the same ones they had occupied separately when they interviewed for a job as telemarketers. Dane thanked his boss for taking the time to talk about, perhaps, only wild speculation. He briefly explained the burglary of months ago. Of course, Mr. Carmona acknowledged a distinct memory if not of the actual event at least the of TV interview featuring Dane. That interview introduced Mr. Carmona to Dane's fluid voice and his potential as a telemarketer.

Dane moved to the edge of his chair. "I have a question that has something to do with that sad event."

Carmona frowned. "Sure, ask away."

A serious look clouded Dane's face. "This afternoon when I parked in the parking lot, I saw these two men raking debris from the grass around here." He paused to swallow. "I suppose I could be imagining things, but one of those guys looked like the guy who wanted to shoot me."

Carbona's mouth fell open; he pinched his chin with his thumb and forefinger. "Really? That's not good." He sat back in thought. "Or maybe it is good. I think I can find out from the management company here whom they hired to do this clean up."

Dane's face lightened. "If you could do that, I'd really appreciate it."

Carmona smiled. "Anymore questions?"

The next day Mr. Carmona reported the names of the two men hired for clean up: Tony Harris and Sylvester Ramirez.

Chapter 17

Dane cradled the phone in his hands, debating about making the call. Learning the names of the two maintenance guys at the strip mall where he worked renewed the urgency of discovering the culprits who ended his career in the convenience store business. Still, he hesitated, reluctant to prolong his involvement in the case. It wasn't his problem. Let Chester Reynolds take care of it. But in the weeks since the incident, little had happened except a threatening message from the irascible Mr. Reynolds.

Dane returned the phone to its stand. Late morning news offered little interest. He reached for the remote to click off the TV. As usual, this time of day found him home alone, his dad on another trucking assignment and his mom counting numbers at the accounting office. His late afternoon, early evening shift at Fore Sure Telemarketing gave him considerable time alone to contemplate just what he should do.

He eased himself up from the sofa, headed for the kitchen where he reached into the fridge for a carton of skim milk. Restlessness and indecision, not hunger or thirst, attracted him to the kitchen. He poured himself a glass of milk and searched the cupboard for cookies his mother recently baked, peanut butter his favorite. With a cookie in one hand and milk in the other, he returned to the living room to stand in front of the small picture window giving a view of the front yard. He took a generous bite of the cookie. He chewed slowly, his eyes narrowed to a squint.

Almost from a force of its own, the image of the man with the mustache, maybe this Tony Harris or Sylvester Ramirez, played before his eyes. Dane took a drink of his milk wrestling with his suspicions. He doubted he could justify refusing to notify officials simply because he wanted no further involvement in the case. Besides he still couldn't dismiss the mystery of Chester and his possible connection to the guy with the mustache. He jerked his head. "This is nonsense," he voiced out loud.

Plopping the half eaten cookie and the glass of milk on the end table where the phone sat, Dane grabbed the phone and dialed the office of Lt. Lewis of the Minneapolis Police Department. Three rings brought on the line not the gentle voice of the female officer he spoke with before but the nauseating, automated voice with a list of options, Lt. Lewis one of them. Dane punched nine, the number representing Lewis's extension. In seconds the deep, familiar voice answered, "Officer Lewis, how may I help you?"

"Officer Lewis, this is Dane Barton." He reached down to rescue the cookie ready to fall to the floor. Unsure of himself, his usual strong, distinctive voice weak and submissive, he explained, "We talked recently in your office about this Chester Reynolds robbery."

"Of course, I remember you and the case. How're you doing?"

Dane cleared his throat, trying to recapture his vocal confidence. "I'm fine. I, ah, I don't wish to bother you, but I may have useful, ah, ah, useful information."

Detecting Dane's tentative sound, Lewis used his most engaging voice. "No bother. Please tell me your information."

Dane sat down on the chair next to the phone, inhaled then exhaled. In better control of his voice, he said, "I don't know how really useful it is, but a couple days ago in the parking lot where I work, I saw two guys doing some kind of fall clean up of the grounds around the parking lot." He paused, taking another audible breath.

"Remember before, I described one of the convenience store robbers as big with a bushy mustache?"

"Yes, I remember," Lewis replied.

"Well, one of those guys doing the cleaning looked like that guy."

"That is interesting." The information grabbed the officer's attention.

Again an apologetic hint seeped through Dane's voice. "I don't know if this will lead to anything, but I found out the names of the two guys." Dane waited for a response.

Breaking the silence, Lewis asked, "What are the names?"

"Tony Harris and Sylvester Ramirez."

Silence returned to fill the line. "I don't know what those names mean or if those guys are the culprits. I just thought you might want to know." Dane replied.

"Well, you thought right, Mr. Barton. We've had very little to go on in this case. Maybe this can give us a boost."

Dane stood up from the chair, pressing the phone to his ear."

"I hope so."

"Thank you, Mr. Barton. We'll look into those names and see what we can find. Anything else, today?"

"No, I guess not."

"Well, thank you, and if you can think of any other information, don't hesitate to call."

Much more relaxed, Dane said, "I'll definitely do that." He hung up the phone and picked up his cookie and glass of milk. Standing before the picture window now, he decided the world looked a whole lot better than it did only a few minutes ago. Making decisions can clear ambiguity.

The conversation ended, Lt. Lewis pushed his chair away from the desk. He steepled his hands under this chin, contemplating the significance of the names he just heard Dane give him. Of course, he would have his staff trace those names to discover if, perhaps, one or the other or both had any kind of police record. What he would do about the names would depend on what the search uncovered. He moved closer to his desk, his finger punching his secretary's number on the phone, the first step in learning something about Tony Harris and Sylvester Ramirez.

The search in police records revealed nothing about either man. License records indicated an address in western Hennepin County where they apparently lived together. Military records also disclosed their time spent in the Army including their stint in Vietnam. Beyond that, records contained nothing unusual about Tony and Sylvester. Perhaps what the records didn't list carried more importance than what they did. Nothing suggested how either of the men made a living. Neither drew any veteran's disability compensation nor Social Security benefits.

The three days' search into the lives of Tony and Sylvester found Lewis concentrating on other cases. When his secretary delivered the folder containing the report, he paused, trying to remember the significance of the two men. A stack of reports occupying his time he moved off to the side of the desk. In front of him, he positioned the folder labeled Tony Harris and Sylvester Ramirez. Leaning forward, he planted his elbows on top the desk, studying the brief report. Assimilating the information demanded little time. What to do about the information posed the more urgent question.

Chester Reynolds' huge aviation glasses magnifying protruding eyes popped into Lewis' mind. The outcome of the last meeting with Chester rested near the surface of his memory. Reynolds had almost kicked him out of his office. Remembering the hostility of this belligerent man, Lewis smiled. However, maybe Reynolds had reason for antagonism.

The officer sat back in his chair, absently staring at a spot on the opposite wall. He reminded himself that Reynolds was the victim. Yet, he couldn't dismiss the hints of some connection, some collusion, between him and the perpetrators. Officer Lewis rolled his chair away from the desk and opened a lower drawer on which he rested his feet. His fingers combed through his thinning hair. He considered another contact with Reynolds. This case had dragged on long enough. Recent developments, such as the confrontation reported by the young lawyer whose office shared a wall with the one occupied by Reynolds as well as Dane Barton's reference weeks ago to a Reynolds' comment about the big man with the gun and mustache added to Lewis' growing uncertainty. Just another wrinkle in an elusive case that had lingered too long in mystery. Perhaps another meeting would dispel some of that mystery.

Lt. Lewis stamped his feet back on the floor; his hand reached for the phone. Irritated by the case and his inability to resolve it, he commanded his secretary to locate the number and call Chester Reynolds, who maintained an office on south Hennepin Ave.

Reynolds expressed no delight in a call from Lt. Lewis. A vague explanation, new information pertaining to the robbery, failed to weaken his outrage over another police call. A suggestion by the officer that he only wished to resolve the case, that they discuss the information face to face like adults made little difference to Chester. Ultimately, Lewis exercised his authority; either they meet at Reynolds' office or they meet at the precinct office, but they would meet.

The next afternoon Officer Lewis and his partner, Sergeant Manny White, a compact, husky detective in his early fifties and a twenty-five year veteran of the police force, drove to an early afternoon meeting with Chester Reynolds in his office. Without bothering to get up from his desk chair, Chester had blurted out, "The door's open," when the officers knocked.

Dressed in his customary soiled vest and checked flannel shirt, Chester stared at the two officers seated on the other side of his desk. Brief introductions produced only a grunt from Reynolds. He now sat with arms folded across his chest, eyes wide behind large oval glasses, nostrils flared.

"Okay, what's this god damn information that's so important?"

Lt. Lewis opened the folder resting on his lap, for a moment pretending to study the data while waiting for Chester's hostility to subside. With eyes locked on those oval glasses, Lewis reminded Chester of the big man with the mustache who had received considerable attention during the investigation of this case. Chester sat motionless, elusive eyes seeking something to rest on.

Lewis continued, "We have a report from a reliable source that a man fitting the description, bulky with bushy mustache, was seen doing some fall clean up at a Metro strip mall."

Chester rolled his eyes. "So what? A lot of guys have a mustache."

Lt. Lewis nodded his head in agreement and glanced down at his folder. "How many of them have the name Tony Harris?"

Hearing the name sent a jolt through Chester's body. He struggled to control a surge in his throat. He choked.

Suspicion provoked a glance between the two officers.

"I know nobody by that name." Chester corralled his stampeding emotions long enough to make his comment.

"How about Sylvester Ramirez?" This time Sgt. White asked the question.

Chester's radar eyes stared at the officer with disdain as if to question his authority to ask. "Never heard of him." Chester slapped his hands on top his desk. "Do you two think I'd know the assholes who robbed my store?" He looked first at Lt. Lewis then at Sgt. White. "Why are you wasting my time?"

"Mr. Reynolds, we are only trying to solve a crime, a serious crime including homicide. We must follow up on all the leads we have." Lt. Lewis tucked the folder under his arm and braced his hands on his knees. "We've gotten a lead on a possible suspect. We ask only for your cooperation." Lewis stood up followed by Sgt. White. "One more point, Mr. Reynolds. Records indicate you served in the Army at the same time as Harris and Ramirez. Is it possible you could have met up with them there?"

Chester vaulted out of his chair. "Are you guys idiots? Thousands of men served in the Army with me. That doesn't mean I knew them!" His face turned a bright red, his eyes expanded even farther. "Now you've wasted enough of my time so get the fuck out of here before I contact the mayor's office about police harassment." He stood defiant behind his desk, hands clamped on his hips.

Lt. Lewis and Sgt. White turned toward the door. "Like you, we're only interested in resolving this case." Lewis announced.

In response to the antipathy flooding Reynolds' office, they closed the door softly as they left. Chester stood anchored to the floor behind the desk, glaring at the door, his breathing coming in short pants, his stomach in turmoil. "That damned mustache!" he gasped.

The two officers pulled away from the curb, each in his own mind assessing what they had just witnessed. Sgt. White looked over at his superior driving the unmarked police car.

"That guy knows a lot more than he's tellin." Manny scratched his chin.

Lewis studied the street ahead. "Yeah, I can't quite figure that guy out." He repositioned his hands on the steering wheel. "He's resisted the investigation from the beginning. His insurance company, I guess, also stays on the investigation." Another pause. "Some of that may be routine."

Manny pulled on his seat belt snug around his generous stomach. "I was thinking about his victim comment. You know, ah, he's got somethin there." He looked over at his partner. "Kind of unusual for us to question him about the identity of the guys who committed the robbery."

Lt. Lewis nodded his head. "I know. I see your point." He glanced over at White. "What bothers me are a couple things: the comment by Reynolds to Barton about the big man and then the incident in Reynolds' office involving the big man with a mustache." He studied the road ahead. "Could there be something between the perp and the victim?"

The officers looked at each other, shrugged their shoulders, and attended to what they knew for sure, the street ahead and the visit to Mr. Harris and Mr. Ramirez.

Chapter 18

His call to Officer Lewis had squeezed out most of the tension and ambiguity of the day before. Though Dane never expected any type of report from the officer, he assumed Lewis would contact Reynolds or maybe even Tony Harris or Sylvester Ramirez. Police certainly must have access to records establishing a person's residence.

Dane enjoyed a rare opportunity to share breakfast with his parents. Returning only the previous day from one of his truck assignments, his dad did the only thing in the kitchen he did well, make breakfast. This morning he prepared a special breakfast sandwich, Dane expected, patterned after those his dad consumed at truck stops or at McDonald's. Whatever the source, the sandwiches appealed to Dane and his mom, who would drive to work later.

This morning, the conversation around the table concentrated, again, on the robbery, a perpetual topic that refused to fade and recently grabbed their attention again following Dane's shock in witnessing the two maintenance men at the strip mall.

"What did this Lewis guy say when you called? Dane's dad rested his hand next to his plate.

Dane seated across the table, looked over at his dad. "Not much."

"He must have said somethin," his dad persisted.

"Well, yeah, ah, he … he thanked me for the information." Dane took another bite of his sandwich.

Milo wiggled around in his chair. "Didn't he promise to look into the name thing?" With his fork he moved his sandwich around on his plate. "That's his damn job."

"You don't have to be so vulgar." Dane's mom placed her hand over her husband's in a soothing gesture.

Milo looked at his wife then at his son. "How long has this case limped along? What do these cops do all day?" His face turned a shade of red. He had little tolerance for what he viewed as incompetence. "This fuc ... sorry." He glanced at his wife. "Ah, this ... nasty thing has gone on long enough."

Silence settled over the table, all three intent on their own breakfast. Beatrice interrupted the silence. "Son, what are you going to do?"

Dane stared down at his plate. He closed his eyes and jerked his head in a gesture of indifference. "What am I supposed to do?" He shrugged his shoulders. "Let the police handle things."

"Right," Milo agreed. "Dane should just stay out of it. He's done enough already." His eyes skipped from his wife then to his son.

Silence marked the conclusion of the robbery discussion. Beatrice rose from her place, taking her plate to the sink. She turned back to the table. "You guys done?"

"We can take care of ourselves," Milo assured her. "You'd better get ready for work. Somebody's got to make a living around here." His sarcasm punctuated with a smirk.

"I'm going in a little late today. The staff needs time to check over time and trip cards guys like you mess up." Beatrice matched her husband's sarcasm even though her time and trip card comments carried validity.

"And you, son, will spend another evening bugging people about windows or siding or something." Milo made sure he distributed his light sarcasm without discrimination.

"Yeah, Dad. I'll do that while you sit on your butt in front of the TV." Dane's mom joined him in a confirming laugh.

Dane drove into the strip mall parking lot unable to avoid

searching for the two guys cleaning up debris. Seeing nobody dispelled a moment's concern. Climbing out of his car, he gripped his keys and punched the remote, lock control to hear the click. Making his way up the stairs to the area occupied by Fore Sure Telemarketing, he relaxed in the freedom he felt from Tony Harris, Sylvester Ramirez, Chester, and even Lt. Lewis. As he opened the door to the reception area, he faced his boss, Mr. Carmona and the receptionist, Carmen Hinton.

Dressed in his customary dark blazer, gray trousers, and golf shirt open at the neck, Carmona gave tangible definition to meticulous. He smiled at his newest, most promising caller. "Good afternoon, Dane." Carmona stepped away from the reception desk to offer his hand. "How'd that thing go with the names?"

Dane grasped his boss's hand. "Thank you for finding them."

"Oh, you're welcome. It was nothing, just a simple phone call to the management company."

"I called a Lt. Lewis of the Minneapolis Police Department to report what you found out." Dane lowered his arms, palms up. "Now what happens is up to him, I guess."

"Well, let's hope this thing gets resolved soon." Carmona tapped Dane on the shoulder then walked toward his office, leaving Dane with Carmen.

"You look fresh this afternoon," she announced.

"Well, I did shower before I came," Dane laughed. He did take pride in his appearance, basic but appealing. Jeans, loafers, and a Polo golf shirt gave his small stature a casual, distinct look. Obviously, Carmen agreed. Though she lightened in his presence, neither she nor Dane made any attempt to pursue a relationship. With a smile Dane headed for the calling center room. "Talk to you later."

The first person he saw there, Ashley Ryland, had made a big difference to his performance on the job as well as to his time after work. She had played a vital role in his quick acclimation to the world of telemarketing. She also filled a void in his social life, one that had shadowed him for years.

Seeing Dane enter the calling room, Ashley jumped up from her station to meet him. "Hi, I'm curious what you did with the names of those two guys." She stood in front of Dane, her eyes bright and locked onto his.

He took a deep breath as if to prepare for a lengthy explanation. With a hand touching her arm, he grinned. "I called the police." He stood quiet, staring at Ashley.

Her eyes opened a bit wider. "That's all?"

Dane laughed. "Yeah, that's all I did."

She poked him on the chest. "Come on. You're kidding me."

He shook his head. "No, I'm not. I called this Lt. Lewis, on the case since the beginning. What happens now is police business."

Ashley propped her hands on her hips in a gesture of finality. "Then it should be over for you?"

Dane mirrored her gesture. "Damn, I hope so."

The evening calling included the usual routine, some responsive, some immediate rejection even before hearing the spiel, this time about siding, especially designed for Minnesota's harsh winters and hot summers. Over the weeks since Dane started his job as a caller, the number of times he requested help from Ashley declined with increasing speed. He could handle most situations he encountered with perverse call recipients, even situations like the recent woman customer who insisted on making a date with someone with such an eloquent voice. What had not declined were the delightful moments sharing a drink with Ashley at their favorite bar.

Engaged in serious discussions with potential customers, Dane only briefly noticed a gentleman talking with Ashley near the entrance to the calling room. Normally only callers were permitted in the room. This man stood tall and straight, probably forty something and familiar with daily workouts. Dressed impeccably in a dark suit and white shirt accented by a pale blue tie, he stood very close to Ashley, his hands nearly tracing her shoulders and arms. Dark flashing eyes and bright white teeth highlighted a tan complexion under dark curly hair defining precisely the contours of his head. Even from across the room Dane found this man captivating. It seemed by her attention to his conversation, Ashley did too.

The man's conversation with Ashley diverted Dane's attention from his calling. Like a magnet the two standing near the entrance drew his frequent glimpses. When she finally resumed her place at her station next to Dane's, she was prepared to explain this fascinating visitor, an explanation Dane's inquisitive expression obviously expected.

Before she could explain, Dane blurted out, "Who was that charmer?"

Ashley laughed, "Just my next date."

For a second Dane's eyes widened, and his mouth opened in alarm until she laughed again. "Why, Dane, you look jealous." Ashley gave him a playful nudge.

He grinned in self-reprimand, guilty of over reacting to her likely very innocent interchange with this male paragon.

"I'm so happy you care," Ashley added to the charade.

"Who was that guy?" Dane asked, recapturing his composure.

"He's Mr. Dexter Parks, a big wheel at the window company, one of our clients. I think CEO or something."

"I've not seen any clients in the call room before," Dane admitted.

Ashley settled into her chair before her phone. "Not many of them do. They meet with Mr. Carmona and trust we'll take it from there."

"I see," Dane nodded his head. "He seemed to like talking to you." He smiled. "Even his hands liked you."

A blush invaded her face. "I'm irresistible, I guess." She ran her hands over her cheeks in an admission of playful self-promotion.

Dane nodded his head, eyes studying his mentor and, hopefully, someday maybe more. "I'll go along with that."

Chapter 19

Enraged by the two pompous officers, Chester Reynolds stood paralyzed behind his desk. The door left open only added to the seething rage boiling up in his stomach, pressuring his throat. His foot slammed the chair against the wall behind his desk. Stomping to the door left ajar by the departing officers, he raised his leg to blast it shut. He leaned his head upon his forearm braced on the door. His body trembled in anger and desperation. "What the hell had happened to his life, his business, his future?"

The sound of his fist pounding the door echoed out into the hallway. All his life he had worked hard to make a living. In his own mind he had succeeded. Unlike others he knew, he sacrificed, no foreign vacations, no adult toys like boats, snowmobiles, no campers, only dedication to independence and an adequate living. Now all of that was threatened by people he couldn't trust and by the stupid decision to join forces with idiots like Tony Harris and Sylvester Ramirez.

Distraught, he walked back to his desk. With hands spread on the desk top, he leaned forward and closed bulging eyes. In his mind he ventured back to the days growing up in St. Paul. Years had passed since he indulged in any sentimental journey any place, certainly not the home of his youth. For a moment he recalled his parents working hard to provide for his sister and him. This work ethic they transmitted to their son, who sacrificed many of the passages of adolescence, proms, athletics, homecomings, enjoyed by others his age. Instead, he had dedicated himself to making his own living without reliance on his hard working parents.

A short venture into higher education fell short of any degree. It resulted in various jobs as a waiter, a taxi cab driver, and a cashier at a twenty-four hour convenience store where his hard work earned him a position as manager. When the opportunity arose to establish himself in the business world, he captured it with an investment in a convenience store of his own.

Standing straight, Chester breathed deeply, the harsh edge of his anger reduced by the reminder of what he had achieved. Sitting in the chair behind his desk, he envisioned the meeting months ago with Tony and Sylvester. His stores faltered with the sagging economy. The three of them had arrived together at a plausible but daring and risky plan to rescue Chester's convenience stores from bankruptcy. Simple with obvious hazards but worth the risk if it worked, the plan involved Tony and Sylvester robbing one of his stores. Chester then would submit a claim to his insurance company which protected his stores from theft. A good plan, in Chester's mind, confirmed by the success of the first robbery, but after the second attempt, the stupidity of Tony and Sylvester, along with that blabber mouth, Dane Barton, placed in jeopardy all he had worked for.

He removed his glasses, placing them on the desk. His head dropped to his hands. He rubbed his fingers over his temples in a futile effort to allay a pounding headache. Besides the stumbling ineptitude of Tony and Sylvester, the treachery of Dane Barton, and the renewed interest of the police, Chester faced the tenacity of the insurance company that refused to release funds, he declared his, until the case reached some resolution.

Chester ran his hands over his mouth and across his forehead. He rubbed his tired eyes, which gave no relief to his fear over what the hell to do to avert disaster, maybe even prison. The plan to defraud the insurance company he now recognized as blatantly foolish. He reached for the phone to dial the number at the shack shared by Tony and Sylvester. The phone gripped in his hand, he listened to several rings. Moments before he hung up, a blunt voice sounded, "Hello?"

Chester straightened his frail body, cleared his throat and asked, "Tony there?"

A pause followed, then, "Who wants to know?"

Chester then recognized Tony's voice but grimaced having to talk with him. Still, few choices remained. "Chester Reynolds. Tony, right?"

"Yeah," came a grunted response. "You got the money?"

"No, I don't. I got …"

"Why the hell not?" Tony interrupted.

"Because I don't have it yet." The anger expanded again gnawing at Chester's stomach and throat.

"What the hell, you holden-out on us?"

Chester pushed the phone closer to his ear. "Shut your fuckin mouth and listen. God dammit, the police are on your ass. They got your names. Next they knock at your door."

Tony inhaled audibly. "How the hell did that happen?"

"This Barton guy saw you working at some strip mall. The damn mustache gave you away."

"What the hell! I thought … you took care of that bastard."

"Yeah, well … well, you and that partner better get your asses out of town." Chester paused then spoke, "Shave off that damned mustache!" He swallowed bile produced by a stomach in turmoil.

"Where the hell we supposed to go, Mr. smart ass?" Silence claimed the line.

"I don't give a shit where you go. Get out of town before you really screw up everything." The line went dead. "The son of a bitch hung up," Chester mumbled aloud before slamming the phone back on its base.

He clutched the arms of his chair. Questions, such as his partners in crime refusing to leave town or destroying his future if they were arrested, swirled through his troubled mind. He shook his head to renew the self- reprimand. What a stupid decision he had made to think he could trust these mindless bastards to do the right thing. With vaulting desperation chewing at his body, he jumped up from the chair, replaced his glasses, and marched with deliberation to his car parked outside on Hennepin Avenue.

Chester's search, weeks ago, for Dane Barton's phone number also produced Dane's address. With both hands squeezing the steering wheel, he squinted through a windshield marred by a hair line crack right in front of his eyes. Four in the afternoon marked the beginning of rush hour traffic. He drove cautiously, fueled by determination to extricate himself somehow from this god damn mess. In pursuit of western Hennepin County and the Barton home, he pushed on to state Highway 7.

Not familiar with the near rural part of Hennepin County, Chester stopped at an Excelsior filling station for directions, specifically, to the location of County Road 110 where, according to his information, he would find the Barton home. Rural mail boxes, spaced about one mile apart, lined County Road 110, each box labeled with a name and a number. Studying each mail box he passed, he suddenly spotted the Barton name near a short driveway shrouded by pine trees.

He entered the driveway which brought him to a modest two story house with shrubs decorating the front. Anxiety combined with desperation and anger made him question his intentions. If he found Dane at home, what would he say he hadn't already said? He'd come this far. A bang on the steering wheel sealed his resolve.

Standing on the front step, Chester reviewed, for an instant, what he would say to Dane. This time no options except, "Stay the hell out of the case." A knock brought no response. He tried again. This time he heard movement inside. With straightened shoulders reaching for his maximum height, he waited.

The door opened, not by Dane but by a stranger, a man, likely Dane's dad. Milo stared at the disheveled little man with the big glasses on the front step. "I don't know what you're selling, but I don't want any." Not a big man himself, Milo, nonetheless, stood taller and after years of commanding eighteen wheelers, more muscular than Chester.

Chester licked his lips. "I'm not, ah, I'm not selling a damn thing. Is … is Dane home?"

Milo stepped out onto the front step, closing the door behind him. Though Milo previously had not met Reynolds, Chester's appearance, his ragged vest, his owl shaped glasses, offered immediate recognition. Regardless, he asked, "Who are you?"

Eyes protruding behind his glasses, he announced, "Chester Reynolds. Dane worked for me. Who are you?"

Milo folded his arms across his chest, his eyes boring into the little creep in front of him, the threatening phone message fresh in his memory. "I'm Dane's dad. He's not here." He shifted his arms, hands now gripping his hips. "Even if he was, you wouldn't see him. Now get the hell out of here." Milo turned to open the door.

Chester made one step toward Milo, closing his hand on Milo's arm. Milo swung around to grab Chester's wrist. "Don't you ever lay your damn hands on me you little jerk!"

Chester's eyes flared with rage. He pointed his finger nearly in Milo's face. In a strident voice, he declared. "You tell that son of yours, if he knows what's good for him, to keep the fuck out of my business."

Milo grasped the pointed finger, slowly bending it back until it snapped. Chester howled in pain. Milo stood firm on the step. "As I said before, get the hell out of here while you still can."

Chester stumbled backwards, nearly falling to the ground. Clutching his broken finger, he headed for his car. A broken finger made awkward and painful opening and closing the car door. When settled behind the wheel, he leaned his head out the window, proclaiming in a screech, "You bastard! You'll pay!"

Chapter 20

For months Tony and Sylvester waited for the big payoff promised to them by Chester. Each day they anticipated the call that would tell them their venture into burglary rendered its rewards. The few dollars they retained from the actual robbery of Chester's convenience stores they had spent long ago.

The call from Chester only inflamed Tony, who recently realized the entire plan drafted between him, Sylvester and Chester was a stupid mistake. After slamming the phone into its base, Tony growled, "The bastard can't do anything right!" He ran his hands over his face, smoothing the mustache that had taken on such crucial importance. Standing up, he kicked the frail chair into the wall, crossed his arms over his chest, and took several deep breaths to relieve the galloping anger that gripped his body.

Sylvester Ramirez sat across the crowded living room of their humble house, staring at his companion, intimidated by his explosive behavior. Of course, he knew the subject of the phone call but not the details. Challenging Tony's intimidation, he asked, "What was that all about?"

Tony stopped his prowling around the limited space, turned to face his house mate. "That damned Chester is screwing us over," he blurted out then pushed open the fragile door in search of fresh air to calm the turbulence racing through his body. Standing glaring into trees surrounding his meager home, Tony fought the urged to lash out at something, anything, to release the tension that threatened to explode. Deep breaths helped as did the cool, late autumn air. He had to get control of himself, think about what best to do. Shutting up that worm Dane Barton claimed the first priority in Tony's mind. How he would do that proved simple. A few shots through a window would serve as a persuasive warning to keep his mouth shut about the robbery.

Tony relaxed his shoulders, stepping back to lean against the front door. Deep in thought, he closed his eyes, again running his fingers through that critical mustache he vowed he would never shave off. His plan emerged from the cloud of anger that enveloped him. He would drive by Barton's house, using it for a bit of target practice with his trusty hunting rifle. A few shots through the front window, in Tony's mind, would get Barton's attention, would intimidate, would threaten, and would compel him to lay off. After that, dealing with pathetic Chester Reynolds would grab first priority.

Resolved, Tony stepped back into the house where Sylvester stood next to the kitchen sink, holding a cup of coffee. Tony approached him. "Get the local phone book."

Sylvester looked at him with a furrowed brow. "What for?"

Tony stopped in the middle of the floor, glaring at his companion. "Just do it damn it."

"Okay." Sylvester moved toward the small table where the phone sat.

Tony remained standing, hands on hips. "When you find it, look for Dane Barton."

He glanced up at Tony, the question "why" never making it passed his lips. He paged through the narrow volume which included the area near their own house. He ran his finger down the list of names. "No Dane Barton." He glanced up at Tony. "Three Bartons, a Milo, a Frederic, and a Victor."

Tony scratched his head contemplating what to do. "We need to find out where Dane Barton lives."

Sylvester asked, "Why?"

Tony dropped his arms to his sides in a gesture of annoyance. He took a deep breath. "If you can't understand, I suppose I'll have to explain it to you. We need to do what Chester should've done weeks ago, silence that little jerk who can cause serious problems for us." He stepped closer to his friend sitting with the phone book open in his lap. "Now, I want you to call those three numbers and ask for Dane Barton. You should get an answer of some kind. Either he lives there or he doesn't.

Sylvester shrugged his shoulders, reached for the phone and dialed the first number. The first call took him to an answering machine. The second call reached a woman who said he must have the wrong number. He hung up the phone with a smile stretching his lips. "He apparently lives at this address." He pointed to the one listed for Milo Barton.

Tony grabbed the phone book out of Sylvester's hands, studied the address, then ripped out the page. "We're gonna make a visit to our friend Dane Barton. Get the rifle and a few shells."

Sylvester's eyes opened wide but he said nothing.

Locating the Barton home proved relatively easy since it was not that far from Lake Independence near where Tony and Sylvester lived. Sylvester drove as Tony gave him directions to Highway 110. As Chester had done earlier, they drove slowly, watching the names on the mail boxes lining the road. Tony sat in the front seat studying both mail boxes and the property designated by them. In minutes they found the box with Barton printed on the side.

Tony gripped his rifle, a Browning A-bolt action Medallion, a weapon he cherished over years of successful deer hunting, a weapon that received dedicated attention and care. He observed the Baron home partially obscured by trees extending the width of the property. Only the short driveway gave an unobstructed view of the house. Tony smiled. A momentary stop in the driveway entrance followed by several well placed shots at the house should serve as a warning to Dane and his family that he could not screw with the lives of Tony or Sylvester.

Sylvester steered off the road onto the driveway entrance, sitting parallel to the house, clearly visible only a short distance away. Tony inserted a five shot clip, rolled down his window, and took aim. The gun resting on his shoulder felt comfortable, reminding him of the many times he aimed his gun at an unsuspecting deer. He squeezed the trigger. The picture window exploded. He squeezed it again and a bullet ripped through the front door. Three more shots left their marks on one more window on the ground level and two on the upper level. Tony grinned and ejected the clip as Sylvester stomped on the gas, screeching back on to Highway 110.

Chapter 21

While Tony and Sylvester engaged in their plan for intimidation, Lt. Alvin Lewis and Sergeant Manny White of the Minneapolis Police Department drove west into rural Hennepin County and the office of the Hennepin County Sheriff. Equipped with a search warrant, they were scheduled to meet with Melvin Long, a Hennepin County Deputy Sheriff, who would join them in issuing a search warrant for the house shared by Tony Harris and Sylvester Ramirez. From meetings with Chester Reynolds and discussions with Dane Barton, the officials had assembled sufficient evidence suggesting, perhaps, collusion between Chester, the alleged victim of robbers, and Tony and Sylvester, the alleged perpetrators.

Following Sheriff Long's patrol car, Lewis and White discovered finding the home of Harris and Ramirez relatively easy. They drove slowly along the narrow road leading them to the humble house surrounded by stately maple and oak trees now resplendent in late autumn colors. Both vehicles pulled onto the gravel driveway where no other cars sat, and where no life was evident in or around the house. The officers parked, Lewis and White behind the Deputy Sheriff. They emerged from their respective patrol cars to walk together to the front door. Lt. Lewis grasped the search warrant as Deputy Long knocked at the door. The three officers waited, saying nothing. The deputy knocked again. Still no response. He tried the door. Locked.

Deputy Long looked at his partners, shrugged his shoulders. "No one home, I guess."

Lewis folded the search warrant, stuffing it back in his jacket pocket. "I guess not." He looked at officer White then at the deputy. "What now? Do we hang around or do we come back later?"

Deputy Long pulled at his chin with his left hand. "I know very little about these guys. You know ... do they work at a regular job or what?"

"I'm not sure either, except I do know they have done odd jobs around the area." Lt. Lewis paused in thought. "Why don't we park in a less conspicuous place and hang around for a while? Maybe we'll get lucky, and they'll return."

"Sounds good to me," agreed Deputy Long.

The Lt. turned to White, "What do you think?"

With a cock of his head, Officer White concurred, "Fine with me."

Back in their patrol cars, they backed out of the driveway, drove a short distance beyond, far enough to maintain surveillance of the house but still partially concealed by trees.

Dane joined his mother at the kitchen table where they shared a late breakfast. Dane's job at Fore Sure Telemarketing still required him to work late afternoon and into the evening. His mom normally would have departed for work much earlier. A persistent cold and soar throat finally compelled her to take a day off from her accounting work.

Since the confrontation with Chester, Milo had returned to the road on another extended trucking assignment. However, the family had discussed the incident which inflamed Milo and prompted Dane to contact Lt. Lewis from the Minneapolis Police Department to alert him to his former boss's threatening behavior, which now included his family. The Lt. promised to pursue the complaint.

"Have you heard any more from that Mr. Lewis?" Beatrice rose from the table to carry her breakfast dishes to the sink.

Dane pushed back his chair. "No, I haven't heard anything." He collected his dishes to join his mother at the sink. "I'm sorry I've involved you and Dad in this mess." He shook his head. "I can't believe I worked for that guy."

Beatrice squeezed her son's arm. "It's not your fault. You've done all you can to help solve this robbery. Let's just hope something happens soon to end it all."

Dane rolled his eyes. "I don't know what that would be, but you're right. This crap needs to end before someone else gets hurt." Dane turned to his mom. "You'd better get some rest. Get rid of that cold."

"Yeah, I think I'll lie down for a while on the sofa. Get off my feet and rest my eyes." Beatrice placed the dishes in the dishwasher then headed for the living room for a quiet rest. She paused before the sofa when the picture window exploded in a resounding crash. At almost the same time, a searing pain erupted in her right shoulder ripping through muscle and bone. She collapsed on the floor.

Dane rushed from the kitchen to the living room, barely escaping a shot splintering the front door. The shattering of glass heard first from the kitchen then from upstairs nearly paralyzed Dane as he stumbled into the living room to discover his mother sprawled on the floor, unconscious and bleeding from a shattered shoulder. In desperation he kneeled down to shield her from this apparent barrage of gun fire. Dane stayed low, close to the floor leaning over his mother to determine if she was still breathing. Assured that she was, he needed to get to his phone still on the kitchen table where he left it.

On the edge of panic, Dane grabbed from the sofa a pillow and knitted afghan in an attempt to comfort his mother whose shoulder sustained an ugly wound. His heart rattling in his chest, his breathing coming in pants, Dane strained to keep his head despite the devastation to his mother's shoulder. His cell phone. He had to get the damn cell phone. For several minutes he heard no additional shots. Staying low, he crawled back to the kitchen, reached for his phone, and called 911. He explained as clearly as he could what had happened. The operator assured him the dispatch of an ambulance as well as the police. When he returned to the living room, his mother had regained consciousness and lay bewildered on the floor in front of the sofa.

Dane again kneeled down next to her, running his hands over her forehead to push back her hair. She looked up at her son with beseeching eyes as if begging to know what happened. She tried to speak. Words failed her.

"Somebody shot at the house," he explained in a frail voice. "The ambulance should be here soon." He stared down at his mother, pale and so fragile looking. "Can I get you anything?"

She closed her eyes then whispered, "My shoulder."

"I know, Mom. A bullet hit you." He breathed deeply. "This is just crazy."

The sound of sirens in the distance filled the silence that pervaded the living room. In minutes both ambulance and police arrived. The EMT's immediately administered to Beatrice while the officer inquired about what happened. Dane attempted to explain the shots that ripped through the house. He only speculated as to the responsibility for the brutal, senseless assault that could have killed his mother. The officer suggested they discuss possible perpetrators when they got to the hospital.

The ambulance transported Beatrice to the hospital in Waconia, a small neighboring town only a few miles away. After a thorough examination, doctors determined Beatrice did not sustain life threatening injuries. However, she did suffer a major injury to her right shoulder and could possibly lose some function in that shoulder and right arm. Dane contacted his dad to explain what happened and to reassure him that Beatrice rested in good hands. Milo would return home as quickly as he could, convinced this Chester Reynolds creep had something to do with the senseless attack.

Tony and Sylvester drove in silence back to their house. For

Tony some of the glitter of anticipated satisfaction from revenge faded with the realization that serious consequences could follow what he just did. He now realized someone could have seen their car and recorded the license number. Also one or more of the shots could have hit someone in the house. To that concern Tony assured himself that no one likely would be home at that time of day. Already they faced a possible homicide charge. They didn't need another one. Sylvester said nothing, intent on his driving and well acquainted with the truth: Tony does what Tony wants.

After a few miles separated them from the scene of the shooting, Sylvester suddenly blurted, "What now?"

The question jerked Tony away from his thoughts of possible regret. He turned to face his friend. "What do you mean, what now?"

Sylvester slid his hands around on the steering wheel. "I don't know. This gets deeper all the time."

Sylvester's question forced Tony back to thoughts of retribution, to the police connecting them to the shooting. Tony sank lower in his seat, eyes fixed on the road ahead but mind fixed on the question of evidence that could implicate them in the shooting. Of course, there was Dane, who already had caused trouble. However, from what Tony understood, Chester had reached Dane, threatening serious consequences if he pursued the robbery. Still, if anyone would generate suspicion or heap guilt on others, certainly Chester would.

Tony suddenly remembered his most recent conversation with Chester, who informed him the police knew their names and would soon learn their address. Gripped by sudden regret for the senseless shooting, Tony hunched down in his seat. Through his mind rushed thoughts about leaving town, about splitting up with Sylvester, and about never seeing any money from Chester. Soon they would have to make some important decisions. Now they rode in silence headed to Lake Independence and home.

At that home two patrol cars sat waiting for the potential arrival of Tony Harris and Sylvester Ramirez. For over two hours Deputy

Long, Lt. Lewis, and Sgt. White sat patiently in their patrol cars in the event the two suspects returned. Trees partially concealed the officers' presence, leaving them with a clear view of Tony and Sylvester's house and the road leading to it. The officers maintained radio contact with each other.

Almost ready to give up the surveillance, the deputy radioed the police officers that a car approached. They agreed to wait to determine if this car contained the people they waited for. Deputy Long advised, "Let's wait to see if the car pulls into the driveway and the suspects get into the house before we drive up."

"Understood," Lt. Lewis confirmed.

"Look, I'll drive in first and stop behind their car. You follow, but why don't you park at the end of the driveway?"

"Will do." Lt. Lewis answered.

The officers watched as the car slowed then turned into the driveway. Two men emerged, one bigger than the other, one with a distinctive mustache.

"Those are our guys, I'm sure," Lewis announced over the radio.

The officers waited until Tony and Sylvester entered the house. They then pulled up to the driveway the way the deputy had advised. The deputy opened his door to step out onto the driveway. Still standing behind his open driver's side door, the officer cringed as the windshield of his car exploded in a cloud of shattered glass. Another shot whizzed by the deputy's head as he crouched behind the open driver's door.

The Lt. and the Sgt. stepped out of their patrol car moments before the shot shattered the deputy's windshield. Immediately, they drew their guns, crunching behind the patrol car. The second shot passed by the deputy, striking the rear fender of Lewis's car. Lt. Lewis reached for his radio to request back up for a potential stand off near Lake Independence. Another shot skipped off the roof of the deputy's car drawing a barrage of gun fire from all three officers who concentrated their shots at the house's one front window.

Sirens announced the arrival of backup officers. Two more

sheriff department, patrol cars screeched to a stop on the road near the driveway. The additional deputies cautiously stepped out of their cars to approach Lt. Lewis.

"Anything new here?" the deputy asked.

"No, not much action in the last few minutes," the Lt. replied.

"Have you tried to make contact?"

"Yes, but no response."

The now five officers, three deputies and the two policemen, agreed to wait a little longer before attempting to rush the house. No more shots came from the house. They waited only a few more minutes when suddenly the front door swung open. With guns aimed, the officers waited. Slowly the smaller of the two men stood in the open door, attempting to hold up a sagging Tony Harris.

Sylvester slumped to his knees, Tony falling beside him. He pleaded, "Tony's hurt. He needs help."

Deputy Long and Lt. Lewis stepped from behind their vehicles, approaching the kneeling Sylvester, one careful step at a time. Blood trickled from a bullet wound to Tony's head. He lay unmoving in the doorway.

Still kneeling, Sylvester begged, "Can't you do something before he bleeds to death?"

They did something for both of them. Sylvester Ramirez sat in jail. Tony Harris lay under heavy guard at the Hennepin County Medical Center, suffering from not one but two wounds, one to the head and the other to the stomach.

Chapter 22

Dane closed his cell phone and stood in the entrance to the living room of his parents' home.

"Well, what did he say?" Dane's dad turned from his position next to the picture window.

Walking slowly into the living room, Dane looked at his dad by the window then his mom seated in the sofa chair with her arm resting in a sling. "Tony didn't make it, I guess." He moved to the sofa where he eased himself onto one of the cushions. "Apparently, he died … from his shoot-out wounds."

"That's justice in my mind. What about the other guy?" Milo leaned against the wall next to the picture window.

"Lt. Lewis said he's, ah, I guess his name is Sylvester. He's in jail."

"I guess so. Robbery and taking on the police in a gun battle are serious charges."

"Did the Lt. say anything about your former boss, this Chester guy?" Dane's mom cringed when she adjusted the sling protecting her shattered shoulder. After only one night in the hospital to assess the damage to her shoulder from the wild shot that smashed the front picture window, Beatrice returned home where she intended to stay until her shoulder healed. The bullet splintered her collar bone, ripping through muscle and tissue. She would require reconstructive surgery on the shoulder after a brief period to allow a reduction in the trauma to the area damaged by the bullet.

Dane turned to face his mother. "Yeah, he said the guy's not around, some kind of fugitive, I guess."

'Maybe he's looking for some doctor to fix his broken finger." Milo laughed reflecting on his moment of victory when he grabbed and snapped Chester's finger pointed in Milo's face.

Dane grinned in response to his dad's comment. "I don't know about that guy." He shook his head. "The Lt. explained that several attempts to contact him have failed. Sylvester confessed to the arrangement he and this Tony Harris had with Chester."

"Exactly what was that arrangement?" Beatrice asked.

Dane paused for a deep breath. "Something like they rob his convenience store. Chester makes an insurance claim, and they split the insurance."

"You get insurance for robbery?" Beatrice's brow furrowed in disbelief.

"I guess so. That's the explanation the Lt. gave me."

Milo faced his son. "So, we have one of the robbers dead, one in prison, and one on the loose."

Dane nodded his head.

Silence pervaded the Barton living room. Milo turned to run his hand over the molding replaced along with the picture window. Meticulous about details, he had inspected the picture window already several times as well as the front door and second floor window, both victims of Tony Harris' revenge.

"Is the window all right?" Beatrice asked, a grin spreading her lips.

Milo scratched his head. "Could have done a better job myself." Their homeowner's insurance provided the labor for the necessary repairs. He turned again to face his son. "The job you had at that store certainly caused a whole lot of excitement." Milo smiled. "God, I hope this telemarketing thing doesn't give us any more trouble."

"Oh, Milo, stop it. It's not funny. People got hurt, even died as a result of this crazy affair."

"I know. I'm sorry. I'm only kidding. We all know how serious it was." He moved over to stand by his wife, tapping her on her good left shoulder. "We only have to look at you to know how serious it was and how lucky we are."

"Well, let's hope this is the last chapter to the saga." Dane stood up from his place on the sofa.

"I hope so too." Milo bit down on his lower lip. "Son, I don't want to prolong this nightmare, but you've got to remember you were the only witness to the robbery and, more important, to the killing of that young man."

Dane closed his eyes and nodded his head. He exhaled. "Yeah, I know."

"You know you might have to give some kind of testimony sometime." Milo rested his hand on the back of his wife's chair. "The county certainly will prosecute this Sylvester guy. I bring this up not to disturb you, son, just to alert you to what might happen."

Dane again nodded his head, "Thanks." He stared down at the floor then looked up at his parents. "I need to get ready for work. Nobody else works around here." With his facetious comment, Dane released part of the intensity gripping the moment.

"Don't I deserve a day off once in a while?" Milo planted his hands on his hips in good humored defiance.

"I can hardly wait to get back to work," Beatrice announced in a quiet voice.

"By the way," Milo asked, "how's that marketing job going? With all the excitement around here we've kind of lost touch with the real world."

Dane stopped in the living room entrance. "It's great. The people I work with work hard and are very good at what they do. Besides, they're friendly and care about things."

"What things?" Milo too often played the skeptic's role.

Dane braced his arm against the living room wall. "Well, they care about other people, not just themselves. They really were concerned about Mom after the shooting. They still ask almost every day about how she's doing. They even ask about you, for reasons I don't understand." Dane walked over to give his dad a playful punch in the stomach.

"They must know how important I am." Milo grasped his chin in the palm of his hand, his eyes narrowed. "How about the young lady you've mentioned once or twice? Are you still having drinks together or something?"

"Yes, on occasion, we still have a drink together after work. She's helped me a lot in the job. She's a sweet person."

"You'll have to bring her home sometime." Beatrice suggested.

A grin crossed Dane's face. "I'm not sure we're, ah, at that stage in our friendship. Maybe sometime. Right now I've got to get ready for work."

"You thank, ah, I'm sorry … I forgot her name." Beatrice frowned in regret.

"Ashley,"

"You thank Ashley for thinking about us." Beatrice reached across her lap to adjust her right arm.

Walking to his room to change into his work clothes, Dane thought about Ashley and wished their relationship did justify her meeting his parents. Maybe someday.

Chapter 23

The months of work at Fore Sure Telemarketing had boosted Dane's confidence in responding to recipients of his calls. Driving to work over familiar roads at about the same time each day gave him a few minutes by himself to reflect on recent turbulence in his life and that of his family. With relief he thought of his mother's recovery from a potentially fatal gun attack by the infamous, hapless dual, Tony Harris and Sylvester Ramirez.

He tapped the steering wheel in rhythm with the music coming from the car stereo. He shook his head thinking of the imposition of those two duds on him and his family. How things could have been much worse. Now, the probable need for him to give testimony in the prosecution of Sylvester joined the long list of consequences left by that early morning robbery months ago.

Also, out there someplace Chester Reynolds presented a threat. Dane couldn't erase him from his memory. Each day when driving to work, at work, or simply out shopping or something, the image of that man would invade his thoughts. Far too often, driving or walking on the sidewalk, he would see someone who resembled Chester, demanding that he take a second look. The compulsion to take this second look annoyed Dane, but it occurred beyond his control.

He ran his hands through his hair in a gesture of dismissal. Yes, he certainly would thank Ashley for thinking about his mom. He delighted in talking with Ashley about any topic. Over the months at Fore Sure Telemarketing his relationship with her, still mainly professional, had developed into something a bit more personal. The occasional stops for a couple drinks after work attested to that development. Her diligent training had enabled Dane to perform his job efficiently. A grin joined his thoughts about loquacity, that rare quality of voice he presumably had acquired from his mother. He also thought about the glorious moment weeks ago in the parking lot as Ashley reached up to join him in a prolonged kiss. With those two gratifying thoughts, he prepared to serve another shift on the phone.

Dane pulled into the familiar parking lot determined to cleanse his mind of thoughts of Tony, Sylvester, Chester, and convenience stores. Instead, he would concentrate on the job and the people he worked with; he enjoyed both. He zipped up his jacket as protection from the brisk afternoon air and walked to the familiar entrance. At the top of stairs leading to the offices and phone stations of Fore Sure Telemarketing, sat the demure but striking receptionist, Carmen Hinton

"Good afternoon, Dane. How's your mom?" Carmen sat back in her chair behind the reception desk.

"She's coming along fine, thank you." Dane paused in front of the desk, always willing to spend a few extra minutes admiring Carmen's naturally dark complexion, her flowing black hair, and most important her gracious manner. Dane found intriguing how three very attractive women all found employment in a small firm like Fore Sure Telemarketing. That they did certainly made his job that much more appealing. "Are the others here already?" Dane peeked into the phone station room

"All except Emile. He called in sick this afternoon. You and the girls will have to handle things by yourselves." Carmen rested her elbows on the desk, smiling up at Dane.

"Anything serious?" Dane asked.

"I don't think so. Just a cold or something. He sounded kinda hoarse. Not good in this job."

"That's for sure." Dane turned to enter the phone room. "I'd better get in there to help the ladies. Talk to you later."

He entered the phone room to see Misty already engaged in calling from her station. Ashley occupied her usual seat next to Dane's. Already on the phone, she moved her hand in acknowledgement as Dane reached for his chair. Her call ended, she turned to ask about his mother.

"She's fine. A bit sore in the mornings, but maybe that could just be her age." Dane laughed.

"The culprits responsible apparently are paying their price." Ashley leaned back in her chair.

"Yes, one apparently died in the hospital and the other sits in jail." Dane nodded biting down on his lower lip.

The evening shift passed quickly with a heavy schedule of calls. At the conclusion of the shift Dane prepared to secure his phone station and maybe to ask Ashley to join him at their favorite bar. He stood up, repositioned his chair and turned to ask Ashley if she wished to join him. As he turned he caught sight of Dexter Parks entering the call center.

Mr. Parks, of course, was the man Dane first met a few weeks ago when he then observed Ashley intently engaged with Parks in what appeared a serious conversation. Though he refused to admit it, watching her interact with this handsome, debonair executive produced a hint of jealousy.

Typically, clients spent little if any time in the calling room. If they wished to discuss business matters, they did so in Mr. Carmona's office. Mr. Parks, however, displayed no reluctance to spending time in the calling room especially with Ashley. At first glance unassuming, Parks did exhibit a degree of arrogance, likely the result of his elevated position as president of Foster Windows, a leading Twin City designer, manufacturer, and installer of distinctive windows. Of course, Dane was very familiar with the sales pitch for Foster Windows.

Dexter Parks grew up in a modest Minneapolis, suburban home, one of four siblings. An indifferent student, he devoted more time to socializing than he did to studying. Nonetheless he graduated with an interest in college. His choice took him to Duluth and the campus of the University of Minnesota, Duluth where he drifted through four years of academic apathy while relishing an abundance of female companionship. Never establishing any serious relationship with any of the girls he dated, he graduated as unattached as he started four years earlier. His degree in marketing landed him a job in sales for Foster Windows, a company recommended by an uncle who for years worked there himself.

Now at thirty-eight Dexter's dedicated effort and engaging personality propelled him to president of the company. As president he sacrificed none of the magnetism of his college years, but his charm, handsome features and talent never resulted in a wife. He simply lacked interest in serious romantic commitments. Dane questioned that conclusion watching his interaction with Ashley.

Parks walked briskly to Ashley's station. He greeted her with a brief, gentle embrace. A sudden twinge traveled through Dane's stomach.

Ashley stepped back from the engaging Parks. "You remember Mr. Parks." Her eyes shifted from Dane to Parks.

"Sure, I do." Dane extended his hand in greeting.

"Good to see you again," Parks grasped the extended hand, a smile exposing his gleaming white teeth.

An uncomfortable calm settled over the three as they stood around the two calling stations. Dane reached for his chair, pushing it back to the table. He glanced at Ashley expecting some comment. None came.

"I hear your mother narrowly escaped serious injury." Parks broke the silence. "What was that all about?"

Dane rested his hand on the back of his chair. "It's a long story that ended with a couple goons using our house for a target."

A grimace cross Dexter's face. "Yeah, that's what Ashley was telling me. I hope your mother is okay."

Dane turned to face Dexter. "Yes, she's doing fine, thank you."

Silence again surrounded the three. This time Ashley broke the silence. "Time to close down the shop." She diverted her eyes toward Parks, who responded with another gleaming smile. To Ashley he asked, "Mind if I walk you to the door?"

"Sure." She glanced at Dane. "Why don't you join us?"

Dane merely nodded his head, trying to control the pulsing currents of anger.

Ashley moved away from the stations, leading Parks toward the door to the reception area. Reluctantly, Dane followed the two as they walked, casually, hand in hand. He closed his eyes in disappointment. His stomach churned as the audacity of Parks fueled a rush of anger and bitterness, rare for Dane.

At the top of the stairs, silence enveloped the three. Dane stood in ambiguity, puzzled over his expanding disgust for Dexter Parks. Blessed with an undeniable talent to attract people, Dexter presented a threat to Dane. Even Parks' inquiry about his mom who continued to recover from Tony's brutal, rifle assault on the Burton home failed to allay Dane's suspicion about Parks' sincerity.

Dane leaned against the stair railing, shoulders drooped, debating why the hell he just didn't go to his car. He felt unwanted in this trio. Ashley turned to Dexter, placing her hand on his arm, in Dane's opinion, a gesture of affection. He looked away, trying to conceal the resentment bubbling in his mind. Recently, Dane's relationship with Ashley had gradually weakened from one of mutual attraction to one of simply fellow employees in the telemarketing business. That perceived weakening dragged on Dane's heart, on his confidence, and on his vision for the future.

He turned to take the first step down the familiar stairway leading to the Fore Sure Telemarketing offices. A brief pause invited thoughts of the countless times he descended those steps, content in his good fortune: a good job, a happy home and a pretty girl as both mentor and occasional companion. In his mind he savored those times when at the end of a calling shift, Ashley had joined him for an escape to their favorite neighborhood bar.

"Nice seeing you again. Good to hear about your mother." Parks folded his arms behind his back and straightened his shoulders in a commanding presence.

Dane looked up at Parks at the top of the stairs. He forced a grin. "Thank you." His eyes found Ashley standing too close to Parks. "See you tomorrow?" expressed more as a question than a mere statement.

Ashley crossed her arms over her breast. "Of course. I think we share tomorrow afternoon's shift." Her arms dropped to her side.

Dane nodded his head. "Good. See you tomorrow." He led the way to the parking lot. Sensing Parks lingering behind him with Ashley by his side ignited a flame that spread from his chest around to his back. He resisted the urge to punch the wall, wishing to avoid any display of jealousy to Parks and Ashley, who followed him closely down the stairs.

Rarely had Dane engaged in any physical conflicts or even verbal ones. His easy going disposition more than his small size combined to determine that. Now anger simmered, threatening to create an embarrassing scene right there on the stairs and right there in front of Ashley.

At the exit door, Dane slammed his hand against the release bar; the door burst open with a bang. He rushed out without even a glance at Parks and Ashley behind him. Anger blended with embarrassment as his unnaturally hostile behavior pushed him to reach his car without incident. About the time he pressed the remote unlock, Dane heard, "Hey, want to join us for a beer?"

The question registered the final click on Dane's temper. He yelled, "Go to hell!"

Silence settled over the near empty parking lot. Dane braced himself with hands pressed against the roof of his car. Only a few yards away, Parks shrugged his shoulders. "Hey, that's no way to talk. Would you like to join us or not?"

Dane pushed himself away from his car. "No, I wouldn't want to intrude on your date." Though his temper had cooled some, resentment and bitterness remained.

"Where did you get that date business?" Parks' voice rose in volume.

Dane kicked at the blacktop. "I don't give a damn what you call it. She's all yours."

From out of the fading light of early evening, Ashley reprimanded Dane. "Dane, stop this nonsense. Dexter just asked you to join us."

Surprised at his own sudden belligerence, Dane replied, "He's been after you for weeks. Now stop the bull shit and leave me alone."

Parks rushed toward Dane. "You're not talking that way around her. Now apologize to Ashley."

In the dim light Dane stared with burning eyes at Parks, just inches in front of him. "Why don't you just forget it and get to hell out of here."

Parks grabbed Dane by the shoulders, pulling him away from the car. With little experience in physical confrontations, Dane pushed back at the taller Dexter Parks, who stumbled to one side then pushed vigorously on Dane's shoulder, causing him to fall forward striking his head on the parking lot curb. Dane emitted a loud groan, tried to raise himself with his hands, then slipped face down onto the hard blacktop.

Ashley silently watched the struggle, then screamed, "Stop it!" As two grown men behaved like teenagers. When Dane fell striking his head on the curb, she yelled, "Oh, my god!" and raced to where he lay unmoving on the blacktop, blood oozing from a gash on his forehead.

She kneeled down to whisper in his ear. "Are you all right?" The question produced no response. She gripped his shoulders. "Can you hear me?" she pleaded.

Dexter kneeled next to Ashley. "God, I'm sorry. I didn't mean to push so hard."

Ashley glanced over at Dexter beside her. "That doesn't matter right now. We need to get him to the hospital. Drive your car over here and help me get him into the backseat."

For the third time in his young life, Dane occupied a room at Methodist Hospital in St. Louis Park.

A slight movement of his head sent pain surging above his eyes and around his temples. Intravenous tubes restricted movement of his right arm. Monitoring devices blinked on the stand next to his bed. A dim light above the bed revealed details of Methodist Hospital room 436. Besides the bed and monitoring equipment, the room included two straight back chairs, a TV mounted on the wall opposite the bed, a closet and a small bathroom. A table on wheels stood at the end of the bed.

Slowly, a growing awareness gave Dane some idea of what had happened and where he was. Through the haze of his memory, he remembered talking with Ashley and Parks, of the uncharacteristic anger gnawing at his stomach, of the belligerent responses to Dexter Parks, and the moments of pushing. Dane closed his eyes, lost in the entire sequence of events of the last several hours and of the last few weeks at Fore Sure Telemarketing.

The anger and bitterness he remembered perplexed him. Never a hostile person, he accepted the reality of his small size and of his accommodating personality. Turning his head reproduced the pain above his eyes. He thought of Ashley, one of the few women with whom he had discreetly pursued a relationship. Then Dexter Parks, a wealthy executive of a telemarketing client, stepped into their lives. Without question that intrusion into his relationship with Ashley made a bigger difference in his life than he realized.

A tap at the door of his hospital room preceded the entry of a tall, slim, nurse with long blond hair framing a slender face. Dressed in the standard blue and white uniform, she carried a clip board tucked under her arm and held a small tray of medications.

"Excuse me, Mr. Barton. I'm Nora. I'll be looking after you while you recover from a nasty fall." She moved closer to the monitoring device. "How do you feel?"

"A little drowsy but okay, I guess." Dane managed a faint smile.

"Good. Everything looks in order here." She reached for a small bottle resting on the tray and extracted two pills. "Here, I want you to take these. They should help to clear some of the haze from your head." She inserted a straw into a plastic glass and assisted Dane in raising the pills and glass to his mouth.

Dane swallowed the pills and looked up at the nurse. "Thank you."

Nora smiled back, "Oh, you're very welcome." She placed the plastic glass on the nearby table then turned to face Dane. "You'll be happy to know that your parents will arrive soon. The young lady who brought you to the emergency room, Ashley, I think, called them. Doctor Hunter issued orders for no visitors until your condition stabilized. Happily it has. They are on their way now."

Dane shared another smile. "Thank you."

Nora stepped toward the door. "Anything more I can do right now?"

With a tiny shake of his head and a soft voice Dane said, "No, thank you."

With that Nora reached for the partially open door. "I'll check back later. Now, try to rest while you wait for the arrival of your parents."

"Dad, I'm just not sure how it all happened. It was, ah, kind of sudden."

Milo leaned against Dane's hospital bed, careful to avoid disrupting the intravenous tubes. "Who is this guy who pushed you?"

Dane eased himself up on his pillow. Initial expressions of concern, especially from his mother, Dane allayed with assurances that he would recover completely. At least Dr. Hunter gave that assurance. He reminded his parents that Dr. Hunter would explain his condition and that Dr. Hunter was the same doctor who treated him after the convenience store robbery.

"He's an official of one the companies that uses Fore Sure Telemarketing."

A puzzled look settled over Milo's face. "How the hell did he get involved in some pushing match in the parking lot?"

Standing near her husband, Beatrice rested her hand on his arm. "Maybe we should wait on some of the details. Dane needs his rest."

"It's okay, Mom." He concentrated his attention on his dad. "I guess it has something to do with a woman." Dane grimaced. "I talked about Ashley many times before. I work with her." Dane paused, closed his eyes then opened them. "I thought we had a relationship that went beyond mere friends." Another pause and a grin. "This Parks guy changed that."

Milo stepped back from his place by the bed and grasped his hands behind his back. "Sounds like the classic love triangle." He shrugged his shoulders. "So, what did the rumble in the parking lot accomplish?"

Dane gently turned his head to stare at the blank TV screen mounted on the wall across the room. In a weak but firm voice, he uttered, "Probably nothing."

The arrival of Dr. Hunter precluded for the moment the discussion of the "rumble" as Milo described it. With mutual greetings and recognition of Hunter's previous treatment of a Dane concussion, the discussion focused on the current one. With disturbing familiarity, the Bartons listened to the doctor's diagnosis of a mild concussion. The abrasion on Dane's forehead would heal quickly with only minor scarring. The concussion would take more time as the Bartons were aware. According to Dr. Hunter, Dane should spend a couple more days in the hospital for careful observation. After his release he should rest and avoid any strenuous activity. In two weeks he should return to discuss his recovery and his resumption of work.

Following his extended explanation, Dr. Hunter made eye contact with Dane's parents. "Are there any questions?"

Milo and Beatrice exchanged glances. Milo looked at the doctor and shook his head. "I don't think so." He looked over at his son then back to the doctor. "Can you do anything about Dane's crippled relationship with Ashley, the woman, ah, kinda at the center of things?"

Beatrice nudged her husband on the shoulder. "Milo, stop it. This is serious business."

Milo reached for his wife's hand. "I know, but the woman must also be serious business."

Dr. Hunter chuckled. "I'm sure that's true. Unfortunately, my training doesn't include dealing with such complicated issues." He nodded at Dane sitting upright on the bed. "Dane is probably more than capable of handling that part of his life."

Dane smiled, thinking, "If only that were true."

Chapter 24

Chester slammed the phone back on its base, frustrated by the call he just ended, the fourth time attempting to contact Clark Walker. Like Chester, Clark Walker had lived at the fringes of the teenage social structure. A tall, skinny kid, he possessed an amazing artistic talent to create false ID's for his classmates who strived to experience the adult world of liquor and cigarettes. His talent gained him a measure of popularity with his classmates and a degree of suspicion from school officials. However, discretion enabled him to survive unscathed those late teen years.

Though inexperienced in the life of a fugitive, Chester understood the need to change his identity, at least identifying documents, such as a driver's license, thus the calls to Clark Walker, whom he hadn't tried to contact in years.

Desperate, angry, and resentful, Chester slumped on the sofa, besieged by details of the last two days. So far he had miraculously escaped confrontation with police. Nonetheless, it was inevitable that unless he got out of town, the knock at the door would come.

So far on TV he learned the fate of his coconspirators, Tony and Sylvester. His was suspended in doubt. With some remorse he heard of Tony's death from police bullets. Only with regret did he greet the survival of Sylvester, who possibly held Chester's future in his hands. His testimony could most certainly implicate Chester in the whole sordid affair, assuring the arrival of that knock on the door.

That door belonged to the home Chester grew up in. Along with his sister and parents, he shared a home of compatibility and comfort. A 1950s style rambler, the house offered Chester an inviting refuge from the turmoil of growing up in St. Paul's east side. With three bedrooms, living room, kitchen, and two baths, the house afforded the Reynolds family privacy when they needed it and companionship when they needed that.

Never a popular adolescent, Chester devoted much of his time to visions of independence and to a pursuit of a career in something. He failed to identify what, just something. His ultimate career destination ended with the ownership of three, twenty-four hour convenience stores, that destination now crumbling, destroyed by the stupidity of a plan to avoid foreclosure and bankruptcy.

Prior to the death of his parents, he had divided his time between his modest office on Minneapolis' Hennepin Avenue and an efficiency apartment off Lake Street. After the death of his parents, about ten years ago, he had moved back into his family home. Shortly after high school, his sister had moved out to pursue a life of her own. A licensed cosmetologist, she eventually married, and with her husband moved to Colorado where she still lived. Chester and his sister agreed, with little discussion, on his decision to buy her share of the house and property. Since then he spent less time at his meager office.

Chester eased himself from a living room chair, stretched, and stepped to the picture window giving him a view of his familiar neighborhood, emerging from a long winter. Blended with nostalgia, his angst dragged him to the vivid truth of his situation; he would have to leave behind all that he had worked for. He would not hang around to face prosecution which could include the charge of fraud and accessory to murder.

Removing his glasses, Chester rubbed his burning eyes. The last several nights found him struggling in attempts to sleep. Thoughts of dire circumstances left him staring into the darkness of his bedroom. He shook his head, then replaced his glasses. Falling victim to self-pity, to life in the past, would resolve nothing. Fleeing the Twin Cities as soon as possible was emerging as his only sensible option.

He dropped back into the chair, folding his hands in his lap. In recent weeks he had thought little of his convenience stores. Somehow they survived thanks to loyal employees, not traitors like Dane Barton. He clinched his hands, trying to erase the profound regret of losing what he worked so hard to create. However, his life was more important than his stores. That life demanded his undivided attention.

Chester raised his head, stared blankly at the wall across the room, then reached for the phone. He punched in Clark's number again. Gripping the hand set, he listened as he counted the rings. Suddenly, after the sixth one a voice said, "Hello."

Chester pushed the phone tight against his ear. "Is this Clark?"

"It sure is." Clark confirmed.

Chester cleared his throat. Reaching for his most distinct voice, he announced, "This is Chester Reynolds." He paused anticipating a response. None came. "I'm sorry to disturb you," he apologized, "but I need your help."

Chester and Clark did not share a close friendship in high school or after. Nonetheless, they did occasionally meet, usually by accident. This meeting on the phone definitely was not by accident.

"Hey, Chester, long time since I've heard your voice. What can I do for you?" Clark asked.

Possessed with little tact, Chester again cleared his throat and jumped to the point of his call. "Ah, are you still in the business of fake ID's?"

Clark chuckled. "Not presently. Most of my former clients don't need them anymore."

Chester managed a quiet laugh. "I understand." He inhaled then slowly released his breath. "I think I do."

Slowly and succinctly, Chester explained his problems and his need for special ID's. Clark listened without comment.

When Chester stopped, Clark responded. "You know, I think

I heard about or maybe read about those robberies. God, I never thought you were involved."

"I was. I am. I need to get out of the Twin Cities. Except for misleading the insurance company that certainly doesn't function on strict honesty, I'm innocent." Chester swallowed. "Unless … unless I get lost, I'm afraid the authorities won't see it that way and will lay false charges on me."

"That's bull shit," Clark declared. Following an annoying confrontation with police regarding a disputed DWI arrest, Clark retained no affection for law enforcement officials. After a moment of silence, he asked, "What specifically can I do for you?"

An audible sigh preceded Chester's answer. "I guess the usual personal ID's. Ah, ah, maybe a passport."

"Wow, that's a load." Clark confirmed. "I suppose I'll give it a try. But in the mean time if you need to get out of town, my family owns a small, primitive cabin near Pelican Rapids. Up there you're anonymous, no neighbors in sight."

Chester inhaled so fast he choked then uttered, "Damn, that'd be great."

Encouraged by the conversation with Clark, Chester rushed into organizing essentials he would need at Clark's remote cabin. What he forgot he would buy someplace. Knowing nothing about Lake Lizzy, the area of the cabin's location, Chester assumed the heart of the lake country certainly would offer numerous chances to fill in for what he may have forgotten. Though the poor performance of his stores over the last few months eroded his income, he still retained enough to get by, most of it in cash to avoid ATM or credit card identification.

Chester hurried through his home, collecting clothing and personal items he considered important. Not a man of fashion, these items accounted for very little. Nonetheless, abandoning where he spent so many years gave him moments of regret. His life had changed now, ruled by a different set of priorities. When he would ever return to this house he had no idea. Protecting it from the vagaries of weather involved shutting off the water main and all other major appliances that fed off that main water source. Beyond that the house would have to survive on its own.

A restless night of regrets about the past and apprehension about the future ended before day light. Chester eagerly packed the few essentials in his faithful Mazda 626. One last stroll through the house stirred emotions he seldom felt. A final farewell pat on the garage door prepared him for his race to the cabin near Pelican Rapids, a shield from potential, criminal prosecution.

Early departure avoided the morning Twin City rush. As the sun peaked over the eastern horizon, Chester headed northwest on I-94 for the approximate two hour drive to Clark's family cabin on Lake Lizzy. The drive was not Chester's alone. Each mile brought more memories of life in St. Paul, of reaching for independence, of operating a business, of a future fraught with uncertainty. Chester studied the road ahead, aware that life didn't promise anything. Life only offered opportunity. He had captured that opportunity only to let desperation destroy it.

Approaching the turn off leading into Pelican Rapids, Chester delivered a firm slap on the steering wheel, dragging him away from his revery, his melancholy, his self-pity. He reached for the directions Clark provided, according to Clark, guaranteed to deliver him to the cabin. A confirmed city dweller, Chester had little experience with life outside the Twin Cities. Though he had heard about places like Pelican Rapids, a small town of three thousand people located in central Minnesota, he had found no reason to travel there, most of his time dominated by operating his stores. This first time introduced him to the rural beauty of the area adorned with dense groves of trees surrounding large and small bodies of water, part of the 10,000 lakes punctuating Minnesota's landscape.

Following Clark's directions, Chester drove out of Pelican Rapids for about three miles to a narrow road marked "Thompson Road." Lined on each side with pine and oak trees awakening from winter's rest, the road carved its way ahead. Despite Clark's reminder of the cabin's remoteness, with each passing mile, Chester grew increasingly wary that he would end up lost in the middle of nowhere. Clark instructed him to look for a mail box formed in the shape of a fish. Chester studied the road, seeing no mail boxes at all, anxiety cramping his stomach.

He needed no more stress but searching for the mail box produced more tension in his stomach which now rumbled in protest. Sighting the fish mail box sent relief flooding through Chester's frail body. He slowed to make the turn onto a mere trail, two tracks separated by grass and small weeds. He advanced slowly, eyes peering through the trees hugging the trail.

Though it seemed much longer, in just over a mile the trees opened up to reveal a small clap board cabin resting on a cement block foundation. Chester pulled up close to the only visible door. He sat for a moment studying the extent of the cabin, apparently perfectly square with small windows on each side of the door.

An hour later Chester rested on a lounge chair positioned against one wall of the assumed living area. Since his arrival, he had gotten acquainted with the two room cabin. One room served as kitchen and living area, the other as the bedroom. Outdoor plumbing introduced Chester to primitive sanitation he had only heard about. In back of the cabin a well with a pump delivered cold water to those willing to pump the handle and tote water in a large pail back to the cabin.

Surveying his small, crude domain, warmed by a struggling propane stove, Chester smiled, content for the moment that he enjoyed, as Clark promised, complete anonymity. Now he would await word from Clark regarding his special ID's that could chip away at the ambiguity of his future.

Chapter 25

During the months working for Fore Sure Telemarketing, Dane's schedule had varied little, late afternoon to early evening. His mom leaving for work early and his dad often gone for several days on trips in his eighteen wheeler gave Dane the entire house for himself most of the day. At times the hours languished, leaving Dane free to examine the events of the passed few weeks, events indelibly imprinted in his memory: the robbery, his injury, the threats from Chester, the discussions with the authorities, and, of course, the assault on his home which left his mother severely injured. And now the incident in the parking lot.

Oblivious to the TV, Dane allowed these thoughts to filter through his mind. He moved restlessly on the sofa, tapping his foot on the floor, running his fingers through his hair, or crossing one leg over the other then switching legs. He leaned back on the sofa, closing his eyes only to see Ashley Ryland, plans to bring her home to meet his parents still unfulfilled. For how much longer, he hesitated even to speculate. Thanks in part to Dexter Parks, a relationship with such promise, at least in his estimation, had faded, only adding to Dane's anxiety and regret. It also induced thoughts of another job, as well as his need to seek, finally, a place of his own. He loved his parents who had provided well for him. Nonetheless, at twenty-four years old he believed he had lived long enough in the shelter of his parents.

Suddenly the landline phone interrupted the images flowing through his head. He jumped up quickly, pausing to regain his balance before moving to the phone. Considering the seriousness of recent events, a phone call could insight concern, even fear.

A glance at caller ID identified the caller as Lt. Lewis of the Minneapolis Police Department, the officer who, from the beginning, supervised the investigation into the robbery at the convenience store where Dane had worked and subsequent developments.

Dane reached for the phone. "Hello."

"Hello, is this Dane?"

"Yes, it is." Dane briefly tensed, curious about the reason for the call.

"This is Lt. Lewis from the Minneapolis Police Department. How are you?"

Dane breathed easier. "I'm fine, thank you. How are you?"

The Lt. laughed. "Still locked in this stubborn case that started with you."

"I'm Sorry," Dane answered, joining in the facetious nature of the Lt.'s comment.

"Only kidding, of course," the Lt. admitted, not accustomed to playful conversation. "Sorry to interfere with your day, but I wanted to check with you about the elusive Chester Reynolds." He paused. "Have you heard anything from him or about him?"

Dane sat down on the straight backed chair next to the telephone. The mere mention of Chester Reynolds caused a sensation in the pit of his stomach. "No, I haven't seen him or heard anything from him, thank god. I only know what you people have announced on TV."

"That's good, I guess, if he hasn't tried any retaliation." The Lt. explained.

"No, fortunately, I've heard nothing," Dane confirmed.

"I presume you have heard what happened to his buddies, Tony and Sylvester."

"Yes, the TV has kept us informed."

For a moment silence crowded the phone line. Then the Lt.

continued. "Regarding Sylvester, his case is pending. I can't say too much about it, but I do need to remind you again of your potential role in his prosecution. I don't know what his legal future includes, but keep in mind the county attorney's office will likely contact you. You're the only eyewitness to the shooting that occurred during the robbery."

"I understand," Dane acknowledged, slumping in the chair. "By the way, I think I heard on TV that Chester is, ah, ah, a fugitive."

"You're right," the Lt. affirmed. "He's disappeared somewhere. No sign of him at his office, his home in St. Paul or any place else. I called in the remote possibility he had tried to contact you." In cases still under investigation the Lt. could reveal only minimal information. He did not mention Chester's cleaning out both his personal and business bank accounts, nor did he mention the status of Chester's convenience stores now in the hands of the state.

Dane cleared his throat. "I'm sorry your search has not located him. I guess I'm glad he's made no attempt to contact me."

The Lt. agreed. "Well, I'm glad for you too. Look, if you ever hear or see anything about him, please contact me immediately."

"Oh, you can be sure I will do that."

"Thank you. By the way how's your mother getting along?" The Lt. asked.

Dane rose from the chair. "She's doing fine. Once in a while she suffers a twinge in her shoulder, and the injury restricts her from raising her arm above her head. But she's doing okay. Thanks for asking." Obviously, the Lt. knew nothing about the incident in the parking lot. Dane shrugged his shoulders, thinking, "Why should he?"

"You're welcome. I won't take any more of your time. Please keep in touch if you learn anything. Thank you."

"Thank you too and goodbye." Dane placed the phone back on its base. He checked his watch, time to prepare for his evening of calls to people who didn't often receive his calls with pleasure.

The drive to the Fore Sure Telemarketing studio still included Dane's sensitivity to the sudden appearance of Chester Reynolds. Since the robbery and most definitely since the shots fired at his home as well as the shoot out near Lake Independence, Dane had driven with vigilance, wary of spotting the piercing eyes of Chester Reynolds. Haunted by the thought of Chester Reynolds, on the side walk, on the drive to work, or in a store, Dane often looked twice at men who from a distance resembled Reynolds.

Today, however, Dane thought about Ashley Ryland, his colleague and mentor at Fore Sure Telemarketing. A relationship with such promise had recently faded. At least from his perspective it had faded, culminating in a pushing match in the parking lot. Gone were the moments of personal conversation about family and friends replaced by strictly professional talk about their calls each shift. Gone also were the occasional stops at a local bar to share a drink after a long shift on the phone.

Dane parked in his usual place near the building where he worked. For only a few seconds he anticipated walking into the calling center to meet Ashley. He shut off the car, stepped out onto the blacktop, and closed the door with finality. Shaking his head, he tried to dismiss the clouds that shrouded his life beginning with that damn robbery.

"Good afternoon, handsome." Carmen Hinton, company receptionist, each day greeted him with such glee, delivered with a gracious smile. Other members of the telemarketing staff knew about the parking lot incident but knew few details.

"Good afternoon," Dane mumbled.

Carmen's eyes opened wide. "Something wrong?"

Dane shook his head. "No, I'm sorry." He grimaced. "Maybe I got up on the wrong side of the bed." He gave Carmen a brief wave and walked to the calling center.

A quick survey of the room confirmed the presence of all three of his colleagues. Ashley occupied her place next to his, Misty and

Emile their places across the room. Ashley turned to greet him as he approached.

"Ready for a big night?" She joked.

"Hi, yeah, always ready for a big night."

"How's your mother doing?" Ashley asked.

"She's fine, thanks." Dane seated himself in front of his calling station.

"How are you doing?" Ashley inquired.

Silence invaded the space around their stations, each reaching for the prepared calling manuscripts.

"I'm fine, too, physically anyway."

Ashley looked away, intent on her phone and scripts for the evening.

For most of the shift, calls demanded the attention of both Dane and Ashley, leaving little time for them to talk. One call recipient asked so many questions that Dane had to seek assistance from Ashley. Only rarely did he request help from his assigned mentor. This time offered the chance for some personal contact.

Toward the end of their shifts, calling slowed. Despite the intrusion of Dexter Parks, Dane refused to abandon a closer relationship with Ashley. During one short lull, Dane decided he would try again to suggest their sharing a drink after work. Too many previous requests had met with excuses about prior commitments. What kind of commitments she never clarified.

Reaching for courage, Dane turned to face Ashley. "How about a drink after work?" he blurted.

She looked up from her phone station, smiled and announced, "Sorry, tonight's a bad time."

Dane hung his head, a smile concealing his disappointment. "You sure do have a lot of commitments lately."

Ashley closed her eyes and licked her lips. "I'm sorry, Dane, but my life has taken on some complications."

Dane looked surprised. "What kind of complications?"

Ashley exhaled deeply. "It's … it's family stuff. I'd rather not get into it."

Dane locked his eyes on Ashley seated next to him. He simply needed to know the truth. At the risk of sounding rude, he asked, "Does that include Dexter Parks?"

Ashley's mouth dropped open; her shoulders slumped. "No, Dane, no. It does not include Dexter Parks."

Chapter 26

"Good morning, Chester. How are you this morning?" A short, slim waitress dressed in a plain blue dress with an apron around her stomach stood before Chester's table. Her hair encircled her face like a frame. Her eyes twinkled in the small diner's lighting. A tag attached to her apron carried the name Irma.

He looked up through his more contemporary glasses, ones with dark brown frames that reduced the intensity of his stare. He forced a smile. "Fine, thank you."

In the three days since he arrived at the Lake Lizzy cabin, he decided he would risk eating out rather than trying to cook for himself on a small propane stove. The cabin offered few comforts, but served the next most vital requirement for Chester, a temporary hiding place. Quickly, he had learned to tolerate the outdoor plumbing as well as the outdoor well. Moments in the cramped outdoor toilet elicited the question about just what happened in the dead of winter? Certainly, Chester did not plan to occupy the cabin in the dead of winter.

With reluctance he ventured into Pelican Rapids the morning after his arrival. He needed to eat. The town impressed him with its main street lined with small businesses, not one of them a twenty-four hour convenience store. A quick recall of what he left behind in the Twin Cities produced fleeting regret. Life produced unexpected consequences. Weeks ago Chester had surrendered to the truth that in life shit happens. Learning to deal with it demanded patience and ingenuity. Patience he lacked. Ingenuity produced three convenience stores.

Only a block from one of the two traffic lights along main street, Chester found a quaint, unpretentious restaurant with an attached sign proclaiming it as Sadie's Diner. A man of basic culinary tastes, he quickly concluded eating there would pose no threat to his identification. The few times he visited the restaurant had proven sufficient to establish him as a good customer. Though hesitant about giving his name, he decided revealing his first name would create no problem.

Irma smiled. "Coffee?"

Chester nodded his head.

She carried a glass carafe of coffee which she placed on the table, reached to turn over his coffee cup, then carefully filled it. She stepped back. "Now, how else can I help you this morning?"

Ignoring the menu next to his plate he announced, "How about scrambled eggs and bacon?"

Irma jotted down his order on her pad of paper. "Anything else right now?"

"No." Chester shook his head and turned to gaze out the large window onto a tiny slice of the Pelican Rapids world.

Irma moved to the small counter behind which stood the kitchen area. In full view of customers, the kitchen was dominated by a large grill, serving as the major method of food preparation. A gaping exhaust hood absorbed much of vapor and aroma of frying eggs, potatoes, bacon, and other miscellaneous breakfast specialties, leaving a faint remnant of that aroma to drift around the small dining area.

Chester reached for his coffee cup, took a swallow, then relaxed in his chair of simple wooden construction with a pad that failed to soften the hard seat. He ran his hands across the plaid oil cloth cover draped over the round table, large enough to seat four. Only five other tables made up the diner's capacity except for the counter in front of the kitchen area which provided seating for four more customers. On this early morning, customers filled most of the places.

Chester leaned back in his chair looking again through the large window with the view of the main street surprisingly heavy with traffic on this morning. The tantalizing aroma of fried food filtered through the crowded diner. The sound of muted conversations filled the air. A smile spread Chester's lips, a rare expression, for the moment revealing his satisfaction with his circumstances.

On a shelf across the room from Chester's table sat a TV, its screen large enough for watching from any of the tables. Not since his quick departure from St. Paul had he watched much TV, his only chance now at Sadie's Diner; the cabin offered no TV. This morning the news included reference to the approaching spring and needed preparations for that inevitability in Minnesota's vast lake country. Allusions to a winter, reluctantly giving in to spring, made Chester shake his head. He could never spend winter confined to a primitive cabin with few amenities and already responsible for an incipient claustrophobia. Nothing else in the news attracted his interest.

With quiet efficiency, Irma delivered Chester's breakfast. "More coffee?" she asked.

He nodded at the glass carafe on his table. "I can help myself, thank you."

Irma stepped back and smiled. "Enjoy your breakfast."

Chester, indeed, enjoyed his breakfast. With no reason to hurry, he took his time, savoring every bite, wondering why food tasted no much better in this tiny, rural restaurant. In between bites he glanced at the TV. An inviting tropical scene filled the screen. It captured his attention in view of his need to find some sanctuary someplace. He studied the TV, catching bits of information delivered by a smooth, resonant voice. The picture on the screen displayed a sprawling structure surrounded by palm trees and other tropical foliage.

Chester listened more carefully as the announcer described a magnificent tropical resort on a bay whose name he couldn't hear, in the Mexican city of Puerto Vallarta. Though he heard the city's name, he couldn't remember ever hearing it before. Nonetheless, it virtually ignited in his mind a possible destination protecting him from the fangs of Twin City police.

He signaled to Irma, who responded instantly. On a piece of paper she handed him, he wrote down the essential information, an eight hundred number as well as an email address, about the resort. Chester was no desperate romantic in search of a place of his dreams. He was, instead, a desperate fugitive in search of a place to hide.

Back at the cabin, Chester sat idle, studying the piece of paper which just might rescue him from a future shrouded in fog. Dedicated more to financial independence, his life included virtually no time for travel, certainly not to Mexico where he heard repeatedly about murders and drug cartels. He possessed enough business sense to realize real estate companies would avoid property development in areas infested with drug cartels engaged in drug wars.

The more he thought about the TV ad the more it lured him to consider how to get to Mexico undetected by authorities. The details about the resort, the fact that it featured private ownership of expensive condos he ignored. His blind commitment to finding some safe haven made him oblivious to a litany of other possible problems, such as transportation to Mexico, language, culture, and monetary issues.

Chester had withdrawn a considerable sum of money, enough, he believed, to get by for a while. Again the urgency of his need for a hiding place obscured practical thinking about suddenly ending up in a foreign country. Of course, he needed altered ID's. That he recognized immediately, and Clark Walker was working to produce those altered ID's. It suddenly occurred to Chester that maybe Clark Walker could also work on a plan that would transport him to Puerto Vallarta, Mexico.

Chapter 27

Seldom did the Barton family share a meal, especially a breakfast. Saturday morning witnessed the confluence of schedules for Dane and his mom and dad. Milo returned late the night before from his latest trip. Beatrice's job included only a Monday through Friday schedule. Dane worked only on those Saturdays when a client demanded it. To the satisfaction of each family member, Dane's latest concussion no longer occupied a central place in the family's conversations.

Seated around the kitchen table, they ate in silence, fried eggs, sausage, toast, and apple juice capturing their attention. Milo placed his fork on his plate and reached for his napkin to dab his mouth, then looked up at Dane across the table. "I hear that Lt. Lewis called again."

"Yeah, he did." Dane returned his dad's eye contact.

"What'd he want this time?"

"Ah, ah, to check on Mom's shoulder." He grinned, reaching over to touch his mom's arm. "No, he asked if we'd heard or seen anything of Chester Reynolds." Dane leaned forward in his chair, taking another bite of his breakfast.

Milo shook his head. "Haven't they found that little creep yet?"

Dane moved closer to the table. "I guess not. He's skipped the country, found someplace to hide."

Milo used his fork to cut another chunk of sausage. "One of

those guys, one of the robbers, got his reward from a police bullet or two, right?"

"Yeah, that's right." Dane reach for his glass and a drink of juice.

"What about the other guy?"

"He's in jail. He goes to trial sometime, I think." He rolled his eyes. "I may have to testify since I'm the only eyewitness."

"Do you have any idea when that will be?" Dane's mom joined the conversation from her place at the end of the table.

Dane shook his head. "No, none. Lt. Lewis has reminded me twice about the testimony but said nothing about when."

"Did Lt. Lewis have any idea about this Chester guy?" Dane's mom asked.

Again Dane shook his head and shrugged his shoulders. "He didn't say anything other than what I've said already." He smiled. "He did ask about your shoulder."

"Yes, you said that. It was nice of him to ask." Beatrice smiled. "Did he ask about your concussion?"

Dane just shook his head, a bit surprised that his mom would even bring that up.

Silence returned to the table as the Bartons resumed their breakfast.

Beatrice reached over to touch her son's arm. "By the way, when do we get to see your friend from work. What's her name ... Ashley isn't it?"

Dane shot his mom a quick stare, not eager to address that subject and puzzled by why his mother would even ask. He wrinkled his brow. "I don't know," he mumbled.

"Something the matter?"

Dane exhaled; again he leaned back in his chair, thinking, "Of course, something's the matter. It's called Dexter Parks." Instead, he answered, "No, nothing's the matter. Just some family problems, I guess. I, ah, I don't know any more details."

"Maybe you should impress her with your loqua ... what's that word?" Milo looked to his wife for confirmation.

"Loquacity, but stop it. It's not funny." She reprimanded.

Milo squeezed his lips in a grin. "Sorry."

Dane slid from his chair, collected his dishes, and placed them in the sink. His mom followed, carrying both her dishes and her husband's. Placing a gentle bump on her son's hip, she asked, "Any plans for the weekend?"

"No. There's a small chance I might have to work for a bit tomorrow, an insistent client."

"On Sunday?" his mom declared.

"Only a slight chance as far as I know."

Beatrice placed her hand on Dane's shoulder. "You need a date." A smile spread her lips.

Dane looked away. "I suppose. Any suggestions?"

The Sunday shift never materialized, leaving Dane spending time watching TV, part of the Twins game, and wasting time in his room thinking about his future with Ashley Ryland and with Fore Sure Telemarketing as well as the possibility of a move to his own apartment.

Chapter 28

"Does that include Dexter Parks?" Dane's question rumbled through Ashley's mind depriving her of much needed rest. Distraught and restless, she moved from her back to her stomach, stretching out on her queen-size bed. She stared into the darkness of her bedroom, reaching for calm that would allow her to fall asleep.

A life that offered, at least temporarily, satisfaction had recently shadowed her with misgivings, frustrations, and maybe even mild depression. To think about suffering from depression frightened Ashley, recalling the days her mother had struggled against its debilitating effects.

She rolled onto her side, pushing the blanket back with her legs. Perspiration collected around her neck and under her arms. Swinging her legs over the side of the bed, she sat up rubbing her eyes and shifting her brief cotton pajamas. With feet firmly on the floor, she walked across her small bedroom to the door to the second of two bathrooms in her apartment. Reaching around the open door, she switched on the light. She blinked as the light rushed to her tired eyes. On her right stood the tub and shower enclosure. Straight ahead a large mirror over a double sink counter took up most of the wall.

She approached the mirror, ran her fingers through her dark hair suffering now from the effects of a restless night. The image in the mirror disappointed her. Through her young life she took pride in her clear skin virtually without noticeable blemish. Now faint lines emanated from her dull, red eyes, over the past few weeks too often deprived of renewing sleep. She touched her cheek, her hand tracing small creases accentuated by the touch. She grimaced, seeing the difference a few years had made on her skin.

With hands braced against the counter, she gazed down at the empty sink. For most of her twenty-five years life had offered her some sense of fulfillment. Now she confronted misgivings and anxiety. To her, part of the problem rested with three men in her life. Dexter Parks' troubling attention, Dane Barton's obvious interest beyond a professional relationship, and her father's falling victim to Parkinson's disease combined to drag her into moments of tension and mild depression. The recent parking lot confrontation between Dexter and Dane only added to the turmoil of her life.

All through high school and college she enjoyed mostly exciting but often brief relationships with boys and men. Never did she feel threatened by physical or psychological dominance. Why she did now puzzled her.

The mere thought of depression alarmed her. Vivid in her memory were those days when her mother struggled under the burden of depression. As Ashley progressed through adolescence and mid teens, she gradually concluded, at least in her own mind, the source of her mother's depression, dominance. Even as a young high school student she found difficult addressing this condition which deprived her mother of a happy life. Only with reluctance now would she even pronounce the word. Its connotation simply too painful.

Her father provided well for his family, a local real estate agent in the small, northern Minnesota town where Ashley grew up. He also showed love and affection for Ashley, her younger brother, and her mother. Never did she hear harsh words between her parents. Never did any member of the family face any physical deprivation.

The problem she ultimately realized rested with her father's dominance over her mother and over his children. Denied a sense of independence frequently pushed her mother into periods of depression, sometimes lasting only a day, sometimes lasting longer. Ashley could not remember her mother seeking medical help. No doctor ever explained to Ashley the reason for her mother's falling into periods of gloomy, doleful behavior often accompanied by tears. Years of observing her mother's struggles, her submission to her father, her reluctance to exert her will dragged Ashley to the conclusion about her father's unrelenting control of the family.

Ashley looked at herself in the mirror, tears forming in the corners of her sad eyes. She would not allow anyone to deprive her of her independence. At twenty-five years old she could conduct her life unattended. Dexter Parks, from her perspective, supplied the biggest threat to her freedom. Yet, he treated her with respect and only hinted at a more serious relationship. As an executive with a major Fore Sure Telemarketing client, he represented for her the control she remembered in her father. She stepped away from the sink and made another futile attempt to tame her hair, wrestling with how to deal with Dexter Parks without creating resentment.

She ran her hands under the cold water faucet, pressed her fingers gently into her eyes, and around her mouth. Dane Barton she considered a sweet, considerate man. With regret she thought about those moments when she paid little attention to his attempts to talk with her or when she refused to join him for a drink after work. The realization of her role in the parking lot confrontation between Dexter and Dane added to that regret. Her behavior was guided not so much by her unwillingness to engage him in conversation or join him for a drink but by a feeling of confusion, of apprehension about what to do to rescue herself from what she viewed as a dilemma.

Finally, only months ago doctors confirmed that her father suffered from Parkinson's disease which added another layer of worry and misgiving. Her mother had emerged as the strength of the family, providing for her dad's every need while they confronted this brutal illness.

Ashley turned to the door and reached to switch off the bathroom light. Carefully, she followed the familiar route back to her bed. She lay back against her pillow, hands clasped behind her head. Eyes wide, she gazed into the darkness of her bedroom, only a sliver of light sneaking around the edge of a window shade. She thought about the promise offered by her successful high school career which prepared her for success in college. More important, her early successes helped establish a sense of independence and confidence, qualities missing in her mother's life, qualities she desperately wished to serve her all through life.

She turned onto her side, determined to take control of her life rather than let it drift into daily frustration and depression. She closed her eyes to wait for that elusive sleep.

If he would listen, she would explain to Dane about Dexter Parks, about her father, and about herself. Candor, she could think of no better way to deal with her dilemma. Suddenly as if a screen clicked on in her mind, a hospital scene captured Ashley's attention and refused to release her. On that screen the entire scene played out.

"Boy, you look great. They certainly must be treating you well around here." Ashley stopped short of Dane's hospital bed.

"Yeah, twenty-four hour room service." Despite his sensitive head, Dane laughed, sitting upright, braced by pillows.

"If care gets too good, you might not want to leave." She paused and moved closer to the bed.

Dane shook his head without creating an explosion of pain. "No, I don't think so. A bit too confining here."

In a more tentative tone, she announced, "Incidentally, Dexter sends his good wishes."

A scowl crossed Dane's face.

Ashley looked down at the floor, recognizing his dismissive response to the mention of Dexter Parks. "When do you get to leave?"

"I think tomorrow, depending on what Dr. Hunter says." Dane smiled. "Interesting that Dr. Hunter is the same doctor who treated me after that other concussion I had."

"What a coincidence." Ashley folded her hands across her stomach. She shifted nervously from one foot to the other. Looking up at Dane, she confessed, "I'm so sorry for what happened the other night. I, ah, I just don't know how things got so out of hand."

Dane breathed deeply. "I'm not sure either, but, Ashley, part of it had to do with you."

"With me?" Ashley's mouth dropped, and eyes opened wide. "Really, if I was the cause, I'm so, so sorry."

Dane pulled on the sheet covering his legs. "Ashley, I don't mean it's your fault. If anybody's, it's mine." He ran his hand over his lips. "Maybe I assumed too much. I thought we had a special relationship beyond just fellow employees." His eyes dropped to the IV tubes attached to his arm.

Ashley stepped closer to the end of the bed, grasping the end railing. "I thought we did too, but recently I sensed kind of a resistance, a, ah, a hesitation in our relationship."

Dane took another deep breath. "Yes, that's my fault. Look, Ashley, I need to be absolutely honest. I'm sorry." He rested his hands on top the sheet. "I saw what I believed to be a growing relationship between you and Dexter Parks. I kinda resented that. Just pure jealousy, I guess." Dane slumped back into his pillow.

For a moment silence filled the space between them. Dane fiddled with the corner of his sheet. Ashley tapped her fingers on the bed railing. She then made eye contact with him. " I'm so sorry that I disappointed you. It wasn't intentional. Believe me. I obviously misinterpreted your intentions, stupid me."

The acknowledgement of their relationship realities helped reduce the tension swirling around the room. "Our problem is that we were both stupid." Dane smiled, "Dancing around our feelings like middle school kids. Ashley, I've enjoyed the time we've spent together both professionally and socially. Maybe we can preserve some of that."

Ashley dropped her hands from the railing. "I certainly don't know why we can't. I think I told you before about a bit of confusion

I've suffered over the three men in my life. You know who they are. My father hangs in there in his fight against the Parkinson disease." Moving around to the side of the bed, she placed her hand on Dane's arm. "Honestly, Dane, I don't know what to do about the other two men. I know I don't want them hurting each other."

She shook her head. "I'm not asking for sympathy. I'm an adult. I need to behave like one. Right now all I want is for you to recover and to get on with your life as I will get on with mine." She straightened her shoulders, standing firm next to the bed. "At the risk of getting philosophical, the seeds for a lasting relationship have been planted. Time will tell whether they will flourish or wither."

Dane blinked a tear from his eyes. He reached for Ashley's hand. "Thank you. What a great way to put it. You don't know how important it is to hear you say that." He squeezed her hand. "To slip in a little philosophy of my own: 'The future will see us through'."

Chapter 29

Paralyzing boredom found Chester fastened to his chair surrounded by four bare walls and a couple cloudy windows. His only diversion a drive into Sadie's Diner for meals, the days dragged onerously. His conversation the day before with Clark offered a degree of reassurance of ID documents needed to get him out of the country.

These documents would contain the name Charles Randall. As the investigation of the events of the past weeks intensified moving dangerously closer to Chester, he decided new ID documents would not offer him needed protection. Familiar with the machinations common in the business world, he determined a name change was essential. Though the decision caught Clark by surprise, he didn't question it. If Chester needed a new name, Clark easily could apply it to the altered documents without asking questions. For the agreed $500.00, he could consider Chester's needs none of his business.

Clark promised he would deliver a driver's license, passport, and auto insurance verification all under the name Charles Randall. Chester could hardly tolerate another day confined to the cabin. No outdoorsman, Chester viewed as intimidating the dense, pine forest surrounding the cabin. The lakeside of the property gave some relief from the dense forest with a dozen feet of sand, a prelude to the cold waters of Lake Lizzy. Other than on the shore line, thick with decades old towering pine trees interspersed with smaller oak and maple trees each displaying a new growth of leaves, the area teemed with potential hazards besides simply getting lost. Nonetheless, claustrophobia compelled Chester to do something besides staring at bare walls. Breakfast complete and lunch hours away, he made a sudden decision to venture outside for a brief walk staying close to the cabin.

He stepped out the only entrance to the cabin, stood for an instant determining in what direction to walk. To his left was the lake. To his right stood less thick foliage. Still, besides the low hanging bows of pine trees, sharp twigs and branches of the oaks and maples, exposed roots and half buried boulders demanded extreme caution.

Chester advanced, each step carefully measured. After a few minutes he stopped and inhaled the fresh forest air, a distinct contrast to his recollection of air in the big city. Looking around, he moved ahead. Suddenly, he heard a sound off to his left, something rustling in the underbrush. He stopped to listen. He stepped forward. Distracted, he stumbled on an exposed root and fell, striking his head on a partially submerged boulder. He sprawled on the rocky ground, his glasses landing in the ground cover

Pain erupted in his head, rendering him immovable. He lay in semiconsciousness, throbbing pain crashing through his head. He attempted to raise up on his knees. The intense pain in his head forced him back on his stomach. He dropped his head onto the ground, his indispensable glasses loose on the forest floor. He lay there confused, in pain and nearly motionless.

Sixty-eight year old Omar Trulson, a third generation Norwegian, each day walked with his dog through the forest separating his cabin from the one occupied by Chester. A bachelor and confirmed outdoorsman, Omar retired ten years ago after a long career as a local cement contractor. Rumor hinted that he made the foundations for more buildings and homes than anyone else in Todd County, the home county of Pelican Rapids.

Even at sixty-eight still a powerfully built man over six feet tall,

Omar had square shoulders, long arms, and huge hands, all essential for his years of working in concrete. A man who lived his life his own way, he ignored social convention, content with his long gray, stringy hair reaching his shoulders and his full, bushy beard of the same color. Under the long stringy hair, his gentle eyes betrayed his obvious physical strength. Hidden beneath his full beard lurked a friendly smile that knew no favoritism. Omar represented the veritable mountain man who lived no where near a mountain but thrived on the shores of Lake Lizzy.

Despite his successful career in the concrete business, Omar lived modestly for over twenty-five years in a two bedroom cabin on the shores of Lake Lizzy. About one half mile from the cabin Chester used, it sat close enough for Omar to know what went on with his neighbor. Omar knew someone occupied the cabin owned by the Walker family, but he refused to intrude.

On this morning's walk with his faithful Black Lab, Omar followed the dog who exhibited a nervous insistence on going his own way. That way led to Chester still on the ground, semiconscious. Accustomed to taking care of himself, Omar knelt beside Chester, touching him on the shoulder. A huge bump on his forehead disclosed what likely had happened. Assuming this was his neighbor in the Walker cabin, Omar attempted to talk with the man sprawled on the ground. The man only moaned incoherently. Gently, Omar moved the man over on his back, his Black Lab standing guard close by, nosing Chester's glasses in the nearby ground cover. Omar reached to pat the head of his helpful companion.

Aware of the potential dangers of a concussion, Omar sat on his knees watching this strange man until he could notice a gradual return to full consciousness. Omar reached down to nudge Chester's shoulder. "You okay?" He asked.

Chester gazed with vacant eyes at this strange man hovering over him.

"Look, I'm Omar Trulson. I live a ways over there." He pointed in the direction of his cabin. In his hand he held Chester's glasses. "I guess these belong to you."

Chester tried to sit up, confused by what had happened and by this big man who kneeled next to him. He grasped his glasses, an essential part of his life. "Thank you," he mumbled.

Omar's immediate diagnosis, a concussion, prompted his recommendation to take Chester to the hospital, a recommendation Chester in his weakened state vehemently rejected for reasons he refused to disclose, a rejection Omar refused to pursue. Chester did manage to identify himself and his place at the cabin.

Omar's independent existence had prepared him to deal with a range of pains and accidents. However, anything he could do he could only do in his own cabin. Not in any condition to refuse Omar's offer for help, Chester submitted to Omar's practically carrying him to his cabin where he would receive the minimal care Omar could supply.

At Omar's cabin, Chester received a special concoction Omar claimed derived from ancestral Norway and served over the decades as treatment for any number of maladies. Chester remained under Omar's care over night, rendering him sufficiently healed to return to the claustrophobia of his own cabin.

After helping Chester return to his own cabin and with a promise to check on him, Omar left him with a small container of the special, family concoction. Chester understood a concussion carried potential long term consequences. Of course, he received no professional diagnosis of a concussion. Besides by the next day he felt much better, even well enough to visit Sadie's Diner for lunch. Feeling an uncharacteristic gratitude, on his way home he stopped by Omar's cabin to do just that, express his gratitude. With eyes wide and tail wagging, the Black Lab sat before Chester as if waiting for his thank you. After all he discovered the injured Chester. In appreciation, Chester scratched the dog under his chin. In response, the dog licked his hand.

Back in the lonely cabin, Chester contemplated the immediate future. Clark indicated he would complete shortly the critical documents, driver's license, pass port, and auto insurance confirmation all in the name of Charles Randall. Clark reserved comment on learning of Chester's Mexico destination though he, too, had seen the promotional ad about the tropical resort in Puerto Vallarta. For Clark, this whole agreement with Chester carried with it more intrigue all the time which made little difference to Clark. Besides, for the $500.00, he didn't need to learn all the details of Chester's plan.

Clark did remind Chester of obvious risks in getting to Mexico, especially from the airlines and border authorities. Nonetheless, he agreed that if Chester had to find some place to hide and if the journey proved successful, Mexico offered a safe haven. Maybe during the coming weekend Clark could drive to the cabin with Chester's new name, critical documents and any advice Clark could offer about the best way to Puerto Vallarta.

Chapter 30

Dane's preoccupation with certain people in his life shadowed his short drive to the Fore Sure Telemarketing office. His recovery from the parking lot fall left him crowded with misgivings about Ashley despite the discussion of their relationship while he recovered in the hospital, with suspicions about the fate of Chester Reynolds, and about his job. Spring at one time served as one of Dane's favorite season. The beauty of renewed foliage on trees that flourished around his rural Hennepin County, family home often found him as a teen standing in his back yard marveling at the splendor of nature. In recent years other elements in his life dominated his attention.

He pulled into his usual parking place, still vivid in his mind the glimpse of Tony and Sylvester collecting debris around the parking lot and, of course, his more recent parking lot fall. Stepping out of his car, Dane decided not to succumb to all the peripheral things in his life. After all, he enjoyed good health, a sound relationship with his parents, and a job which almost satisfied his immediate needs. He straightened his shoulders and walked to the entrance to the Fore Sure Telemarketing offices determined to concentrate on his job.

"Good afternoon, Mr. Barton." Carmen, the receptionist, possessed a marvelous capacity for congeniality. Inevitably her welcome always lifted Dane's spirits.

"Good afternoon to you." Dane paused in front of Carmen's desk. Dressed in a sleeveless, light pink top with matching tasteful ear rings and necklace, her smile served as a memorable introduction to Fore Sure Telemarketing, even for Dane, who experienced it each day he worked.

"Everybody here?" Dane asked.

Carmen glanced down at her hands folded on the desk in front of her. She looked up with a tight smile. "Yes, plus one," she announced with clinched teeth.

Dane rolled his eyes, aware of what Carmen implied with her comment. Around the calling center few secrets stayed that way. Dexter Parks' interest in Ashley was one of those secrets. Dane shrugged his shoulders. "Yeah, I know." Then he turned to enter the calling center, fully aware that the parking lot confrontation would not remove Parks from his life.

Ashley and Dexter Parks stood next to her calling station adjacent to Dane's. In conversation, they failed to notice Dane's approach. When they did, the conversation stopped, replaced by broad smiles.

Dexter stepped forward with hand extended, natural behavior for a corporate executive. "Good to see you again, Dane." He deliberately avoided any reference to the parking lot clash.

With suppressed reluctance, Dane offered his hand. "Good afternoon."

Ashley reached out to place her hand on Dane's arm, reluctant to expose her ambivalence regarding her relationship with the two men who stood beside her. "All set for another hard day on the phone?" Her attempt at humor failed.

Dane closed his eyes and nodded agreement. "Somebody's gotta do it." He pulled out his chair and sat down to prepare for his evening shift.

Ashley nodded her head, touched Dexter's shoulder and settled into her place next to Dane. Dexter walked out on his own.

Dane concentrated on his script for the evening, positioning his head set and automatic dialing control, refraining from any more conversation with Ashley.

She halted her preparation for calling then looked over at Dane. "You okay?" she asked.

"Yeah, I'm fine." Dane pushed his chair closer to his desk. With a hint of sarcasm, he commented, "I thought clients weren't permitted in the calling center."

Ashley exhaled and touched her chin. "He was only clarifying details about his latest window product."

"Oh, I see." Dane's response signaled an end to the conversation.

Through the evening their calls consumed their time, Dane discovering moments of impatience with the abrupt rudeness of some of his call recipients, a feeling new to his experience as a telemarketer. A periodic glimpse at Ashley only a few feet from him served as their only contact.

Near the conclusion of their shift, a calm settled over the calling center, callers exhausting their lists of recipients. Dane pushed back his chair, folding his hands behind his head. He dropped his chin on his chest.

Ashley rested her elbows on the arms of her chair. She took a couple deep breaths. "I'm sorry, Dane."

Her admission caught Dane by surprise. He straightened up. "What are you sorry for?" his question laced in bitterness.

She adjusted her chair to face Dane. "I'm sorry that something keeps straining our relationship." She folded her hands in her lap. "I'm sorry that our hospital conversation has done little to change our relationship."

Dane studied his close partner. "I'm sorry too. Maybe we just have to give it more time." He stopped to scratch his arm in response to a nonexistent itch. "Parks hanging around here doesn't help."

Ashley sat back in her chair. 'Dane, Dexter is a friend and an important client for the company. I don't think our relationship goes beyond that." She spread her arms in a gesture of surrender. "I don't know what to think about ours either." She hung her head and pushed a tear away from her cheek.

"I guess I don't either." Dane leaned forward with hands resting on his knees. "Since we both don't know what happened maybe we should sit down at the bar and search for an answer?"

Ashley looked into Dane's eyes. Her smile exposed her compliance with his suggestion. "You know, that's a damn good idea. Excuse the language."

That evening at the conclusion of their shifts, they made good on Ashley's suggestion. They met at the same bar that had brought them together earlier. In a quiet corner they sipped their drinks, wine for Ashley, beer for Dane, stretching their time together. Though busy on this week night, the bar still offered a suitable place for two people to engage in important conversation. The atmosphere of the bar and, perhaps, the capacity of their drinks to suppress inhibitions allowed them to speak candidly about themselves, their families, and their futures.

Ashley, with little hesitation, discussed her dilemma involving the three men in her life: her dad, Dexter Parks, and Dane Barton. Dane spoke of his reservations about his job, about the elusive Chester Reynolds, and about his squandered opportunities. He also talked about his emerging desire to move out on his own, leaving the only home he ever knew. He avoided any response to the subjects of Dexter Parks and Dane Barton, expressing interest only in the condition of Ashley's father as well as their future at Fore Sure Telemarketing. After two hours of soul cleansing, they raised their glasses in a toast to the future.

In subsequent days, Ashley and Dane enjoyed a much more amiable relationship based on a tacit understanding to allow that relationship to advance gradually and naturally, to comply with Dane's comment to Ashley while he lay confined to a hospital bed: "The future will see us through."

Chapter 31

Driving west to the cabin, Clark Walker squinted into the low spring sun inching its way to the western horizon. His planned meeting with Chester Reynolds was delayed by Chester's fall. However, a brief discussion with Chester that morning confirmed Clark's drive to deliver Chester's new documents.

A bright, insightful, congenial man, one of Chester's high school classmates, Clark chuckled to himself as he drove west to Pelican Rapids and the family cabin. How many times over the years he had made the drive he had no idea. However, he knew this represented the only time to deliver false identification documents.

From the time he received Chester's call about his need for modified documents, Clark entertained a playful suspicion. He did remember hearing about the robbery and its consequences. The incident, in Clark's mind, rendered Chester a victim, not a perpetrator. Clark simply refused to dwell on why Chester needed the new documents. That he needed them and would pay $500.00 for them satisfied Clark's playful curiosity. Besides he welcomed the excitement of working in the shadow of suspicion.

Dressed in his Vikings uniform, sweat pants, sweat shirt, and cap, Clark relaxed driving over very familiar roads. A slender man from a long line of slender men, someone once reminded him, he stood about five feet ten, his slender frame making him look even taller. Even with his heritage of slenderness, in later years he developed a slight bulge around the middle, a physical feature he worked to control three times a week at a St. Paul fitness center.

A row of white hair encircled Clark's head leaving the top bare. Beyond that he looked much younger than his sixty-five years. Most of those years he flourished as a graphic artist, capitalizing on his natural artistic talent. He considered this mission simply a favor for a classmate whom he knew little about.

When Clark drove into the sheltered driveway and stopped behind Chester's car, Chester, dressed in his usual baggy pants, wrinkled shirt, and vest dotted with stains, stood in the cabin's entrance ensuring the identity of his visitor. Chester stepped out the door to greet Clark, his glasses doing little to conceal a dark, purplish bruise across his forehead and around his left eye. "Good to see you." Chester announced before Clark emerged from his car.

"How you doing, Mr. Woodsman?" Clark asked playfully.

"Okay, I guess." Chester ran his hand gingerly over his forehead.

"That looks painful. You all right?" Clark moved closer to observe Chester's wound.

Chester adjusted his glasses. "Yeah, thanks to Omar next door." He tilted his head in the direction of the Norwegian's cabin.

Clark nodded. "Yes, he is quite a guy. Always willing to give a hand."

Chester led Clark into the cabin where they found space at the small, narrow kitchen table. Clark inquired about Chester's accident, receiving a brief description about what happened. He then reached into a larger envelope to withdraw the documents Chester so desperately needed and had impatiently waited for.

Clark carefully explained each document, especially the passport, the most critical of the documents considering Chester's determination to travel to Mexico. The explanation complete, Clark sat back in his chair.

Chester shuffled through the documents. "These look great. So now I'm Charles Randall." He rubbed his hand over the colorful passport. "I don't know how you do it."

Clark smiled. "It isn't easy. Do you have any questions?"

Chester's face tensed; he bit on his thumb nail. He removed his glasses to rub the discolored eye. "I don't think so." He rested his arm on the table. "It's just, ah, ah, what do you think is the best way to get to Mexico?"

Clark inhaled then scratched his bald head. "I don't know. Under the circumstances you should probably avoid airports." He paused to retrieve a thought. "I don't think you should drive your car. The registration wouldn't match your driver's license." Clark pushed the envelope in which he brought the documents across the table toward Chester. "That doesn't leave much choice except the bus."

Chester wiped a spot off his glasses. "Buses go all the way to Puerto Vallarta?"

Clark shook his head at Chester's remarkable naivete. "Yes, I think so, but not the same company."

For several minutes they talked about Chester's Mexican destination. Clark vaguely remembered hearing the tropical resort ad played on Twin Cities TV stations, dismissing it as just another property exploitation. Nonetheless, he respected Chester's decision to make Mexico his ultimate destination. What role the resort depicted in the ad would play in Chester's future, Clark had no idea. Knowing a little about Chester's limited travel, Clark harbored skepticism about Chester's awareness of what he faced when he arrived in Mexico. Ultimately, Clark decided that was Chester's concern, not his.

Eventually, the conversation settled on a plan. Chester would park his car in the shadow of the cabin, perhaps as remote and secure a place as any. He would ride back to the Twin Cities with Clark. At Clark's home in St. Paul, they would explore routes and bus transportation all the way from St. Paul to the Mexican border then across Mexico to the Pacific and finally south to the tropical city of Puerto Vallarta.

Sitting in Clark's home office, Chester only blinked his eyes as

Clark navigated his computer in search of bus information and a suitable border crossing. In an hour Clark had tentatively identified a route and a carrier all the way to El Paso, Texas, a busy crossing into Juarez, Mexico, and a bus connection to Mazatlan and south to Puerto Vallarta. Next Chester would have to secure ticketing from various bus companies both in the U.S. and Mexico.

Clark leaned back from his computer desk to look over at Chester waiting anxiously for the conclusion of Clark's searches. "Well, buddy, the rest depends on you. A couple clicks here will confirm ticketing to El Paso. Beyond that you will have to fend for yourself after crossing into Mexico." Clark stood up, stretched and moved away from his computer. "I've never taken a bus to Texas, certainly never to anyplace in Mexico. I, ah, ah, would suggest once over the border check with border officials. They should direct you to bus transportation." He stood facing Chester seated beside the computer desk. "I guess once in Mexico your real adventure begins."

Chester rested his arms on his knees. "That's all I need is more adventure." He rose from the chair with hand extended. "Thank you, Clark. That adventure could never happen without you."

Chapter 32

Dane waited for the green light. Relieved to face the end of his calling shift but missing the shared drink with Ashley, he smiled at the near full moon visible in the low Southern sky. That along with the encouraging and satisfying conversation with Ashley inspired Dane's thoughts of his future.

Uncertainty shrouded that future. He hoped maybe it included some relationship with Ashley. His future definitely needed a more secure and lucrative job. His clear, convincing voice, the one described by his mother as blessed with loquacity, perhaps, might lend itself to more employment options. The advertising business intrigued him. Telemarketing did, too, despite an expanding discontent with rude, sarcastic people who hung up without a one word response.

Nearing the Highway 12 freeway exit, Dane combed his hand through his hair, merged into the right hand lane taking him to the Highway 12 exit. The rest of the drive home took only minutes on County 110 in western Hennepin County.

At 10:00 he pulled into the driveway of the only home he'd ever known, another aspect of his life seeking more of his attention. His mother's car was parked in front of the garage, his dad out on the road piloting his eighteen wheeler. A quick look at the large picture window dominating the front of the house, awakened that horrible memory of gun shoots shattering the glass and his mother writhing in pain on the living room floor.

Since his last conversation with Lt. Lewis days ago, Dane strived to erase thoughts of Chester Reynolds as well as Sylvester languishing in jail waiting trial for robbery and accessory to murder. Nothing in Dane's life prepared him to deal with such egregious events. Determined to suppress these thoughts, Dane punched the steering wheel before shutting off the car. He stepped out onto the driveway and slammed the door. Too damn much of his life included memories of that meaningless job at the convenience store.

"How was your evening on the phone?" his mother asked as Dane walked into the kitchen.

Dane shrugged a shoulder and wrinkled his brow. "Oh, really exciting."

Beatrice turned around from her position by the sink. "Something wrong?"

Dane laughed, extending his arms to the side in a gesture of conciliation. "No, no, ah, it's, ah, it's just sitting in front of that phone for hours doesn't count for much excitement."

Beatrice picked up her cup of coffee from the counter and moved to the kitchen table. "Want some coffee?"

Dane placed his hands on his hips. "Uh, yeah, I guess I can handle a cup of coffee."

Beatrice started to get up from her chair.

"No, sit down. I can get my own coffee." Dane stepped to the counter, reached for a cup from the cupboard, poured his coffee, and joined his mother at the table.

For a moment they sipped their coffee in silence. Beatrice studied her son. "You haven't said much lately. How is the job going?" The subject of Dexter Parks was not popular in the Barton home.

Dane took another sip and wiped his hand over his mouth. "Mom, it's okay." He set his cup down. "I just don't know how long I want to continue doing it."

"Have you talked to Mr. Carmona?"

Dane shook his head. "No, not yet, but I think I will soon."

Beatrice took a swallow of coffee. Still holding her cup in both hands, she allowed a furtive grin to enliven her face. "What about that girl you promised to bring home?" For years Beatrice had encouraged her son to seek a girl friend. In her mind, he never even tried, despite, in his mother's opinion, an engaging personality and handsome appearance.

Dane slumped in his chair. He blinked his eyes. "I don't know. Someday, maybe."

"Is there a problem?" Beatrice asked.

Dane hesitated, turning his cup around on the table top. He had shared with nobody his intimate conversation with Ashley. Right now he debated the wisdom of sharing the details with his mother. Considering the lift it had afforded him at the time, he concluded discussing it with his mother would cause no harm. He straightened up in his chair, hands clasped in his lap. For the next half hour he described to his mother the details of his candid conversation with Ashley at the bar. He finished with explaining their mutual agreement to let their relationship evolve on its own.

Without interruption Beatrice listened to her son's narrative. When he finished, she sat without comment, eyes fixed on her son. A few seconds passed. She reached to touch Dane's hands now folded on the table. "Thank you, son. Thank you for your honesty. I admire what you and Ashley did." She rubbed a finger under her eye. "It's what mature people should do."

Dane smiled in response to his mother's compliment. "Well, now you know about the chances of Ashley's visit here."

Already past her bedtime, Beatrice squeezed her son's hand, rose from her place by the table, and rinsed the two coffee cups in the sink. "I'm sorry but 7:00 comes early in the morning. I think I'll head to bed."

"Me, too, in a little while. Don't make any noise at 7:00." Dane laughed.

After his mother left for bed, Dane moved into the living room, switched on the TV to a David Letterman rerun. More interested in lingering thoughts than attending to the TV, he settled into the sofa with a deep sigh. He leaned back on the sofa cushion, content with having shared those thoughts with his mother. What he hadn't shared with his mother were his thoughts about finding a new job or about finding an apartment of his own. Certainly, he had plenty time to address those thoughts.

A glance at the TV gave him the rare opportunity to watch David Letterman throw a football at a richly decorated cake positioned on top a ladder. Such ingenious TV programming.

Chapter 33

"Say, Dane, have you read the new script?" Ashley turned in her chair to face him.

"No, not completely. I'm working on it." He reached for his copy of the script. "I think this place is the same place advertised on TV a while ago, some tropical lure."

Ashley gave the script another glance. "Sounds really exotic and not a bad deal if you win." She cocked her head. "I wouldn't mind spending an all expense vacation for two for a week in tropical … let's see, tropical Puerto Vallarta, I think."

Dane nodded his head. "I guess so."

Since their intimate conversation days ago, their relationship offered hope of possible endurance. Entering the spring season meant three important promotions at Fore Sure Telemarketing: windows which had dominated their time for weeks, furnaces and air conditioners, and what Dane termed tropical lure. The latest of the three was the promotion of a tropical resort in Puerto Vallarta, Mexico, named "Mi Casa by the Bay."

For the next several days all four callers toiled with each evening's list of calls. The calls dubbed "tropical lure" received the best response. Dane alone recorded eight recipients willing to sit through a presentation and qualify for a drawing to determine the winner of the one week all expense paid vacation for two to Puerto Vallarta.

The pitch was not complicated, just a brief but vivid description of the exclusive resort composed of one hundred condominiums available for purchase through the Tropical Real Estate Company. An agreement to attend an information session at a local motel would create the chance to enter the drawing for the vacation. That evening Dane drove home satisfied with the shift, with Ashley, and, for now, his job.

Several days passed, each one busy at the calling center. The pace of the evening calls restricted much conversation among the four callers. The response to the tropical lure exceeded that from the other two promotions which pleased Mr. Carmona as well as the Tropical Real Estate people whom none of the callers had met. Unlike Dexter Parks, client representatives rarely entered the calling center. At least Dane found that proper and acceptable.

Following a particularly brisk calling evening, Dane and Ashley decided to meet again for a drink after their shift. Unlike the last time, they sat relaxed at the familiar bar. They avoided discussion related to their future relationship, or to Dexter Parks, or to their future with Fore Sure Telemarketing, or to living arrangements that had captured their last visit. Instead, content with a review of some of their more interesting, evening calls, they quietly sipped their drinks.

Dane sat back in his chair. "I'm sorry I haven't asked, but I assume your dad's doing okay."

Ashley dabbed her lips with a napkin. "Yes, thanks for asking. He just spent some time at a Duluth hospital for further testing and, ah, ah, I guess some refinement of his medication. Apparently he's doing okay."

"That's good. How's your mother handling all this?"

Ashley smiled, her eyes diverted upward with a frown. "She hasn't always handled adversity very well. But she seems to handle my dad's situation quite well." She paused. "Incidentally, what about your mom?"

"She's doing fine, only a hint of stiffness when she reaches above her head."

Ashley cupped her chin in her hand. "Maybe I shouldn't even bring it up, but have you heard any more about that whole robbery mess and what's his name, Chester something?" She took a swallow of her wine.

Dane closed his eyes and lowered his chin on his chest. He looked up. "No, not since the call from this Lt. from the Minneapolis Police Department. I guess the guy took off, a fugitive. To think I worked for this goon." Dane shook his head.

Ashley reached to touch Dane's hand. "We all make mistakes," she laughed.

Finally, their conversation did drift into a casual consideration of their futures at Fore Sure Telemarketing with Dane hinting again about seeking his own apartment. Neither topic generated much attention. With one swallow left in their respective glasses, they saluted the evening with a quick toast to the future. They walked hand in hand across the parking lot to their cars, content with the world and content with each other.

When Dane arrived at work the next afternoon, Carmen greeted him with her usual sparkle, welcoming him to another evening on the phone. Dressed in a stunning lavender top allowing an enticing peek at her cleavage, she challenged Dane, who stood before and slightly above her as she sat behind her desk, to focus his eyes on her face, not on her chest.

Her face assumed a serious look. "Mr. Carmona made sure to remind me to tell you he'd like to talk to you when you arrive."

Dane's body tensed. "Did he say why?" Dane wondered if he had done something wrong.

"No, he didn't, but he does have a meeting with, ah." She glanced down at notes on her desk. "With a Mr. Perez. I think he's big in this Tropical Real Estate Company."

Dane stepped back from the desk. "I wonder what that's all about?"

Carmen displayed one of her seductive smiles. "The only way to find out is to walk over there and knock on the door." She pointed in the direction of Mr. Carmona's office.

Dane shrugged his shoulders and headed toward that door. He stopped in front of the door. Gingerly he raised his arm to knock. A faint voice from within invited him to come in. When Dane opened the door, Mr. Carmona rose from behind his desk to greet him.

"Thank you for coming." Mr Carmona dressed immaculately in khaki trousers, blue blazer and beige polo shirt open at the neck, reached out his hand. Dane did the same.

Dane only smiled as they shook hands.

Carmona turned to the gentleman standing next to the desk, a man in his thirties, brown skin declaring his Hispanic ancestry, with thick curly hair, dark eye brows over deep black eyes, and sparkling teeth, indeed a handsome man.

"Mr. Perez, I want you to meet Dane Barton, one of our outstanding telemarketers."

"My pleasure." Mr Perez reached out his hand to shake Dane's.

"Thank you. Good to meet you too." Dane shifted uncomfortably on his feet.

The cordial introduction removed much of Dane's misgivings about the meeting. Still, nerves tingled in his stomach as perspiration gathered around his neck. Mr. Carmona turned toward his desk. "Gentlemen, please take a seat." He gestured to the two chairs positioned before his desk. All three seated, Mr. Carmona shifted some papers on top his desk. He looked up, gaining eye contact with both his guests.

"Dane, we've asked you to meet with us today because Mr. Perez would like to make a proposal involving you. You know for the last several days we have had the privilege of promoting one of Mr. Perez's prime properties." He paused directing his attention to Dane. "Dane, you probably have pronounced the name 'Mi Casa by the Bay' countless times."

Dane nodded his head in agreement.

Mr. Carmona looked over at Mr. Perez, who took that as a clue to make his pitch. He turned to face Dane. "Mr. Barton, maybe it's a bit melodramatic, but it is a great resort development with impressive potential. My company, The Tropical Real Estate Company, looks at the resort with pride and boundless expectation." Perez's dark eyes danced with excitement. "Mr. Barton, Dane, I'm aware of several people you have called describe to me how impressed they were with your articulate presentation and professionalism. These are people who because of calls from people like you have agreed to attend the more detailed presentation and have entered the drawing for the all- expense vacation for two at the resort."

Dane moved uneasily in his chair, slightly embarrassed by the compliments. He blinked his eyes and smiled, "Thank you."

Mr. Perez folded his hands in his lap. "Mr. Carmona has graciously given me permission to invite you to join our sales team at Tropical Real Estate. We believe your salesmanship and your articulation can prove invaluable assets for you and for our company."

Dane sat stunned, looking first at his present boss, Mr. Carmona, and next at his potential future boss, Mr. Perez.

Noting Dane's unease, Mr. Carmona cleared his throat. "Dane, you've served this company well in the short time you have worked for us. Only with reluctance would I see you leave." He squeezed his lips together. "Dane I don't wish to stand in your way of another opportunity in the advertising world. If you consider this something you would like to pursue, by all means take it." He leaned foreword in his chair, placing his hands flat on top his desk.

Quiet filled the office. Carmona stared at Dane. "Well, what do you think, young man?"

Dane furrowed his brow and shook his head. He cleared his throat. "I'm not sure what to think." A sensation trickled through his stomach. Perspiration collected under his arms and just below his hair line. He squeezed his nose with his thumb and forefinger, then licked his lips. "I'm overwhelmed with your offer Mr. Perez and with your generosity and understanding Mr. Carmona." Dane looked down at the floor then made eye contact with each man. "Maybe you could give me a little time to think about the offer and acquaint me with more details about what the position entails."

"Of course, you need time to make a decision," agreed Mr. Perez. "Take your time. Why don't we plan to sit down together in the near future so I can lay out the details of the position."

Dane left the office with an entire new perspective on his future.

Chapter 34

Throughout his life Chester (aka Charles Randall) held firmly to his independence, his striving for self-sufficiency and self-fulfillment. The last few weeks and months had tested that commitment. The events compelling him to flee had drastically transformed his life beyond anything he could have imagined. The last five days marked the epitome of that transformation.

Through large round sun glasses over his regular glasses, Chester squinted into the brilliant Puerto Vallarta sun, bathing in its late spring rays the city's Gustavo Diaz Ordaz International Airport. He stood bewildered by what he saw, by what he had never seen before. The last leg of his five day journey took him from the small village of Tepic to the drop off site near the Puerto Vallarta airport.

The short ride from Tepic to the airport featured an enormous sign, covering the entire median of the four lane highway and reading "Bienvenido a la Puerto Vallarta." The sign confirmed that he had finally arrived at his destination and that he faced life in a country never before visited with a language and culture he knew virtually nothing about. Still, he considered gaining freedom from the predators back in the Twin Cities justified the ambiguity he faced.

He leaned back against the wall of the compact bus stop decorated with posters advertising several products whose names Chester didn't even try to pronounce. If he so desired, from this bus stop he could board a bus to El Centro, the name he learned that applied to downtown Puerto Vallarta. Unaware of where he would go or what he would do downtown, he took a deep breath, exhaled, thankful, at least, for Clark's invaluable help in getting him out of the country.

The five days on the road had begun at the St. Paul bus terminal where under the name Charles Randall, Chester, with his back pack and a small carry-on boarded a bus that would take him to Oklahoma City. After a night in a dingy motel with soiled sheets, a heating system that rattled all night, and a bathroom sink corroded with a yellow film, he climbed aboard another bus that took him to El Paso, Texas.

The border crossing in El Paso caused Chester to suffer a severe anxiety attack. According to Clark, this crossing into Mexico could expose Chester to the most complete security. Standing safely in Puerto Vallarta, he could now reflect upon those tense moments in the middle of a long line of people waiting to cross into Mexico at one of the pedestrian crossings. Remembering the ease of that crossing, Chester rubbed his nose and adjusted his double pair of glasses, a smile replacing residual misgivings.

Beyond El Paso he discovered the gracious assistance of the Mexican authorities at the crossing and at the Mexican bus terminal in Chihuahua. From there, for a remarkably small fee, a bus took him across Mexico all the way to Mazatlan on the Pacific Ocean. From Mazatlan he headed south for the long ride ending in Tepic from where he rode the city bus to the airport. Not at all certain of his destination in Puerto Vallarta, he decided to stop at the airport bus shelter to assess his alternatives.

Chester looked around the area where he stood in the bus shelter. Though during his bus ride in Mexico, he had adopted a few simple Spanish words and phrases, such as "Hola," "Gracias," "¿Cómo está?" "Buenos díez," and "Buenas noches," his inability to ask even about food or lodging drastically limited his options. His survey of the area around the airport spotted a familiar sign advertising a Comfort Inn motel. With renewed energy, he picked up his back pack and grabbed the handle of his carry-on, the two pieces containing practically everything he now owned, and moved out of the shelter in the direction of the motel only a few blocks away.

Next to Clark, no one had offered more essential assistance than Raul Rivera, the manager of the Comfort Inn. Tired, hot, stiff, and burdened with lingering apprehension, Chester pushed open the door to the five story motel proclaiming on a huge outdoor sign a free breakfast and free high speed internet service. The breakfast appealed to Chester; the internet service didn't.

Cool, comfort greeted Chester as he stood inside the door searching for the registration desk. Only three years old, he later found out, the motel featured a contemporary lobby with two conversational settings furnished with sofas, lounge chairs, and small tables with subdued, lamp lighting. Off to his left the registration desk contained two stations, only one served by an attractive young lady with flashing eyes joining her flashing white teeth.

Fluent in English, the attractive young lady, a name tag identifying her as Martina, wore a plain white blouse accentuating her smooth, light brown skin, and a black skirt. An engaging smile, flashing dark eyes and the ubiquitous "Hola" welcomed Chester to the motel. With little hesitation he approached the registration desk to secure a room in the name of Charles Randall.

A typical motel room, king size bed, dresser, TV cabinet, small fridge, closet and a bath with tub and shower, it offered Chester more comfort than his own bedroom at home in St. Paul. Stretched out on the bed with hands clasped behind his head, he stared into the empty space above him, thinking about the emptiness of his mañana, and the next, and the next. Rather than protecting his identity, his major concern now was how he could survive in, so far, a friendly but foreign culture.

Chapter 35

Well, Mr. Importance, was it good news?" Carmen stood up from behind her desk and watched Dane approach, a wide grin highlighting his face.

Dane wrinkled his forehead and tightened his lips, sustaining the grin. He only nodded his head.

"Can't you tell me?" Carmen begged, packaged in her most engaging voice.

Dane moved closer to the charming receptionist, gently placing his hands on her shoulders. He exhaled. "That was the head of Tropical Real Estate, our newest client." He locked eyes with Carmen, and in a voice strained by excitement, announced, "He offered me a job in sales for his company."

Carmen's sparkling eyes reinforced her generous smile. "Gee, that's great, isn't it?"

Dane stepped back, dropping his arms to his sides. "Yes, I certainly think so. Soon I'll meet with Mr. Perez to discuss details of the job."

"Exciting." Carmen shared Dane's obvious enthusiasm. "What did Mr. Carmona say about, maybe, losing his star caller?"

"He said he would never stand in the way of my professional advancement." Dane shifted from one foot to another.

"That's fantastic." Carmen returned to her desk. Sitting down, she looked up at Dane. "When do you start?"

"I'm not sure. It's, ah, ah, kind of sudden. I need to think about it a bit. I'm sure sitting down with Mr. Perez to talk about the job will help me decide." He grasped his hands behind his back. "I suppose I have to talk to my parents about the whole thing too. They're always worried about their little boy." He laughed.

"Well, congratulations anyway. I'm proud of you."

"Thank you," Dane smiled again and walked into the calling center. There, too, his colleagues greeted him with eagerness and curiosity. Word had obviously traveled fast about his meeting in Mr. Carmona's office.

Ashley jumped up from her station to greet Dane. Both Emile and Misty turned in their stations to hear what transpired at the meeting. Ashley rushed to confront Dane.

"Is something wrong?" The question came with a strained look on her face.

"No, I just got fired is all." Dane stared at Ashley in false sincerity.

"You what?" she asked, eyes wide, mouth open.

His shoulders slumped, Dane reached for Ashley's hands. "I'm sorry. I'm only kidding." He straightened his shoulders. "I was offered a job with the Tropical Real Estate Company. You know, our newest client."

Ashley playfully poked Dane in the stomach. "You stinker, for a moment you had me worried."

I'm sorry. It's just, it's just so unexpected. It's hard to know how to react."

Ashley stepped closer to Dane and kissed him on the cheek. "That's really a tribute to you. I'm so happy for you."

Both Misty and Emile walked over to add their congratulations to Dane's good fortune. With his three colleagues standing near, he explained, as he had to Carmen, the conditions that could lead to a new job and maybe a new future.

Calls that evening received an added touch of clarity and eloquence as Dane's private celebration extended to the tone of his conversations with call recipients. By the time his shift ended, the events of the evening nearly drained his energy. Still by the time he reached home, the need to tell his parents about the job offer renewed his excitement.

Their schedules often conflicting, rarely did Dane have the chance to discuss anything with his parents at the end of his evening shift, virtually never during the day. On this evening both parents sat watching TV when Dane entered the house, eager to share with them his meeting with Mr. Perez. Standing in the entrance to the living room, Dane beamed with delight. His parents sensed something different about their son who rarely allowed expressions of emotion. He stopped before entering the living room, suddenly speechless, eager to explain his news, the words elusive.

His mother detected something unusual about her son's behavior. "Well, are you coming in or not?" She asked.

Dane walked to a sofa chair across from his parents seated on the full sofa. He sat down and stretched his legs out in front of him. "I got offered a new job tonight," he blurted out.

The content and tone of his statement captured the attention of both his parents. In unison they asked, "What is it?"

For the next half hour Dane explained again the circumstances of his meeting with Mr. Carmona and Mr. Perez, the owner of the Tropical Real Estate Company, as well as the yet unscheduled meeting with Mr. Perez to outline the details attached to the new sales position.

Always the skeptic, his dad asked, "Do you know anything about this tropical company?"

"A little, the company is the most recent client of Fore Sure Telemarketing." Dane relaxed, the anxiety of the return home fading.

"When do you have this meeting with, ah, what's his name?" Beatrice leaned forward on the sofa.

"Mr. Perez, Miguel Perez." Dane offered. Getting up from his chair, he stated. "I'm not sure, maybe in a few days. He should contact me tomorrow."

"Well, son, I always knew something good would come of your loquacity. Thanks to your mother." Milo laughed, then pushed himself up from the sofa and faced his son. More serious, he admitted, "You know, Dane, most of your life, your mother and I have been proud of what you have done." He rolled his eyes. "Your work at that damn convenience store a possible exception." He stepped closer to his son, placing his hand on his shoulder. "This may be the opportunity you've waited for. We can only wish you good luck and hope for the best."

Dane hung his head and rubbed his eyes. Displays of affection between father and son were rare. This time called for, at least, a brief hug and mutual pats on the back.

Beatrice rose from the sofa to approach her son with arms wide. Dane quickly opened his arms to receive his mother's tight hug. "We are proud of you, dear. We'll be interested in hearing the details of the meeting with Mr. Perez."

Dane added a special squeeze for his mother. "Thank you, Mom. Maybe a new job could lead to an apartment all by myself."

"That would be something." A playful comment added by his dad. Again a more serious look crossed his face. "By the way, son, would this job require you to travel to foreign countries?"

"Good question, Dad. I really don't know. The company's corporate office is located in Puerto Vallarta, Mexico, a big tourist city on the Pacific." Dane shrugged his shoulders. "We'll have to wait and see, I guess."

Milo acknowledged his son's comment with a nod of his head. He looked at his wife. "I don't know about you, honey, but I don't think I can take any more news tonight. I do have an early morning, besides."

"Yes," agreed his wife. "I need to get to bed myself. Good night son and congratulations."

"Good night, Mom and good night to you also, Dad." Dane returned his dad's playfulness.

That night during those quiet moments before sleep, Dane envisioned what life might entail working for a dynamic international real estate company or what life would be like working in a foreign country?

Chapter 36

In the morning a call from Mr. Perez scheduled for the next day the meeting that would give Dane the details of the proposed sales position. His company offices in Puerto Vallarta, Mexico, compelled Perez to secure meeting space in a small, north St. Paul motel. Perez chose not to accept Carmona's offer to use his office for the meeting. He preferred a more neutral setting. Besides, his company rented space at the motel for the presentations to prospective buyers who agreed to attend with the chance to win an all expense trip for two to the Mi Casa by the Bay. Perez concluded that since the motel space was paid for, why not use it?

With little difficulty, Dane found the motel, a two story, L shaped building with parking around the perimeter. On this midmorning, only eight cars occupied parking spaces. Dane parked a few feet from the front entrance, a double glass door with "welcome" printed across both doors.

Dressed in a dark blue sport coat, gray trousers and a white shirt and tie, Dane felt slightly conspicuous but confident in his professional look. He walked to the registration desk where he explained to the young man behind the desk his purpose for being there. The young man graciously directed Dane to a small conference room only a few steps down the hall from the desk. Butterflies returned as Dane stood before the conference room door. He knocked. In seconds the door opened to a smiling Miguel Perez, dressed in a light blue golf shirt and black trousers, his thick black hair glistening with some hair product.

"Welcome, Mr. Barton. Thank you for coming on such short notice. Please come in and make yourself comfortable."

A cramped conference room, it contained a rectangular table surrounded by fourteen, executive type chairs, those with arm rests and wheels. On one wall a window overlooked the parking area. On another hung a projection screen. On a corner table sat a pitcher of ice water, glasses, a phone, and a cup filled with pens advertising the motel.

Dane lowered himself into a chair across from Mr. Perez, who reached down to grab a thick folder which he placed on the table in front of him. He looked up at Dane. "Obviously you faced no problem in finding this place."

"No, it was really easy."

Perez nodded his head. "That's good since we use this motel for our presentations." He laughed. "We don't want potential clients getting lost."

Dane smiled in agreement, a tension still gripping his stomach.

Perez sat up closer to the table, opened the folder to withdraw a brochure describing his company's prize property, Mi Casa by the Bay.

The property, as Perez described it, was carved out of the jungle across Banderas Bay, one of the deepest in the world, from the city of Puerto Vallarta. Designed as an exclusive retreat for those who sought privacy as well as companionship, the property offered one hundred one, two and three bedroom condominiums priced from two hundred thousand to near a million. According to Perez, the complex would provide some of the best accommodations in the world with amenities for casual living and pleasure. As he described the property, his voice gained clarity and animation reflecting his dedication to the project.

Shifting in his chair, Perez explained the relatively brief history of the Tropical Real Estate Company. From a modest start in

Puerto Vallarta, it had expanded to international operations while retaining the corporate offices in Mexico. Dane listened intently to the details of the company and especially to the details of his potential responsibilities. These responsibilities included, at first, making the presentations, at this motel, to those people agreeing to attend and wishing for a chance at a free trip to Puerto Vallarta. Though eventually he would probably spend time in Mexico, his early responsibilities would keep him in the Twin Cities.

Perez wheeled his chair closer to the corner table where he refilled his glass with water. "Would you like more?" He asked Dane.

Dane handed him his glass, "Please."

Perez wheeled his chair back to the table. He paused, on the table threading the fingers of one hand with those of the other. A sudden, serious look controlled his face. "Dane, believe me, this place is as close to paradise as any of us can reasonably expect to get. I'm convinced that eventually it will be known around the world as a legitimate Shangri-La." He breathed deeply and exhaled. Sitting back in his chair, he asked, "Any questions?"

Dane wrinkled his brow and pinched his lower lip between his thumb and finger.

Perez detected Dane's hesitation to respond. "Hey, I'm sorry. You probably have a host of questions. You just need time to digest all this information and detail."

Dane relaxed his shoulders and nodded his head. "Yes, there's a lot to learn, but it, ah, it sounds like a fabulous place and a fine company."

"It certainly is even now as it grows out of the jungle."

At the conclusion of his narration proclaiming the grandeur of Mi Casa by the Bay, Perez reached beneath the table for his laptop computer, slipped in a DVD, and gave Dane a chance to view the step by step progress of the resort project which literally did emerge out of the jungle.

Unable to find words suitable for describing the project, Dane just shook his head. Perez smiled and pushed his chair away from the table. Silence dominated the room for a few moments. A brief discussion ensued addressing specifics of wages and benefits, both better than at Fore Sure Telemarketing.

"When do you need my decision?" Dane inquired.

Mr. Perez stood up and moved around the table to face Dane. "You take your time. I don't wish to rush you into a decision as important as this one. Talk it over with friends at the telemarketing firm and with your parents. Let me know your decision as soon as you feel comfortable to make it."

Mr. Perez accompanied Dane to the motel's front entrance where they shook hands, closing one chapter in the drama of Dane's life and maybe opening another.

Chapter 37

Chester(aka Charles) rested in his motel room, his feet propped on the window sill. The fifth floor room gave him an excellent view of part of the golf course winding its way through the heart of Marina Vallarta, an affluent sub-section of Puerto Vallarta and the location of the Comfort Inn. In the week since his arrival in Puerto Vallarta, his familiarity with this dynamic, vibrant Mexican city had made progress. Much of that progress happened with the help of Raul Rivera, the manager of the Comfort Inn. Short, mid-forties with a pouch squeezed over his belt, and a receding hairline, Mr. Rivera's sharp, black eyes testified to his affability. In Chester's opinion, Raul, next to Clark Walker and maybe Omar Trulson, represented one of the most helpful persons in memory.

Still, the last week found Chester confined to his room for long periods during the afternoon and evening. Never one with a sharp social instinct, the periods of seclusion engendered restlessness. His view of the golf course confirmed Raul Rivera's detailed descriptions of the beauty of Puerto Vallarta as well as Marina Vallarta where Chester now spent his time.

Over a free breakfast of quesadillas and coffee, Chester sat with Raul, listening to his interesting narrative about his city in which he obviously took great pride. Chester learned about Puerto Vallarta's past as an agricultural center of the area, squeezed between the Sierra Madre Mountains and the vast Banderas Bay. In the area small farms grew a rich variety of fruits and vegetables sold in stores and by street vendors scattered throughout the city.

Despite its location on one of the deepest bays in the world, fishing did not serve as a major part of the local economy. However, the increase of tourism fueled the popularity of sport fishing. A boon to that increase was the filming of the movie, The Night of the Iguana, in the mid-sixties. From that time Puerto Vallarta had emerged as a prime tourist destination and grown in population from some sixty-thousand to over three hundred thousand in only a few decades. On other mornings, Raul took time to talk with Chester about life in Puerto Vallarta and how it might differ from life in the U.S. or how it might resemble life in the U.S.

Chester's languid stay in Puerto Vallarta caused his fear of arrest to fade. In its place returned his petulance and impatience. That he spent an inordinate amount of time in his motel room added to his agitation. With Raul's help, Chester acquired minimal familiarity with very basic aspect of life in a popular tropical city. Taking the bus, visiting El Centro, the name given downtown Puerto Vallarta, and Old Town, a favorite destination for particularly younger tourists, observing popular restaurants only blocks away in the Marina and grocery stores, one next door to the motel, all added to Chester's expanding familiarity with his adopted city.

A little of that familiarity and too much impatience led Chester to a confrontation with a city bus driver. Nothing like the motor coaches transporting him across Mexico, the city buses lacked the simplest comforts with hard plastic seats, virtually no suspension, and driven by men obsessed with speed.

On a recent trip to downtown Puerto Vallarta, Chester climbed aboard a city bus packed with tourists as well as obvious native workers going to or returning from work. Forced to stand in the aisle, Chester gripped the handrail above him. At each stop the driver applied brakes with an abrupt halt and accelerated as if on a race track. The stop and go motion of the bus bounced Chester into those passengers standing around him despite his futile attempts to steady himself holding the handrail.

About half way to El Centro, the bus emptied to give Chester access to the driver. Ignoring the sign above the driver's head which cautioned no conversation with the operator, Chester stepped beside the driver and in very slow, deliberate and loud English, the style chosen by those who believe volume will transcend linguistic difference, supported by hand gestures, he urged the driver to slow down or suffer a report to the bus management.

The bus driver understood enough English to comprehend Chester's unusual request. He took his eyes off the road for an instant to glance up at Chester standing next to him. He pointed to the sign and instructed Chester to find a seat or get off the bus. The few, mostly native passengers remaining on the bus watched in amazement at the strange action at the front of the bus.

Chester's eyes opened wide. Nobody talked to him like that, especially not a common bus driver. When Chester refused to move, the driver pulled up to the next bus stop, opened the door, and told Chester to get off or he would throw him off. Hearing the threat, Chester flinched. His slight frame, of course, produced no threat to the driver. When Chester refused to move, the driver shifted into neutral, got up from the driver's seat, and reached his hand toward Chester's shoulder.

Chester glared at the driver, much taller than he appeared sitting down, much younger than Chester and much more muscular. Redness filled in around Chester's neck and ears. Recognizing finally the danger he faced, he pushed the driver's hand away, mumbling, "Go to hell," as he jumped off the bus.

He hailed a taxi back to the motel where his temper still simmered over the audacity if this petty bus driver who showed no respect. The next morning he described the incident to Raul, who advised him to forget reporting the driver to the bus company management. The office would likely do nothing about it anyway. Chester grumbled something incoherent and dug into his free oatmeal.

Chester's days dragged on. Sitting by his motel window gradually lost its appeal. Even the beauty of a tropical setting can lose its splendor through tedium. The events of the past few months dimmed in his memory as concern for his immediate future took over. In his need to blend into the Puerto Vallarta life style, he had overlooked that TV ad he watched with such promise weeks ago while hiding out at Clark's cabin. Now he recalled vividly the beauty of the tropical resort promoted in the ad. He would have to ask Raul about the resort.

The next day, on his way out of the motel, Chester saw Raul taking his turn behind the registration desk. He walked over to lean his arms on the counter.

"Buenas tardes, Senior Randall (aka Reynolds)." Raul closed the folder that lay before him on the counter. "¿Cómo está? this fine afternoon."

"Okay. Awfully slow day." Chester moved back a step. "I have a question."

Raul laughed. He'd grown accustomed to Mr. Randall's questions."

Chester wiped the edges of his mouth with his hand. "Back home in the states, I saw an ad on TV for some great resort someplace in Puerto Vallarta." He scratched his head. "Something called, ah, ah, Mi Casa or something. Do you know anything about it?"

Paul clinched his teeth in a moment of concentration. "Yeah, I've heard about it. I suppose almost everyone has. I've not seen the place. I don't know anybody who has. All kind of private right now. Kind of the jewel in the jungle."

Chester shrugged his shoulders and adjusted his glasses. "I don't know why the jewel doesn't get more attention. Don't they expect to make money?"

With a chuckle, Raul responded, "Everybody around here expects to make money, even me. I think the developers would rather not have sightseers around during construction. I'm not sure."

Chester tugged on his belt, lifting his sagging trousers. "Where exactly is this place?"

Raul stretched his arms against the counter. "Well, it's north and west of here, across Banderas Bay from downtown. You can't see it. The bay is too far across. Besides there's always a haze hanging over the mountains."

"How do you get there?"

After a deep breath, Raul explained. "Well, you go to the Main Marina, just about a mile down the road, where the cruise ships dock. I think you can catch a ferry over there. That's what I've heard. This kind of secrecy thing doesn't help in getting such details."

Chester shook his head. "Kinda damn stupid if you ask me. Have you come cross a name or a phone number a guy can contact?" Chester's interest swelled the longer they talked.

Raul repositioned a display of brochures listing amenities at a Comfort Inn Motel. "You know. I did hear a name, supposedly the guy in charge out there. Something like Frost or Foster, I think. I heard that name mentioned by one of our guests." He paused, pinching his skin under his chin. "Stupid of me. I should have thought of this before. I think the company that's building the resort has an office here in Puerto Vallarta." He glanced over at the front entrance as a man and a woman each pulling luggage on wheels entered the reception area. He closed his eyes in thought. "I think the company is something like Tropical Properties or Real Estate. I probably can find the number in the phone book." He shook his head. 'I'm sorry. I don't know why the hell I didn't think of this before."

"Don't worry about that. You don't have to be sorry." Chester stepped back from the counter to give space for the couple to register.

With their registration completed, the couple obviously just arriving tourists dressed in long parts and sweaters, grabbed their luggage to head to the elevator.

Raul dug through the shelf under the counter to come up with the Puerto Vallarta phone book. With only a few minutes search, he found the phone number for the Tropical Real Estate Company. With the phone number in hand, Chester returned to his room to stand in front of the window to the world, eager yet hesitant to make the call. Maybe the name Foster would serve as an adequate introduction. He had to make a decision. The view from his window was rapidly losing its charm.

Dressed in sandals, shorts and a T-shirt, Chester inched his way forward toward a tiny ticket booth tucked between a service station and a marine storage building. Yesterday's phone call to the Tropical Real Estate office acquainted him with the only public access to the resort where construction neared completion. The call also required him to explain his reason for visiting the site. He said he needed a job. The person he spoke with, a fluent female voice, took his name and gave him a number. She explained where he should purchase the ticket for the ferry that transported only those involved in the construction or sought employment. She advised him to give his name and number to the attendant at the ticket booth. She also told him, when he reached the site, to ask for Thurman Foster, the man in charge of the project.

Chester fingered the pesos held in his hand. With very little confidence in his understanding of Mexican currency, he selected from the bills in his hand the one with 100 pesos printed across the front. That familiar tingle in his stomach returned, a sensation he experienced often in recent months. He stepped up to the narrow counter to hand the 100 peso note to the attendant, a young woman with typical black, Mexican eyes and chocolate skin.

She asked with hardly a hint of an accent. "Could I have your name and number?"

He stared at the young woman, eyes wide. "Yes." His shoulders slumped in mild embarrassment. He gave her his name and number.

"Thank you, Mr Randall. The ferry leaves in about fifteen minutes from the dock on your left." She handed him a ticket. "Have a nice day."

Chester joined about a dozen others, some dressed in work clothes, some dressed in more business attire and three ladies dressed in an apparent maid's uniform. Waiting to board the ferry, he gazed across Banderas Bay into the haze that shrouded the Sierra Madre Mountains on the other side. He could see nothing of any resort under construction. Wherever it was the jungle concealed it.

Chapter 38

The day after his meeting with Mr. Perez, Dane brought elation but no decision with him to work at Fore Sure Telemarketing. His meeting had addressed most of the major questions related to the position offered by Perez. Still, Dane harbored doubts about accepting the offer. He knew little about Miguel Perez and less about the Tropical Real Estate Company.

His dad's introduction of suspicion about this company hovered in the remote corners of Dane's mind. However, he could imagine no reason to hold onto doubts about Perez and his company. After all, Mr. Carmona obviously found no threat in dealing with him by accepting him as a client of Fore Sure Telemarketing.

Dane's life revolved around a very small world, a world of innocence until the association with Chester Reynolds and his convenience store. Though that experience introduced more caution into Dane's relationship with others, it failed to extinguish his fundamental integrity and trust in others. That the job proposed by Mr. Perez could expand his small world both excited and worried him, excitement emanating from meeting challenges and worry from misgivings about his adapting to significant changes in his life.

Joined by Ashley at their favorite bar, Dane felt absolutely, at the moment, no apprehension about anything. Ashley created that atmosphere for Dane. The evening in the call center differed little from previous evenings except his preoccupation with leaving the job and sacrificing a possible closer relationship with Ashley. Since the parking lot incident, he had the feeling that their relationship had grown closer. As the evening drifted to the end of calling, he and Ashley made an arrangement to share a drink at the bar.

"Well, any further thoughts about your meeting yesterday?" Ashley, attractive in a plain white blouse under a gray sweater, took a swallow of her wine.

Dane studied her from across the booth. He closed his eyes and pursed his lips. "I don't think so. You know, there're probably all sorts of questions I should be asking." He shook his head. "I just can't think of any right now. Maybe a little naive."

Ashley reached across the table to grasp Dane's hand. "I don't think I'd call it 'naive,' just honest and trusting."

Dane squeezed her hand in reply. His brow wrinkled. "Thank you."

Ashley inquired in a little more detail about the position. Dane, during idle moments earlier that evening in the call center, explained briefly some details of the meeting and the position offered.

"What do you think you'll do?" Ashley moved her wine glass aside and rested her elbows on the table, resting her chin on fingers laced together.

Dane studied her again, her question exposing decisions only he could make. Nonetheless, he reversed the question. "What do you think I should do?"

A benign smile traced her lips. "It's a decision you have to make, but since you asked me, I guess I would have to say, 'go for it'."

Dane slumped back in the booth. "Thank you for your frankness. It seems to me, too, the right thing to do." He ran his hand over his lips. "Two things bother me, one a little bit and the other a lot. The little bit has to do with something my dad said when I discussed the job with my parents. He asked if I knew anything about this Perez and his company. I guess I don't know much." He shifted in the booth. "The other thing that matters a lot is what happens to our relationship?"

Ashley lowered her eyes then looked up at Dane. "Dane, if our relationship has any validity at all, a different job shouldn't make all that much difference. I mean, you're not going to the moon." She laughed.

Dane shared her laughter. "God, I hope not."

Ashley sipped her wine. "By the way, if your dad's comment bothers you, why don't you google this Perez. That might quiet some of your concern."

Dane's eyes brightened. "Yeah, good idea. I might do that."

They ordered another drink. Their conversation changed to discussing prospects for the summer just waiting to make its appearance in the Twin Cities. Their drinks emptied, they walked together to the parking lot and their respective cars. Since the fall in the parking lot, that survived as their routine. In that regard, theirs was a strange relationship, missing physical tenderness. Dane was reluctant to pursue more physical tenderness, and Ashley seemed reluctant to offer it. For him their relationship represented an important part of his life, a part he refused to jeopardize.

A brief stop at Ashley's car, a tender hug and light kiss on the lips represented the extent of their emotional contact. Yet, he found in Ashley a wonderful young companion with whom he would delight in spending more time. Intrusions, such as the one by Dexter Parks, had threatened that desire.

Dane helped close Ashley's driver side door. "Goodnight. See you tomorrow."

Through the open window, Ashley, with an encouraging smile, said, " Goodnight, Dane. It'll all work out."

He walked to his car, troubled but hopeful of the future.

The next morning alone in the house as usual, his dad on another drive to Chicago and his mom already at work, Dane stood by the kitchen counter waiting for his toast to pop up. Still in his short, summer pajamas, he took a generous swallow of his apple juice, images of his taking Ashley in his arms and pouring out his feelings for her commanding his attention.

He thought about their brief parting kiss the evening before. He saw other couples holding hands, walking arm in arm, hugging and even kissing in full view of the world. Why he and Ashley did virtually none of that puzzled him. His only conclusion: their relationship did lack validity even if he wasn't headed to the moon. Besides the decision he needed to make regarding the Perez offer, he resolved to discover the truth about his relationship with Ashley.

He took the last bite of toast and drank the last swallow of juice. Counter wiped clean and glass in the dishwasher, Dane retreated to the kitchen table where he had placed the family's laptop computer. He would take his dad's advice reinforced by Ashley's suggestion and google Perez's name. Confident he would find nothing criminal or even unethical in Perez's background, Dane opened the computer, clicked on Safari, and typed in "Miguel Perez" on the search line.

Four references to "Miguel Perez" suddenly appeared on the screen. Dane clicked on one of them. He learned that Perez grew up in very humble circumstances in a small Mexican village south of Mexico City. Though sketchy, the detail did depict Perez as an ambitious kid who joined the parade of young kids forced to work to help support the family. For Perez that family included his parents and two siblings, a younger brother and sister.

Beyond that, the information traced his advance, apparently without the benefit of much education, to an executive position with an international investment company. Dane sat impressed with the obvious drive that carried Perez from selling vegetables on the street to executive in an investment company with offices in Mexico City.

Dane decided to try one of the other Perez sites. This one said little about his humble background but introduced to Dane a Perez indicted for fraud and the conspiracy to commit fraud. Along with Perez two others in the investment company, a Thurman Foster, a Canadian, and Jose Hector Martinez, the CEO, faced more serious charges. With mild consternation Dane read the short narrative describing the company, now bankrupt, and the subsequent investigation that apparently exonerated Perez but imposed a significant fine on the company along with restitution to investors and probation for Martinez and Foster. All of this took place over five years ago.

Dane looked away from his computer. He shook his head. "Holy shit," he uttered out loud. Another site did reveal information about the Tropical Real Estate Company listing Perez as owner and Thurman Foster as president. Dane found no other mention of Jose Martinez.

Sitting back in his chair, Dane closed the computer and stared at a nonexistent spot on the opposite, kitchen wall. His decision about working for the Tropical Real Estate Company just acquired more complications.

Dane's shift in the call center came with more anxiety than usual. The few online details he discovered about Perez's background floated through his mind all day and into the evening. Ashley asked about any search he had done, but he graciously refused to admit he had done any. He simply wished to avoid talking about it right now at least until he had assimilated the information he found and its implications and until he had resolved the ambivalence he felt.

He and Ashley mutually agreed to head home at the end of their shift. Each claimed a need to get to bed early. Alone in his room, Dane leaned back on a pillow protecting him from the hard headboard of his bed. In his hands he held a copy of a James Patterson novel, about the only reading he did. However, on this evening he wasn't reading.

His eyes traced the configuration of his bedroom where he had spent most of his nights since a young kid. For as long as he could remember, the same, pale blue curtain covered the window to his left. His dresser with attached mirror stood next to the window. Next came his closet with sliding doors and beyond that a chest of drawers and finally a small desk and straight back chair, his place where his mother thought he did his homework through all those years in school. Most of the time he did.

A smile reflected the mild melancholy as Dane thought about the hundreds of nights over the years he slept in this room. He laid the book aside on the soft sheets his mother took care in providing and stared idly at the Twins' pennant above his desk.

What seemed like such a manageable decision suddenly took on major complications. Dane debated the extent of Perez's involvement in an apparent fraudulent scam to bilk investors of their money. He was exonerated, and the whole affair took place five years ago. He considered in his own sheltered life the need for second chances. Certainly, Mr. Carmona must have done a background check on an important client. If Mr. Perez proved legitimate and trustworthy for Mr. Carmona, Dane considered he had no justification to doubt him.

Dane pulled up his knees and rested his head against them. Only with reluctance would he discuss the information he found online. Maybe it only represented rationalization, but in his mind it would only introduce more opinions and further complications as he reached for a decision, one he had to make on his own. After all he was a mature adult capable, he thought, of making his own decisions. Looking up at his room awakened again the possibility of his own apartment. With the increase in his salary he could easily afford one. The next job's effect on his relationship with Ashley haunted him, but as they discussed earlier, if that relationship possessed any validity, it would prevail.

Dane grabbed the book off the sheet, swung his legs over the edge of the bed, and eased himself up off the bed. He assumed his own apartment would comply with his parents' wishes. His dad had encouraged it for years. Dane stood in front of his dresser. In the mirror he saw what he considered a reasonably good looking man, one who needed to consider his future to forget the past and scum like Chester Reynolds. With a grin he thought about the loquacity his dad liked to make fun of. Still, Dane considered it a special feature of who he was.

Though the Tropical Real Estate Company may not prove his future, it may prove a prelude to that future. Tomorrow he would give Mr. Carmona his two week notice.

Chapter 39

A twenty minute ride over the crisp blue waters of Banderas Bay brought the ferry and its passengers to a pier extending several feet out into the bay and protected on one side by a jetty of huge boulders. Gently moving its way against the pier, the ferry stopped and the two man crew positioned a plank from the ferry to the dock. Along with his fellow passengers, Chester cautiously stepped off the ferry, captivated by the magnitude of the massive structure blended into the jungle around it.

Only a short walk from the shore, three buildings connected in a semi-circle ensured that all one hundred condos included in the development enjoyed a full view of the bay and the Pacific beyond. Chester's mouth dropped open as he stared at the imposing buildings tiered from two to eight stories and constructed with decks and large patio doors giving access to the tropical beauty of the resort. An exterior of gentle tans and greens accented by vivid reds hinted at the grandeur that would distinguish this special, tropical resort.

With construction of the buildings apparently complete or nearly so, Chester noticed the activity concentrated on the pool and on the landscaping where workers arranged and planted dozens of flowers of vibrant reds and pinks. Native bushes and elegant palm trees marked the transition from resort to jungle. Without a refined architectural or landscape taste, Chester, nonetheless, stood stunned at the magnificence of the place, reminded by the ongoing landscape work that the resort had yet to reach its full glory.

Entranced by what he saw emerging from the jungle, Chester found himself standing alone, staring.

"May I help you?" a voice asked.

Chester jumped and turned to look at a young Mexican no more than sixteen or seventeen years old, holding a clip board. On his royal blue shirt, with "Tropical Real Estate" printed across his chest, a name badge declared him Ramon.

"I'm sorry," the young man smiled, apologizing in halting English for startling a visitor, one seeking employment.

Chester studied the young man for only an instant, enough time to wonder if all Mexicans had gleaming white teeth. "I'm Charles Randall. I was told to ask for Mr. Foster."

Ramon glanced down at his clip board. "Can you give me your number?"

Chester complied.

Ramon checked off the name Charles Randall. "Thank you. Please follow me."

Ramon guided Chester to an archway opening to a reception area furnished with luxurious lounge chairs and sofas covered in rich, colorful fabrics. Decorative, native plants, especially bougainvillea in dazzling greens, reds, and oranges, spilled out of huge clay pots stationed along a short corridor. Walls of granite punctuated with mirrors and floors covered with a blend of ceramic tile and plush carpet surpassed even the splendor of the outside of the buildings.

Chester followed Ramon to a door only steps beyond the reception area. Ramon's knock produced a faint invitation to enter. Chester followed close behind his guide who stopped in the middle of the floor in front of an elaborate, dark wooden desk.

"Mr. Foster, sir, meet Mr. Charles Randall."

Thurman Foster, forty-five with Hollywood good looks and charm, stepped from behind a sprawling, ornate wooden desk to extend a hand to Chester (aka Charles Randall).

Foster stood meticulously dressed. A royal blue, Polo shirt with the company logo printed discretely on the left side stretched over his firm body; khaki trousers touched the tops of tasseled loafers shined to a near mirror finish and worn without socks.

Foster turned to face Ramon, "Thank you." And then to Chester, "Delighted to meet you, Mr. Randall."

Chester gripped the smooth, soft hand offered him." Good to meet you, sir," his eyes wide in awe of the extravagant office and the man himself.

Behind the huge executive desk a window offered a panoramic view of the jungle edge and the blue Pacific beyond. Elegant wood paneling covered the walls interrupted by shelves of books, pictures, and plaques. To ensure easy access, file cabinets sat at each end of the desk. The floor featured a combination of plush, light brown carpet and inlaid wooden tile. Two stuffed chairs occupied places in front of the desk. Around the periphery of the office sectional sofas shared the space with book cases. In the ceiling two fans turned lazily, circulating the warm, humid air.

For moments, Foster studied Chester dressed in faded shorts, sandals, and T-shirt, as Chester's eyes bulged in wonder over the palatial office. He then returned to his place behind the desk, directing Chester to one of the stuffed chairs. He seated himself. He reached for a folder, paging through its contents before selecting one page which he examined for seconds.

"Well, Mr. Randall, it says here you seek employment."

Chester squirmed in his chair, then nodded his head, entranced by this man seated behind the desk in front of him.

Through the years Thurman Foster had entranced dozens of people. A product of a middle-class family, he grew up in Toronto, Canada. Besides his parents, he shared his childhood home with a younger brother and two older sisters. Probably some of his drive and ambition derived from familial competition, at least competition from his perspective. Despite his perspective, he grew up in a supportive home which prepared him for relative academic and athletic success in school. More remarkable was his social success.

By high school Thurman already had grown to an impressive six feet tall with a medium build nurtured by a workout routine still important to him. Closely trimmed, brown hair with a hint of gray contrasted with his youthful appearance. Pale blue eyes charmed those caught by his magnetism. Losing a tooth from an errand hockey stick and replaced by the talented hands of the family dentist did nothing to distract from his charming smile. A tiny scar under his left eye, another hockey injury, added to the fascination of Thurman Foster.

He learned early that personality could make a tremendous difference in his relationship with others. Perhaps the familial competition he felt or perhaps his genes imbued Thurman with an insatiable thirst for success. Whatever the source, as he advanced in age the successes transformed from scoring the winning hockey goal to making money. Furthermore, as he advanced in age, that drive for success obscured his notion of truth and honesty.

With his dynamic personality, his engaging style, and his determination, he acquired skill in persuading people to do, not necessarily what they wanted, but to do what he wanted them to do. In short, he matured into the quintessential salesman, a characteristic which found him following a series of sales jobs, including cars, homes, and boats, to an association with Miguel Perez and Jose Hector Martinez. That association, an international investment company, suffered from poor management, inept record keeping, and careless disregard for maintaining an image of respectability. The company failed with all three top executives indicted for fraud. That failure engendered in Foster an even stronger desire for success, which to him translated into money. With the penalty, restitution and probation, satisfied by him and Martinez, they joined their former associate, Perez, who for reasons Foster couldn't explain enjoyed exoneration, in a second chance venture called the Tropical Real Estate Company.

"Exactly what kind of employment are you seeking?" Foster leaned forward, placing his elbows on the desk. He watched as Chester fumbled for an answer.

Chester moved restlessly in his chair. Not in years did he have to answer that question. For most of his adult life he asked the questions. He ran his hand over his balding head. "I, ah, I guess it depends on what you need."

Foster laughed. "Sir, we need just about everything in the realms of service and maintenance. What have you done in the past?"

Fearful of what Mr. Foster knew about his background and the mess created by those two goons, Chester explained his career in the convenience store business.

Foster's blue eyes brightened. "Eventually, we will have a convenience store on property that might need some organization and direction. Maybe there would be a place for you there."

Chester took a deep breath and edged up on his chair. "Yeah." He adjusted his glasses. "That's sure a possibility."

"Right now, though, we need desperately those willing to work in maintenance and landscaping."

Chester glanced down at the rich inlaid tile around the desk. "I think I could do that."

"Great. Look, Mr. Randall, why don't you plan to return tomorrow when we have more time to talk about what needs doing around here."

As the ferry pulled away from the dock, Chester stood staring at what, at least for a while, would give him added shelter from the authorities.

Chapter 40

The morning sun, a welcome sign of impending summer, peaked under the windshield visor of Dane's car. Awakened at six a.m. by anticipation of his eleven a.m. meeting with Miguel Perez, his new boss, Dane adjusted his seat belt to gain a more comfortable position as he headed east on I-394 then to I-94 and on into St. Paul.

Confident in his decision to join Mr Perez and the Tropical Real Estate Company he represented, Dane still suffered moments of anxiety ever since he submitted three weeks ago his letter of resignation from Fore Sure Telemarketing. He considered his new position would offer him a better chance at achieving, at least one goal, securing his own apartment. For months he had discussed that goal with his parents and with Ashley. All agreed that having his own apartment freed him from reliance on his parents and granted him a level of independence previously limited.

Driving cautiously through the late morning traffic, Dane reflected on the brief but memorable farewell party organized by his telemarketing mates and lasting last night a bit longer than it should have. All the staff, Ashley, Misty, Carmen, and Emile, at Fore Sure Telemarketing, including Mr. Carmona, joined Dane at that favorite bar where he and Ashley cultivated their relationship. The conversation around the table sparkled with descriptions of sometimes humorous, sometimes rude, and sometimes simply vulgar phone calls they all had experienced. Dane offered his favorite call to a woman who refused to listen to the spiel. She insisted on learning more about the caller whose voice intrigued her, sounding, in her estimation, just like Paul Newman.

As the time rushed by much too fast, the group finally surrendered to the burdens of a long day at the calling center and decided to say their goodbyes to one of their calling colleagues. Before they prepared to leave, Ashley reached under the table for a small box wrapped in paper resembling a telephone directory. Standing up, she turned to Dane seated next to her.

"Mr. Barton, you know Fore Sure Telemarketing will survive in your absence." She looked around at the others who joined in a chuckle. She placed the small package on the table. "More important," she continued, "the place where for the last several months you have sat spreading the good words from Fore Sure Telemarketing will always survive as Dane's place." Applause sounded around the table.

Ashley handed the package to Dane. "In recognition of your contribution to the telemarketing world, please accept this gift as an expression of our pleasure in having shared the calling center with you."

Dane stood up from his chair, emotion threatening to cloud that loquacity some claimed he possessed. "Thank you for the kind words." He gently touched Ashley's shoulder. "These last few months have been interesting and gratifying. I've enjoyed each day I've joined all of you at the calling center and each day I've had the privilege of a greeting from Carmen, the most gracious receptionist in the Twin Cities." Again quiet applause circled the table. "Also I want to thank Mr. Carmona for his willingness to take a chance with a refugee from a twenty-four hour convenience store." More applause.

"Open the gift," urged Misty.

Dane smiled, reached for the gift, and removed the clever wrapping. He stopped to examine the box, about the size of a shoe box. He lifted the cover to discover more wrapping paper. Pushing it aside revealed an ancient phone, one that predated even the common desk phone. In its time it was mounted on the wall; it had no rotary dial, only a small crank which enabled the caller to make calls by turning the crank in a series of long and short rotations.

All eyes focused on Dane as he picked up the small, ancient phone, moving it from side to side. "I think I've heard about this thing." He shook his head. "It certainly wouldn't have made our job any easier."

Approaching the turnoff for the route to the small, north St. Paul motel where he would meet Mr. Perez, Dane relived the warmth of hugs from his calling colleagues and their insistence that he keep in touch. He assured them he would. Without question he would keep in very close touch with Ashley.

In minutes he pulled into the parking lot of the motel where he previously met with Mr. Perez, who at that meeting discussed in general terms the job he offered Dane. A modest two story building surrounded by parking spaces, now mostly vacant, the motel served as a base for the operation of Tropical Real Estate in the Twin Cities. Modest but comfortable, the motel offered meeting space for groups of twenty or so, adequate for the needs of Perez's promotion of a private, luxurious resort in popular Puerto Vallarta, one of the world's favorite tourist destinations.

Dane entered the registration area of the motel where a young receptionist directed him to the meeting room a short distance down the adjacent hallway. The door to the room open, Dane timidly peeked around its edge. Mr. Perez pushed aside the material that sat before him, rose from his chair and stepped to greet his new employee.

"Good morning, Mr. Barton. You faced no traffic problems getting here?"

"Good morning," Dane responded. "No, the traffic was really very light."

"Please take a seat and we'll get started with our review of the project and your role in it."

Dane pulled out a chair and positioned himself off to one side of Perez, who repositioned the folders in front of him then opened one of them.

Perez looked up at Dane. "Mr. Barton, in this room will begin an exciting, rewarding time for you and for Tropical Real Estate. This project surpasses anything I've been associated with in my career. That you will enter our group at this point will serve you well, I'm sure."

Dane nodded his head and positioned his hands on the dark wooden table around which sat twelve chairs. He waited for Perez to continue.

"Today I wish to acquaint you with your role in this exciting project." He leafed through his folders extracting a series of pages and a DVD. He leaned back in his chair, hands resting on the chair's arms. "It is here where all those people secured by Fore Sure Telemarketing will meet to hear about the wonders of Mi Casa by the Bay and to have the chance at an all expense-paid trip to experience the resort first hand." He slid a page across to Dane. "This is a brief outline of what I expect you to cover with each group that assembles in this room. These groups will rarely exceed ten prospective investors at a time. We wish to keep these meetings personal and intimate, reflective of the philosophy of the resort itself."

Dane glanced at the page listing clearly the various points he would cover in his presentation and discussion.

Much of the subsequent discussion concentrated on the absolute splendor of the resort, now reaching completion across Banderas Bay from the vibrant city of Puerto Vallarta. Perez glowed with pride as he described the lush vegetation both natural and man made that surrounded the resort. He spoke of the pools ringed with colorful tile, of cushioned lounge chairs, of richly patterned umbrellas shading small round tables, and of a beverage and snack bar clinging to one side of the expansive pool.

With increased relish he talked about the dedication to detail in each of the one hundred condos ranging in size from one bedroom to three bedroom penthouses. He returned to the themes of the personal and the intimate in discussing the philosophy dominating the project. He described the atmosphere as one of commonality, friendship, one where residents can experience renewal of youthful instincts and possibly relive past moments of exuberance.

During this recital of the glories of the resort, Dane sat entranced by the passion in Perez's delivery, a passion which he had never observed in anyone else. For but an instant he thought of Chester Reynolds and the profound contrast he brought to his special convenience business.

After nearly one half hour of energetic description, Perez stopped, took a deep breath and leaned back in his chair. "Sorry, I sometimes get a bit carried away."

"It's all very interesting," Dane acknowledged. "A lot to learn."

"Yes, but don't worry; you have convinced me you have the commitment to learn it."

Dane glanced down at the table. "Thank you. I will try not to disappoint you."

"Enough words for now. I have a DVD which you, of course, will use during the presentations in this room. The DVD follows the progress of the resort from the initial excavations to what you will see as an architectural rendition of this magnificent, tropical paradise." He paused. "Right now the resort nears completion approaching its ultimate magnificence."

They watched the DVD, both intent on the screen set up at one end of the conference room. The DVD captured Dane's attention from the very beginning, refusing to release it until the very end when the camera panned back to give a breathtaking view of the resort. Without question the DVD confirmed Perez's passionate descriptions.

At the conclusion of their meeting, Perez reviewed the mechanics of the drawing for the lucky person to receive the all expense paid trip to the resort. Only briefly in the discussion did Perez reference critical matters of cost, of financing, of mortgages, of titles, of details of Mexican property laws, of relevance of time share. Perez dismissed those concerns as the responsibility of other staff members. How he might deal with such questions from those attending his presentation gave Dane pause. However, he assumed Perez knew what he was doing.

As Dane walked out of the motel, the overwhelming splendor of the resort dominated his thoughts.

Chapter 41

Dane leaned against the door frame of the same motel, conference room where only days before he had met with Miguel Perez to listen to the passionate Perez extol the boundless virtues of Mi Casa by the Bay. Since that meeting Dane had studied the details supplied by Perez to augment what he felt he lacked, confidence and familiarity with the project.

On this Saturday morning he would meet five men and four women, prospective investors in the exclusive resort on Puerto Vallarta's world renowned Banderas Bay. He glanced down the narrow hallway to observe a maid meticulous in her determination to keep in order on her cart all the items for cleaning and resetting a sleeping room. Since he had never before seen any of the people scheduled to attend this first meeting, he watched carefully for anyone walking in his direction. For now he saw no one except the maid.

Satisfied no one headed toward his conference room, Dane stepped back to examine again the arrangement of the large conference table surrounded by fourteen aging executive chairs. Upon his arrival much earlier, he had inspected the conference room, a space not much bigger than a private living room, but still one suitable for the purposes of the Tropical Real Estate Company for whom Dane now worked. A rectangular room with a large, partially curtained window overlooking the parking lot, it featured minimum furnishings other than the large conference table and accompanying chairs. Light beige walls helped brighten the room, assisting the recessed ceiling lights.

Dane made a quick check of the folders placed before nine of the chairs. These folders contained critical information about the route to investing in the luxury resort by the bay. It also contained name tags which Dane will suggest each attendee attach to add a slight personal touch to the meeting. A computer sat at one end of the table pointed in the direction of a screen open at the far end of the conference room. Satisfied with the arrangements for the meeting, Dane returned to his position by the door to await the arrival of his guests.

While he waited, he reflected on the stress of the last few days produced by his anticipation of this first meeting. The images of his final moments with his colleagues at Fore Sure Telemarketing especially those moments with Ashley raced through his mind. A tingle inched its way up his back as he briefly contemplated his decision to join Mr. Perez and his marketing project. More than once he questioned the wisdom of plunging into the field, the foreign, real estate field, he knew very little about. Nonetheless, with support from his telemarketing friends and from his mom and dad, he made the decision. And now he waited with anxiety joining anticipation to meet his first group.

Scheduled for ten o'clock, the meeting began at ten fifteen, two of the attendees arriving a few minutes late. Dane stood at his place at the end of the table to welcome again the nine potential investors in the project. Looking out at those seated around the table, Dane smiled. "Welcome to my office," he joked. Laughter filtered through the conference room. "I thank you for taking the time on a Saturday morning to spend time listening to what I have to say about a great opportunity."

Several of the guests thanked Dane, some repositioning themselves on their executive chairs whose wheels permitted a degree of freedom of movement.

Upon their arrival Dane had requested his guests to find their places by the table and attach the name tag. Now Dane stood at the head of the table his eyes making contact with each person. "I see you all have pinned on your name tags. Thank you." He paused, looking down at papers lying before him on the table. "Sorry, but I have to check-off your names on my list here just to make sure I have a record of your attendance." He paused with another smile. "I suppose some of you have your sights on that all expense paid vacation to tropical Puerto Vallarta?"

"No, we're here only because we like to spend our Saturday mornings in motel rooms." The facetious comment came from a heavy set man with the name "Ernest" attached to his shirt.

A few other similar comments floated around the table before Dane requested that they acknowledge their presence as he read their names. Each complied with his request. In addition, when he announced the name "Claudia Upton," she inquired about the phone call she received promoting the tropical resort. "You sound just like the guy who called me on the phone." She wrinkled her brow in reflection. "I think only a couple weeks ago."

Dane laughed. "Yeah, I probably was that guy. I did work for a telemarketing firm before this."

"I think I recognize that voice, too," agreed a slender, young man whose name tag identified him as "Fernando". "By the way when do we find out who wins the trip?"

"Good question. I'm sure you've all wondered that." Dane looked quickly around the table. "We have a few more meetings like this one scheduled over the next two weeks before the drawing. You all will receive an invitation to that drawing. If you chose not to attend, you each will receive confirmation of the results. Any questions about that?" Some shook their heads. Others sat unmoving. Dane consulted his list and continued with the roll call.

With the conclusion of the roll call, Dane explained the purpose for the meeting and plunged into a brief history of the resort project and its international flavor. For the next half hour he talked about the Tropical Real Estate Company and its headquarters in Puerto Vallarta, Mexico. A matronly Millie asked Dane to explain exactly where in Mexico Puerto Vallarta was located. He directed the group to a map in their folder that located this famous vacation destination on the Pacific side of the country.

Dane's narrative outlined the extent of the resort, explaining it would include one hundred condos ranging from one bedroom to three bedroom penthouses. He also explained the attractive amenities that the resort will feature for its guests. Descriptions of the condos and the various amenities, such as pools, recreation areas, fitness center, restaurant, bar, clothing shops, and a variety store all emphasized the luxury of the resort.

A well-muscled Chip raised his hand to interrupt Dane's descriptions. "What do these condos cost? Nothing has been said about that."

Dane leaned forward resting his hands on the table. "I was getting to that, but first I wish to explain that financing details and options are available from Mr Perez, the finance officer of the company. I will give you contact information before you leave today." He waited for any response. "I can say that the condos range in price from one hundred fifty-thousand for a one bedroom to about seven hundred fifty-thousand for a three bedroom." Quiet expressions of alarm floated around the table. "You need to remember specific details about financing will allay some of your fears, I'm sure. I'm sorry I can't relate to you those specific details, but, ah, ah, I guess that's not my role." Again Dane's eyes circled the table.

"Okay, if there aren't any more questions for right now, I ask that you turn your chairs around to face the screen at the back of the room. I have a DVD showing the architectural rendering of the resort as well as the current progress of development. The group watched with interest as the DVD displayed the designers' vision of the resort and then the actual construction which revealed near completion of the condo complex and the surrounding tropical beauty. A soft round of applause greeted the ending of the DVD.

Confirming the contact information for Mr. Perez, reminding each person to take the folder placed before them on the table, and assuring each member of the group of their chance to win the all expense paid trip to Puerto Vallarta, Dane stood by the conference room door to offer another thanks to each person for spending Saturday morning with him.

With the room now empty, Dane stepped to his place at the head of the table. He paused to stare at the blank screen at the back of the room. For a moment he closed his eyes and exhaled, an expression of relief at completing his first meeting as a member of the Tropical Real Estate Company. He gathered up his materials closed the computer and walked out of the room, content for the moment with his decision to accept Mr. Perez's offer, but still in the back of his mind rested a question about these people vying for an all expense trip to a tropical paradise and their willingness or capacity to invest in a very expensive resort so far from home.

Chapter 42

Dane hunched over the kitchen table, the daily paper spread out in front of him. He gazed at the full page listing of available apartments in the Twin Cities area. Not accustomed to searching for an apartment, he was amazed by the extent of the list. He ran his finger down the listing of apartments in the suburbs surrounding Minneapolis on the West and South. These areas afforded some familiarity for Dane. Definitely, the listed rental prices did not. He simply failed to realize the vast range in price from one suburban community to another.

Dane sat back in his chair, the house quiet except for the soft background music emanating from the family Bose radio in the living room. He ran his fingers through his hair, his attention drifting away from apartments and toward not one but two concussions. Not often did he pause to reflect on those incidents, either one which could have killed him. The recent good fortune in his life, the new job and a renewed confidence in his relationship with Ashley ironically pulled his attention back to those potentially fatal moments. He shook his head to dismiss those thoughts of the past, remembering, nonetheless, that those thoughts reminded him of his complete recovery from both concussions.

He rose from his chair, stepped to the kitchen cupboard for a glass. From the front door panel of the refrigerator first ice tumbled into his glass then water. He returned to his place by the table, took a long drink of the cold, refreshing water, set the glass on the table, and resumed the perusal of the list of apartments.

Since taking the sales position with Perez and the Tropical Real Estate Company, Dane had conducted six information sessions attended mostly by people introduced to the Puerto Vallarta resort through Fore Sure Telemarketing. Though the first two presentations found him hindered by anxiety and misgivings about the extent of his knowledge of the project, he soon gained more confidence and composure imparting general information about the project while leaving a vivid description of the splendor of Mi Casa by the Bay to the DVD which produced "oohs" and "awes" from the eight to ten potential investors.

He also attempted to answer questions about cost, ownership, and financing, hastening to inform the gathered group that details of that nature would follow. Why Perez failed to provide Dane with that information troubled him, but he said nothing about it, satisfied with his role to concentrate on resort appearance. Furthermore, except for one woman in the first session, the same woman who claimed when Dane called her from Fore Sure Telemarketing, that he sounded like Paul Newman, others attending accepted his explanation about ownership and related financing details.

With his more flexible hours his new job allowed him, Dane found more time to join his parents, particularly for dinner. For the Barton family dinner provided the perfect opportunity to discuss family matters. Dane's future accommodations certainly qualified as a family matter.

Last evening around this table where he now sat, his dad, home after three days on the road, inquired about Dane's job.

"So, just what do you do to justify getting paid?" Milo rarely discussed anything without a hint of facetiousness.

Accustomed to his dad's habits, Dane replied, jerking his head off to the side, "Stand in front of about ten people and demonstrate how much I know about a place I've never actually seen."

The comment produced a grin from his mom seated next to him.

Milo took another bite of his dinner. "Okay, but what do you do. I'm just curious."

Dane rolled his eyes and slumped back in his chair to explain again what he thought he had explained at least twice before.

The conversation had moved on to two other favorite dinner table topics: renting an apartment and Ashley Ryland. Both his parents had encouraged Dane in the past to consider a place of his own. Not that they no longer wanted him in the family home, they simply wished for him to enjoy more privacy, independence, and freedom from parents. That conversation resulted in his present search of rental, apartment listings in the paper.

The subject of Ashley rarely lent itself to any resolution. She and Dane enjoyed frequent contact by phone or by sharing lunch or a drink. Nonetheless, their relationship refused to advance beyond close friends despite Dane's desire to see it flourish and to expect "the future will see them through." Apparently, that future, for now, excluded competition from Dexter Parks.

With a red marker in hand Dane scanned the rental listing for communities around Lake Minnetonka, only a short drive from where he grew up. Listings for Mound, Excelsior, Deephaven, Wayzata, and Minnetrista attracted most of his attention. They also revealed the most expensive monthly rents. Despite that, he determined he would make no decisions until he had the chance to look at some of the listed apartments. Besides, though an important one, cost was not the only factor in that decision. With his red marker he highlighted seven possibilities he would visit.

Dane and his dad grasped the deck railings to peer through the trees, catching a glimpse in the distance of the south shore of Lake Minnetonka. In the small suburb of Deephaven Dane located what he considered an apartment he could afford and one that offered him comfort and at least a tiny view of Lake Minnetonka. On the second floor of a four unit complex, the apartment contained one bedroom, a good size combination living, dining and kitchen area, a bath with tub and shower, and laundry facilities available. In addition, its location gave quick access to major shopping areas as well as to a route to his current job site in St. Paul. In his mind it served Dane's needs better than any others he had looked at.

"Well, what do you think?" Dane faced his dad joining him on the deck.

"Looks good to me." Milo glanced through the patio door into the empty space inside. "What about furniture? Not much here."

Dane braced himself against the railing. "I thought maybe I could bring some of my furniture at home with me. At least the bedroom stuff to start with."

His mom stepped onto the deck. She eyed her husband and then her son, both with such serious facial expressions. "What's the problem?"

Dane moved closer to his mom. "No problem. We just talked about furniture or lack of it."

"That's not a problem, is it? You can easily take some from home."

Dane and his dad exchanged glances. Both smiled.

Beatrice folded her arms across her chest. "What's so funny?" She asked feeling like a victim of some joke.

Dane reached out to pat his mom's shoulder. "Nothing's funny. It's only that your solution to furniture matched mine exactly."

All three reentered the apartment, took one more look around, headed for the exit, and thanked the caretaker who gave them access to the unit. As they drove away from the complex, Dane's mom asked, "Well, when will you make up your mind?"

Dane hesitated. "I, ah, need one more opinion, Ashley's."

Chapter 43

The next morning found Dane alone in the house, Dad on the road, Mom on the accounting books. Preoccupied with his search for an apartment, he slumped on the living room sofa, the TV on but ignored.

The Deephaven apartment impressed him as it did his parents. The rent, of course, was an important consideration but not the determining factor. He intended as he told his parents the day before to seek Ashley's opinion. In the back of his mind floated the idea that maybe someday they would share an apartment. She had said or done nothing to reinforce that idea. It simply captured Dane's attention. Perhaps just wishful thinking, but to him it carried exciting potential.

Since leaving Fore Sure Telemarketing, Dane accepted a stable relationship with Ashley. That they resolved to allow their relationship to develop gradually quieted Dane's misgiving about their future. As far as Dane was concerned, Dexter Parks had, at last, faded into history. He assumed Ashley shared his opinion though they agreed to refrain from discussing the subject. The condition of her father commanded far more importance. So far he held his own in his fight against Parkinson's disease.

Dane stretched out his legs, resting back on the sofa cushions. A commercial marked the end of another morning talk show which he considered food for the weak-minded. A smile prefaced his thought of Ashley, who in a day or so would join him in another inspection of the Deephaven apartment. The thought added to his anticipation of living in his own place.

He leaned his head back on the sofa cushion, contemplating another afternoon presentation for Mi Casa by the Bay. So far the presentations had garnered compliments from participants and from his boss, Mr. Perez. Comments from participants highlighted his composure and his articulate delivery. Never presumptuous about his speech, he paid special attention to his preparation for each presentation. His one major reservation stemmed from his inability to answer questions about finance, to Dane a critical part of the program. Apparently, Perez wished to reserve, for whatever reason, financing matters for himself.

Although not relevant to Dane's role, Pedro, a young Mexican employee at the St. Paul motel where Dane conducted the meetings, had talked with him passionately about billion dollar resorts in his home city when members of his family struggled to find food. The plight of this man's family alarmed Dane, but he confessed he possessed no power to stop the resort construction.

The phone rang. Dane sat up, slowly moving toward the landline phone stationed on a small table across the room. He checked caller I.D. The name of Lt. Lewis filled the small screen. Dane lifted the receiver.

"Hello."

"Hello," came the firm voice of the Lt. "Is this Dane?"

"Yes, it is." Dane pressed the phone to his ear. Talking with Lt. Lewis always awakened bad memories from the past.

"It's been awhile. How are you doing?"

"I'm fine." Dane sat down on the chair next to the phone table.

"Look, I won't take much of your time." The Lt. typically concentrated on business rather than on casual conversation. "I did want to alert you to a call from the Hennepin County Attorney's office."

Dane sat a bit more rigid even though he understood the reason for the call. "Yes, I kind of expected that since you did mention it months ago."

"Well," the Lt. explained, "the hearing for Sylvester Ramirez finally will happen in a few days. The attorney's office will ask you to testify regarding the robbery and homicide at the convenience store." He paused. "Insurance investigations and the fugitive status of Chester Reynolds have delayed the litigation."

"I understand." Dane released a quick breath. "Thanks for the alert. I'll expect the call."

"Thank you," the Lt. repeated. "If you have questions, give me a call. I think, though, the attorney's office will advise you completely."

"I'm sure they will. Thank you. I'll expect the call."

Dane replaced the receiver on its stand and for a moment relived that horrible instance when Tony Harris pointed a gun in his face and Sylvester Ramirez shot the young man at very close range. Along with Tony and Sylvester came the elusive Chester Reynolds, now only a vague image of a little man with piercing eyes and huge glasses that lingered in the depths of Dane's memory.

Dane drove east to St. Paul for his meeting at the motel where he made his presentation for the exotic Puerto Vallarta resort. His role in the promotion now settled into a routine. According to Ashley, time devoted by Fore Sure Telemarketing to the Tropical Real Estate Company had dwindled. That didn't alter the eight to ten prospective investors who attended Dane's presentation, most enticed by the chance of the all expense trip for two to visit Mi Casa by the Bay.

Arriving a good half hour before the scheduled three o'clock presentation gave Dane the time to prepare handouts, name tags and set up the DVD machine and screen. Motel staff greeted him at the door, now expecting him for his frequent visits. Walking to the conference room, he saw Pedro, part of the motel's maintenance staff, emerging from the room. In charge of ensuring the comforts of the conference room, Pedro had talked with Dane before about the plight of his family who, back in Puerto Vallarta, hardly had money to buy food. Dane sympathized with Pedro but confessed he could do nothing to stop the project. He rejected as futile directing Pedro to contact Perez. Today Pedro greeted Dane with a smile while assuring him the conference room stood ready for his meeting.

As usual, Dane positioned himself by the door of the conference room to greet attendees and to check off names. Today nine people showed up, three women and six men. How some people found time in mid-afternoon puzzled him. But he didn't set the schedule. He just did what he was told.

At the head of the conference table, Dane scanned the nine people who sat in front of him. He smiled, "Buenas tardes." He injected a bit of Mexico into the setting. "Thank you for coming. Please, would you write your names on the small tags by your folder. Then if you would open the folder, we can get started." A shuffle of papers confirmed the compliance with Dane's instructions.

Barely started with his opening comments, Dane jumped back from the table when the conference room door slammed open and Pedro burst in. He stopped, framed by the entrance, his breath in loud pants.

"Do you people have any idea what you're doing to my family?" He spoke with only a slight accent, saliva gathering at the corners of his mouth.

Dane moved quickly to intercept the passionate young man before something tumbled out of hand. Pedro ignored him, obviously his earlier friendly greeting dissolved by his vehement objection to the project.

Pedro took one step into the room. "You can give money to build million dollar resorts while my family starves! Some of them have to live on the street and nobody does anything about it!"

Dane faced Pedro. "Pedro, Pedro, stop it." Dane commanded. "These aren't the people you need to talk to." He breathed deeply, looking over the assembled guests. "I'm sorry, but they know nothing about your family."

"I don't care!" Pedro screamed. "Somebody's got to do something!"

Dane directed a woman seated close to the phone to call the desk. Overcome with emotion, Pedro braced himself on the door frame, his chin resting on his chest. In a show of contrition, he ran his hand over his mouth then rubbed his eyes. Another motel staff member appeared behind Pedro. He placed his hand on Pedro's shoulder, urging him to follow. He did without protest; his passion exhausted.

The interruption filtered through the rest of the presentation, much of the time the attendees forced a discussion of the problems which Pedro so ardently addressed. They talked in general terms about poverty in Mexico; however, most of them knew very little about life in Mexico except what media chose to disclose. None of the attendees had spent much time in Mexico. When they did, they witnessed only that part reserved for tourists. The abbreviated presentation left out nothing of importance about the project. The meeting concluded with those in attendance learning, perhaps, of something more important than million dollar resorts.

The motel staff apologized to Dane as he prepared to leave. Accepting that apology left Dane with an altered perception of the Tropical Real Estate Company and the exclusive project it pursued. Absorbed by the lure of a new job, the chance to obtain his own apartment, and the possibility of travel to tropical Puerto Vallarta arrested his attention, diverting it away from any concern for the economic and societal problems in Mexico. Presumably it did the same for Miguel Perez.

At home for the evening, Dane called Perez to report on the interruption of the presentation. Perez acknowledged it but considered it nothing to impede the progress of the project. He reminded Dane that the plight of some people in Pedro's native country could not preclude important economic development which created jobs for people like those in his family. The response did little to allay Dane's awakened awareness of poverty.

Dane also discussed the situation with his mother who confessed her ignorance of dire human suffering around the world. In bed Dane stared into the darkness of his room, trying to imagine the condition of the lives of Pedro's family in the splendor of tropical Puerto Vallarta.

Chapter 44

Chester's shoulders slumped, pain streaked through his back, blisters on his hands imposed restrictions on what he touched. Ten hours of onerous, physical labor had pushed him to the edge of giving up on this damned resort. Never had he resisted hard work. His life reflected a dedication to achieving what he wanted, hard work or not. He was a lot younger then.

With measured steps he walked along the shadowed passage to the dock where he would catch the ferry back to the Main Marina. As he approached the dock, the ferry pulled at its moorings, buffeted by the Banderas Bay surf. Several others waited to board the ferry, most workers at the resort, others there for reasons Chester neither knew nothing about nor cared. He stepped gingerly onto the plank connecting the dock and the ferry, his balance noticeably shaky.

About twenty-five feet long, twelve feet wide under a flimsy canopy and missing any first class amenities, the two level ferry provided a series of hard benches aligned across the center of both levels. If preferred, riders could stand next to the railing encircling the deck. Chester was one of those who found more comfort crossing Banderas Bay standing up. After many crossings he decided standing up enabled him to better tolerate the persistent rolling motion.

With eyes focused on the receding shoreline graced by the nearly completed resort, Chester studied the massive condo complex, the colorful landscaping, the jungle and mountains beyond conceding to himself that the setting was truly beautiful. If only he didn't have to work so damn hard for the privilege of looking at it.

A sudden bump from the surf brought Chester back to the reality of his return to the Main Marina and his home since his arrival in Puerto Vallarta, the humble but accommodating room at the Comfort Inn. His reality included more than the often bumpy ride across Banderas Bay. It also contained a growing concern for the future in Puerto Vallarta or any place else his complicated life would take him.

For an instant, nostalgia for all he left behind in the Twin Cities corralled his thinking. At one time his convenience stores thrived affording him confidence in the future and a satisfactory life style. He shook his head in dismay considering the stupidity of his attempt to rescue the stores from bankruptcy. Would he ever erase from his mind the image of two goons, Tony Harris and Sylvester Ramirez, he enlisted to join him in his fraudulent scheme? Tony certainly paid for his transgressions. Sylvester likely would eventually spend the rest of his life in prison. The thought of prison sent a chill through Chester's body despite the heat of the tropical sun. He realized that his future, to some extent, hinged on Sylvester but even more on Dane Barton. As long as he was around, Chester's freedom hung in jeopardy. However, those who could curtail his freedom were over two thousand miles away. From this he found some comfort.

Chester squinted through his large, round sunglasses as the ferry neared the Main Marina docks. Occupying a huge portion of those docks floated a sprawling cruise ship, its engines rumbling in preparation for departure for the open ocean. With no experience on a cruise ship, Chester wondered how living on a virtual floating city could have such appeal. But then he never indulged in any fantasies about travel and adventure except out of necessity which brought him to Puerto Vallarta.

In minutes after leaving the ferry, Chester, Charles Randall to everyone in Puerto Vallarta including his friends at the Comfort Inn, arrived at his Mexican home.

"Buenas tardes, señor Randall." Martina Leon, the attractive front desk receptionist greeted him with a classic smile. Unquestionably the prettiest thing he'd seen all day, the smile and the young lady responsible for it helped to clear his mind of the melancholy that shadowed him on the ferry ride.

"Buenas tardes, to you." Chester grinned in pride over his use of the common, native afternoon greeting.

In perfect English, Martina asked, "Did you have a good day?"

"Yeah, now that it's over," he grumbled.

Her dark, perfectly shaped eye brows arched and creases crossed her forehead. "Something wrong, señor?"

Chester walked toward the elevator to take him to his fifth floor room. "No, a hot day does that to me."

"I'm sorry, señor. Maybe you should take some time in the pool." Another radiant smile lightened her captivating face.

Chester looked up to study her with his piercing eyes. "You know, maybe that's not a bad idea. Gracias señorita."

"De nada, señor."

In weeks since his seeking refuge in Puerto Vallarta, Chester endured hours of boredom engendered by his reluctance to venture out too far from the familiarity of the Comfort Inn. With directions from Raul Rivera, manager of the motel, he had walked to the Marina, a narrow promenade bordered on one side by dockage for private fishing boats and luxurious yachts and on the other side by restaurants, small variety shops and message parlors. Not much of what the Marina offered appealed to Chester's limited entertainment or shopping habits.

Sitting now at his favorite motel room window, he watched action on the golf course adjoining the motel property. Never having played golf either, his watching only served as a context for another slide into reverie. His legs stretched out against the window sill, he pushed to exercise his back. He studied his blistered hands, victims of the only two tools he used on the job at the resort: a shovel and a wheel barrow.

Not in years had he found necessary using either one. Nonetheless, his current job at the resort entailed his helping in the completion of the elaborate landscaping. What he would do after that, he had his doubts. An earlier comment by Thurman Foster, coordinator of construction of the resort, hinted at a future variety store in the resort. That comment gave Chester a ray of hope that he would have a job after landscaping. A smile narrowed his lips. He would have to talk again to Mr. Foster about that possible job.

"Dammit, this is a spectacular view." Jose Martinez patted Thurman Foster's shoulder. "You did a great job in selecting this location."

"Thank you. It wasn't my decision alone. Miguel played a part, a big part." Foster grasped the deck railing outside an eighth floor penthouse.

Martinez placed his hands on his hips. "I don't know about you, but I had doubts about this place. Lots of money and lots of maneuvering around ocean front property rights." He scratched his head. "Without the help of the clan, this place likely would never have happened."

Foster turned to face his partner in the Tropical Real Estate Company. "Yeah, I had my doubts too." He shrugged his shoulders. "So far, so good."

The day before Jose Martinez called to set up an appointment with Thurman Foster to address the status of Mi Casa by the Bay. With the backing of a powerful cartel, the project, after a stumbling start, rapidly approached completion when financial and legal obstacles mysteriously vanished. Now attracting investors, discreet investors who sought relaxation and pleasure rather than simply fun under the sun faced Perez, Foster and Martinez.

Both Foster and Martinez turned to grasp the railing. Silence filled the space between them. Together they drank in the beauty of the setting like thousands each year who visit Puerto Vallarta, seeking reprieve from a frigid winter. From the advantage of the eighth floor deck, the two men gazed down on Banderas Bay, its waters sparkling in the brilliant tropical sun. Across the bay the city of Puerto Vallarta spread, squeezed between the bay and the Sierra Madre Mountains beyond. Below the deck, they studied the property landscaping replete with native palms, large and small as well as colorful flowering bushes. A shimmering L-shaped pool defined the front edge of all three sections of the complex. To the West the Pacific Ocean blended with the far off horizon creating some of the most glorious sunsets in the world.

"How could anyone resist this breathtaking view?"

"Let's hope they can't." Foster turned to face the penthouse patio door.

"Tell me, Thurman, just how close are we to open house?"

"Well, except for a touch of paint here and there and the replacement of a few cracked tiles, we're about ready to go."

"That's great. The guys will be glad to hear that."

The "guys" was euphemistic for "cartel." Jose Martinez represented one of the biggest cartels in Southern Mexico if not in all of Mexico. After the failure of the investment venture, the bankruptcy, and fulfillment of penalties, Miguel Perez, Thurman Foster, and Jose Hector Martinez withdrew into anonymity, emerging later as the Tropical Real Estate Company. Martinez's connections with the cartel served as an introduction to a potential source for financing an exotic resort on the shores of Banderas Bay.

A series of meetings established a committee to explore the resort idea, the cartel unaccustomed to supporting a losing proposition. The cartel leadership insisted on a significant role in the control of the project, financing of condos, and the future of the resort. Part of that control assured the cartel of a market for its most lucrative product, cocaine straight from the fields of Central America.

The planners envisioned a resort with appeal to prudent, tactful tourists dedicated to relaxation and pleasure. The relaxation derived from the cocaine. The pleasure derived from beautiful, seductive women both native and foreign. This combination of relaxation and pleasure would find its blending In the Enchantment Room, a small auditorium featuring seating for fifty, an elaborate stage, an orchestra pit and a series of small rooms across the back of the facility for those seeking privacy.

Martinez guided Foster toward the patio door. "What about staffing? How are we fixed there?"

Foster stepped into the vast emptiness of the penthouse condo unfurnished but resplendent in colorful tile and stainless steel appliances. "I think we're in good shape. Many of the guys working on the landscaping have agreed to continue on the maintenance staff. We still need additional, maid service staff."

"I assume Miguel is taking care of supervisory positions."

Foster walked toward the condo exit. "Yes, he's already located people, discreet people who will do their jobs without blabbing details to those who might pose a threat. I've even heard Miguel, maybe, has someone to manage the variety shop."

"Really, I wasn't sure about that part of the facility. But I agree. It can serve a valuable function. We wish to be as self-sufficient as possible." Martinez faced Foster for emphasis.

"Yes, indeed." Foster stopped just outside the condo. "The guy's name is Charles Randall, an American who has worked on the landscaping crew for a while. He's mentioned working with convenience stores. Why he ended up in Puerto Vallarta I don't know. Our research has turned up nothing suspicious about his background. Our research found very little information at all about his back ground."

The two men left the condo and headed to the elevator.

Martinez draped his arm around Foster's shoulder. "You've done well, Thurman. The guys depend on your good judgement in selecting staff. You simply can't emphasize security enough."

Foster smiled as they stepped into the elevator.

Chapter 45

Life for Dane had taken on a little more excitement. His preoccupation with the Deephaven apartment evolved into a near distraction, edging out the presentations for Miguel Perez and the Tropical Real Estate Company. The approval of his parents made his decision about the apartment even more tantalizing. Now he needed to seek Ashley's opinion. That would happen in the morning before her afternoon shift at Fore Sure Telemarketing.

Dane studied his notes for his afternoon session in the unpretentious motel in St. Paul. The several presentations he had conducted removed much of the anxiety that accompanied the first ones. This afternoon Perez would join him for the session when finally Perez would draw the name of the winner of the all expense paid trip for two to tour the resort in Puerto Vallarta. About seventy names were locked in a basket secured by the motel staff. All seventy people received an invitation to the drawing.

Dane folded his notes, placing them on the sofa end table. Not unusual, his parents left for work, giving him command of the house. Of course, that meant very little since that pattern had existed for years.

Besides the drawing and Ashley's joining him at the apartment, the Hennepin County Attorney's office did call to inform him of the preliminary hearing for Sylvester Ramirez. The hearing was scheduled for 10:00 a.m. the day after tomorrow at the Hennepin

County Court House in downtown Minneapolis. The attorney's office expected Dane's presence to testify as the only eyewitness to the robbery and homicide.

Of course, the request left him with no choice but to testify. Nonetheless, that failed to alter the awakening of those drastic images of guns, blood, death, weeks of recovery, and of bullets ripping through his home injuring his mother. Nothing could completely erase from his memory the convenience store debacle.

As Dane headed east to St. Paul, more anticipation than usual went with him. Eleven potential investors made up the day's list, not including Mr. Perez, who only twice previously joined him at the presentation. Today, though, brought the long-awaited drawing with the possibility of a much larger group to learn of the winners. The motel staff would direct those arriving for the drawing to the more spacious dining room.

When Dane arrived, Mr. Miguel Perez sat in a corner chair off to one side of the conference room table. With a smile and an outstretched hand, He rose quickly to greet Dane. "A big day for a lucky couple."

"Sure is." Dane placed his folder at the head of the table.

Perez moved to stand next to him. "Do you want to do the drawing first or last?"

Without hesitation, Dane replied, "At the end, not to disappoint those invited to this information session and wish to attend the drawing. Besides it will keep up the suspense."

Perez tapped his hand against his forehead. "Of course, how stupid. I didn't think about that." Dane joined him in a chuckle.

He assisted Dane in distributing materials and name tags for the eleven people expected at the meeting.

The meeting progressed without complication after the assembled group learned of the drawing at the conclusion of the meeting. One of the participants, a robust senior with gray hair hanging to his shoulders and who apparently enjoyed having his way, campaigned for an earlier drawing. The others rejected his campaign.

At the end of the meeting an aura of anticipation spread over the small group Dane and Perez ushered to the dining room. In the dining room roughly forty people sat in nervous expectation for the big moment.

Perez motioned to a motel staff member who turned and left the room through a side door. He reappeared carrying a small round basket half full of white slips of paper. A buzz traveled around the room as the motel employee handed the basket to Mr. Perez. Dane stood to one side, arms folded across his stomach, a smile across his lips.

Placing the basket on the table in front of him, Perez looked out over the room filled with anxious people. "Ladies and gentlemen, thank you for coming and thank you for your interest in Mi Casa by the Bay. We believe it will become one of the favorite tourist destinations in the world."

The group responded with light applause.

He continued. "Before the drawing, and I'm as excited as you are, I wish to acknowledge and thank the young man standing next to me for his vital role in communicating the details of our important project."

Dane blushed when the group treated him with a brief ovation. He looked out over the group and announced a clear and resonant, "Thank you."

Perez gave the round basket a few turns, stopped, unlatched the access door, inserted his hand then looked up at the group.

"Are you ready?" he asked.

The group emitted a roar of approval.

With that he sifted through the slips of paper until his hand emerged grasping only one. Silence dominated the dining room. He unfolded the slip of paper, studied it briefly, and announced, " The winners are Mr. and Mrs. Harvey Gunderson."

In the far corner of the room a scream echoed against the dining room walls as two apparent seniors released a flood of joy and excitement. Requested to come to the front of the room, the jubilant couple learned a few details about their journey to Puerto Vallarta, Mexico.

Driving to pick up Ashley for their planned inspection of the Deephaven apartment, Dane reflected on the long series of meetings he conducted and the boundless excitement displayed by the winning couple. He also thought about the many people who had attended his presentations. Knowing what he did about the resort, he recently had misgivings about the compatibility between the resort and the people who had expressed an interest in it. But he determined that wasn't his concern. Right now he considered the drawing a great way to close out those presentations. Their end, however, created another change in the role Dane played for the Tropical Real Estate Company. In a few days he would meet with Mr. Perez to discuss that role.

"Hey, I like this area, quiet and all these beautiful trees." Ashley stretched her neck to look out the car window. "I can almost see the edge of Lake Minnetonka."

"Yes, that got my attention too the first time I looked at the place."

Dane pulled up in front of the two story building divided into four apartments, excitement growing with his need to gain Ashley's approval. Behind that need rested an ulterior motive. Maybe, just maybe, she would someday share the apartment with him.

After a walk through the apartment with special attention paid to the bathroom and the kitchen, Dane and Ashley stood side by side on the deck.

Dane reached for Ashley's hand. "Well, what do you think?"

"It's perfect." Like Dane's dad she asked about furniture, rent and utilities, questions which revealed her experience with renting apartments.

Another moment on the deck and another casual inspection of kitchen cabinets, closets and the bathroom, Dane paused by the door leading out to a narrow hallway.

He reached again for Ashley's hand. "You can see this apartment is big enough for two people." He gritted his teeth in a tense smile.

Ashley squeezed his hand but said nothing. They walked to the stairs and out to the car.

At a small restaurant only minutes from the apartment, they shared a table on the deck. They sipped on ice tea.

"Well, when do you move in?" Ashley moved her glass off to the side.

Dane wrinkled his forehead. "Soon, I hope." He stared out over Lake Minnetonka just beyond the edge of the deck. "A lot depends on my next assignment with Perez. We meet in a couple days to discuss that."

Ashley studied Dane. "I think it's a great place, but the $1500.00 monthly rent certainly is a factor."

"For sure it is, but I think I could handle it." The thought of sharing that rent raced through his mind, but he refrained from bringing up again the subject of sharing.

While they ate lunch, their conversation drifted away from the apartment with more attention to family and job future. Dane already spoke of his meeting with Perez. He hinted that maybe that meeting would send him to Puerto Vallarta for an inspection of the resort he had promoted for weeks. He also mentioned the impending testimony at the Sylvester hearing, and the complete recovery of his mom from the senseless rifle assault on their home.

Never having traveled much herself, Ashley greeted with excitement Dane's reference to traveling to Puerto Vallarta. She reported her father's improvement in his health. She also confirmed her commitment to the telemarketing business which she admitted treated her well with no help from anyone like Dexter Parks.

Chapter 46

Very likely for the last time Dane drove east to St. Paul and the motel that had served as the site for his many presentations. According to Perez, the project would now advance to the next phase. Today Dane would learn the details of that phase.

The light traffic made the drive effortless, inducing a few minutes of reflection on Dane's recent testimony at the Sylvester Ramirez hearing. The whole procedure conducted at the Hennepin County Courthouse in downtown Minneapolis awakened in vivid detail that fateful early morning months ago. Few of those details had dimmed over the intervening months. However, deliberate suppression helped to prevent them from intruding into his daily life which now lay before him with a range of possibilities: his future with Perez, his future with Ashley, and his future with his own apartment the most important.

Before the hearing, Dane met with Anthony Palmer from the Hennepin County Attorney's office. Mr. Palmer acquainted him with the format of the hearing, briefly describing Dane's part, an obvious one since he was the only eyewitness to the robbery and homicide. He advised Dane to describe the events of that early morning succinctly. The presiding judge as well as the court appointed attorney for Sylvester, perhaps, would seek occasional clarification of Dane's testimony. However, as Mr. Palmer pointed out, the hearing served only as a formality but a required one. In Mr. Palmer's opinion, the facts left no question about Sylvester's guilt.

Dane maneuvered lanes preparing to exit the freeway in route to the familiar motel. He adjusted his sun glasses as his mind skipped to the courtroom scene. Besides the judge, a court reporter, a security guard, Dane and his attorney and Sylvester and his, the only other person in the room sat hunched over in the back row of seats available for observers.

Brief and articulate, Dane's testimony caught Sylvester refusing to gain eye contact with him. Instead he stared most of the time at the table where he and his attorney sat. Only once did the judge call for clarification of a minor point in Dane's testimony. At the conclusion of that testimony the judge thanked him for his help then dismissed him. Mr. Palmer walked him to the court room exit. At the time Dane found strange the behavior of the one person seated in the back of the court room. Thinking about the guy again only renewed the mystery of his behavior.

As Dane and Mr. Palmer approached the back of the court room, this man, Dane assumed in his late forties or early fifties with dark hair pulled into a pony tail touching his shoulders, and dressed in a sweatshirt over plain overalls, locked his eyes on the two men who approached him. His lips moved soundlessly, an intimidating scowl distorting his face.

Dane glanced at Palmer, who shrugged his shoulders, his eye brows lifting in doubt. When they walked by, the man stood up. In a voice strained by anger, he muttered, "You bastards ain't gonna get away with putting my brother in jail."

Dane and the attorney paused in slight shock at the audacity of this man whom nobody knew anything about. Palmer glared at the man standing in front of his seat. He said nothing but rested his hand on Dane's shoulder guiding him through the court room exit. In the hallway Dane and the attorney looked at each other seeking maybe some explanation.

Dane spoke first. "I knew nothing about any of Sylvester's family."

Palmer rolled his eyes. "Neither did I." He urged Dane to move farther away from the court room entrance. "I don't like threats even those from crack pots like the guy in there." He ran his thumb and forefinger over the edge of his lips. "Look, Dane, I doubt if this guy poses any danger, but I'll look into it to determine if we have anything on another Ramirez."

"Thank you." In appreciation, Dane reached out his hand to shake the attorney's. "Let me know if you find out anything."

With that thought Dane pulled into the motel parking lot, secured his car, and headed to his meeting with Perez and likely with his future.

"It's been a long time since we first met in this room." Perez rose from his place next to the conference table. "How did the hearing go the other day?"

"Quick and painless." Dane avoided any reference to the action of the guy who claimed to be Sylvester's brother.

"That's good. Maybe that marks the last chapter to your extended saga." Perez returned to his chair.

"I certainly hope so." Dane selected a chair across from Perez.

For moments Perez paged through a folder opened on the table before him. "Well, young man, today we'll talk about the future, not the past."

Dane nodded his head and smiled.

Perez fixed his eyes on Dane. "First of all, thank you for the contribution you've already made to this project. From the telemarketing to conducting all the presentations, you have performed admirably, really justifying our mutual decision to work together." He smiled. "A couple unfortunate incidents interfered only briefly."

Dane's grin forced creases across his forehead.

"But as I just said, today is about the future, not the past."

Perez pulled from the folder a sheet of paper. He studied it for a moment. "Dane, it's time for you to gain first hand knowledge of the resort. Sure, you have viewed the video numerous times." Perez shook his head. "Not the same." He settled back in his chair. "The project has reached completion. It now awaits investors, owners, or renters. That's where you come in with your charm and convincing articulation."

Dane shifted in his chair, the comments a bit embarrassing for him.

Perez continued. "I expect, with your approval, to arrange in the next few days for your flight to Puerto Vallarta. The staff there is prepared to join you in welcoming the first potential clients arriving to inspect our wonderful creation."

Again Dane nodded his head in approval, for the moment incapable of finding the right words to respond.

"I realize you have lots of questions, but do you have any that we can deal with here and now?"

Dane leaned his elbows on the table. "Yes, very likely my limited understanding of parts of the project makes it hard even formulating questions."

Perez smiled in understanding.

Dane straightened up in his chair. "One thing that has concerned me is the economics and the financing available to prospective investors. Also, were those people we called from Fore Sure Telemarketing the kind of people who could afford one of the condos?"

Running his hand through his thick dark hair, Perez studied Dane. "The whole business of financing is more complicated than what can be explained here. Basically, various options are available leading to a shared ownership, sole ownership, or short term renting. Our company has access to financing at very competitive rates."

Of course, he avoided any reference to the cartel, largely responsible for those rates. Perez continued. "When you get set up on site, the management staff will acquaint you with more specific financing details. You'll do just fine once you have the chance to deal each day with these issues."

At the end of the meeting Dane learned of an income increase that would more than cover the cost of his own apartment. In addition, Perez assured him of occasional flights back home to the Twin Cities. For Dane, Puerto Vallarta would not serve as some permanent residence. Perhaps the apartment in Deephaven would.

Chapter 47

The morning sun light peeked around the curtain's edge in his bedroom. In his bed Dane rested with his hands clasped behind his head. He smiled, feeling the excitement suddenly consuming his life. In days his new job would transport him to Puerto Vallarta, a destination only months ago he had scarcely heard of.

He eased himself up on his elbows, reached over to the lamp table next to his bed, and grabbed a business size envelope propped against the lamp. Inside that envelope his fingers touched a single sheet of paper representing one of the most important developments in his life, a signed one year lease for the Deephaven apartment. Withdrawing the single sheet of paper, Dane perused the details for, at least, the tenth time, amazed at all that constituted a simple rental agreement.

The meeting with the management company for the apartment complex, the discussion of rental details, the submission of the security deposit, the first month's rent, and, at last, his signature will dwell vividly in his memory for a long time.

With legs hanging over the side of the bed, Dane noted the September 1 occupancy date, one selected to blend with his pending assignment in Puerto Vallarta. Though moving immediately was his preference, job responsibilities gained priority. Besides the return at the end of August to begin the move added excitement to the flight home from his first round of duties at the resort.

At dinner the previous evening, Dane relished the chance to share his joy with his parents. They joined in his delight regarding the apartment. With a bit more reserve they responded to his traveling to distant Puerto Vallarta for work. Dane assured them of his ability to take care of himself despite his years of dependence on his parents. This morning found him alone again, his dad off on another trip with an eighteen wheeler, his mom off to her duties in the trucking firm's accounting office. Their previous approval of the apartment had reinforced his confidence in a decision to sign the lease. Support from Ashley added to that confidence.

Standing before the bathroom sink, Dane liked what he saw in the mirror. Rarely did he think about his appearance, content to accept the way he looked. The intermittent periods of joy and sorrow of the past months had changed little his youthful appearance. He rubbed his hands over his eyes and around his mouth, noting, maybe, some accentuation of those lines that extended away from his eyes and around his mouth. He also noted his smile enhanced those lines, but smiling was an important part of his personality. He didn't intend to stop smiling only to erase a couple lines in his face.

Rolling his eyes at the silly distraction of looking at himself in the mirror, Dane placed his hands on the edge of the sink and stretched his arms. He recounted in his mind the things needing attention before his departure for Puerto Vallarta in just four days. Discussing furniture to take with him when he moved into the apartment would have to involve his mom, at least. Packing and preparing for Puerto Vallarta also required special attention, especially because of Dane's limited travel experience. This left to last, perhaps, the most important event, his luncheon with Ashley. That luncheon required him to spend less time in thought and more in action or end up late in picking her up for their date.

At noon Dane stopped in front of Ashley's apartment, a duplex. She occupied one half of the building, the owners the other. Before he could knock on the door, Ashley appeared in front of him.

"Right on time." She greeted him with a smile. "Why don't you come in for a few minutes? I have to remove some clothes from the dryer. Sorry."

With his arms around her, he whispered, "Don't be. We have plenty time."

Ashley moved away to a main floor closet where a washer and dryer sat squeezed together. She glanced back over her shoulder. "Have a seat. I'll be right back."

Dane settled into the sofa positioned under a large picture window overlooking the front yard, very similar to the arrangement at home. An arch led to a dining and kitchen area. A short hallway led to the one bedroom and one bathroom. Ashley's share of the duplex gave her a restful, homelike place to live and only a short drive to the office of Fore Sure Telemarketing.

Not often did their respective schedules permit sharing lunch. Today their schedules did, their destination a small, rustic restaurant named Charlie's Bar and Grill straddling the border between Hennepin and Carver Counties. For years popular with people living on the fringes of both counties, the restaurant was only a few minutes drive from the Barton home, a drive they rarely made. On advice from a neighbor, Dane with his parents shared dinner there recently. Impressed with its quaint ambience and its good food, he wished to share his discovery with Ashley. Today marked the first time they would eat lunch there together.

A basic, wooden structure with faded siding and a few wrinkled shingles, it retained a remarkable capacity to welcome the most sophisticated customers. Of course, a high level of sophistication did not characterize Charlie's Bar and Grill. Serving tantalizing food did.

Dane parked in a space next to the restaurant. Several cars preceded him. A large entrance door stood open, the dining area protected by a heavy screen door allowing for a blending of indoor and outdoor air. Dane and Ashley entered the restaurant to see booths extending around the periphery of the dining area, several tables arranged on the wooden plank floor, and a bar offering seating for six more customers. With most booths occupied, they selected a table near the entrance. Shortly after they sat down, a stout waitress, probably in her fifties, stood next to the table. With a big smile and bigger breasts stretching the name Charlie's Bar and Grill printed across her top, she welcomed her latest customers.

Intrigued by the rural, unpretentious atmosphere of the restaurant, Dane and Ashley relaxed with two drinks before ordering a special Charlie's sandwich. As they savored their lunch, other customers began to leave, their exit taking many of them by Dane and Ashley's table.

As Dane lay down his napkin next to his plate, he glanced up to see walking toward them a vaguely familiar face. Suddenly, recognition of the face clicked. With eyes open wide, Dane muttered, "Holy shit." Ronald Ramirez stomped toward their table.

For an instant Dane debated what to do, remembering Sylvester's brother and the hostility in his voice and the hatred in his eyes. Dane wished to avoid any scene or place Ashley in any danger. He just sat finishing his sandwich.

Ashley detected Dane's unrest. "What's the matter? You see a ghost?"

He tried to share her humor. "I guess nothing."

As Ronald Ramirez walked by, he deliberately bumped Dane's chair, nearly tipping him over. Ashley covered her mouth to muffle her alarm. Dane stood up to face the angry intruder.

"Watch where you're going." Dane cautioned.

"Who says so?" Ramirez bellowed, attracting the attention of the bar tender as well as two other men seated at the bar.

Breathing deeply, eyes fixed on Ramirez's face distorted by rage, Dane pleaded, "Look, I don't want any trouble. Just go."

Ashley stood, moving away from her place by the table.

Ramirez grabbed Dane by the front of his shirt, shouting, "Screw you, you piece of shit, telling all those god damned lies about my brother." He pushed Dane who stumbled over his chair and sprawled on the wooden floor. Ashley watched in horror unable to do anything.

"Hey!" came the thundering voice of the bar tender. "Knock it off."

Instead Ramirez stood over Dane, delivering a powerful kick to Dane's back. He groaned in pain, arching his back to absorb the pain. That brought two men from the bar to Dane's defense. While they surrounded the seething Ramirez, the bar tender called 911. In minutes two sheriff patrol cars screeched to a stop outside Charlie's Bar and Grill.

As quickly as it started the incident ended with sheriff's deputies hauling Ramirez away in hand cuffs. As the deputies dragged him out to the patrol car, he yelled, "You god damned liar!"

With a pain streaming through his back but otherwise unhurt, Dane with Ashley by his side leaned against the bar talking with the bartender and the two men who came to his rescue. They admitted seeing this Ramirez guy before but knew little about him except that he lived someplace near the restaurant.

Following brief introductions, Dane described his encounter with Ramirez at the courthouse. The conversation inevitably recounted the whole sordid affair including the robbery, homicide and subsequent events. The bartender declared that he now remembered reading about the incident.

Dane explained the report, he recently received and desired to forget, from Anthony Palmer of the Hennepin County Attorney's office regarding both Ronald and Sylvester Ramirez. For Ronald, Palmer reported a DWI, a license revocation, and a disorderly conduct arrest at a Minneapolis bar. Records revealed very little else about this volatile man. For Sylvester, Palmer reported a conclusion to his case. He had pled guilty to a lesser charge, second degree murder. With the implication of Chester Reynolds in the insurance fraud, Sylvester received a reduced sentence of thirty years. This report only made Ronald's vehement behavior more futile since his brother no longer would benefit from anything he could do. The case was closed.

The conversation concluded over a free glass of wine and two bottles of beer courtesy of the management who apologized for the disruption of their lunch. Dane and Ashley thanked them for their courtesy, their rapid response, and for the delicious lunch. With a measure of regret they drove away from Charlie's Bar and Grill, fearing that the image of the distorted face of Ramirez would outlast the memory of the lunch.

Chapter 48

"Mom and Dad, this is Ashley. Ashley meet my mom and dad." Dane rested his arm around Ashley's shoulder. She squeezed her hands hanging at her sides.

Beatrice reached out to embrace Ashley in a gentle hug. "So happy finally to meet you."

Milo took Ashley's hand in his. He grinned. "We thought Dane was ashamed of us or something."

"Maybe in the past but not any more." Dane shared his dad's humor.

"So happy to meet you despite this guy." He tilted his head toward his son.

"My goodness, we don't have to stand by the front door." Beatrice guided Ashley toward the living room. "Let's sit down in here where we can relax and talk."

Dane and Ashley took the sofa while his parents each sat down in the sofa chairs. A nervous silence filled the room.

Milo broke the silence. To Ashley he commented, "I understand you've seen the apartment."

She moved forward on the sofa. "Yes, I did. I like the area as well as the apartment itself."

Milo nodded his head and glanced at Dane. "We did, too, eager to get our son out from under our feet."

"Milo, that's not funny," Beatrice scolded.

"What is funny," Dane countered, "is my putting up with parental abuse."

Ashley shared a laugh with him.

The evening passed with more serious conversation about the future and about the next day, a momentous one for Dane. His Delta flight to Puerto Vallarta was scheduled to depart at 11:15 in the morning. To celebrate this important event in the lives of all of them, Beatrice insisted on sharing dinner at the Barton home.

Around the dinner table topics ranged from getting acquainted to the prospects of Dane's assignment in Mexico and the eventual move to the apartment. Milo politely inquired of Ashley's background in the Duluth area, comparing it, couched in humor, with that of Dane's who hadn't ventured too far from the home he grew up in. Dane mostly listened to the discussion even when his dad brought up his loquacity.

With dinner complete, dishes stacked in the dishwasher, the evening resumed back in the living room. Though they all agreed that the future qualified as far more important than the past, attention to the events of the last several months intruded. Dane emphasized the need to move on, relieved at the resolution of the Ramirez saga.

Dane's mom and dad exchanged with Ashley expressions of delight over the chance at last to meet. At the door Ashley even received a gentle hug from Milo, not one inclined to displays of affection. They agreed to get together soon certainly upon Dane's return to make the move to his apartment.

Dane and Ashley rode the half hour drive to her apartment in near silence, their thoughts dominated by the meeting of his parents, the events of the next day and those of several weeks after that. He steered the car to the curb and turned off the engine and lights. With his seat belt unlatched, he draped his arm over the seat back and faced Ashley.

"I enjoyed the evening. I finally lived up to a promise I made my mom months ago to bring you home to meet her and my dad." He tapped her shoulder. "I hope my dad didn't embarrass you with his sometimes caustic tongue."

Ashley unlatched her seat belt and slid closer to Dane. She laughed. "He's definitely entertaining but not offensive, just playful. He seems to get a kick out of life."

"Maybe. Sometimes it's not always life he gets a kick out of. It's more like making fun of people." He ran his hands across his mouth.

"Do you want to come in for a while?" She placed her hand on his knee.

"Of course, I was waiting for your invitation."

Out of the car, they walked hand in hand to the entrance to her half of the duplex she shared with the owners. They tightened the grip on each other's hand. A sensation drifted from Dane's stomach down to his groin. In the months of their fluctuating relationship, they had avoided any intimacy, only occasional, innocent making out and a few roving touches.

Ashley unlocked the door leading Dane into the living room where they stopped. Months of expectations of tenderness exploded as they leaped into each other's arms, his hands searching for access to her breasts. She breathed heavily. Her hands reached around to unhook her bra. A long, moist kiss brought their bodies together in a near perfect physical blend. He reached inside her bra to fondle her breasts, firm yet soft, yielding to his touch.

She reached down to unbuckle his trousers, her hand inching toward his throbbing erection. Shivers traveled through their bodies. He moved her toward the sofa where in an emotional frenzy, they discarded their clothing to plunge into the world of ultimate euphoria.

"The cabin door is now closed. Everyone should be seated as we prepare to take off." A deep voice drifted through the plane.

Dane listened to instructions about safety, about evacuation, about seat belts, and about remaining in his seat. A hectic morning ensuring his luggage contained everything he had listed, making sure he carried his passport, saying goodbye to his parents, and waiting for Perez to take him to the Minneapolis/St. Paul International Airport, Dane tried to relax in his aisle seat, not easy since he found relaxing elusive, challenged by this major change in his life.

Not an experienced traveler, only once before had he taken a flight to Chicago with his parents, Dane suffered tension over getting to the airport on time for his international flight. Perez convinced him they had plenty time and when they arrived at the airport, he dropped him off at a curbside check-in site, thus avoiding a long line awaiting check-in inside. He did avoid that line but not the one through security. He found his gate without difficulty where he plunked down to wait one hour before boarding his flight.

The plane raced down the runway creating a pull on Dane's stomach as the view from his aisle seat spread out to encompass nearly the entire Twin City area. Within minutes the plane broke through the high cloud cover into a burst of morning sunshine.

Dane settled back in his seat, making sure his seat belt stayed fastened. He rested his head on his seat back, the image of last night's sensational goodbye with Ashley suppressed all the morning tension. He closed his eyes to savor the memory of Ashley's fragrance, her softness, and the splendor of their union. For several minutes he relived that glorious evening.

Minor bumps jolted him back to reality. He looked around at those seated near him. Seat backs prevented seeing much of any other passengers except those next to him. Settled back again in his seat, he tried without success to resist thinking of other recent events. The flight offered little to distract him. He wrestled to suppress the images of the clash with Ronald Ramirez. Remembering last night's conversation at the dinner with his parents and Ashley, he relived the relief that the case against Sylvester Ramirez was finally closed. The surprising encounter with his brother clouded some of that relief. However, as far as he knew, Ronald was in the hands of the county law enforcement officials.

The flight attendant passed by, pushing a narrow cart,

momentarily rescuing Dane from his thoughts. The attendant moved on after leaving a cup of Sprite on ice and a tiny bag of pretzels on his pull out tray. Munching the pretzels diverted his thoughts away from the Ramirez brothers and toward more immediate concerns, such as his landing in Puerto Vallarta and the sequence of events that supposedly would end with his arrival at the resort.

Perez had explained to Dane the predatory welcome he likely would receive from the timeshare salesmen and taxi drivers who together formed, at the airport, a virtual gauntlet through which passengers had to pass. With assurance Perez also informed him of the young man, Ramon, who with a name sign would meet him near the terminal exit. He breathed deeply struggling with apprehension about all the details that would hopefully deliver him to his final destination, the resort where he would contact Thurman Foster.

An uneventful flight, it arrived on time at Puerto Vallarta's Gustavo Diaz Ordaz International Airport. Dane followed the crowd, clutching his immigration and customs declaration papers as well as his passport. Passing through the immigration station without delay, Dane faced a short walk to baggage claim area that further reduced his tension when he found his two pieces of luggage waiting for him next to the conveyor. Through the security light which blinked green for him, Dane faced the gauntlet of salespeople Perez warned him about. Ignoring their aggressive tactics, he emerged into a large receiving area where on the other side of a retaining rope stood a young man holding up a sign reading, "Welcome, Mr. Dane Barton."

The young man immediately reached for Dane's luggage, "Buenas tardes, señor. Good afternoon, Mr. Barton." The young man smiled, his tan face accentuating his white teeth. In clear English the young man identified himself as Ramon then asked, "Did you have a good flight?"

Dane shouldered his brief case, staying close to Ramon. "Yes, it was. A bit long but otherwise okay."

"Good. Just follow me, and I will get you to where you want to go."

Where he wanted to go was the resort. Before he arrived there, he had a very short ride to the Main Marina and a longer one with Ramon by ferry to the docks serving Mi Casa by the Bay.

Dane gripped the railing of the ferry, gazing around at the fascination of the Puerto Vallarta shoreline and the mountains beyond. In front of him spread the blue waters of Banderas Bay and the mountains towering in the distance.

Standing beside him, Ramon announced, "Beautiful, isn't it."

Dane nodded his head. "It certainly is."

Half way across the bay, Dane could discern in the distance a break in the jungle boarding the shoreline. With each passing minute that break enlarged revealing this magnificent resort carved out of the jungle. He stood in awe as the ferry glided to the dock. He couldn't take his eyes away from the luxurious palm trees and flowering bushes teaming with blossoms. Guarded by the bushes and palms, the sprawling pool shimmered in the bright tropical sun. Dane caught his breath as he viewed the towering three sections of the resort decorated in red and yellow accents. The DVD images Dane had viewed numerous times failed to capture the splendor of the resort.

Dane followed Ramon on the tiled path leading to the main entrance of the resort which housed the management contingent that would strive to make it a prime destination for tourist from around the world. Inside the main entrance more splendor greeted him. Decorative flowers, colorful tile, rich wooden furniture and a reception desk welcomed arriving guests. At the desk Ramon dropped off Dane's luggage.

To one side of the reception desk a hallway gave access to directors' offices where Ramon now escorted Dane to the one with "Thurman Foster" attached to the door. A light tap on the door produced a firm, "Come in."

Ramon entered first holding the door open for Dane. As he

did from the dock in first viewing the luxury of the resort, Dane absorbed the opulence of Foster's office. From behind his expansive desk positioned in front of a huge window affording a view of Banderas Bay, Mr. Foster rose from his chair.

Ramon announced, "Mr Foster, please meet Mr. Barton."

Pushing back his chair, Foster came around his desk with hand extended to shake Dane's. "So happy finally to meet you. I've heard good things about you from Mr. Perez."

Dane gripped the hand of his new boss. "Very happy to be here. Thank you."

After thanking then dismissing Ramon, Foster directed Dane to sofa chairs positioned on one wall of the office. Settled in their chairs, Foster rested his chin in his hand. "You've had a long day. I don't want to make it any longer. We do have many details to discuss but for now let's just get you settled in your office and in your home away from home."

A small room but nonetheless impressive in its decorative appointments of tile and wood, it contained the basic essentials for an office. A highly polished desk, executive chair, file cabinets, a small book case lining one wall and a view across the pool and out to the bay, the office impressed Dane with its simple comfort and utility.

In the evening Dane rested in his one bedroom condo, a marvelous accommodation nearly the same size as his apartment in Deephaven. Unlike his apartment, though, this condo gleamed in fresh paint, polished tile, stainless steel appliances, plush furniture, tasteful wall decorations and a huge king-size bed. Events of the last twenty-four hours skipped through his mind, as did those of the next day dedicated to a complete orientation to Mi Casa by the Bay.

Chapter 49

Dane stared at the fan above his bed, slowly pushing around the warm, humid air. Though his condo came equipped with air conditioning, he simply hadn't taken time to learn how to turn it on. He blinked his eyes to ensure the reality of the last twenty-four hours.

The magnificence of this place he found difficult to comprehend. In the next two months he expected to find this stunning beauty part of his routine, most of which he had yet to understand. He did understand the comforts and conveniences of his condo, located he discovered only two floors above his office and like his office giving him a splendid view of the pool and Banderas Bay.

The bedside clock reminded him of the nine o'clock meeting with Mr. Foster, an imposing man who on first sight reminded Dane of John Wayne. Of course, John Wayne belonged to an earlier generation, no longer attracting large audiences. Nonetheless, Dane grew up on classic western movies. Today Foster intended to take him on a tour of the resort, introduce him to other administrative staff, and discuss his link in the chain dedicated to the success of Mi Casa by the Bay.

Dane showered and dressed quickly for a day packed with importance. His knock on Foster's office door produced the same firm response as yesterday. Dressed in a polo shirt declaring Tropical

Real Estate across the front, jeans, and loafers, Foster welcomed Dane.

"Did you get a good night's sleep?" Foster extended his hand to grasp Dane's.

"I sure did after some of the excitement of the day wore off." Dane's plain blue polo and shorts failed to identify him as one of the staff.

Foster pointed to Dane's shirt. "Pretty color," he chuckled, "but we've got to get you one that tells everyone who you are."

Dane nodded his head and smiled.

Moving toward the office door, Foster urged, "We have a busy day today. We'd better get started first with a walk through the property."

"I've been waiting for it. The video I've seen numerous times, but it doesn't do justice to the real thing."

"I agree."

They passed by the reservation desk. "We may as well start where everyone else who expresses interest will start." Foster signaled to an attractive, Mexican woman occupying a position behind the highly polished reception desk. "Diana, I want you to meet our newest staff member."

She emerged from behind the desk to reveal her slender figure enhanced by her firm fitting company shirt and tactfully tight jeans. Advancing toward the two men, she reached out her hand to grasp Dane's.

Foster did the introductions. "Diana, meet Dane Barton. Dane meet Diana, director of reception and registration."

"So happy to meet you, Dane." She gripped his hand with both of hers. "I look forward to working with you."

"Thank you." Dane gave Diana's hand a slight squeeze. "I, too, am eager to get acquainted and to get started."

Diana walked back to her station, turning when she reached the desk. "Have a good day, and I expect to work with you often."

Around the corner and several steps down a narrow hallway, an older woman with nearly white hair paged through papers on her desk. Foster approached that desk.

"Excuse me, Lorena, I want you to meet the latest member of the administrative staff."

Dane joined Foster in front of the desk. With his hand placed on Dane's shoulder, he stated, "Lorena, please meet Dane Barton, one of our financial staff." He then looked to Dane. "Dane, please meet Lorena, director of the maid service available to our guests and residents."

Lorena stood up. In heavily accented English, she replied, "So honored to meet you. I hope you'll enjoy your work here."

"Thank you. I'm sure I will."

From the reception and maid service desks, Foster guided Dane to the front entrance where they started a slow walk around the exterior property. With Dane's awe of the resort diminished somewhat from the day before, he still found the entire setting stunning, particularly the vast collection of palms and native flowering bushes. At poolside, he stood amazed at its size and the array of pool furniture precisely arranged around the pool's edge.

On the exterior tour Dane had the chance to meet two more administrative staff, Ricardo in maintenance and Juan in security. Both men in their late thirties, Dane assumed, they, too, extended a warm welcome to their colleague.

Back inside, they visited the restaurant and kitchen where Dane met Alvaro, the food service director. A full service restaurant with an impressive menu, its design, nonetheless, was influenced by the realization that many potential residents would prefer eating in their condos and that the Puerto Vallarta area offered dozens of fine restaurants.

From the food service department, Foster directed Dane to a small auditorium separated from other first floor facilities by a long corridor lined with tropical images of beaches, bikinis, and palm trees. At the end of the corridor, two large, imposing doors opened to the auditorium. Dane and Foster paused just inside the doors.

For a few moments they studied the colorful decorative drapes over windows with a view only of the nearby jungle, the rows of deeply cushioned chairs, and the ambiguity of the small cubicles lining the back of the auditorium their apparent privacy ensured by more decorative curtains.

Foster urged Dane to move into the auditorium. "I expected Marcos, our entertainment director, to guide us through this place, but he had a conflict. I'll do my best." He pursed his lips.

"This," he explained with some hesitation, "is the Enchantment Room." He pointed to the stage on their right. "This is where those who wish can enjoy entertainment, group or individual." Foster's voice assumed a more serious tone. "Maybe you remember some words from our advertising campaign, words like 'relaxation and pleasure'." He glanced at Dane. "This is the place for pleasure."

Dane's eyes traveled over the auditorium, his mind trying to envisage just what kind of pleasure guests could find here. He smiled but made no comment.

Foster detected Dane's skepticism. Reluctant to pry to deeply into the intent of the Enchantment Room, he explained elusively, "We have signed a contract with a Mexican company that can supply entertainers, seductive entertainers. We feel this can be an important selling point for those seeking some adventure."

Dane, in silence, contemplated just what Foster tried to explain without specificity.

Foster urged him back to the entrance. "Maybe the purpose of this place will become clearer after we get underway."

The last stop on the tour was at the variety shop, the type quite familiar to Dane. Though this shop failed to qualify as a convenience store, it still carried many of the same miscellaneous items. At this time the shop stood empty and locked. Foster admitted that the manager, a Mr. Charles Randall also from the states, must have gotten sick. He hadn't shown up for work in three days. A call to his condo in the Marina Vallarta produced no response. Foster assumed security would have to look into the mysterious Mr. Randall.

Following a lunch in the restaurant, Foster and Dane returned to Foster's office to discuss the specifics of Dane's role as a member of the resort's financial team. Seated in front of Foster's executive desk, Dane prepared himself for the details of his new position. He never considered himself any kind of financial genius. Back in the Twin Cities Perez obviously recognized that limiting his involvement in the financial options of Mi Casa by the Bay would focus Dane's presentations on the physical attraction of the resort.

Behind his desk Foster reached for a folder, placed it in front of him, then opened it. He looked across the desk at Dane, radiating a sense of authority. "Let me assure you we would never assign you to our financial department without confidence in your ability to fulfill the demands of the job. Let me also assure you that, at anytime, you have access to me if you need assistance."

Dane nodded his head. "Thank you." He moved nervously in his chair.

Foster sat back. "Basically, you will be responsible for presenting an initial outline for prospective clients of ownership or rental options and their costs. It's not science. It's common sense. Living in luxury does not come cheap." His fingers counted off several pages in the folder. "I want you to study a few pages I'll leave with you today. In a couple days we'll sit down together to discuss any questions." He pushed the papers across the desk, allowing Dane to grasp them.

Dane sat up straight. "I really appreciate all your time, thank you. I'll get right on these pages. I definitely will seek answers to any questions."

Foster rose out of his chair, placing his hands on the desk top. With eyes fixed on Dane, he stated, "I don't know how much you understand about the money behind this project and behind the Tropical Real Estate Company." He bit his lower lip. "Suffice it to say the people with influence over this project wield a hell of a lot of power." Foster stood up with arms at his side. "I don't tell you this to intimidate you. I tell you this for your own information."

Alone in his condo, Dane rested with a Corona on the small

deck off the living area. The day engendered thoughts on a range of subjects from facilities to directors to finance. Foster's final comments hovered over other concerns. Who exactly were these powerful people? For an instant he thought about the missing manager of the resort's variety shop. That awakened questions about the fate of another person intimately connected to a variety shop.

Chapter 50

Chester (aka Charles Randall) slammed his fist hard on top the table. The phone tilted then tumbled to the tiled floor.

"God damn that little shit!" He bent over to rescue the phone. For three days calls came from the resort. The variety shop needed his guidance. Dane Barton had screwed that up too as he did Chester's Twin Cities convenience stores.

Recalling the meeting only days ago when Foster announced the impending arrival of another administrative staff by the name of Dane Barton, Chester relived the shock created by that name and all it represented. In the days since that meeting he wondered how the hell Barton ended up at the same place where until now Chester had sought and gained refuge.

In recent weeks his job at the resort diverted his attention from the events of the past, events which dramatically altered his life. The agony of people like Tony Harris, Sylvester Ramirez, and Dane Barton compelling him to sacrifice all he had worked for faded some with his adjustments to life in the tropics. Now that life, too, abruptly disintegrated with the mere mention of the name Dane Barton.

Chester collapsed in the soiled sofa chair which added little to the decaying efficiency apartment he now lived in. Located only blocks from his original home at the Comfort Inn, the apartment saved him money while giving him the minimal comforts he required.

Only slightly bigger than his room at the Comfort Inn, the apartment included three rooms, the only one with a door the bathroom and rusty shower. The bedroom, scarcely big enough for a double bed, offered privacy with a moveable, folding partition. A combination living, dining, and cooking area completed the modest apartment. One small window in the living area gave a narrow view of the Marina Vallarta promenade below.

Chester removed his glasses, rested his head in his hands, rubbing his tired eyes. In dismay he contemplated what he would do now. He explored the options as he perceived them. He could flee the immediate area, one he knew very little about. "Where would he go?" His fugitive status eliminated a return to the states. He could confess his association with Dane Barton, the robbery and his refuge in Puerto Vallarta. His knowledge of the role played by a cartel in the resort and the anticipated distribution of cocaine and likely marijuana, maybe, provided a shield from Foster and others from exposing him as Chester Reynolds rather than Charles Randall.

He took a deep breath then exhaled; his musing reduced the earlier tension. Slumped back in the chair, Chester considered another option, one probably too preposterous to think about. But he would think about it anyway. Maybe he and Dane could establish a truce, each leaving the other alone, each burying the past. That option assumed the threat of Chester's exposure would balance the threat to Dane whom the cartel would need to muzzle if he ran to the states to rat on Chester Reynolds.

Chester shook his head, seeking more control over his thoughts. To himself he confessed little confidence in any of his options. He reached for his glasses. At the discolored sink, crowded between a meager fridge and a cupboard, he poured himself a glass of slightly cool water. A glance out the one available window to see the usual stream of tourists walking the Marina promenade did little to assuage his anxiety and apprehension over his future. Confinement to his cramped apartment did no better to quiet the ambiguity of his life. Plagued with indecision, he slipped from his apartment down to blend with the evening crowd milling around studying the menus of the numerous restaurants lining the Marina.

He maneuvered his way through the thick crowd, leaving the area for the bus stand a block away on Paseo de la Marina Sur, Marina Vallarta's main street. Where he would go he wasn't sure, probably El Centro or even Old Town, just away from his apartment where his troubles only seemed to multiply.

Earlier in his escape to Puerto Vallarta, Chester discovered the adventure of riding a city bus. Drivers tended to pride themselves on speed, quick stops and starts, and on threading their way through Puerto Vallarta's congestion. Some buses old, some new, they all had one thing in common, squeaky brakes.

In minutes the blue and white Marina bus pulled up to the stop. This evening a combination of tourists and natives nearly filled every seat. Chester climbed the steep steps to hand the driver the seven and one half pesos fee to ride the bus, if he chose, to the end of its route in Old Town.

Leaving Marina Vallarta, the bus raced along the Blvd. Francisco Marina Ascencio, the main artery to Puerto Vallarta's commercial and entertainment center, weaving around other buses, trucks, pickups, and cars. Designed for speed and convenience, the bus offered little comfort for the passengers pushed together on hard plastic seats. The ride took Chester by familiar scenes of elaborate, condo complexes reaching over twenty stories clinging to the shore of Banderas Bay and of squalid buildings crumbling in abandonment. He paid little attention to the scenery, preoccupied with what the hell he would do and where the hell he would do it.

Winding through the narrow streets of El Centro, the bus bumped to a stop at intersections where bunches of people waited to cross for access to the Malecon, a popular, scenic, public walkway boarding the shoreline of Banderas Bay. At last the bus crossed the bridge over the Cuale River dividing Old Town from El Centro and the end to its route. Later it would retrace the route back to Marian Vallarta.

Stepping off the bus, Chester quickly oriented himself to the attractions and culture of Old Town, a distinct district of Puerto Vallarta. He glanced first to the left then to the right. He would find the beach on his right. With a measure of confidence he stepped over the curb and onto the sidewalk that would take him to the beach. He had formulated no plan for what he would do there except to blend in with the often rowdy crowds that gathered around the restaurants, bars, and vendors that added to the vitality and charm of Old Town.

Ahead he saw the first of several sidewalk vendors, a preface to many more along the way. Chester needed nothing from any of the vendors. He needed a plan, one of the few he had pondered while still in his apartment. Sidewalks crowded with revelers and those seeking a place to eat and drink made his progress halting. At least these crowds would shield him from anyone who might recognize him, in his mind highly unlikely.

He followed the sidewalk as it rose toward the foothills of the Sierra Madre Mountains, like most of Puerto Vallarta squeezing Old Town between them and the bay. Feeling the strain imposed by the rising elevation, Chester walked slowly, pausing to catch his breath. In the next block he saw, to his surprise, a horse munching on grass in an empty lot. He found curious the presence of a horse amid the crowds of tourists, vendors and barkers committed to luring people into a restaurant or bar, but the Mexican culture featured its own unique qualities. Standing next to the horse a man held tight to the reins.

Chester approached the man, not much bigger than himself with a slender build and thick black hair tinged with gray. The man greeted Chester with, "Buenas noches, señor."

In the time Chester had lived and worked in Puerto Vallarta, he learned a few common Spanish words and phrases. "Buenas noches," he replied.

A smile acknowledged the greeting. "Montar a caballo, señor?"

Chester stared in confusion. He shrugged his shoulders and turned to leave.

The man reached out to touch Chester on the arm. In clear English he asked, "Do you want to ride a horse?" A smile punctuated the request.

Not sure what to say, Chester moved from one foot to the other, looked down at the ground and back up to the man's very dark eyes.

"Well, what do you think? Two hundred pesos for half an hour."

Never in his life had Chester ridden a horse. Never had he stood so close to one, at least in recent memory. He considered the ride might take his mind off all this problems. "Okay." He nodded his head.

"Bueno, good, gracias"

The ride did not start there. Instead, the man first identified himself as Toni. He then assisted Chester up into the saddle before leading the horse with Chester on top a few blocks farther up the foothills to a small corral, home to a half dozen other horses. Toni selected one, fitted it with a bridle and saddle. Toni mounted the horse to guide Chester on an interesting ride through the dense jungle and over a gentle stream only a short distance from the cacophony of Old Town crowds and the fascination of Chico's Paradise, a popular restaurant cradled on the banks of a meandering stream.

Chester found the fascinating half hour ride much too short. He talked Toni into extending it a few more minutes. The ride concluded, Chester joined Toni in exploring the corral, a small horse barn, and the humble house that made up an almost miniature ranch. The setting intrigued Chester who found great relief in the quiet seclusion of this place. Maybe it offered some answer to his dilemma.

Chapter 51

Dane closed the folder. Across his desk Edward and Harriet Bennett exchanged glances; Edward pursed his lips in thought.

With hands clasped on top the folder, Dane studied the older couple, the owner of a successful plumbing company in suburban Chicago and his wife, a petite woman with attractive blonde hair and a captivating twinkle in vivid, blue eyes. Used to assuming control, Edward found his robust size, broad shoulders, and big hands an asset in managing his crew of ten plumbers. A receding hairline directed attention to his inquisitive eyes which now locked on Dane.

"Do you have any more questions?"

The couple exchanged another glance. "I don't think so," Edward tightened his hold on his wife's hand.

In five weeks Dane had learned fast the strategies and related techniques to help clients make a decision about their future at Mi Casa by the Bay. Most of the initial weeks he devoted to adaptations to this foreign world and to learning about these strategies and financial policies of the Tropical Real Estate Company. The Bennetts represented the third opportunity to discuss options with prospective residents. The previous week he registered his first success in securing owners for one of the superb two bedroom condos.

With no more questions to answer, Dane eased himself off his chair to walk around to congratulate Edward and Harriet on their attentiveness to his explanation and to their tentative decisions to purchase a two bedroom condo. Before they took the final step of conferring with Mr. Foster, they wished to view one more time the condo they had selected for possible purchase. Dane took great pride in showing these luxurious yet functional condos with stainless steel appliances and colorful tiled floors all waiting for new owners to provide the furniture. After this second review of the condo, Dane guided the Bennetts to Foster's office to conclude discussion of ownership details and to reach a final decision. Though sales had dragged at first, recent days hinted at encouraging signs for greater success. The Bennetts were part of that encouragement.

Early in Dane's assignment to the resort, the urgency of learning the lay out of the complex, the configuration of the various condos, and more important his role in the finance department diverted his attention from other aspects of his life, such as the future of his relationship with Ashley, his move into his own apartment, and fragments of the Chester debacle that lingered in his mind. Foster's mention of the mysterious absence of the manager of the variety shop Dane dismissed, at the time, as none of his business. However, lately, curiosity about that person captured his attention more often than he liked. What he liked was burying that sordid event in some remote chamber of his memory. Still, each time he met with Foster the thought of the mysterious manager hovered close by.

At least two or three times a week Dane contacted his parents as well as Ashley. Since his schedule varied, the agreement with those important people at home determined that he would call them when he found time in his schedule, mostly late afternoon or evening. In these calls he never alluded to what he labeled as preposterous suspicion over the missing manager.

Besides his gaining control over his responsibilities as part of the finance staff, Dane gained a greater understanding of the totality of the resort's operation, particularly that of the enigmatic Enchantment Room. The brief exposure to the Enchantment Room when Foster conducted a tour of the property only proved another source of uncertainty. Of course, without residents, the room served no purpose. With the arrival of either owners or renters, or both, indeed, a definite purpose emerged.

On the tour taken with Foster weeks ago, Dane missed meeting Marcos, the entertainment director. Since then, however, Dane had not only met Marcos but had established a friendship with him. Born and raised in Puerto Vallarta, Marcos, in his early thirties, brought with him experience in the entertainment world. Before taking the job with Tropical Real Estate, he managed a sophisticated men's club located in the mountains above El Centro and popular with many of the more important men in Puerto Vallarta. The club featured stunning dancing girls dressed in provocative costumes covering very little of their shapely bodies. Marcos also brought with him connections with Mexican agencies that provided a source of gorgeous dancing girls, some of whom possessed no reluctance to go beyond mere dancing.

Brief contacts with other members of the management staff established a compatibility between Marcos and Dane. Despite the vast differences in nationality and background, they shared a commitment to making Mi Casa by the Bay one of the top tourist sites in the world. This relationship produced several discussions between Marcos and Dane about attractions of the resort, particularly the Enchantment Room. That discussion prompted Marcos to encourage Dane to visit one of the programs which had only begun since guest attendance at the programs depended on occupancy. During prospective clients' orientation to the resort, they would meet with Marcos to learn about entertainment options including the Enchantment Room which at first received a measured response from residents. However, word spread rapidly about the spectacular shows available there as well as about something called "enchantment enhancement," ranking it as the most popular entertainment option.

Marcos made a special invitation to his friend for Saturday night's show featuring six young women from Mexico City, ranging in age from late teens to mid twenties. Dane's rather conservative if not sheltered background limited his imagination to envision what the shows entailed. Saturday night arrived and Marcos greeted Dane at the ornate entrance doors to the Enchantment Room. Entering the room, Dane stopped, eyes wide open drinking in the splendor of lights, of music, and an aura of hazy expectation hovering over the small crowd. Marcos ushered him to one side of the auditorium where they enjoyed a clear view of the stage. Just to the other side of the entrance doors, two men in the shadows were seated next to a small table, their purpose not readily recognizable.

His eyes traveling around the auditorium, Dane's face took on a puzzled look. Standing next to him, Marcos noticed Dane's frown.

"Something the matter?" Marcos turned to his friend.

Dane stood straighter, then leaned back against the wall. "No, ah, nothing's the matter." He squeezed his chin between thumb and forefinger. "It's just some of these people seem kind of lost. I thought this was a room of excitement."

Marcos laughed. "Oh yeah, it's a room of excitement all right." He paused. "Excuse me but haven't you heard about 'enchantment enhancement'?"

Dane shook his head. "I guess not. What is it?"

Marcos grinned at Dane's innocence. "Foster didn't give you any details about this place?"

Dane shook his head.

In near conspiratorial tones Marcos explained the powers that controlled the resort and the availability of substances that expand a person's capacity to respond to certain kinds of stimulation. He explained that many of these people sat in a world of sensation all their own.

Eyes widened, Dane uttered, "Really?" his eyes focused on the two men seated at the nearby table.

Marcos nodded his head and repeated with a giggle, "Really." The auditorium nearly full, Marcos estimated thirty or forty people, some obvious couples, some unaccompanied, contained a murmur of multiple conversations masking excited anticipation. For Dane a shiver of anticipation skipped through his stomach.

As the lights dimmed over the audience, spot lights illuminated the stage. Music streamed out of huge speakers positioned around the auditorium. Slowly the curtains parted. Silence gripped the crowd. A long, bronze colored leg extended through a break in the curtain surrounding the stage. Soon two more legs made an appearance. The legs moved in response to the music.

In minutes the curtain parted to reveal six, stunningly beautiful young women dressed in almost formal attire, flowing white dresses accented by vivid colorful scarfs. A wave of applause spread through the auditorium. The women joined hands to engage in an intricate, seductive dance. Soon they stopped with backs to the crowd, alert now to the spectacle occurring before them. The music stopped; silence dominated. Then the dancers untied their scarves which released their formal gowns to expose six exquisite bodies with firm bottoms, perfectly tapered hips and long shapely legs. To the roars of the crowd the dancers in perfect unity swayed to the music while they slowly turned to face the audience, now treated to six sets of firm, erect breasts, pushed out with pride by the dancers who, perhaps even more than the audience, admired their superb bodies. Dressed now in only a G-string, the women engaged in a series of dances and moves that engaged their sumptuous bodies and threatened to drive crazy the men in the audience.

Marcos nudged Dane whose eyes never left the stage. Dane looked over at his friend standing next to him. He shook his head in amazement at a true spectacle of female beauty. The show lasted about a half hour with the dancers displaying their exotic sexuality and the audience thrilled with the display, the thrill apparently enhanced by those special substances available to them.

At the conclusion of the show, curtains opened to the cubicles at the rear of the auditorium, those Dane observed when he first visited the Enchantment Room. At the time Foster had hinted at private pleasure, but Dane formed no conclusion about exactly what he meant. Now he realized what he meant. The six girls moved seductively to those small rooms, assuming positions in front of six of the cubicles. In near nakedness they offered an irresistible lure for those men in search of extreme private pleasure.

Marcos bumped Dane on his arm. "What do you think, my friend?"

Dane ran his fingers over his forehead and eyes, searching for words to express what he thought. "Incredible," is what he said. What he thought related more to how long this entertainment could last before authorities arrived to investigate.

Chapter 52

Chester wrestled an aging wheel borrow over the rock path leading to the corral. Before the gate he stopped, released the wheel borrow, removed his glasses, and whipped a soiled handkerchief over his forehead and around his neck. Each day the horses needed hay. Each day he delivered it to them in this ancient wheel borrow.

Both hands and his back sore from the physical demands of his menial job, he stared at the six horses waiting for their hay. In three long weeks, Chester had adapted, temporarily, to another life, one he previously hardly imagined existed. Of course, he felt the same way about his recent life at the resort.

He shook his head at the sudden intrusion of that recent life. Not a day passed without his constant vigilance over some accidental identification by someone from the resort or someone like Dane Barton. Chances were incredibly slim for that to happen. Still, a shiver invaded his back at just the thought of people like Foster learning of his fugitive status. As far as Chester knew, Charles Randall no longer existed in the minds of those at Mi Casa by the Bay.

Shortly after leaving his apartment in Marina Vallarta to catch a bus to Old Town where he met Toni, he returned to collect his meager personal belongings. He entered the apartment quietly and left quietly, contacting no one. As far as he could remember, he had paid the rent. However, he felt no compulsion to ask. Since then he joined Toni in caring for the horses and readying them for tourists seeking a few moments of adventure. A cot in the horse barn next to the corral replaced his apartment. As far as he knew, no longer did the people at the resort attempt to find him; besides he no longer cared.

Chester slipped the latch on the gate and maneuvered the wheel barrow over the rough surface of the corral to dump the hay in the manger shared by all the horses waiting patiently for their breakfast. With an empty wheel barrow, he left the corral to seek another load of hay.

At the stack of hay, Toni used a pitch fork to push the hay into a more defined pile. Hay was expensive; they couldn't waste any. He turned to face Chester(Charles to him).

"Buenas días, señor. ¿Como está?"

Chester spoke little Spanish, but over the time he had lived in Puerto Vallarta, he acquired a growing vocabulary.

"Muy bien." he replied.

Since that night he met Toni on the edge of Old Town, they formed a close friendship. Toni's gentle disposition soothed Chester's irascibility. Chester avoided any mention of his background either in the states or in Puerto Vallarta, and Toni avoided asking any questions. He simply invited him to stay; he needed the help. His small ranch enjoyed a brisk business and provided him with an adequate living, his horse back rides and tours popular with tourists who spilled out from Old Town's Romantic Zone. He appreciated Chester's willingness to help in exchange for food and shelter.

Toni rested on his fork. In very clear accented English, he explained, "Last few nights have really been busy. I could use your help on the tours."

Fearful of too much exposure to the public, Chester hesitated. With reluctance he accepted.

His chores completed, Chester retreated to his cot in a corner of the house barn that served as his bedroom. As he did with increased frequency, in idle moments he examined his options. He considered if he would spend the rest of his life fleeing a justice system stacked against him. He rubbed his tired eyes. Maybe he should try to explain to Foster the danger Dane Barton posed to the resort. Exposing his fugitive status would also jeopardize the impending drug culture planned for the resort.

He sat up on the wiggly cot, feet touching the dirt floor. His life was simply a damn mess. Spending what's left of it in the present turmoil presented a grim future. He resisted desperation so far. Suggesting a compromise with Barton, compelling each to keep his mouth shut bordered on desperation. Chester harbored little hope of Dane's agreeing with that plan. In his troubled mind he admitted that Dane had little reason to accept his compromise except if Dane believed in a threat from the cartel. Chester might help to establish that threat.

He slumped over with elbows resting on his knees. Exposed and under interrogation by Twin Cities authorities, considering what Chester knew about the role heroin played in the resort's relaxation and pleasure component could create a threat to the future of the resort and to the Tropical Real Estate Company and its cartel backing.

"Hey, señor." Toni entered the horse barn, squinting into the dim light.

Chester jerked his head up, reaching for his glasses. "What do you need?"

"Some help to saddle the horses." Toni stood in the double barn door, the sun casting his shadow on the dirt floor.

Chester walked with Toni to the tack area of the corral. The horses greeted them with quiet whinnies, cooperative while the two men tossed saddles over their backs.

As Toni promised, the afternoon and early evening produced a sequence of riders. Chester devoted most of his time attending to the horses in between rides and short tours. Toni's chunk of the extreme southern edge of Puerto Vallarta contained narrow trails through the jungle and a meandering creek that tumbled over small rock formations. The area never ceased to impress Chester, a former product of the big city. To his relief he met no one who could recognize him.

The time spent in reviewing his options finally pushed him to some decision. Though Chester related well to Toni and to Toni's slice of an area including Chico's Paradise, a classic, jungle restaurant, he needed something more permanent. He refused to dwell on the options that danced in his mind.

The next morning while servicing the horses in preparation for another busy afternoon, Chester consulted Toni about something more permanent. Toni hinted that his operation might serve that purpose. Chester didn't dismiss the suggestion but still pried for more options.

"Okay," Toni conceded. "I think you might try El Tuito"

Two days later Chester boarded the bus for the one hour ride to El Tuito, a classic Mexican, mountain village complete with cobble stone streets, a town square, and a population of friendly engaging people. Staring out the cracked window next to his seat, he watched as the narrow road, lined first with palm trees then with mountain pine trees, climbed higher into the mountains. He closed his eyes, thinking that his options were running out. If this didn't work, what then?

Chapter 53

Up early in anticipation of his first visit back home, Dane shuffled through papers on his desk. Those papers represented a busy week, one that tentatively captured four more resident couples. He arranged the papers in chronological order to file until Foster consummated the deals.

A tap at his door distracted him. He expected no one. Besides his one p.m. flight imposed limitations on his time.

"Come on in." Dane announced.

The door opened. Marcos peeked around the partially opened door. "Am I interrupting anything?" A close friendship had developed between Marcos and Dane. Amiable, competent, and helpful in Dane's grasp of the many details associated with the resort, Marcos gave him someone to turn to with questions about the resort and about life in Mexico.

"No, just getting things organized so when I get back, I'll know where I left off." Dane rose to greet his friend by the door. "Did you need something special?"

Marcos shook his head. "No, just wanted to wish you a good flight."

Dane made a slight bow of his head. "Why, thank you. I didn't think many people knew of my brief timeout at home."

Marcos laughed. "Oh, it's going around the whole resort."

Dane grinned, "Yeah, I bet." He paused in a moment of

reflection. "You know, I've meant to ask you something for a long time." He turned back to the desk. "Why don't we sit down for a minute." He guided Marcos to the cushion chairs in front of his desk. Seated they exchanged glances.

"Ask away," Marcos nudged Dane's leg with his foot.

Hesitating with almost a reluctance to ask for fear of what he would find out, Dane scratched his eye brow, the one stitched up twice in the past. "Did you know this guy who was the variety shop manager?"

Marcos slouched in his chair. "I guess I saw him a few times, but never met the guy."

"Do you know what happened to him?" Dane asked.

Marcos shrugged his shoulders. "He just up and left a few weeks ago, shortly before you arrived, I think."

"What did the guy look like?" Dane pushed on.

Marcos closed his eyes, a scowl drawing his eye brows closer. He looked at Dane. "I don't know. Kind of a scrawny guy, mostly bald head." He paused. "Oh, he wore these big round glasses."

A shock raced through Dane's body, carrying with it the possibility that the missing manager could be the elusive Chester Reynolds.

Marcos noticed the impact his description had on Dane. "Did I say something wrong?"

Dane drew a deep breath and released it slowly. "No, just some excitement about my flight scheduled in about three hours."

"Good." Marcos eased himself out of his chair. "You'd better get going." He moved toward the door. "Have a good flight and greet your special people for me."

Dane grasped him around the shoulders, a typical gesture between men in Mexico. "Thank you. Take care of things while I'm gone."

The hectic preparation for the ferry and taxi rides to the airport diverted Dane's attention from the information Marcos supplied about the missing manager. Checking in, clearing security and waiting nearly an hour before boarding his non-stop flight home, he now tried to relax in his seat.

The preposterous notion that Chester Reynolds had made it all the way to Puerto Vallarta tumbled through his mind. A litany of questions crowded Dane's mind. First among them was deciding what to do assuming the validity of what he had learned about the missing manager. At the moment he couldn't grasp the full implications of Chester eluding justice, hiding in Mexico, and working for a company backed by the cartel.

Dane shut his eyes in an attempt to block out any more thoughts of Chester Reynolds. Instead he forced his mind on the impending reunion with Ashley at the airport and later with his parents.

A brief case draped over his shoulder, Dane stepped on the escalator delivering him to baggage claim at the Minneapolis/St. Paul International Airport. At the bottom of the escalator ride, Ashley studied the descending passengers until she spotted Dane. A smile lightened her face, her hand moved in welcoming him home. When he picked Ashley out of the small crowd waiting, he waved vigorously, a broad smile reflecting his joy at seeing Ashley for the first time in two months.

Dane burst through the doors to baggage claim and into Ashley's open arms. Dropping his brief case, he embraced her in a firm hug.

"God, it's good to see you," he whispered in her ear.

She leaned away for a moment then licked her lips ready for a passionate kiss. "Welcome home. I've missed you too, so much. How was the flight?"

"Long, but it's the only way to get here." He laughed.

His one piece of checked luggage slid down the conveyer onto the carrousel. He grabbed it and followed Ashley out to the parking lot and the ride home. Heavy rush hour traffic delayed the ride, giving them the chance to update their lives despite their frequent phone conversations during his absence. The move to his apartment dominated the conversation.

That evening, dinner at home gave Dane the chance to discuss his function in Puerto Vallarta with Ashley and his mom and dad. Questions bombarded him about his new life and new job. He tried to answer all of them in as much detail as possible. Of course, the move to the apartment finally prevailed.

Milo returned from a trip the day before, grateful that he could be there to join the discussion and the important move to the apartment. He drank a swallow of milk, locking his eyes on his son. "I've kind of planned on the move tomorrow. I realize that's a day early, but I've got to leave again the day after tomorrow."

"That shouldn't be a problem. I've communicated with the management company. I think they're flexible about the move-in date." Dane assured his dad.

"Good. I can get a small truck from the garage to hall the furniture you intend to take from here." He paused directing a glance at Beatrice, a grin narrowing his lips. "Just remember, kid, you can't have it all."

The next day as Dane and his dad muscled furniture from Dane's room to the truck, it seemed as if they were taking all of it. Dane couldn't avoid the rush of excitement he experienced with each piece of furniture they hauled to the second floor apartment. Though most of what they hauled ended up in the bedroom, Dane thrilled over his vision of what the living room and kitchen would eventually look like. Toward that goal, he and his dad drove to the Ikea store in Bloomington to secure a table, four chairs, a few dishes and a set of silverware to fulfill the needs of both the kitchen and the dining room. The final load for the day brought to the apartment Dane's clothes, miscellaneous personal items, and his mother's touch in the form of bed clothes, towels, and a few kitchen utensils. That evening Ashley joined the Barton family in a moving celebration of Dane's new home.

The excitement of the move and of the reunion with Ashley and his parents helped to suppress Dane's thoughts about the missing manager and about Chester. In one week he would return to Puerto

Vallarta to resume his duties there. Before that return, he intended to discuss his suspicions with Ashley and his parents. Before that, though, he wanted to spend time with Ashley perhaps to renew the splendor of their last night before he departed for Mexico. Also he intended to visit the Fore Sure Telemarketing facility to greet his former colleagues, whom he missed more than he admitted.

What better place for a gathering to send Dane back to Puerto Vallarta than his newly occupied apartment. The night prior to his departure his mom took charge of the dinner. Some of her preparation took place at home. Most, however, used the facilities of the apartment. By seven o'clock in the evening the four, Ashley, Dane and his parents, joined to share another meal.

The special baked chicken breast, roasted potatoes, and mixed vegetables satisfied the palates of all. Milo severed the grip of silence the meal exerted around the table.

"Beatrice, you outdid yourself." He smiled at his wife seated across the table. "A great meal. Do you suppose the new kitchen had something to do with it?"

"I don't think so, but you can show your appreciation by taking care of the dishes." Beatrice responded to her husband's humor.

Conversation ebbed at the table, all cleaning the last of the meal from their plates. Maybe Beatrice did not intend for Milo to take seriously her comment about the dishes, but he rose from his place to begin the collecting, rinsing, and stacking the dishes in the dishwasher. Dane joined his dad. Ashley and Beatrice backed their chairs away from the table in anticipation of the resumption of conversation. Their bussing function completed, Dane and his dad returned to their places by the table.

Dane settled into his chair. "I'm sorry about the lack of more comfortable places to sit. It's either here or in the bedroom."

"It doesn't matter," countered his mother. "What counts is sharing dinner together as a family."

Dane shot a glance at Ashley, who responded with a generous smile.

Brief silence returned to the table. "How about some coffee?" Beatrice broke the silence.

Milo sipped his coffee then placed the cup on the table. 'What time is that flight again?"

"About eleven thirty tomorrow morning. I need to get to the airport about nine thirty." Dane did a quick nod of his head.

"I can take you." Confirmed Ashley, who had spoken little during the dinner, content to listen to the Bartons.

Earlier in his short visit home Dane described to his parents and to Ashley the specifics of his job at the resort. He avoided discussing facilities like the Enchantment Room as well as the mystery of the missing manager.

"How long do you think you'll stay with this company?" Milo took another sip of coffee.

Dane moved his cup around on the table. "I don't know. I suppose it depends on the response from prospective clients." He shifted in his chair and took a deep breath. "Something has bothered me almost since the time I arrived at the resort."

All eyes locked on Dane. All cups set aside.

He moved his chair away from the table. "Part of the management staff included a supervisor of the variety shop. Mr. Foster, you know the project manager, told me my second day there that this manager had not shown up for several days. Nobody seemed to know much about him or what happened to him." Dane paused to look across the table at his dad. "This manager, a Charles Randall, came from the states. Foster knew very little more about him. During my brief assignment, the guy, so far, has never shown up."

Beatrice squinted her eyes in thought. "Have they tried to find the guy? He must live someplace."

Dane shook his head. "I guess so but not many people talk about him."

"Why does this guy bother you?" Ashley moved her chair to look directly into Dane's eyes.

Dane grinned. "Oh, maybe I'm just paranoid, but I can't help wondering whatever happened to the notorious Chester Reynolds." Finally the mention of his name released months of pent up tension.

Milo sat up straight. "You mean to say this Randall guy might be Chester Reynolds?"

Dane blinked his eyes. "Yes, the thought has kind of haunted me for quite a while particularly after one of my colleagues told me what the guy looked like, short, scrawny, and with big glasses." He shook his head. "It just bugs me."

"Have you talked to this Mr. Foster about your suspicions?" Beatrice inquired.

Dane rested his elbows on the table to voice his concerns about exposing this man as the fugitive Chester Reynolds and the possible retaliation from the powerful cartel backing the resort. He also spoke of the potential consequences for him, considering the details he possessed about the flow of cocaine. The cartel and the Tropical Real Estate Company would not look with favor at anyone jeopardizing their lucrative enterprise.

Those around the table stared at Dane in silence. "Damn, that is a mess." Milo asserted. "Do you really think you face some kind of risk?"

Dane shrugged his shoulders. "Honestly, I really don't know. It still bothers me."

"I'm sure it does." Ashley added, reaching out to touch him on his hand.

"What are you going to do?" Beatrice asked.

Dane pushed away from the table and rose out of his chair. "That's something I have to determine. If my suspicion holds up, I'll need to decide on doing the right thing or the safe thing. Should I let the little jerk get by with murder to protect myself or should I turn him in and face the consequences?"

The others also moved away from the table. Milo approached his son, placing an arm around his shoulder. "I don't pretend to have the answer. I do know that as far as we are concerned, you come first, always."

Chapter 54

The morning sun peeked under the over hang shading the public plaza. Small groups or individuals scattered around talking, playing cards, playing dominos or simply resting. Chester Reynolds(Charles Randall) was one of those simply resting.

There for only three days, he already joined, in a daily routine, the mostly senior citizens of the classic, mountain village of El Tuito. The public plaza reserved the honor of the most popular destination for the locals. A near perfect rectangle, the plaza adjoined a traditional, Mexican cobblestone street. A traditional paint made from several local clays gave the buildings around the plaza a tan exterior.

Chester dozed on a sagging rattan chair off by itself on the plaza. Now months of residence in the Puerto Vallarta area had calmed some of his petulance replacing it with increased patience and contentment. Only the misgivings about the discovery of his fugitive status intruded on the contentment. In El Tuito he found basic lodging at a type of boarding house recommended by the bus driver who delivered him to this mountain village. With dwindling funds he would have to find some kind of employment. At this moment in his life, he didn't care what kind of employment.

He tipped back in his chair, reviewing what he knew about El Tuito from a brief, halting conversation with two natives who spoke a little English. At more than two thousand feet above sea level,

El Tuito was distinctly different physically and culturally from the cosmopolitan Puerto Vallarta, the only other Mexican community he knew anything about. Considered one of the oldest mountain villages in that part of the Sierra Madre Mountains, El Tuito served as the home to about five thousand people, most of them making a living on local ranches, plantations, and breweries producing a classic moonshine called raicilla. Those unemployed devoted most of their time to the plaza.

Nearly every day about mid-morning, Chester observed a robust man driving a late model pickup pull up next to the plaza in search of day laborers. Exactly what kind of labor Chester did not know until one day he asked.

His name was Stan Robinson, kind of an expatriate from Canada who as a young man vacationed with family in Puerto Vallarta, developed an intense fondness for the people and the culture, and eventually made the decision to settle in El Tuito with its expanse of agricultural land. A tall, muscular man, he towered over the shorter Mexican men. Hours out in the tropical sunshine and clear mountain air had tanned his face, to some extent, blending him with the natives.

In his late sixties with a body accustomed to physical labor, Robinson sported pure white hair and thick white eye brows over vivid blue eyes. The white hair served to accentuate his tanned face. A firm jaw gave him a look of control. However, his calm, confident demeanor dismissed any hint of intimidation.

The owner of a large plantation specializing in oranges, bananas, and a variety of agave plants popular throughout Southern Mexico, Mr. Robinson very often needed day workers to help in his many agricultural enterprises.

In need of money and in need of some more productive way to pass his time, Chester volunteered to join a half dozen other men for a day on the orange plantation. A short ride in the back of Robinson's pickup brought the laborers to an impressive adobe type house surrounded by several other buildings, primarily for fruit storage and processing for shipment. On the first day for Chester, the gang gathered at an expansive grove of orange trees to pick those oranges ready for market.

A product of the inner city, Chester rarely spent time in the sun. His arrival in Puerto Vallarta changed that. He now rarely spent time out of the sun. On this day he noticed a distinct difference between the sun in Puerto Vallarta and that in El Tuito, the two thousand foot elevation accounting for the much cooler, drier El Tuito conditions. Chester's recent introduction to shovels and wheel barrows helped prepare his aging body for the job of picking oranges and placing them in baskets set among the rows of trees in the orchard.

Robinson mingled with the natives with whom he conversed fluently. His friendly nature gave comfort to the natives eager to earn a few pesos and likely a free meal. He found intriguing an American among his workers. Over rest breaks he inquired of Chester about his journey that brought him to El Tuito. Measured in his response, Chester fabricated an explanation based on some nascent sense of adventure.

As Chester and the others moved through the rows of trees, he noticed on adjoining property an impressive building surrounded by vast gardens of native flowers and plants. Several people followed narrow paths among the exquisite displays which Chester later learned was the popular Puerto Vallarta Botanic Garden.

At the end of the day, Robinson treated his crew to a lunch of chicken and shrimp tacos. A short ride in the back of the pickup delivered Chester and his companions back to the plaza. The next few days Robinson returned in search of more day workers. Chester volunteered each time, creating some identity with Robinson and appreciation for the few pesos. Pleased with Chester's willingness to work without constant supervision, Roberson approached him at the end of a day picking oranges to ask if he would agree to work full time on the plantation. Without hesitation Chester accepted.

Chapter 55

Despite the morning crowd, Dane agreed to meet Marcos for breakfast in the resort's restaurant. In only a few weeks, occupancy in the resort climbed to forty percent. Many of those new arrivals nearly filled the restaurant.

Dane reached for his glass of apple juice. Seated across from him, Marcos poured syrup over a stack of pancakes. Setting the syrup bottle aside, he looked up at Dane.

"How was your short trip home?"

Dane chewed a bite of fried eggs and swallowed. "It was great, made even better by the move into my apartment."

"That's right. You told me about that." Marcos wiped his mouth with a napkin. 'I think I know how you felt about the move. Not too many years ago I moved into my first house." He furrowed his brow. "Now, moving out also is exciting."

Dane cocked his head to one side. "Where you going?"

"No place, really. It's just my girl friend insists on a bigger place." Marcos smiled in obvious submission to a greater authority. "Everything's okay with your family and ah,"

"Ashley." Dane rushed to the rescue.

"Yes, Ashley," Marcos repeated. "And your parents are fine?"

Dane nodded his head. "Yes, happily everybody's good."

For a moment they concentrated on their breakfast, a murmur

of conversation surrounding them. Marcos set down his fork and dabbed his napkin against his mouth.

"Dane, I have a question to ask."

Dane slid his plate aside, eyes on his friend. "Does it have anything to do with finances?" He laughed.

Marcos joined in the humor with a brief chuckle. "No, it doesn't, really." He paused with a hint of reservation. "Remember just before you left for home, you asked about this infamous missing manager."

Dane nodded his head, concerned for where this topic would lead. "Sure, I remember."

Marcos explained. "My brief description seemed to produce a visible reaction. Is there something you know about that man? Charles Randall, I think was his name?"

Dane squeezed his lips together. He exhaled, a momentary debate tumbling around his head over what to reveal about his suspicions. "No, I don't think so. It's just kind of a coincidence that just days before my getting here he disappeared."

Marcos sipped more coffee. "I don't know about a coincidence, but the deal is a mystery. Nobody has seen or heard from this guy in weeks."

Dane quipped. "I guess the tropical lure just kind of ate him up."

Marcos laughed. "Yeah, that's one explanation. By the way have you mentioned anything to Mr. Foster?"

Dane shook his head. "No, I don't what to bother him. He has enough to take care of."

Satisfied with avoiding anymore discussion of Mr. Charles Randall or whatever his name, Dane pushed himself away from the table. He explained, "Look, I have some catching up to do in the office. Progress didn't wait for my return. We can talk more later."

"Sure. I've got to get busy myself, another big show this weekend." A salacious smile punctuated the remark.

Images of the line of seductive, young beauties danced through Dane's mind.

Marcos laughed. "You know all about that. Look, before you

rush off, do you know anything about Puerto Vallarta's Botanical Gardens?"

With immediate surprise over the question, Dane shook his head. "No, I don't."

"I'm no devoted crusader for trees and flowers, but my girl friend is. She wants to visit the garden only about an hour out of Puerto Vallarta. She suggested I invite you for a little insight into a part of Mexican culture and to give me some companionship." He laughed.

"Sounds interesting," Dane conceded. "Let me know when you intend to go."

"Rosa, I want you to meet Dane Barton, my first real American friend." Marcos emphasized his introduction with a tap on Dane's shoulder. With his arm around Rosa, Marcos faced Dane. "Dane, please meet my favorite girl, Rosa Vargas." He pulled her close. "Today she will be our guide through the Botanical Gardens."

"So happy to meet you Dane." With a smile characteristic of the Mexican culture, Rosa held out her hand grasped by Dane.

About the same size as Ashley, Rosa's dark, inquisitive eyes highlighted her deep tan and her flawless, delicate skin. Black hair, drawn back into a pony tail, hung to her shoulders. Dressed in white shorts accentuating shapely legs and a royal blue top snug against modest breasts, Rosa could easily join the glamor of the Enchantment Room. Dane later found out that at one point in her career, she did exotic dancing. Now she sold cosmetics at the Liverpool, a huge department store near the Main Marina.

Dane climbed into the back seat of Marcos' Nissan. Marcos and Rosa occupied the front seat. He navigated the crowded weekend streets of Puerto Vallarta, through El Centro and Old Town, turning onto Highway 200 toward the gardens and the mountain village of El Tuito.

As they made their way south out of Old Town, Rosa explained the short history of the Botanical Gardens. About twenty-seven acres mostly of trees, flowers, and bushes, the garden attracted visitors from around the state of Jalisco. She explained its award-winning displays were heralded by the state's horticultural society as some of the most attractive and inspirational in all of Southwestern Mexico.

She further touched on the historic, classical village named El Tuito, only a brief drive from the garden. The village rested at the center of a flourishing agricultural region over two thousand feet above sea level, a jewel tucked in the Sierra Madre Mountains.

The orange grove adjacent to the Botanical Garden served as the work site most days for Chester Reynolds, still Charles Randall for now. Perhaps by necessity, the time spent in Mexico softened his rough edges, mellowed his irascible propensities, and reduced his fear of discovery. The determination that propelled him all the way to ownership of convenience stores weakened as he realized contentment in working for amiable bosses like Toni and now Mr. Robinson.

Days passed quickly, refreshed by the clear mountain air. Chester's work in the orange groves proved interesting and gratifying, providing him with a meager salary and, more important, a place each night to sleep, free from the worry over capture.

About the time Dane and his friends reached the Botanical Gardens, Chester and three other workers advanced to the fence dividing Robinson's orange groves from the garden. Curious about this popular place of trees and flowers, Chester paused in his picking oranges to lean against the fence to watch the garden's visitors.

Dane, Marcos, and Rosa walked the path around the garden headquarters and administrative offices. Rosa took the lead followed by Marcos then Dane. Only a few feet from the fence, Dane noticed a frail man braced against it on outstretched arms. Two more steps and Dane stopped, shivers racing through his body. Large round glasses shielded the man's eyes. Dane caught his breath; his heart raced.

Chester watched as three garden visitors made their way toward him, guided by this stunning Mexican woman. At about the same time, recognition registered for Chester as it did for Dane.

"My god!" Dane mumbled as the shock of recognition momentarily paralyzed him. "He's been here all along?" Dane whispered.

At the other side of the fence Chester's mouth dropped open in consternation. Instant recognition of Dane, his arch-enemy who could sentence him to prison, left him speechless. He turned abruptly to disappear in the orange grove, his recent security potentially shattered.

The remainder of the garden tour found Dane in a fog of indecision. If Rosa and Marcos noticed, they said nothing. As before he refused to involve his friends in this protracted nightmare.

Late that afternoon, standing before his condo window to the world and staring at the magnificent sunset, Dane made a monumental decision. He would do what was right. He reached into his pocket for his cell phone. In the phone's directory he located the number for Lieutenant Lewis of the Minneapolis Police Department.

Chester slumped in his bunk bed provided for Robinson's crew. He removed his glasses and rubbed his eyes, weary of the toll the events of months ago took on his frail body, on his life. He closed his eyes, uttering, "To hell with it all. If they want me, by god they can come and get me. I'm done running." He lay back on his pillow to await the arrival of an elusive sleep.

Printed in the United States
By Bookmasters